Strangers in Our Heads

BRI EBERHART

Strangers in Our Heads

Copyright © 2023 by Bri Eberhart

All rights reserved.

No part of this publication may be reproduced, distributed, or transmitted in any form or by any means, including photocopying, recording, or other electronic or mechanical methods, without the prior written permission of the publisher, except as permitted by U.S. copyright law. For permission requests, contact the author at brieberhart.com.

The story, all names, characters, and incidents portrayed in this production are fictitious. No identification with actual persons (living or deceased), places, buildings, and products is intended or should be inferred.

Editing by Jennia Herold D'Lima

Book Cover by Emily's World of Design

Paperback ISBN: 979-8-9887571-0-8

Hardcover ISBN: 979-8-9887571-1-5

First edition: November 2023

Content Warnings
Car accident, death of parent, death (including death of a sibling),
fire/fire injury, panic attacks/disorders, profanity, grief, violence

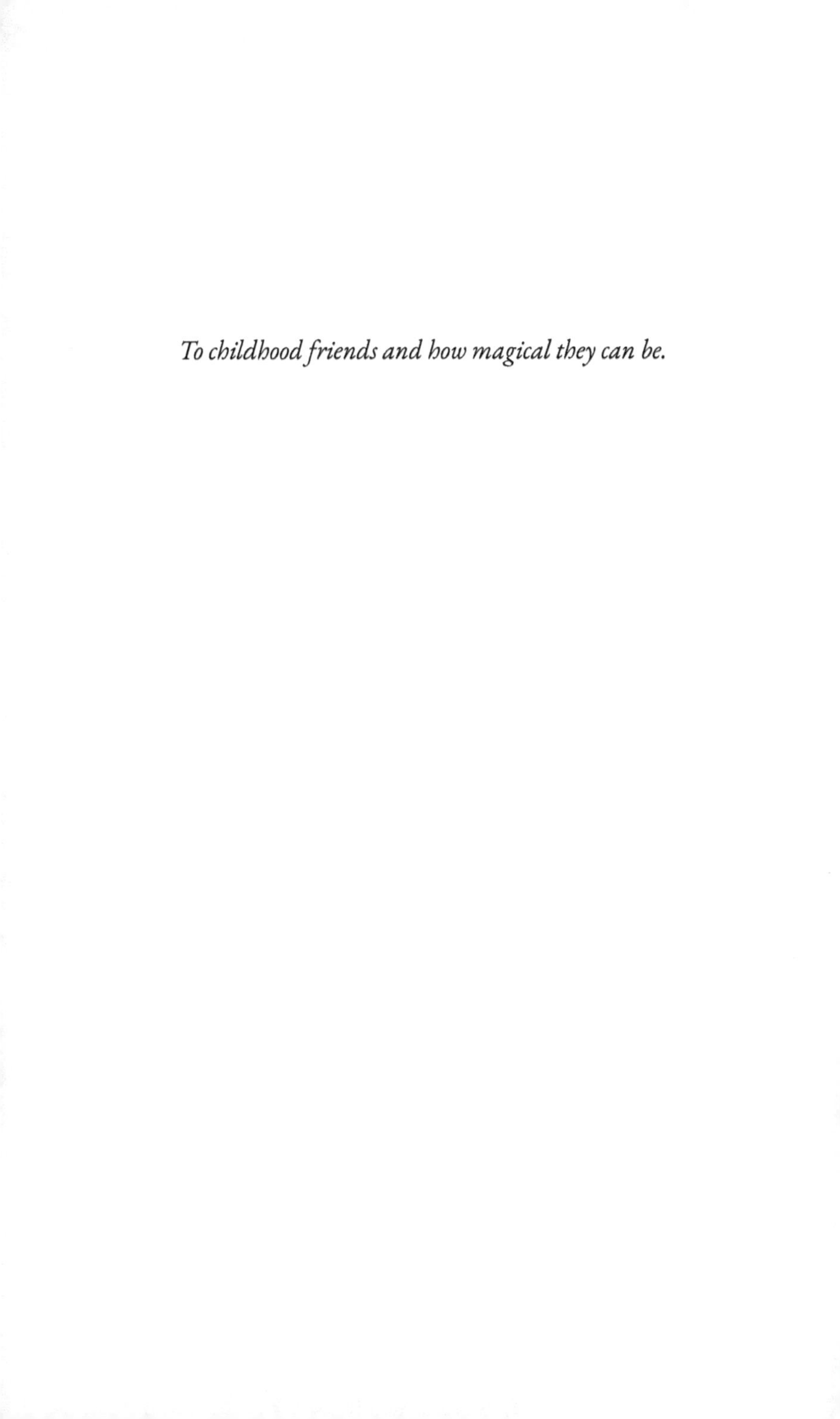

To childhood friends and how magical they can be.

Chapter One

Gemma

Should it take four months to adjust to a routine?

My older sister, Olivia, and I have been with the McIntyres since summer started. But our daily schedule still doesn't feel natural after nearly seventeen years of living with foster families who didn't care what we did or when, so a routine feels weird.

Everyone eats breakfast together before going to school or work. Then, we're all expected back at the table in time for dinner. And the parents, not *our* parents, but the foster parents—Judy and Dennis—always ask about our days, taking in the good and the bad and figuring out any problem-solving needed.

It's nice, but again—weird.

Much to my surprise, Olivia doesn't seem to mind the routine. I've tried to get a good read on her to see if she's somehow blocking her real emotions about the situation from reaching me, but I don't think that's it. I think she actually likes living here.

Amber's the only other kid in the house besides us—she's been with the McIntyres a lot longer, but the official adoption is on hold due to needing to terminate her birth parents' rights or something. I'm not entirely sure. Not everything is spilled at the dining room table, just like how they don't know my hands randomly glow purple from time to time. Some secrets are better left unsaid.

As I make my way toward the kitchen, I spot Olivia and Amber bickering in hushed voices at the bottom of the stairs. Annoyance and a bit of sadness tangle in my chest, and I have to block them both out. These aren't my emotions. If I had to guess, Olivia is the annoyed one.

Not only do my fingers like to glow, but I'm also an empath. *It's great.* My hand slides down the banister as I approach them.

"What's the problem?"

"I know you two are skipping school today." Amber lifts her chin to drill me, and a curl of her dirty blonde hair escapes from one of her space buns. "Let me come with you."

"We—" I glance at Olivia as she dutifully rolls her eyes. I don't even want to skip today. It's not that I'd rather hang out with the kids at Willow High School, who all think I'm a pariah, but Olivia wants to find dresses for the homecoming dance tomorrow, and I *really* don't want to do that. Finding a dress means I'm an eager participant, and to be completely honest, I'm still trying to think of a way out of it.

"We're not doing anything exciting," I finally say.

"And like I said before, you're not even going to the dance," Olivia chimes in.

"So?" Amber puts her hands on her hips, jutting one out like she's made her point. "I still want to go shopping."

"Girls!" Judy beckons us from the dining room.

Olivia makes an exasperated noise, disappearing down the hall with Amber hot on her trail. Instead of following them, I head to the kitchen, offering my assistance to Dennis. His wide build towers over the stove as he finishes making scrambled eggs. I can't see past him, but since he makes them every single morning, it's not hard to guess what he's cooking on the stovetop.

I pull a large plate out of the dishrack and approach him, holding it aloft so he can dump the food onto it.

He gives me a double take, like he's surprised I'm standing there, a grin spreading across his face. "Oh, hey, Gemma!"

"Morning, Dennis," I say like always. I can't tell if he's actually shocked I help him every day or if he just likes to stick to what he knows is safe as if he's afraid I'll spook easily if he deviates. Either way, he gives off this warm feeling, like he's genuinely happy to see me.

I won't lie... there's guilt that our conversations never go deeper than this. School is always fine. My day is always good. There's never anything to report. Because what else am I supposed to say? *I had to hide in the locker room showers today because my hands started glowing during gym class when Heather threw a volleyball at the back of my head?* Yeah, like I'd tell them all that. It's better to stick to the same routine.

Like now, as I bring the eggs into the dining room, where Olivia and Amber are already sitting, both annoyed. I don't need to be an empath to notice Amber's crossed arms and pout, but Olivia's mood still reverberates against mine. Judy pours a glass of orange juice from the carton, ignoring them both.

"Morning, Gemma." Judy smiles, her light blue eyes even brighter with the sun shining through the bay window, contrasting against her navy nursing scrubs.

I offer a small one in return as I slide into my usual seat next to Olivia, setting the eggs down in the middle of the table. Moments later, Dennis carries the bacon in. Now we're all here.

Once again.

We're only a few bites in when Amber announces, "Olivia and Gemma are skipping school today to go dress shopping."

Olivia inhales sharply. "You brat."

My hand freezes as I'm about to pick up my glass of orange juice. I hold my breath, waiting for Judy and Dennis's reaction. I might be the only one who can tell Olivia's outburst is all for show, so it looks like she cares if they know about us skipping. Olivia stopped listening to adults a long time ago, and she'd miss whether Judy and Dennis forbid it or not.

Judy gives a strong "Hey!" to admonish the name-calling, but Dennis only chuckles, scooping another forkful of eggs into his mouth.

Her eyebrows raise, and she glances between the two of us. "Is this true?"

My breath loosens, but my shoulders still hunch as I lean back in my chair, letting Olivia take the lead.

"We're not missing any tests and want to go before the shops are slammed this afternoon. We can't be the only ones who've put it off this long." Olivia's pointed look is at me since I'm the reason we haven't gone yet. I've run out of excuses for not attending the dance, and she knows it.

"I don't like the idea of you two missing class—"

"Oh, let them go," Dennis interrupts. "Don't you remember what we were like in high school?" He squeezes her shoulder like he's reassuring her one day of skipping school won't kill anyone. "I can take them. I need to go to the barber anyway." He moves his hand to run it over his low fade haircut, then pats his full beard. "It's becoming unruly."

"Oh, so now you're skipping school, too?" Judy tries to scoff, but her lips twitch. It's tough to be mad at Dennis, who also happens to be a ninth-grade science teacher at our school.

"Wait. No, darn it. I'm giving a test today." Dennis gets up long enough to retrieve his wallet from the kitchen, pulling free a credit card as he comes back in and holds it out to Olivia. "You can take this. *If*"—he pauses as she reaches for it—"you take Amber along with you."

Olivia narrows her eyes as her fingers close around the card. "Deal."

"Amber, do *you* have any tests today?" Judy gives her a stern look as if silently informing her to choose wisely.

"Nope." Amber bites off a piece of bacon before beaming at Olivia. My sister ignores it, not taking the bait.

Thankfully, Dennis willingly provided his credit card; I don't want to entertain the idea of how Olivia would have obtained our dresses without it. We do have some money since the state pays the McIntyres to take care of us, and they trickle it down to us so we can save for our future. But Olivia has sticky fingers, and Dennis would be easy to steal from since he never has his wallet physically on him.

We're so close to aging out of the system that I don't need her messing things up now.

"Thanks, Dennis." I stand to clear the plates, but Judy stops me, pulling the dishes out of my hands. Olivia and Amber race each other out of the room, both calling dibs on the two bathrooms in the house.

"Go have fun, Gemma." She gives me a slight nod like she understands I need actual permission to let myself enjoy anything.

"Thanks, Judy."

I probably sound like a robot to them, but it's easier this way. We just have to get through senior year, and then we'll be free from everyone, and I won't have to worry about my secrets spilling out in front of prying eyes.

APPARENTLY, WE'RE NOT THE only ones who had the bright idea to skip school to go dress shopping.

Modern Moda is the only place in town to get formal attire, and it's already swarming with girls our age picking out outfits.

"I hope something good is left," Olivia grumbles as we stroll through the aisles, skimming our fingers over ribbons and lace.

Even though she has a dance recital tomorrow night in the next town over, Amber's fully invested in digging through the hangers. She eventually pulls out a black gown covered in tulle and gold sequins and beams at me. "This is perfect."

"Amber, you're not even going to be there." She's been practicing her routine all week; she couldn't have suddenly forgotten.

"Not for me, silly. For you!" She pushes the dress against my chest. "Go try it on!"

I hold it out at arm's length, my stomach free-falling as I take it in. It's too fancy.

Olivia nods in approval. "The brat has good taste."

Amber scowls for the tiniest moment. "Stop calling me that. And I know I do. At least better than Gemma's," she says sweetly like she's not actually insulting me.

I sigh, slipping into a dressing room before any of the other students can take too much notice of me.

The dress fits perfectly, curving in all the right spots and brushing the floor. It's short enough not to need heels; I can get away with wearing my high tops. But no, I shouldn't buy it, it's too expensive—anything here is too pricey, I don't even have to look at the tags—and it's too *nice*. People will notice me in it.

My pulse thrums in my ears as I study my reflection. I look different when I'm not hiding under layers of clothes, trying to blend into my surroundings. I might even consider myself pretty. Maybe not as stunning as Olivia with her golden waves, green eyes, and curves, but I'm definitely not the hideous creature I make myself out to be. The problem is, I can't let anyone else see me like this—this dress is the opposite of blending in. I take a deep, steadying breath. Don't panic. Not here. I'll tell them it doesn't fit. Everything will be fine.

When I slip out of the dressing room, back in my jeans and T-shirt, a chorus of voices swells from an aisle over.

Olivia's shout rings out loudly over all of them, "Ladies! It's just a dress."

I push through a handful of students as anger radiates through my bones. I try to brush it to the side, focusing on the scene in front of me—two girls scrapping over a hot pink dress clenched in both their hands, playing tug of war with the fabric. Olivia is wedging herself between them, trying to break them up.

My fingers begin to tingle, the negative emotions swelling into me too much to bear. I need to get out of here. I need—one of them slaps Olivia across the face.

Olivia gasps, and the world around me goes black.

I DON'T KNOW HOW much time passes before my vision clears. *Did I just black out from rage?* Shattered glass litters the carpet. I peek at the two girls who had been fighting, but now they're sobbing with blood dripping from cuts on their arms.

I stand in place, nails biting into my palms at my sides, trying to take in the scene with my eyes, not the emotions swirling around me, which are mostly confusion and worry.

No one seems to know what happened.

My gaze falls on Olivia, hovering over Amber as she sits against the wall, her legs tucked against her chest, staring at me. Blue eyes blown wide open in fear.

"You didn't see *anything*," Olivia hisses. "Do you hear me?" She shakes Amber's shoulders, and her gaze finally snaps to Olivia's face. "Do you understand?"

Amber nods, her lip slightly trembling.

I examine the shattered glass around me, glancing at the broken bulbs above.

Did I do that?

Dread coils in my gut; it's my own anxiety this time. It starts deep in the pit of my stomach and doesn't attack me from the outside like other people's emotions do.

What have I just done?

Olivia drags Amber to her feet, grabs my arm, and storms toward the door. "We have to go. Now."

Chapter Two

THEO

I KEEP MY BACK pressed against the stone wall, waiting for the door to open.

Every night, a La Liga Steakhouse worker takes out the trash, locks the door, and heads for the parking lot. Finished with their shift, they're ready to go home, meet their friends at the bar, or whatever the hell normal people do after work. I'm sure they don't stake out restaurants waiting for scraps.

Moths flutter around the only light casting a glow over the alleyway, closer to the dumpster than me, so I'm hoping Nora and I won't be spotted. Still, I pull my hood tighter around my face and shuffle deeper into the shadows, the stone behind me scraping across my old leather jacket. It's seen better days, but it's gotten me through the past few winters on the streets, and I won't do a run without it. It's my good luck charm. I pull a lighter from my pocket and spin it in circles, focusing all my fidgeting on this one movement to keep the rest of my body still.

The food we steal tonight won't keep us for long, but we haven't found a place I can hit up where it won't trace back to us if we take too much. Those jobs are bigger and more dangerous, and I do them alone, unlike tonight.

I narrow my gaze, focusing on the darkness in front of me. Odd shapes of varying sizes bleed into one another, and I have to blink a few times to spot Nora hidden between two... wooden crates? A small, pale hand lit by the streetlight shoots out from the center, holding up a single finger telling me one minute.

Sighing, I lean my head against the wall. With a big run, we'd be set for a few more months.

My stomach clenches at the thought.

A few months. That's all we ever get. Mere weeks of alleviation before wondering where our next meal is coming from. Days of rationing so we don't run out too fast. Nights spent hungry so the younger two can eat.

I don't know how long we can keep going like this. It's been five years since it was Elise and me. Three since Nora found us. But we're pushing on a year with Zay now, and that kid eats *a lot*.

Shaking my head, I peer down at my watch.

Three... two... one.

The back door swings open, thudding against the brick wall as the employee grunts, throwing a bag over the railing and into the dumpster. My shoulders tense when he looks in my direction, but he can't see me. Or, at least, I hope not. After a second, he sweeps his gaze toward the parking lot, digs into his pants pocket, and pulls out a pack of cigarettes and a lighter. He lights a smoke and locks the door. My heart beats in sync with each second of the watch ticking as he stands there lingering.

Leave, asshole.

I stay as still as I can. After what feels like an eternity, the man disappears into the parking lot. A car starts. Music blares from its open windows. Tires peel away. I step forward, but Nora shoots a hand out again, fingers splayed—*stop*. The melody playing from the vehicle grows again as I blend into the shadows. The same guy runs up the steps, unlocks the door, and disappears inside, but only for a minute before he's back out with a cord dangling from his hand.

This time, when he leaves, Nora reveals herself. She's a whole foot shorter than me, but she looks up, giving me a smug grin. "We're clear now, Theo."

Her ability to see the future has saved us countless times, like how she just rescued me from having to deal with an awkward encounter explaining why I'm digging through their trash. Or worse, if he decided to call the cops for trespassing. I motion her forward with a 'by all means, ladies first' hand gesture.

She snorts, taking off her backpack as she heads toward the dumpster.

I've learned certain things while trying to survive before becoming so desperate we started digging through the trash. My decisions are always based on the severity of our situation, rated one through five. How desperate are we? Five? We'll eat anything to stay alive.

We're probably nearing a two right now, so we can be a little pickier.

I once was surprised at what restaurants threw away, but now it doesn't shock me at all. Some are decent enough to donate their scraps, but we're not lucky enough to obtain them.

We're the invisible, the lost, the ones hiding under the radar. Society forgot us long ago, or maybe they never even knew we existed. Either way, we're no one.

And *no one* gets stuck with the trash.

I pocket my lighter as I rush up the steps where Nora is already waiting and lean over the railing to see how full the dumpster is. Ideally, I'd like to pull the bag *out* so I don't have to go *in*. And this is one of those lucky nights where I can do just that.

Hauling the bag upward, I place it back on the stairs and tear it open—a mixture of relief and disgust twists inside me when I spot an abundance of bread. Every table gets dinner rolls, most of which go untouched; what a waste.

The same goes for tortilla chips and any bruised fruit or vegetable. Most of those are edible even when you don't want to eat them—desperate times.

Once Nora's bag is full, she stands up, brushing her hands on her jeans. She's developed a poker face for our trips and doesn't let an ounce of her emotions flicker across her face when we do the actual job. I'm sure her feelings aren't much different than mine, though. I don't think anyone would be thrilled to dig through the trash to find their next meal.

I test the weight of my backpack, already laden with expired soup cans we got from the supermarket's trash earlier. It's heavy—knots were forming in my shoulder before I filled it with the take—but it's a good sort of heavy, a relieving heavy. Dumping the remaining trash back into the dumpster, I also wipe my hands on my pants.

"Ready to head back?" I ask Nora. She nods but doesn't say anything as she fiddles with the bag's straps on her shoulders.

The reality of our situation always tends to hit a little harder once we've found food. The four of us only have ourselves to rely on. No parents, no other outside connections. Unless I count the girl who exists in my head, but I don't, considering she's not real, as much as I wish she were.

Some—like me—left our old lives by choice, while others—like Elise—watched the Authorities, who hunt down and kill people like us, slaughter their families.

All because we're a little different.

No one in the crew actually *knows* I can enter other people's dreams. I've kept my ability to astral project to myself, but they know about my little sister, Ril—no. I don't want to think about her. Not right now. Not when she'd be the same age as Nora, and if I had just done anything different that night, she'd be here, too.

Nora and I walk in the direction of home. *Home.* I inwardly scoff to myself. I'm glad I didn't say that word aloud. If Nora heard me call it that, she would've told the others, and they would all congratulate me for arriving at their sentiments. "Home" is a condemned, abandoned mansion we dubbed the "Rib House" since the entire structure looks like it's made of skeleton bones that will crash around us at any second. But we've been there for eight months now, and it's the longest we've ever stayed in one place. *Home.*

"You did good today," I finally say, breaking the silence as the parking lot ends and the grass begins.

She gives me a sidelong glance like she wants to say something but doesn't.

I slow to a stop. "What is it?"

Nora pauses for a moment, chewing her lip. Finally, she admits, "I think my visions are getting stronger."

"How so?"

"They're becoming... more prolonged. Instead of flashes, they're starting to unfold like scenes. I'm seeing a lot more."

"Well... that's good, right? It'll help?"

She shrugs before heading into the woods. "I guess we'll find out."

Adjusting the backpack's weight on my shoulders, I lower my gaze to avoid tripping over jutting tree roots and follow her into the dark.

Chapter Three

Gemma

WE'RE ROAMING OVER, UNDER, and around southern live oak branches in the middle of the night, an accident waiting to happen. What could possibly go wrong for a clumsy girl with two left feet? I roll my eyes at Olivia's need for adventure.

We shouldn't even be here after what happened yesterday at the dress store. That's the first time I ever exploded something with my mind. I don't even remember what happened. The girl slapped Olivia, and then... nothing. I was no longer present.

By the time the—what? Anger? Shock?—whatever it was cooled in my system, the damage was already done. According to Oli, Amber witnessed my hands sparking to life, and the lights above exploded when I balled them into fists.

Olivia's best guess is that I was already dangling over the cliff with everyone arguing around me, the negativity driving its way in, so when I saw someone hurt her, it pushed me over the edge.

It makes sense, I guess. But that's not good. At all.

I barely have control over myself already, let alone with whatever cursed abilities I have growing into something worse.

What if I can no longer hide?

What if someone catches me?

My stomach drops. Someone already did catch me. Amber. She promised she wouldn't tell Judy or Dennis, but it's not something she'll likely forget.

She's barely made eye contact with me since it happened.

For the hundredth time tonight, my feet tangle in the hem of the black gown Amber picked out before it all went wrong. A soft yelp escapes my lips while I reach for a low-hanging bough. After catching myself, I quickly shake out the purple emitting from my fingertips in case there are any peering eyes. I scan the trees, goosebumps rising on my arms as I wait to be caught, but then the color fades.

And thankfully, no one comes.

I don't know how Olivia managed to get the dresses. I assumed the store would have closed to clean up, but apparently not. She left shortly after dragging us home, delivering Amber and me to our rooms, demanding we stay quiet, and then showed up just in time for dinner with both dresses zipped up in a garment bag.

She returned the credit card to Dennis, thanked him, and didn't even bat an eye, like the most insane afternoon didn't just happen.

Even now, she's waltzing through the woods as if I'm not a ticking time bomb. I shake my head in awe at her compartmentalization skills.

The tree trunks here are massive; it'd be impossible to reach around and brush my fingertips together. Their limbs sprout in all directions—a monster with an infinite number of arms, waiting to yank someone off the ground and devour them. At least, that's what I imagine others think of them as.

Not me, though. I'm not scared.

The trees soothe me, lulling me into a silent comfort. They're always there, nice and sturdy, growing for hundreds of years. They were here long before I was born and will hopefully remain long after I'm gone. This forest is their home—a true home—something Olivia and I have always lacked. No matter where we end up, which foster home, or in which state, nature is always there in one way or another. I can count on the trees being there when I need to take a break from pretending not to be me for a little while.

And I could use that refuge right now.

I glance up at the night sky, barely visible through the tree branches, and take a deep, steadying breath. *Let the darkness take me and forget all about yesterday.*

Moonlight slips through the gaps in the leaves and highlights the gold sequins covering the outer layer of tulle as I wipe my now dirty hands on my hips.

"I look ridiculous," I mutter to myself. Traipsing through the woods in a ballgown; what a night. I need to draw less attention to myself, *especially* now, but Olivia wouldn't hear of it.

With apparent sonar hearing, she whirls around and struts toward me. Resting her elbow on one of the monster's forearms, she tucks her fist under her chin and smiles. "You look beautiful, Gemma." Quickly scrunching up her face, she adds, "But those shoes are still ridiculous."

I hike up my dress to show off the pink high-tops and grin despite myself. She might've gotten me into this dress, but at least I was able to negotiate something about my outfit.

"No one can see them, and they make me feel better."

Dropping the material back onto the ground, I stomp ahead of Olivia to escape whatever lecture regarding my fashion choices she's about to start.

Following a winding path—if that's what you want to call it—further into the dense groves, yesterday's events continue to flash in my mind, causing my heart to skip a beat.

"What if it happens again?" I ask. I don't have to elaborate; she already knows this has haunted me since it happened.

"It won't." Her voice sounds so sure, I almost believe it myself.

"This really isn't good, Oli."

"Nothing happened," she states matter-of-factly. "We don't even know if it was you. Okay? Yes, Amber saw your hands. But I don't think she'll tell, or she would have by now. The lights could have been a fluke."

"A fluke," I deadpan, slowing to a stop.

"Nothing. Happened." She gives my shoulders a shake. "Stop overthinking it."

I bite my lip, trying to keep the uneasiness at bay. "But what if you're wrong?"

Olivia ignores the question, forging ahead.

Noise filters through the foliage, and with a sinking realization, I discover we made it to the right spot—the masquerade ball's after-party. We'd never been to a school with such a fancy homecoming, and I loathed every second of it: too many sweaty people grinding on each other to terrible music, the fighting over dresses, the pressure to find a date; needless to say, I'm a bit inexperienced in that department. And, of course, the drinking. I'd rather have spent the night curled up in bed with a good book, but no. That's far too simple for a Friday night, according to Oli.

After the dance, I tried escaping back to the house, but Olivia begged me to go to the after-party. Judy and Dennis were out for the night since they took Amber to her recital. And I knew she would inevitably drink while here, so I might as well keep an eye on her.

As the giant branches clear, revealing a wide-open space, Olivia squeals and skips in her equally embellished dress, though the one she chose is rose-red, the upper half covered in lace. Her long, straight blonde hair lays smooth against her shoulders, while my loose brown curls have already frizzed in the humid Florida night air. The red complements Olivia's piercing green eyes, while my midnight-colored dress only makes mine appear even darker.

I cling to the edge of the forest, still sending silent pleas into the night for the trees to take me as one of their own so I don't have to mingle with people I don't like, as Olivia makes her way to the largest part of the group, filled with giggling cheerleaders surrounding some jocks. I don't care enough to figure out what sports they play, but they definitely aren't a bunch of nerdy kids all getting wasted together. Some of the lower social groups might filter in and out tonight, but no one parties like the popular kids.

"This is when the fun begins," I grumble to myself.

After circling the party a few times, my eyes land on an abandoned chair near the massive fire. We're in the middle of a vast field, the grass brown and dying from the clinging summer temperature, even though it should have started cooling down by now. The fire—too large to be legal and probably a bit dangerous considering how dry everything is around us—is raging, orange flames licking the night sky. Clusters of kids are in smaller groups, spread out across the lawn, all drinking from plastic cups.

Plopping down into the seat, I fixate on Olivia in all her glory, already with a red Solo cup in hand. A grin spreads across my face as she twirls her perfect hair, her shoulders shaking with laughter while flirting with some boy who isn't half as cute as the one who visits me in my dreams.

I lean back and sigh; he's so—the thought halts as I notice a few nearby jerks pointing in my direction. My fingertips tingle, and I quickly hide them under the layers of my dress.

"Not here, not here," I whisper.

They can't know that what happened at the shop was because of me. If it even was. It's impossible. Only Amber noticed my hands; the rest were too busy ducking out of the way. It's fine. Everything is fine. Like Olivia said—nothing happened.

My face flames as the kids now laugh. They're making fun of me, as usual, but there isn't anything I can do about it. *There's never anything I can do to make them stop.* I guess I can't blame them, though. It doesn't matter which school I'm in; they always tend to hone in on my differences. They might not realize *how* different I am, but it's like a beacon—the girl who hardly talks and always has her hands curled into fists, avoiding eye contact. I'd think I was a freak, too. They only tolerate me being here because of Olivia.

They might point and laugh or whisper behind cupped hands while nodding in my direction, but Olivia has been the yin to my yang since we were kids. The more closed off I became, the more she opened up to those around us, helping draw the attention away. She's Miss Popular, and being Miss Popular's sister makes me less of a target. As long as she's nice to me, the others will follow suit to the best of their abilities. Or at least that's what I tell myself. It could always be worse, especially if anyone linked the dress shop disaster back to me.

As if sensing my anxiety, Olivia appears beside me. "Back off," she barks at the cluster, and they scatter, seemingly too afraid of upsetting the queen of Willow High.

"How do you do that?" I ask, amazed even though this isn't a new occurrence. "We've only been at this school for a month, and you're already their leader. It's a new record."

Olivia shrugs, handing me a drink. "I'm charming."

I glance between the cup and where my hands are stuffed under me, unsure if it's safe for me to reach for it. My fingertips could be glowing again, and I don't need *that* to be widely known. I don't think Miss Popular could save me from that one; they might come with literal sticks and stones. *But words will never hurt me*—what a lie.

Biting the inside of my cheek, I whisper, "My hands..."

Immediately understanding, Olivia sets the drink on the ground and peers around. "No one's looking," she murmurs under her breath.

I slip a hand out from under my thigh and take a quick peek, sinking back in relief when my fingers appear perfectly normal, and reach for the drink to quell my nerves. I'm aware of my limits from being dragged to equally daunting parties. One cup won't hurt; I can still keep an eye on Olivia without getting messy myself.

She saunters off to find another chair and drags it back to sit next to me. We both watch the fire silently, but my heart swells, knowing Oli is only doing this to make me more comfortable.

Minutes pass before she picks up our earlier conversation. "Amber won't tell anyone. She's now terrified of you." She tries to laugh it off, but it comes out forced.

I frown, the guilt eating away at me as I toy with the lip of my cup. "I don't want her to be scared of me."

"She thinks you're a witch."

"I'm not," I hiss, but the uncertainty remains thick in my voice. Although honestly, I'm not sure what I am. I gaze down at my fingertips, counting my breaths to quiet the panic, waiting in case they spark to life again.

While glass exploding around me is new, the actual glowing phenomenon isn't; it began when I was ten years old, after I almost drowned. I don't know how to get it to stop, though. I've never been *normal*, but I could at least pretend I was before then. I've always wondered if my powers were because of my near-death experience, but I can't be the only one who's faced mortality. Wouldn't there be a ton of people out there like me if that was the reason for having powers?

Ever since that day at the beach, my fingertips glow purple whenever I feel a rush of adrenaline or a too-extreme negative emotion. It doesn't matter which one—sadness, anger, fear—but any flare causes my hands to light up with electricity. The sensation only feels like dull pins and needles, but I'm too afraid to touch Olivia when it happens. Just because it doesn't hurt me doesn't mean it wouldn't harm someone else. Instead, I bury my hands in the nearest hiding spot and wait for it to pass or, if no one is around, shake them to get rid of the tingly feeling as if they're only asleep. Either option is hard to do while at school with people watching.

At least there's a plus side to this dress; the voluminous skirt made it easier to hide my hands tonight.

"What am I supposed to do now? What if the lights were because of me?"

"We do nothing. Like always."

"We should tell someone."

"Yeah? Who?" she snaps. "We're just going to go tell Judy and Dennis your hands glow? Or you might've exploded some light bulbs, which I'm still not convinced was you. How do you think they'd react?"

I open my mouth, but no words come out.

"They'll ship you off to God knows where, and I'm willing to bet I won't be able to come with you. No." Her jaw clenches shut. "I'm not letting that happen."

The evening breeze ruffles my dress as I shake off a chill. Crossing my arms, I rub the goosebumps away. "You don't know that." My voice is timid and weak with defeat—the bonfire crackles, wood exploding from the heat. Something is burning inside of me, too. "What if someone can help me? What if there are others like me?" I stop speaking aloud, but my thoughts continue, *What if I can get rid of this?*

Olivia shoots me a glare, but I don't dare look away. We hold each other's gaze as unspoken words pass between us—my defiance against Olivia's stubbornness.

"I thought *I* was helping you," she finally lets out, effectively blowing out the flame inside my heart.

She's right. She does help me. Even though she's only eleven months older, Olivia's mostly been the one who raised me in the countless foster homes we've been bounced around to since I was a year old. She's the only one who knows my secret, the one who protects me. She even stayed by my side when I tried to get away from her—back when I was the mess, and she was the one who took care of me.

"Oli..." Stopping, I struggle to form my thoughts into words. "You help me more than you can imagine, but you don't know what this is like. There has to be someone else out there who's like me, who understands what's going on. Maybe they can fix me; maybe I can be normal again?"

"Or you can just embrace it."

I grimace, afraid of what I'll say next because speaking it into existence will make it harder to ignore. The thought of being a freak keeps me up at night, haunting my dreams and quickly taking over my life in the last seven years. The more my hands glow, the faster my fear consumes me.

"I'm not embracing this. I don't want to become a monster." My mind drifts back to the live oaks disguised as beasts and how I wished for them to take me away. *Maybe I already am one*, I think bitterly.

"Don't you even want to know what you could be? What if you could control it? Then you wouldn't have to hide. Lean into it a little, and a whole new world might open up." Olivia's voice is dreamy, like my cursed abilities are a once-in-a-lifetime opportunity. Even though she said herself that Dennis and Judy would ship me off somewhere, this isn't the first time Oli's acted like I'd be some sort of superhero if I mastered it—whatever *it* is. In secret, of course. So, more like a vigilante, I guess.

"No, absolutely not. I want nothing to do with this," I finally answer, my tongue pressing against my top teeth as I blink away the tears. If I'm not careful, the glowing is going to come back. For a minute, I forgot we were even at this stupid party. "Don't you have somewhere to be? Some guy to make out with?"

Olivia gives me a sarcastic smile as a thrum of anger pushes against my senses. She stands up, fixing her hair. "That power is wasted on you." Turning on her heel, she leaves me slack-jawed and alone.

I'm fixed on the glow of the fire, mesmerized by the pieces of wood splintering off, embers shooting into the night sky. I focus on my breathing so the prickle doesn't reappear in my hands. I shouldn't have riled up Olivia, but I couldn't resist. Over the years, every once in a while, she falls into these moods where she seems insanely jealous of me and my powers. She doesn't understand I'd do anything to get rid of them, no matter how I explain it to her.

I can't imagine Olivia having these abilities, though. She's her own sort of superhero *to me*, but she's also kind of a mess. However, if our roles were reversed, she wouldn't have ever gone down the wild path she did to protect me from being discovered. If the spotlight is on her, there's less chance of anyone noticing me. We've been in this unfair game for a while now, and I struggle to imagine any other scenario.

But if we could just both be normal, that would be great.

I didn't realize anything was wrong before my hands started glowing when I was younger. It took me until my early teens to put a word to it, but being an empath who bounced around to different foster homes is a bitch. Back then, I didn't realize not everyone lived through every feeling and experienced every hit. Apparently, I was the *lucky* one. It didn't matter if they belonged to me or not. I sucked up emotion and pain like a vacuum, and all I ever wanted to do was bury it; push it so far down that I was ordinary and just like everyone else, praying every night my ability would disappear.

But God let me down, and I stopped believing in him.

Instead, I put my faith in my sister. She's the one constant in my life who has my back—who will never leave. Well, her and the trees. But it's okay; we can handle ourselves. We don't need a real family, one with two parents, a white picket fence, and a dog. We have each other.

A wooden log cracks under the heat, a loud *pop* dragging my thoughts back to the present. I frown at the flames, waving away the smoke filling my lungs, coughing slightly. My mind continues to race a million miles per second as I question if yesterday's disaster was me and why Olivia is always so eager to take on my burden.

Protective sibling or not, I wouldn't wish this on anyone, especially when we know so little about it. If only we had answers as to why I'm like this.

I guess we can add that to the other questions we've shared most of our lives, wondering who our parents were and why I was cursed, but Olivia was spared.

Chapter Four

THEO

ONLY ELISE IS IN the kitchen when we get to the Rib House.

She has my earbuds in, her light blonde hair stuck high in a ponytail that bounces around as she bobs her head while doing the dishes. I can't tell what she's listening to as she half-whispers incoherent lyrics, the words bleeding together in a hushed breath.

Nora studies her with flushed cheeks as her face twitches like she's trying to refrain from smiling. I can practically see hearts floating above her head.

Elise pauses the iPod when she finally turns and notices us standing there, pulling the earbuds out of her ears. I wait for her pink skin to darken, but it doesn't. I think it might actually be impossible to embarrass her.

"Zay passed out about an hour ago."

I nod as I gently drop my backpack onto the kitchen floor, afraid the clanging cans will wake him. Peeling the jacket off, my shirt clings to me, soaked with sweat. I collapse into a chair at the kitchen table, and my back spasms from the release. Nora hands her backpack to Elise and bids us goodnight, slipping from the room. She was quiet most of the walk home, but she usually needs a night for our crushing reality to wear off, and then she'll return to normal.

"The tarp fell again," Elise adds.

I grunt in response; I'm not surprised because most of the house is unusable. Parts of the structure are missing entirely, nature crawling its way through broken windows. We moved everything we could into the main rooms and blocked out the rest, using tarps we'd carried from place to place and cement blocks from the crumbling house. I'll have to figure something out soon, though. It'll be snowing before we know it. The tarp won't keep out the bitter cold, and our solar panels only heat so much. We can use the fireplace, but that would mean resorting to everyone sleeping in the same room again. It's always an option, but I don't like the idea of smoke billowing out from the half-decimated chimney. There's no one around for miles, so it should go undetected, but still. Better safe than sorry.

I lean over to flip the light switch, and the bulbs dimly flicker to life, the power coming from the solar panels I stole on a previous run. At least we have utilities, something we haven't always had. Elise and I have survived some dark times—literally. Our luck changed when we met Nora.

My state of mind continues to plummet as my eyes scan the faintly-lit room. Elise strung up the white Christmas lights to make the place homier, but it's still pretty bleak. The living situation, the lack of food, the colder weather approaching; none of it is good. I don't know what our next move is.

Maybe Nora's visions can manifest the next place we stay at. Not that she has total control over what she sees. There are some things, like knowing whether that restaurant worker would come back so soon, but for the most part, things randomly trickle in with no rhyme or reason. And it's usually much harder to decipher. But still, if her power is growing, maybe we can use it to pick our next location.

Letting out a sigh, I sweep the hair out of my face. "I need to make an actual run soon. This isn't going to last us."

Elise bobs her head in silent agreement, grabbing the food and putting it into containers to stay fresh a day longer.

"We should think about leaving..." I start, but she shoots me a glare with her sharp emerald eyes. I clench my mouth shut, too exhausted to have this argument with her again, so I don't.

I should tell her what Nora told me and how it can maybe help, but it's not my secret to share. If roles were reversed, I wouldn't want Nora to blab to everyone about how I can dream hop.

Instead, I hastily stand up, brush past Elise, and head to my room to avoid the oncoming speech about how we need to stay in this God-forsaken place, skipping over soil and rocks from missing floorboards.

No matter where we go, we'll never be able to put down roots. And they all know this, but I'm the bad guy for moving us all the time. It's whatever. They'll thank me when we don't end up dead somewhere—or worse. Who knows if the Authorities keep people like us alive for some sick reason? The only people I'm aware of who died at their hands are Elise's parents and Ril... It's like her name gets stuck on the way out, and I'm forced to choke it down, like the smoke I inhaled all those years ago. But there has to be more. We can't be the only ones who are unlike the rest. Or have the Authorities killed them, too?

I fish the lighter from my pocket, gripping it tightly as I close the bedroom door. I lean against the cracked wood for a moment, steadying my breath.

Riley, Riley, Riley.

Her name was Riley.

The Authorities killed her after discovering she could make fire with her mind.

So no, we can't stay here. Roots lead to comfort, which leads to our guards slipping. One mistake—that's all it takes. One mistake and the Authorities who keep people like us a secret from the rest of the world will know where we are.

And then they'll come to kill us, too.

Chapter Five

Gemma

One hour bled into two as I fidgeted in my chair, having dumped the warm beer from my plastic cup long ago. It tasted like garbage anyway.

Olivia's voice is becoming louder and louder, signaling it's almost time to go. It'll be game over if I don't get her back soon. Either the poor drunken girl will puke, or Judy and Dennis—home from the recital by now—will catch us from her obnoxious singing. She always chooses to belt out, "Lloyd, I'm Ready to Be Heartbroken," every time I drop her into bed. Olivia has only seen *P.S. I Love You* once and still became obsessed with this song for whatever reason. Not to mention, they think we're sleeping at one of Olivia's friend's houses tonight. I'd rather they not find out otherwise and catch us.

I lean closer to the dying fire. No one has tended to it for quite a while; they're all too busy being drunk and stumbling around, laughing with each other. The wind is picking up, and the air is thick with the scent of warm rain. Placing my hands as close to the flames as possible, I soak up the last of the warmth before I need to find my way through the trees with my favorite drunken party girl. Jittery, I'm almost excited to return to the oaks—more at peace with nature than I am with humans.

The ash at the bottom of the pit glows red; smoke surrounds me as I gaze at the pile of soot. My mind leaps back to earlier when I was rudely interrupted while thinking about *him*. He came to me again in another dream last night. He's been away for months now, and I assumed he was gone for good, but then he appeared out of nowhere, taking my breath away.

I have no idea who he is, but I'm certain he doesn't exist outside of my imagination.

Olivia knows I often dream of the same person and have for years, but neither of us understands why. The older I get, though, the more I keep his appearances to myself. He's my handsome and mysterious secret, and it often leaves me reeling when I wake up and remember he isn't real.

The dreams are difficult to explain. I can see him; I'm aware he's with me. But that's it. I don't even know his name, just that he appears whenever I need him. He's around my age, maybe a year or two older. Lean but muscular, with tattoos starting at his hands and covering both sun-kissed arms and light brown hair just long enough that a few loose curls lay across his forehead. I've been close enough to him once to notice the gray in his eyes and the freckles that dot his slightly crooked nose—like it was broken at one point—but we're never able to communicate. He's more like a ghost that drifts in and out of my subconsciousness.

In a way, he's a comfort to me. He would appear if I ever had a rough night or if there was violence or too much screaming inside whatever home I was staying at. We would sit together for hours, never saying a word. Or maybe he'd speak when I wasn't paying attention, focusing on our surroundings and whatever spot we'd hang out in—the woods, a field of wildflowers, the scenery changing whenever he arrived—but I can't ever hear him. I gave up trying to have a conversation, figuring the odds of him being able to listen to me were the same on his end.

Thunder rumbles overhead as I chew on the inside of my lip. He's mostly stayed away since we've been at the McIntyre's, which I guess is good. It means I haven't needed him. But I always want him. When he's not there, I find myself wondering about him. And when he does show, I long to speak to him, touch him. *But he doesn't exist*, I remind myself, unlike this incoming storm, which is definitely real.

I shake my head, trying not to laugh. Or cry. My subconscious created a person to check in on itself, and I'm obsessed with him. Go figure.

In the beginning, I thought I was going mad. Was he an imaginary friend I conjured up in my mind? I couldn't see him during the day, only during my dreams. I couldn't wrap my head around how it worked, but I was glad it did. Eventually, the intrigue wore off, and now he's a close, ghostly friend who pops in and out.

Loud cheering snaps me out of my reverie, my pulse racing when my eyes land on the commotion. Olivia is puking, and her so-called friends are around her, chanting. *Great.*

Bolting out of my chair, I hold Olivia's hair back until the gagging ebbs away, staring daggers at those still lingering until they all disperse.

When it's just us, Olivia knocks my hand away. "I'm fine. Leave me alone."

It's going to be one of those nights, then.

Grabbing Olivia's shoulders from behind, I direct her toward the dirt path leading back to the parking lot. From there, we only have to walk a mile or so until we're back at Judy and Dennis's. I've dealt with worse behavior and longer walks. This will be easy and give her time to sober up.

Stumbling over tree roots, I do my best to keep Olivia upright, eventually giving up and letting her sling her arm around my shoulders as she leans into me. Meanwhile, she's slurring so much that I can't comprehend the words. Occasionally, "powers" and "waste" pop out, giving me the impression she's still bitter about our earlier fight.

Keeping my mouth shut so we can make it there in one piece, I continue to tug her along, tempering my anger by reminding myself she doesn't mean any of this. My gaze flickers between my feet and the monster trees, their arms twisted like pretzels, covering us up from above like they're a protective shield.

We make it to the parking lot when Olivia starts to slip and brings me down with her. I haphazardly attempt to break our fall, but we end up sprawling onto the hard asphalt anyway. Olivia is on her back, chuckling while I curse under my breath and call her a lush.

Brushing pebbles off my skinned arm, I sit up and straighten out my dress, which is undoubtedly torn by now. Olivia continues lying there, releasing a mix of a laugh and a cry. My anger bubbles to the surface, and the tingling in my fingers races back. Clenching my hands into fists, I will it—along with my annoyance at her—to disappear.

Her incoherent outbursts drag on as purple sparks flick to life on my palms. *Fantastic.*

"What is your *problem*?" I finally snap, no longer able to control my irritation. "Why are you acting like this?"

Olivia struggles to sit up, leaning all her weight on her elbows, and looks me in the eye. "You don't get it."

"Get what?"

"All you want to be is…" Her words slur off into nothing before she can finish the sentence, but I understand what she's getting at. I've told her enough times now over the years.

All I want is to be normal. And Olivia wants to be anything but.

I hold up my palm, which is now encompassed in a purple haze swirling around my skin, emblazoned by a mixture of feelings. It started as anger, but now it bleeds into annoyance, bitterness, and guilt, absorbing Olivia's emotions as much as my own, and I can't decipher whose is whose anymore.

"Nothing good will ever come of this."

"You don't even know what *this* is," Olivia argues.

I study my hand a moment longer, then slip it under my thigh again, half worried about other kids coming across us in the parking lot. I let one shoulder rise and fall, accepting we'll never see eye to eye on this. "It's my curse, so it's my choice what to do with it. Sorry, you don't have a say anymore."

I can maybe accept Olivia is right, and nothing did happen. Perhaps I'm not responsible for those lights exploding. But if there's the slightest chance this is worsening, I'm not following through to find out what else I can do. No way.

Standing, I brush off my destroyed ball gown, tattered and covered in mud. My eyes rake over my drunk sister, and a mixture of pity and revulsion pulses through me. Why does she always have to drink so much? Sighing, I place both arms under hers and scoop her up into a standing position. After steadying her, I let go and head toward the direction of the house.

We walk in silence, the echoes of a waterfall burbling in the distance. I'm six feet ahead but constantly glancing over my shoulder to ensure Olivia's still behind me. She trips in her obnoxiously high heels, forcing me to stop to help her.

I sigh. "Just take off your shoes."

"No."

Failing to control the annoyance in my voice, I bite out, "It'll be easier for you to walk if you're not stumbling around in four-inch heels."

Olivia shuffles past me, heels still on, head held high. I stand there in disbelief, watching her go, plotting ways to get back at her in the morning and developing a plan for when she's nice and hungover. I'm thinking... bright lights and loud noises.

We don't go at each other like this a lot. Our fights are few and far between, but when we do argue, it's when Olivia has had too much to drink, and it's always about my curse.

Clucking my tongue, I'm frozen in anger, which puts too much distance between us. With a chill running up my spine, I hike up my dress and increase my speed to catch up with her. It's well past midnight now, no one is around, and the fog has descended over the sloping hills. Olivia's nearing a bend in the road.

I'm going to lose sight of her.

My heart thumps harder, and I can't figure out why. Almost like a haze, confusion fills my head, and it's now my turn to feel intoxicated. My lips are numb as I break into a run. My throat constricts, and I'm panicking.

This isn't my fear. It's someone else's.

Tires squeal; a sudden crash rings in my ears. Gasping, I fall to the pavement, clutching both sides of my head. The pain is unbearable, and I don't know what hurts worse: my skull that's been drilled into or my cracked open chest. I open my mouth to scream, but nothing comes out.

Seconds pass before I have enough clarity to realize the pain isn't mine. Physically, I'm fine, but emotionally... I rise on shaky legs, calling out for Olivia.

Just as I make it around the bend, a red pickup truck with a broken headlight and a cracked windshield races past me. Dazed, one hand still clutching my chest, I search for my sister.

"Olivia?"

Nothing but the wind rustling against the leaves answers me.

The physical pain is at bay, but it's draining away. Whoever or whatever is hurting is losing the battle. The panic, however, is raging. My entire body trembles; I spin in circles as tears blur my vision.

"Olivia?" I yell. "Where are you?"

Too distracted to care that my hands are glowing, I spot a crumpled mass on the side of the road. Approaching it as if it's a wild animal, I have to stop a few times to work up the nerve to continue. Lead fills my legs, making them nearly impossible to move. With each step forward, I jolt to a stop, shaking my hands out, before moving another hesitant foot closer. I gulp down air, fear radiating from my body.

When I'm close enough to make out the shape, a scream dies in my throat. Covering my mouth with both hands, I collapse to the ground. My hands shake as I reach out and clutch Olivia's broken body to my chest, gently rocking her, trying to rouse her.

"No, no, no," I cry. "Wake up, Olivia. Please don't leave me. Please."

My begging is for nothing since I'm already sensing Olivia's gone, but I can't stop the words from pouring out of my mouth. Over and over. A piece of me is missing.

She's gone.

A guttural scream tears from my throat, and the ground beneath me vibrates. Tree limbs snap off, blown away from the sudden velocity of my cries, mimicking ferocious winds.

Nothing matters, not anymore—not without her.

Purple mist encircles my entire body in a fierce storm, mixing with a dark fog that spins like a tornado. My hair whips around me, and tears freeze on my cheeks.

Olivia can't be gone. *She can't.*

I let out another wail, unable to stop my primal cries.

With her death, something inside me breaks loose.

Something uncontrollable.

Chapter Six

Theo

Something terrible is going to happen.

I'm not sure what exactly, but whatever it is, it's knocking me off kilter, like things are no longer lining up correctly. It's as if the world is tilted off base, like gravity is keeping us grounded for now, but our reality might change at any moment.

"What Ever Happened?" by The Strokes plays on my iPod, but I grit my teeth at the crackling that comes through the broken headphones. We haven't had internet in years, so there's no updating my music anytime soon, but that's fine by me. The headphones, though, have to go.

I stare at the ceiling but am too restless, so I'm on my feet again, pacing in small circles in my room. Not long after, I collapse with a huff onto the bed again.

If only I could figure out what Nora saw in her dream.

Something's not right.

Last night, I was sucked into Nora's head as she slept. For the first time in years, I couldn't control whose mind I entered, and she had a vision while I was in there. I've never been privy to them before, but from what I've heard from her, the flashes of images usually line up to form one big picture. Or at least until recently, when she informed me they were becoming more prolonged. This one, however, was still indiscernible.

All I remember is darkness.

And a scream.

Then, the world shone purple.

I woke up clutching my chest, the pain unbearable. Covered in sweat, I panicked for a moment, thinking I might be having a heart attack. Right on cue, Nora came barging into my bedroom, blinding me with lights, fear scrunching up her round face.

"What is it?" I sat up on high alert, not wanting to let it slip that I was in her head, sharing her vision with her. That's my secret to keep. While I would die for anyone in this crew, the fewer people who know what I can do, the better. Abilities do nothing but paint targets on your back. "What happened?"

"I don't know," she whispered, shaking. "I saw you, and then you were just gone. Someone was screaming. Then, there was a burst of purple; I couldn't see through it. I thought something might've happened to you."

I reached for a shirt, pulling it over my head while Nora sat on the edge of my bed, gnawing on her lip. She saw me because I was there, not because it had anything to do with her vision. I choked down the truth. Whatever else she saw—or didn't see, for that matter—must be significant to have her rattled.

"Don't worry about it." I gave her the most reassuring smile I could muster. "I'm fine. It was just a bad dream."

"What if it wasn't?"

I put out my hand, motioning it toward my body, indicating that I was clearly alive. "Not a scratch on me."

"What if it's just a vision of something that hasn't happened yet?" She picked at her cuticles until they bled.

I studied her briefly, her wide eyes and shaking hands, her fingernails dotted crimson. I've never seen her this troubled from one of her visions. I threw the covers made of old clothes sewn together off me and headed for the door.

"Nothing bad is going to happen to me."

Nora followed me out of the room until I walked down the warped hallway to hers. After watching her crawl back into her makeshift cot comprised of musty couch pillows, I leaned against her doorway, arms folded, and smirked to lighten the mood.

"You're not getting rid of me that easy, you know. Now go back to sleep."

She's silent for a moment before finally accepting it with a stiff head bob. "Fine."

I bit back a laugh from how clipped it came out. "Goodnight, Nora."

Once I was back in my room, though, I lay there unblinking until dawn. The memory of smoke burning in my lungs kept me on alert, uneasy about falling asleep for even a moment.

We both knew it wasn't a dream.

I understand Nora's gift as well as she does at this point. But worrying over what we don't know or can't control is useless.

But still, even if it has nothing to do with me personally... *Something's not right.*

I yank off the headphones as the claustrophobia wins, and I can't leave my bedroom quickly enough. The pent-up energy and the sense of something *wrong* have me wired. I need answers but don't know where to begin. What I do know is that I need to plan my next job.

By the time I make it to the kitchen, Elise is cooking breakfast, which is more or less just heating up what we found yesterday—the odor of burnt toast lingers in the air. Nora is at the table with Zay, helping him study.

"Zay, *focus*," Nora urges. Her amber eyes drill into his.

"I am, but it's not going to grow! I'm not there yet."

"You are, trust me. You can do this."

Zay holds his hands over the potted plant as his gaze settles on the stem. His mouth moves, but no words come out. He shifts his head slightly, his coiled corkscrew hair bouncing along with him as he tries to convince the plant to grow. I lean in closer to see if he'll do it this time, but thirty seconds later, he slumps back in defeat.

"I told you I wasn't ready," he whines.

I slap him on the back and sit beside them at the table. "Don't worry about it, kid. You'll get there."

"Maybe." Zay sighs, picking at the plant stem.

It's sometimes easy to forget how young he is until he's defeated like this. His gaze falls to the table, his lower lip jutting out enough for me to know he's upset. I study the few freckles dotting his brown skin just around his cheeks, and a pang of guilt twists in my stomach. His childlike wonder fades the longer he stays with us, and I wish it could be different. He just turned fifteen last month, but we found him and this house at the same time nearly a year ago. Zay went from a boy who ignored his ability and whose biggest concern was beating video games to a "man" desperately wanting to figure out his powers to help out. He thinks if he can master plant roots, he might be able to stabilize parts of the house by using the trees outside.

I don't know what he is or isn't capable of, but he should get a handle on his powers anyway. The more control he has, the better he'll be able to hide them.

His grandmother passed away a week before we found him, and he had nowhere else to go, so he ran. But, unfortunately, she was the only one who knew his secret—his ability to manipulate nature—and as she raised him, she made him promise never to tell another soul, so he ended up at the Rib House alone. It took us a long time to convince him to trust us.

We were passing through then, and Nora had a vision of him. She guided us here, and we never left.

That has to change. Being comfortable will ruin us. The longer we sit in one place, the easier it can be for people to track us.

"Did you do your math homework yet?" I ask, interrupting their bickering that must've started after I zoned out.

Zay scoffs. "Aw, come on, man. I'm already failing enough."

"Ha ha," Nora mocks as she flicks his ear. "You have to do your homework."

Elise brings over a plate of food and tugs on one of Nora's auburn pigtails. "I don't know why you're laughing; you haven't finished yours either."

Zay points at Nora, taunting her right back, but Nora slaps his hand away, her cheeks turning red as she tries to collect herself.

"I don't know why you're making us do this," Nora argues. "I'm sixteen, almost seventeen. If I were in school right now, I could just get my GED."

"Well, you're not, so..." I spin the textbook toward her. "Plus, you have to be eighteen in most states."

Nora opens her mouth like she's going to fight me on this, but it's pointless; we've been through this. She'd need permission from a superintendent to get a GED before she's eighteen. To do that, she'd have to be enrolled in school. She'd have to give her name. She'd have to join the system, and then the Authorities would have access to find out about her.

She's never completing that test.

"If we're never going to be *regular kids*, why do we have to go through all this?" Zay asks.

I shrug. "Education is good for you. You don't know what the future holds. Maybe things will be different someday." Resting my elbows on the table, I cover my mouth so they can't see my frown. It's never easy to lie to them. But I can't bring myself to tell them things are never going to change. At least not for people like us.

My eyes flicker to Elise's, and we share a mutual understanding in one look. Fake it with the kids; they don't need to know how dire our situation is. Not yet. We're not much older, only eighteen, but we've come to terms with the fact that we need to lead the group. They look up to us in more ways than one.

The only difference is Elise thinks we should stay here, and I don't.

Nora and Zay understand the lack of food and the lack of comfort. They're fully aware we're in a terrible situation and will be for some time.

However, they don't know how *deadly* the Authorities are. They know they exist, and that we have to hide. But we don't want to tell them their lives are in danger. Yet.

That's why I have rules.

If only they'd actually follow them.

Zay and Nora have gone back to arguing, and Elise is filing her nails, ignoring them.

I sneak outside to start planning.

Once I'm behind the shed, I rip the green tarp off of the old, beat-up Ford I picked up from a farm a few years back. I stole the plates from a different state, so it's harder to track. We hardly take it out unless we leave a place for good; the risk is too great. The only other time I use it is when I go alone on bigger hauls. Elise knows to move on if I'm not back within two days. Unfortunately, it'd have to be on foot.

The tank is half full. But four five-gallon gas canisters are in the back of the cab, so I can make it about 400 miles without running into trouble.

Grabbing a map of Indiana from the dashboard, I glance at the pistol beneath it. Reaching over, I open the magazine to make sure it's still loaded. I have two more guns in the house, hidden, but they're for the end of the line. If we ever get caught... My throat constricts, and I shake out a clammy hand as the other tightens around the grip before putting it back into its spot.

We can't get caught. But if we do, I'm not going down without a fight.

I spread the map open onto the truck's hood. Leaning over, I trail my finger down until I land on an area remotely near Thornbrooke and assume that's where we are. There are no real roads out here to mark our exact spot, only a dirt path that eventually crosses Route 74. It's the trip Nora and I make through the woods for things we can get on foot.

For this, though, I'll have to go as far as possible. I can't risk getting caught too close to home. If something happens, I'll need to be on my own so I won't unintentionally alert anyone to the others being nearby. The Authorities can look, but they won't find them if I'm far enough away.

I let out a breath, my heart thumping, and start tapping my fingers restlessly on the hood. Leaving them defenseless isn't a great option, but bringing everyone with me is even worse. I try to reassure myself they'll be fine, blocking out the darker thoughts that try to follow.

After studying the map for nearly an hour, I decide where my next target will be. It's a little over three hours away and won't use up all my gas. According to the map, it appears to be in the middle of nowhere, and the more rural, the better. The chances of being spotted as an outsider are greater, but there's likely to be less security. Backwoods towns tend to have fewer alarms, with citizens relying on their personal weapons instead.

I can handle those. I can't handle the Authorities.

I map out a route that keeps me off the main roads, fearing a cop scanning my license plates and noticing they're stolen. There's always a danger with each of these runs, but there's also no other choice. We can't live on restaurant garbage forever.

As I begin folding the map back up, a voice startles me from behind.

"I don't like it," Nora says.

I turn toward her, plastering on a fake smile as I stick the map in my back pocket. "You know I need to go."

"After last night, though..." Her beige skin loses its color. Her eyes glisten as if she's still shaken by what she saw.

"You don't remember anything else?"

She shakes her head. "You popped into my head; then someone started screaming. You clutched your chest. It looked like you collapsed, and then you were just... gone. I couldn't find you anywhere in the purple light."

"Well... that's all right," I say flatly. I have no idea what that means, but it probably isn't good. I did wake up with chest pain but didn't realize I showed my hand to Nora in the dream. I school my features into what I hope is an expression of indifference. *Don't let her know you were there.*

"Everything is going to be fine. I'll be back tomorrow."

"Promise?"

I don't make promises. I promised Riley I would always watch out for her, and look where that got us.

Gazing over her head, I stare into the tree line. "Tell you what, do you see anything?"

Nora chews on her chapped lip, concentrating hard, a *V* forming between her eyebrows the more she focuses. Reluctantly, she shakes her head.

"Then see? Everything's fine."

She sighs. "You know that's not how it works."

"I know, but it's better than nothing, right?"

She stomps toward me as if annoyed she's actually going to help me with this. She reaches around, yanking the map out of my pocket and smoothing it onto the hood.

Much shorter than I am, she has to stand on her tiptoes; her finger lands on the spot I've already chosen, with no hint from me on where I'm going.

"There's a gas station named Hilda's. It has everything there, no alarms."

"Good to know." I'm unfazed by her information, learning a long time ago to trust whatever she sees. Her specialty is people, but sometimes, there are gems like this that help us.

She slams the map against my chest, her face turning stony with her all-too-familiar valor. "You better come back."

I mimic Elise from earlier and tug on Nora's pigtail, then slip into the truck and escape her deadly glare. I'm not ready to leave yet; I have to wait until it's dark, but she takes the hint. As she turns away, I remind her through the window, "Elise knows what to do if I don't."

Chapter Seven

Gemma

I'm trapped in stunned silence as the storm around me rages on. Clutching Olivia's broken body, I refuse to let go. A tiny voice in my head tells me to find help, but there are no cars around, and I don't have a phone with me since it died, and I left it back at the house. I can't leave her here alone. I'm frozen, yet the world around me continues to spin.

The purple exuding from me blends with the fog, whipping around me in a frenzy. Lightning cracks overhead as the sky opens up, and the rain plummets down, dousing me and my emotions. The colored gloom slowly seeps back into my trembling body as if I'm weakened by the amount of power I drained.

There's nothing but destruction around us. The trees are gone, wiped away from existence. The ground is scorched; the only two things left untouched are us.

I haven't let go of Olivia since I found her.

Emergency lights flicker into view, and only then do I realize I'm still alive. That this is real life and not some terrible nightmare I can wake up from. Olivia's gone, but I'm not. Another sob racks my body.

How is this happening?

A cop pulls me away from Olivia's body, but I refuse to let go of her, screaming at him to get off me. He doesn't listen. An ambulance arrives, and they begin resuscitation measures, and this time, I'm forced to let go.

Save her.

Deep down, I already know they can't. I felt her leave, her soul vanishing the moment her heart stopped beating.

An EMT leads me to the back of another ambulance, but my gaze remains glued to my other half. Someone wraps a jacket around my shoulders, but it doesn't stop my shivering. A cop is talking to me, asking me things I can't comprehend right now.

Moments later, Olivia's placed on a gurney. Someone covers her with a white sheet. She'd hate that. She's claustrophobic. She wouldn't want anything covering her face. Her hair spills out from under the fabric, just as glossy and beautiful as ever—making it hard to believe how broken she is beneath the sheet.

Snapping out of whatever slow-motion blur I'm stuck in, I race to the ambulance they're loading her into.

"Please, let me stay with her," I cry.

They tell me to sit up front, away from Olivia, but I refuse. Why is no one listening to me? I can't leave her.

"I need to hold her hand; she needs to know it's okay."

The two paramedics give each other concerned looks, eyes filled with pity as they reluctantly allow me into the rear cabin. Sitting on the bench, I find Olivia's hand under the cloth and squeeze.

"I'm right here," I whisper. "I'm right here."

The ambulance turns off its lights, not bothering with a siren. The driver takes their time, going slowly around the bends, roads still wet from the torrential downpour that suddenly stopped seconds before the police arrived.

There's no reason to rush because there's no one to save.

Softly humming her favorite drunken song, I give her hand another squeeze as tears stream down my face. Olivia will never again have a chance to belt that song aloud while dancing around in the quiet of one of our foster homes. And I'll never be able to complain about how it drove me crazy every time she did.

I'd take back every complaint if it meant hearing her sing off-key again.

How can she be gone? Her hand is still so warm in mine. No, this can't be real. This *is* a nightmare. I crush my eyelids shut, springing them back open, expecting to find a new scene in front of me.

Nothing changes.

Guided from the ambulance, I blink up at the entrance doors of the emergency room. They glide open, beckoning me to come in and be heartbroken. We step into a cold blast of air conditioning as a chill shudders through me. My teeth were chattering from before, but now I gnash them together. The cop from the scene arrives, and he steers me in a different direction than where they're wheeling Olivia.

"Wait, no!" I try to pull my arm free, but he doesn't budge.

"I just need to ask you some questions." His voice is calm and soothing.

"But my sister—"

"I'm sorry, there's nothing else they can do, but we need more information about what happened."

The cop guides me along, directing me into a small room at the end of a corridor. A round table with three chairs circles it. In the corner, there's one counter with a tiny built-in sink and a coffee maker next to a bright orange bowl with a mix of coffee and tea.

Olivia hates the color orange. No—*hated*. My throat tightens.

The officer points to the counter. "Want anything to drink?"

Reluctantly sitting down, I shake my head and adjust the coat around my shoulders. I don't want to see my dress; I don't want to acknowledge the damage done—shredded, covered in mud, and now Olivia's blood.

A shudder racks my body again.

"You should drink something. Or do you want something to eat? You don't want to go into shock."

I don't respond. Shock is an understatement. I'm devastated. I'm a dam waiting to break, and when I do, I'll drown.

He sits across from me and pulls a notebook and a pen out of his pocket. "Mind if I ask you some questions?"

I lift my head, giving a stiff tilt in response, allowing him to proceed.

"Do you mind giving me your parents' names so we can inform them? Then we can wait until they arrive before we talk if you'd like."

Throat constricting, I think, *We don't have parents.* I haven't even thought about Judy and Dennis until now. What are they going to do or say? Are they going to get rid of me now? They wanted siblings. I can't be part of a sibling pair without Olivia.

My voice cracks when I try to use it. The bulge in my throat is impossible to swallow, but I can't cry any more, not right now, at least. "We—we don't have parents. We're in foster care. We're living with Judy and Dennis McIntyre."

He leans forward, adjusting his chair to bring it closer to the table. "How long have you been there?"

"About four months or so. We arrived just before summer."

"Do you have a caseworker?"

Nodding, I reply, "Nancy Jacobs."

I remain quiet as the cop relays the information into his radio so someone else can start hunting everyone down.

"Do you want to wait for them before we begin?"

"I just want to see my sister."

"You..." He lets out a sigh. "You do understand what happened?"

"Yes," I snap. My voice is thick. "I know she's gone, but I don't want her to be alone."

"We can..." He moves his chair again, shifting uncomfortably. His concern radiates off him, making my teeth grind. "We can see what we can do when we're done here."

Tears well in my eyes, and I'm afraid I'm going to lose it again. Every moment is a new crack in the concrete. The water is waiting to release, ready to destroy anything in its path.

"I'm assuming you two were walking somewhere, and from the state of your attire, I'm guessing you attended homecoming tonight?"

"Yeah. We went to homecoming and then to a bonfire."

He jots something down. "And where were you heading when we found you?"

"Home. Well, Judy and Dennis's home."

The pen stills over the paper. "They didn't want to give you a ride?"

My head snaps up to look at the cop. Wary, I answer the question to the best of my ability. "They would've come if we called, but we didn't."

"Why didn't you?"

I open my mouth and close it; I have no response for this—not one that will satisfy him, at least. Because Olivia was drunk? Because we shouldn't have been out late? Because we were afraid of what Judy and Dennis would do—ship us off as all the others have? Guilt seeps in when it dawns on me. Olivia would still be alive if I'd only dialed their number from someone's phone.

The cop writes something down again, then asks, "Did you see the vehicle that drove off?"

Wracking my brain, I realize I barely registered anything because Olivia's fear seeped into my own and overwhelmed me. But it's not like I can explain *that* to him.

"Uh... it was a pickup truck. A headlight was out, and I think the windshield might've been broken."

"Did you get a look at the driver?"

I shake my head, choking back a sob. Just another thing I did wrong. Another way I failed Olivia.

"A man, a woman?"

"It was too dark and happened too fast," I whisper. "I didn't... I didn't..."

The dam breaks loose. I sob into my hands, refraining from letting out a scream. The pain is unbearable; I just want it to end.

The cop stops questioning me, placing a hand on my shoulder. It's supposed to be comforting, but the only person who could ever comfort me is lying alone in a sterile room somewhere in this hospital.

Minutes pass, and my cries turn into hiccups. My eyes sting from my tears. I'm so tired; I'd do anything to sleep for a little while, but the need to see Olivia outweighs all of it.

"When can I see my sister?" I ask.

"Soon," he promises. "Was Olivia walking in the road?"

I frown, trying to recall. Licking my lips, I wipe my nose with the back of my hand. "She was a little bit ahead of me, so I didn't see the accident happen. I was still coming up on the bend. But, no. She wasn't in the road before then."

He takes more notes. I want to reach over, snatch the pen away from him, and throw it at the wall. "Was she stumbling?"

She was, but what's this guy playing at? Is he trying to blame Olivia for what happened?

I don't respond, so he asks, "Was she drinking at the bonfire?"

Eyes narrowing, my protective instinct kicks back in. "Does it matter?"

The cop picks at invisible lint on his uniform as he avoids eye contact. The tension in the room builds.

"Well?" I lash out.

"I'm just trying to understand what happened."

"Someone ran her over, and now she's *dead*," I say, low at first, but then my voice begins to rise, hands prickling. *Not here. Not here.*

"I understand that, but I need to know the circumstances. Did she stumble into the road? Did she jump?"

I leap out of my chair, knocking it over, and clench my hands into fists because of how hard they're shaking. "Why does it matter? She's gone. She can't go back and change anything."

I'm pacing the room like a trapped animal. I have enough sense to hide my hands in the jacket, but I'm too afraid to peek to see if they're glowing. "Why are you even in here? Shouldn't you be finding the person who did this?"

The light flickers, and the cop peers up uneasily, but I can't look away from his face, committing it to memory the longer I stare. I'll never forget the man accusing Olivia of wrongdoing instead of looking for her killer.

He's not that old, probably in his mid-forties, but there are bags under his eyes aging him, making it look like he hasn't slept in days. His dark hair is smoothed back but slightly disheveled as if he ran his hands through it too many times and the gel couldn't hold it in place. The shorter bits stick out, adding to his fatigued appearance. He has a stocky build and seems friendly enough, but there's tension in his shoulders like he's carrying around a burden. His name tag reads, "J. Goodwin," and I hate him—the cop who played it friendly only to blame the dead girl for dying.

"I want to see my sister now," I demand as the light goes out.

Officer Goodwin turns on his cell phone, casting an eerie shadow under his face while clearing his throat. He holds my gaze for a moment too long, and it's like he's looking right through me. I break our eye contact, shifting my gaze toward my feet.

"Right..." He stands, then steps over to the light switch, flipping it back and forth. Afterward, he stabs a finger at the coffee maker's power button, which doesn't turn on. "Well, it looks like we blew a fuse. Let me see what's going on. Do you want to switch rooms, or should I leave the door open?"

I don't bother responding. Instead, I tug the jacket harder around me, jaw twitching, and lean against the counter. Officer Goodwin scoops up the chair I discarded, using it to prop the door ajar before disappearing down the corridor. The hallway illuminates the room in one tiny sliver. But when I free my hands from the jacket pockets, a purple glow chases away the darkness entirely.

Chapter Eight

Theo

I ARRIVE AT HILDA's right on time. It's the middle of the night, and no one is around.

Mask already donned—I highly doubt they have cameras, but better safe than sorry—I park the truck near the back entrance and leap out, grabbing the dinner (cold soup in an old margarine container) Elise gave me, and head toward the detached shed about fifty feet away. From here, I can watch the place to make sure no one shows up questioning my truck's sudden appearance.

An hour later, legs stiff from squatting, I stretch out my limbs, pulling myself up and brushing the dirt off my pants.

I'm ready to get this over with.

I make quick work of the back door's lock and hold my breath when I open it. Seconds pass, and no alarm sounds.

Shaking out my fingers and hoping routine kicks in and the jitters leave soon, I prop the door open with a box, the space wide enough to slip through for a quick and easy escape.

Leaving all the lights off, I take a flashlight out of my pocket and click it on, keeping it pointed at the floor so it doesn't flash out the window.

Heart racing, I steady myself.

The clock begins now.

The absolute worst part of these runs is getting gas to make sure I can make it back. It puts me dead center in front of the store, out in the open for anyone to drive by and see. I may as well wear a flashing neon sign asking someone to catch me. But it's the only thing assuring my exit.

With a groan, I flip on the pumps at the register and bolt out the back door. Grabbing two cans at a time from the cab, I fill them all, resisting the urge to turn my head. I don't want to make it even more noticeable that I shouldn't be here on the off chance someone *is* watching me.

After turning the pumps back off, my brain's autopilot turns on. I go through my mental checklist: bottled water, any and all canned food, pasta, energy bars, Pop-Tarts, first-aid supplies, hygiene products, cereal, and whatever else will last us as long as possible. Oh, and a carton of cigarettes that will last until my next run. I don't often smoke, only when I need to stop myself from spiraling. It's more about the lighter or match than the actual tobacco, anyway. It's the only fire I can control.

The guilt eats away at me; I can only imagine the worker's reactions when they show up later to see the place has been wiped clean. I never wanted things to be this way. I don't enjoy stealing from people. It's just a matter of survival. And if it's us or them, I'm choosing *us*.

I step back inside for one last haul. My favorite part of the run.

I've made it a rule: never steal cash from the registers. Most places only leave the bare minimum amount in there anyway, but I won't be that person. I won't let any of us be that person. We don't steal cash. If we find something to pawn, that's a different story. But our snatches are for survival, not pleasure.

It might not seem like a difference to some, but it is for me.

What I do take, though, semi-guilt-free, is comfort food—everyone has something they miss from their "normal" life. Elise is gummy worms. Zay, Cheetos. Nora, king-size Reese's Peanut Butter Cups. And I'm a sucker for hot fries with a Dr. Pepper. It doesn't seem like much, but it's the only thing that lifts our spirits for a while. We're just kids, after all.

I also grab a new pocket lighter and a pair of headphones while I'm here—necessities for me to stay sane.

Headlights flash outside as I'm zipping up my backpack. Ice trickles down my spine. I duck down, creeping silently to the windows for a better glimpse.

The closer I get to the doors, the louder the music becomes—a car parks outside the station.

Fuck.

Spinning, I frantically scan for a place to hide; behind the counter is the nearest spot. In the faint light, I spy a door leading into a kitchen.

It's not a great plan, but it's my only one.

I dart behind the counter as two people approach the front door. The jingling of keys taps against the glass as they unlock it.

I'm doubled over, moving as fast as I can, and the flashlight slips from my sweaty hand just as I turn the corner into the kitchen.

Their slurred arguing blares out, destroying the silence, but thankfully, they don't turn on the lights.

"Just get the beer, wouldya?" a male voice booms.

A second, deeper voice snipes, "Don't tell me what to do."

Shifting, I glance at the flashlight, still on, and my heart rate doubles in speed.

"I'll do whatever the fuck I want."

A grunt, then feet tripping over themselves, a squeak of a rubber sole echoing off the epoxy floor.

Did they just shove each other?

I strain to follow their movement—their bickering fades the tiniest bit the further they move toward the back of the store—and I chance stretching an arm out, fingertips just brushing the flashlight.

Fuck. *Fuck.*

I adjust some, pulling my arm back as I stretch my body across the floor, praying to a God I hope exists right now, and reach out again. Sweat drips from my hairline, and my hands tremble, but I'm able to snatch the flashlight. I switch it off before drawing it close and slinking back; my body is flush against a metal safe.

"When Hilda finds out you took beer again, she'll kill you. And I'm going to let her," the deeper voice belts out, followed by a sickening laugh that makes him seem a bit unhinged.

I close my eyes, wiping my palms on my pants. Then, I inch over, unbearably slow, to get further away from the opening. I let the backpack straps glide off my shoulders to rest entirely on the floor and crouch.

They continue to argue, cracking open whatever shitty beer they took. My back goes rigid when something shatters. The force of an object connecting with a door? A window?

"Hilda can fuck right off," the first man scoffs.

My heartbeat thrums in my eardrums.

They continue to bicker; more indiscernible things break in their path of destruction. An endcap possibly being thrown to the floor, items swiped off the counter, landing with a clang. That hollow laugh bounces off the walls again.

What the hell is going on?

I ball my shaking hands into fists and clench them against my thighs. My knees groan in protest over squatting again, all my weight on the balls of my feet, my body taut, ready to launch.

I don't want to fight my way out of here, but I will if I have to.

Having the element of surprise will help if it comes to that.

Finally, their voices fade.

I unclench my hands and flex my fingers. That was *close*.

Before relaxing, I wait for the headlights to shine through the window, but they don't come. Minutes later, I'm still barely breathing as if they're inside and able to hear me.

I shake my head, silently cursing when the bell over the door tinkles again.

The man grumbles to himself about fetching a pack of cigarettes two feet away from me, only the kitchen wall separating us.

The closer his footsteps get, the more my vision darkens. My head spins, and it feels like I'm falling. I lower my hands to the ground to steady myself but can't catch my breath. My heart ricochets against my ribcage, and once more, the chest pain is so bad I think I might be dying.

What does Nora see right now? Does she see me?

My vision turns from black to a dazzling purple, and I'm no longer in the store. I'm watching her—the brunette girl who's usually only in my dreams. She's laying her head on a table. Her hair is drenched and in knots, and she hides her face under her arm. The color surrounds her, ebbing and flowing as her body shakes violently with a sob.

I want to ask her what's wrong, but we're never able to communicate.

Hesitantly, I stretch out a hand, moving closer. She doesn't notice I'm right behind her. Not knowing how to form the question, even if she could hear me, words die on my lips. I shouldn't be here right now.

How is this possible? I only see her in my dreams. Does that mean I'm sleeping?

When I'm close enough, I rest my hand on her shoulder, breaching new territory since I've never felt her before now. My hand rests on her oversized jacket, but she doesn't notice my touch. I sit in the opposing chair, my heart fluttering when she shifts to look at me. It upticks when she squints like she can actually see me. She stares before shaking her head as if to clear it. Her eyes glow the same purple shade as her hands, currently lighting up the room.

For the past five years, I've only hung out with the girl sitting in front of me while in my dreams, someone I've created entirely in my mind. I think she was my way of coping when I learned not to enter my parents' heads when I slept. I needed a distraction. I needed anyone to take my mind off of Riley, and the more desperate I became not to be alone in the dream world, the clearer she became.

She now looks so broken, so defeated, though. And I hate it. I'll do anything to get her to stop crying and comfort her somehow. The dreams where I create her aren't normally so... somber. I wonder what changed. How did I fall asleep, and why am I making this so tragic?

Something like guilt worms its way into my stomach. I can't help her. I have no power to change the situation, but I can wake up. Maybe that will take away her pain.

This might be my last opportunity to be this close to her since it's never happened before, and it could be a fluke that it's even happening now. I eye the purple, judging the danger, and place my hand over hers.

The faintest of touches singes my skin. Burning through me with a pain I've felt before.

I gasp awake, collapsing onto the floor. Blinking away the darkness, it takes me a few costly seconds to remember where I am.

"What the fuck?" a deep voice growls.

A large figure looms in the doorway, but it's too dark to make out his facial features. I lay there motionless, head spinning. I touched her, she burned me, and now *this*.

This can't be good.

Scrambling to my feet, I punch him with the same hand she burned. Something on his face crunches from the force. I hiss at the impact, knuckles splitting open, as the guy stumbles backward. With him unbalanced, I snatch my backpack from the ground and escape through the back door, kicking the box as I go.

I don't even care how loud the truck is at this point; there's no more hiding now. I start the engine and peel out. My entire body shakes like a live wire from the close call, and I want to take a minute, but I don't have a minute to spare.

Pushing the pedal down to the floor, I leave as fast as I can.

THE SUN RISES OVER the horizon as I berate myself on the drive home. I've had a few close calls in the past, but nothing as bad as that. This was my first time trapped, having to fight my way out. I messed up big time. How did I fall asleep? I don't understand. Or did I faint? The last thing I remember was the pounding of my heart before *her*.

My fingertips tingle as she pops back into my head. I felt her smooth skin underneath mine, and my head swims, thinking of it all over again. That's never happened. I don't know what it means or if there will be another chance to try again.

What am I even talking about? You made her up, fucking idiot. She isn't real.

I rub my fingers together, wincing at the pain from the minor burns that are very much real, left behind from her skin, and I'm taken back to the worst night of my life. My lungs cease to work, choking on smoke that isn't there, and my head starts to spin.

Pulling over to the side of the road, I wrench open the door and stumble out, collapsing to my knees in the ditch to vomit. As I retch, echoes of screams haunt me. I'm not sure if they're mine. They might be Riley's. Both of us are dying in my memories this time. Maybe she never died alone.

After a few minutes, I wipe my mouth with the back of my hand, fumble for the pack of cigarettes, and dig out the lighter. I focus on the flame until it burns the edge of my thumb. Closing my eyes, I finally light the cigarette dangling from my lips and inhale as deeply as possible. The smoke burns, and I let it fill my lungs, then reluctantly return to the truck.

MY HANDS STOP SHAKING before I'm back at the house, which makes unloading the haul easier. By the time the crew wakes up, I can pretend the close call never happened.

When Zay enters the kitchen, his face lights up as if it's Christmas morning, and I chuckle.

"Easy now. We need to make it last," I remind him.

"Yeah, yeah, no, that's cool," he responds as if it's no big deal, but he still eyes everything hungrily.

Nora comes up and gives me a swift, silent hug. Maybe she didn't see anything after all?

Elise fiddles with an energy bar, turning it over repeatedly, eyes flicking between me and the stockpile of food. "How'd it go?"

It takes me a moment to meet her gaze, my lips turning upward, imitating a smile as I shrug. "It was good."

Her eyes flash down to my already bruising knuckles, and I quickly stuff my hands in my pockets. Before she can question me further, I duck out to my bedroom, locking myself in.

The world is still off-balance, like light vertigo is clouding my senses.

Nora saw me disappear.

I fucked up big time today.

What's wrong with me?

Chapter Nine

Gemma

Sitting in silence for too long creates chaos in my mind. I can't stop thinking about what happens next. I can't live here without her. I can't *live* without her. The lights going out only confirms the incident at Modern Moda was me—not to mention the destruction around us after I reached her body. My throat tightens.

What am I becoming?

Regardless of whatever level of freak I am, I no longer have Olivia to protect me. Or keep me grounded. Or tell me everything is fine.

I've lost my sister, my best friend.

Where will I go? When should I leave? Who will keep me in control? Energy runs unchecked through my veins. Grief is powering me more than any emotion ever has. Electricity burns at my fingertips. I should care that my hands are glowing right now, that someone might walk by and see, but the problem is, I don't. I don't care about anything anymore.

I'm unable to wrap my mind around the fact that Olivia is truly gone, but I understand all the same since I can't sense her anymore.

Olivia's emotions were so much my own that it was like two beating hearts inside me. Now I feel empty—hollow—and the echoing of one heartbeat only mocks me, reminding me the other is gone. The frequency I've been attuned to for seventeen years has been changed to another channel.

A cloud is hanging over me, draping me in a blanket. Is that sorrow? Or is it something else? I can't shake the feeling that there's more.

Sensing the gentlest touch on my hand, I let out a small sigh, envisioning Olivia with me. Then I notice a figure standing when I glance up—darkness forms within the purple glow. I squint, shaking my head, and it disappears. *No.* It must've been a trick of the mind. That wasn't her just now, was it? Is this what grief is like? Or am I just losing my mind?

I've almost cried myself to sleep when the lights flicker back on, and the first thing I notice is that the glowing is already gone. Blinking away the spots in my vision, I lift my head from the table to see Judy and Dennis standing in the doorway, watching me. Judy is openly weeping, her face bright red, and her blue eyes dim. Dennis has his arm wrapped around her, his eyes slightly swollen, brown cheeks tear-stained.

My heart fills with hollowness, but I discern something more. Regret, maybe? It must be coming from one of them. Maybe they're disappointed with who we turned out to be and thinking how they could've gotten better kids.

Right now, I don't care either way. I just want to be held.

My lower lip trembles as I stand up and cross the room, wrapping my arms around Judy. She freezes in place, and I realize this is the first time we've ever hugged. A heartbeat passes, and her arms wrap around me, holding me close as I sob into her shoulder. Her wavy strawberry-blonde hair tickles my cheek, but I relish it anyway. I don't want to let go.

"What happened?" Judy whispers.

"I don't know." I shake my head, unable to get the words out. "There was a truck, and I didn't..."

Judy pulls away, looking down at me, sweeping my hair back. "Shh, it's all right. We can talk about it later. Let's get you home."

Home. There's that word again.

Olivia and I've never truly had one, and now I'm positive I never will. How could I have a home without Oli? Dennis lays a comforting hand on my back but doesn't offer any words. He takes the officer's jacket off me, sets it on the table, and wraps me in a sweater he's brought with him.

"Is there any way I can see her?" I ask as they lead me to the front lobby. "One last time?"

"They've taken her to the morgue," Dennis says softly. "But you can see her before the funeral."

Funeral?

That word, for some reason, takes me by surprise. It's natural to have a funeral after someone dies, but I can only handle one minute at a time right now. I can't even process that I'm leaving her behind in the hospital, let alone think of her burial. I try to respond, but I'm frozen.

Judy intertwines her arm with mine and tugs. "Amber is still at the house; we should be getting back."

I don't move.

"You want to bury her?" I finally ask in disbelief.

Judy and Dennis exchange uneasy glances as Dennis stammers, "Well... yeah. I mean..."

"No." The word is out of my mouth before I have time to think. "You can't bury her here. This isn't our home."

Judy softens. "Sweetie..."

"I said no." My anger flares, and I breathe through my nose to keep myself from lighting up again. "I want her cremated. She needs to stay with me."

"We can talk about this back at the house," Dennis adds.

"That isn't our home!" I repeat, almost screaming this time. My home is *gone*—I'm alone now. "I *need* her with me."

"Okay, okay." Judy wraps her arm around my shoulder, tugging me close as if she can't bear to lose me, too. I sink into her as she casts nervous glances around the waiting room, offering a weak, apologetic smile to those watching us depart. Dennis keeps his mouth shut as he opens the sedan's back door when we reach the parking lot, closing it firmly after I climb in.

There's nothing but darkness outside the window. No shapes of houses or curves of trees. Nothing. Nothing's registering but an endless sea of black, void of any light now that Oli's gone.

I don't know what to do, say, or even how to think. Dennis and Judy's concern worms inside my emptiness, and all I want to do is turn everything off and have no emotions ever again.

I've gone over every second of my argument with Olivia a hundred times before Dennis parks in the driveway. Guilt rips me in half, and it's my undoing.

Once inside, I fly past a crying Amber and race up the stairs and into the bedroom, locking the door so no one can follow me. I slump against the hard wooden surface as I face Olivia's unkempt bed. She'll never sleep there again.

Sliding to the ground, I let out a howl and cry for hours.

I FINALLY HAVE ENOUGH sense to pull off this stupid ball gown I've been sitting in this entire time. Balling it up, I force it into the trash can in the bathroom. It's overflowing around it, but I don't know what else to do.

I'd set it on fire right now if I could.

I haven't slept yet, even though it's five in the morning. I'm in a dream state nonetheless, like I'm stranded in a stop-motion animation. All my movements are jagged and slow. I want to sleep but can't close my eyes.

When I do, all I see is Olivia dead in my arms.

Creeping downstairs, I brew a pot of coffee, quietly tiptoeing around the kitchen so I don't wake anyone up. Seconds later, though, the kitchen light turns on. I spin, startled, registering it's only Dennis standing there in his pajamas.

"Hey, kiddo."

"I'm sorry. I didn't mean to wake you."

"You didn't. I can't sleep either." Dennis crosses over to the cupboard and pulls out two coffee mugs. Setting them gently on the counter, he turns away to grab spoons, sugar, and milk. "Want to talk about it?"

I pick at one corner of the kitchen island, studying how the paint flakes off in my palm. I shouldn't be destroying their stuff, but I can't help it. "I didn't mean what I said earlier." My eyes flash to Dennis's. Sadness pours out of him, mingling with my own, and it takes me a second before I'm confident my voice won't come out shaky. "You both have treated us really well here. I'm... I'm sorry. I'm just used to it being the two of us."

Silence hangs in the air, allowing me to work out my thoughts.

"Olivia was the only home I've ever known. We were both so close to aging out of the system. I was going to leave when she did." I lift a shoulder. "Now, I'm lost. I don't know what to do. I don't know how to feel. There's a war waging inside of me, and I..." I teeter off, realizing this is the most I've ever spoken to any of my foster parents, especially about something so personal.

"You'll always have a place here," Dennis says, his voice gruff.

I study him here in this quiet kitchen. Why didn't I let him and Judy in sooner? They're the most decent foster parents we've had in our short lives, and I never even gave them a chance. Dennis's kind eyes are now glistening, and I have to glance away again. It's hard to wrap my head around since he's only known us for a handful of months, but I think he actually cares.

But the damage is already done. As much as I always wanted to be normal, this isn't the life for me now.

There's no going back.

"Thank you," I whisper.

Dennis pours the coffee, and we both sit on barstools surrounding the island, but neither one of us takes a sip.

Instead, we sit in silence, and it takes everything in my power not to cry again. I bite my lip, distracting myself, sealing the dam shut, but the cracks are only being held together by duct tape. There's no way it'll keep for long.

"I'm so sorry, Gemma," he begins. "I can't even imagine what you're going through. But I'm here to talk whenever you need to. Day or night." When I don't respond, he squeezes my shoulder. "Why don't you try to get some rest, okay?"

I avoid his eyes as my vision blurs, and I nod, bolting out of the kitchen and up the stairs. The bedroom door is barely shut when my tears start flowing again. I fall asleep crying, hoping the boy from my dreams will appear tonight. I need someone with me.

I can't do this alone.

Chapter Ten

THEO

I WAKE UP HOURS later with the world spinning around me. After blinking a few times, my vision straightens itself out, and the broken ceiling fan above me comes back into focus.

My hand aches, knuckles bruised from hitting that guy, and fingertips throbbing from the burns.

I roll back over, hoping to block the pain out, seconds before Elise barges into the room.

"Christ," I mutter into the old pillow, all the comfort beaten out of it long ago. I pull the blanket over my head to block her out, too.

"Are we going to talk about what happened last night?"

"Nothing happened."

"Look at your hand."

Opening one eye, I peer at the hand sticking out from underneath the sheets, then pull it under the blanket with the rest of me.

She taps her foot. "Well?"

"It's nothing. Let me go back to sleep."

"I can tell when you're lying. I literally see it."

"You can't see lies." I roll my eyes at her exaggeration, thankful she can't see me doing it.

"Maybe not the *lies* themselves, but you always feel guilty when you lie, and your aura turns pink."

Not always.

Elise huffs. "It's already five in the afternoon. You slept all day."

I peel back the covers and lift my head at this, brushing a curl out of my face to get a better look at the watch on my splintered nightstand. "Shit."

She pushes a pile of dirty clothes onto the floor, sitting in the sole chair, leaning toward me, waiting for the details—the *drama*.

Letting out a sigh, I flop back onto the mattress. "I have to get new plates."

"What happened?"

Gripping the blanket, I clench my injured fist, coaxing the pain to come back as those purple eyes ringed with sadness float in my head. "I punched someone."

"How did you get caught?"

"I—I don't know. He snuck up on me. I wore a mask, but they might've seen my plates."

"They?"

"There was some other guy in the parking lot when I left. They destroyed the place before I left, so I don't think they'll care much that I was there, but—"

Elise makes a noise between a grunt and a sigh. "Theo..."

"I know. I messed up. I'll fix it."

She lets the silence linger between us. I imagine she's trying to develop a plan as much as I am, but neither of us voices it aloud.

Finally, she announces, "I walked to the library today while you were sleeping to see what they had in the free book pile."

"Okay." I close my eyes, annoyed she's still here if she isn't going to help and slightly confused about why she's telling me this.

"I saw a poster."

"Mm."

"A fair is coming to town soon."

I sit up, frowning. "You're kidding me, right?"

"Oh my God. Stop being such a stick in the mud. No one is going to know who we are. It looks like it's going to be big. It's some annual tradition that draws a large crowd every year. Or that's what the sign says. Plenty of cars in the parking lot... maybe even some out of towners..."

She trails off, but the smirk on her face says everything. She knows I'm intrigued by the idea. I'd rather not go to a carnival, but it would be easy to get new plates there.

I nod in reluctant agreement.

"Great! I'll go tell Zay and Nora!"

She hops up and darts out of the room before I can warn her against it. They'd be safer if they didn't come with us, but then again, it's probably fine.

⁂

WHEN WE FIRST GOT to the Rib House, I hung old tires I found from a chain to create a makeshift punching bag. It's not great, but it's an easier way to get rid of my annoyance than speaking with others.

Sweat drips down my back as I work out my frustration by jabbing at it.

I haven't had any more fainting episodes or whatever you want to call them, and I haven't seen *her*.

Each night before bed, I conjure her image, hoping she'll appear when I'm asleep, but she doesn't come. Prior to this, I could change the dream in the blink of an eye, and she'd be there.

I try not to astral project; invasion of privacy, and all that. But sometimes, I can't control it—like how I ended up in Nora's head the other night.

When I first ran away from home, I often ended up in my parents' dreams. Unfortunately, I didn't want to be there. My dad's dreams were chilling. He was always frantically searching for Riley and me in the darkness. I still look over my shoulder, fearing the day he'll catch up to us. He'll turn us in, just like he did Riley.

My mom's dreams, though, never changed. She seemed as unfazed as she was days before the fire.

Either way, I hated being there. Witnessing what I shouldn't. So, I created her. And she's been with me ever since. Someone who brings me peace within the madness. A place to escape when reality becomes too much to bear.

In the past, we've sat on a log next to the shore, walked for hours in the woods, and hung out in my bedroom as The Strokes played in the background, all while never saying a word to each other. Never touching either, like two magnets kept apart, only existing in the same dream universe. It was so easy—one simple thought, and she'd appear.

Two years ago, once I was old enough to convince someone to do it, I started getting our encounters tattooed on my arms to cover the burns left on my hands from my childhood. I decided on her likeness because she's the reason I haven't completely lost my mind. Plus, it helps make her as life-like as possible.

It's pathetic—yearning for someone who doesn't exist. But I want nothing more than to mix in the purple surrounding her the other night and add it to the growing collection of ink staining my skin. Her glow burned me and ultimately brought her more into focus than ever before. The thought sends shivers down my spine.

Now that I can't get her out of my head even during waking hours, she's gone. Like a wall was built, separating us. I can't reach her no matter how hard I try.

What went wrong?

Snapping back into the moment, I let her go as I punch the worn-out rubber.

Everyone else in the crew seems content these days, which I can only attribute to their full stomachs. Zay and Nora continue working on their studies—magical and not—without complaint. Elise seems happier knowing the fair is coming; it gives her something to look forward to.

And I'm just out here.

Fighting with no one but myself.

Hoping *she'll* come back soon.

Chapter Eleven

GEMMA

OLIVIA'S FUNERAL IS TODAY, and I—
I can't.

Chapter Twelve

Theo

Loud music blares as the trees become sparser. We stumble into a clearing, mouths slack as we take in the sight of the county fair in front of us—all bright lights and crowds of people.

Zay's face splits into a grin, but his hands ball into fists at his sides.

"Everything all right?" I ask under my breath.

He shoots me a concerned look, but then his shoulders relax. "Yeah, I'm fine. I'm just..."

"If you feel yourself slipping, let one of us know, and we'll scram. I don't need you dropping a tornado on everyone just because you're too excited." I'm half kidding, but the implication is still there. Zay hasn't mastered nature manipulation yet, so he doesn't always have complete control.

He draws in a large breath, shakily letting it go. "I'm fine. It's just a lot of people."

I nod. The poor kid hasn't seen another human besides us since his grandmother died, and I'm not sure how much socializing he did before then. He liked to play video games, but that's the extent of my knowledge of his past.

"Stick with Nora and Elise, and you'll be fine."

His eyes grow large, flickering between the fair and me. "Where are you going?"

"I have to take care of something, but I'll be here. I'll meet up with you in a few hours."

Before he can respond, I point at Nora with a finger gun. "You good?"

"Mhm." She smiles, pointing a gun back at me, winking as she moves her thumb in a shooting motion.

"All right. Well, I'll see you all in a bit."

"Good luck," Elise responds as we split apart. She's the only one who knows I'm only here to get plates.

As they sneak into the fair, I hang back, leaning against a tree until I can use the cloak of darkness to snatch some plates and hide them in my backpack.

All I have to do is wait.

THE PARKING LOT STRETCHES for at least a mile, maybe more.

I creep along the tree line until I lose sight of the flashing lights, and the merry-go-round music fades into nothing. The only thing I'm still able to spot is the Ferris wheel. My stomach flips as I watch it, imagining myself stuck on top. I hate heights. No, thank you. I'm happy right here on the cold, hard earth.

Shaking my head clear, I get back to business. Rows upon rows of cars sit together, and there's no one in sight. I bend down and hustle to the nearest vehicle when I reach the last line.

Half-running from bumper to bumper, it takes me fifteen tries to stumble upon plates from another state—Kentucky.

Bingo.

I pull a wrench out from my backpack, quickly swapping the plates. I hide theirs away and slap on the old ones from the truck.

Hopefully, they'll be long gone before they realize what I've done since they *almost* look the same—a simple blue-and-white design.

After I'm finished, I disappear into the tree line, blending into the shadows once more, and head back toward the smell of popcorn and cotton candy wafting in the air.

⁂

I CIRCLE THE PERIMETER, deciding on the best place to enter to go unnoticed. The fair is packed with all the staples: food stands, rides, games, a barn full of animals, and long lines of stalls that almost fill half the lot.

Children scream and run around, hyped up on too much sugar; people laugh as they share inside jokes; and carnies in front of the games shout over each other, doing their best to lure customers in to waste their money on a shitty stuffed animal they'll throw out next week.

Ugh.

Elise is probably right, though. This place is so large it'd be impossible to notice us as long as Zay keeps it together.

When I make it to the last section of the fair before it turns into a parking lot again, I spot a big white tent off to the side by itself.

It's as if it's not part of the fair at all.

Intrigue *almost* wins me over, but after a second thought, I jump the railing to the fair and head for the games.

Elise pawned off an old watch she found a few states ago to get some spending cash for tonight, and I'm going to guess they're either playing games or on the rides.

Please don't be on the Ferris wheel.

"Hold it."

Shit.

I turn toward him, my mind racing over what to say. The words tumble out before I can stop them. "Sorry, man, just had to take a piss."

The man sizes me up, and I do the same to him. He towers over me, wearing a suit with a cheap-looking gold chain. He's combed his black, oily hair back on both sides in a way that should make him look presentable, but the toothpick jutting from his mouth ruins that. His gaze lingers on my split knuckles.

"I should be heading back..." I start to leave.

"You fight?" His thick accent makes it hard to understand him. I don't know where he's from, but it's certainly not Indiana.

I lower my head, back still turned to him as I consider my options.

"Only if I have to," I growl.

He lets out a chuckle. "You look like a fighter, and I'm usually right about these things. You interested?"

I fully face him now; brows furrowed in confusion. "I'm not fighting you."

"Not me. You'd be in the ring." He tilts his head toward the white tent behind him as he takes out the toothpick. Then he shrugs as if he couldn't care less. "Unless you're not interested."

"I'm not."

The man doesn't move, so I take a step backward.

The smile on his face is sinister. "Easy way to make a grand."

I stop dead in my tracks, hand gripping the backpack strap slung over my shoulder as his words register. A grand? To fight? I probably *shouldn't*, but a grand?

That's worth bloody knuckles and black eyes.

That'd set us up for a while.

He laughs. "Think about it, kid. With a grand, you wouldn't need to sneak into any more fairs."

It's been a long time since I've fought in a ring. It was our primary source of income when it was just Elise and me, but I stopped after Nora came along. Her visions have helped us survive from run to run by finding places to steal food. Plus, it didn't seem right to drag her along to fights. Elise is different. Nora is like... well, like a little sister I should protect—especially since I failed last time.

I won't fail again.

The tires in the garage haven't been enough for training. This is a terrible idea. There are so many ways this can go wrong.

I narrow my eyes at the stranger. "I'm in."

THE INSIDE OF THE tent reeks of sweat and blood and does nothing to mask the intoxicating excitement radiating from the metal bleachers packed with a rowdy audience eager for the next fight. My gaze snags on the center of the space—it's empty, with a thin layer of rocky dirt covering the grass. It's not the worst ring I've ever fought in.

Sketchy fights like this are never legal, which explains why the tent is close enough to the fair to draw attention but not *too* much attention—blending right in with the rest of the attractions. I just have to get in, make my money, and get out before it's busted. I take quick notice of the two exits, both blocked by bodyguards with guns holstered on their hips.

I turn to the guy with the oily hair, shaking my head, trying to ignore *that* sight. "Who am I fighting?"

He keeps leading people my way, letting them place bets like he's my manager.

"Don't worry about it."

A man twice my size emerges from the other side of the makeshift ring. Speckles of dry blood coat his arms, he's shirtless, and scratches cover his chest. He looks me dead in the eye and spits on the ground.

I glance at the man standing next to me. "I'm worried."

"He's slow. You'll be fine." He puts his hand on my shoulder, leaning close to my face as if we're old pals. I knock his arm off mine. He laughs, then lowers his voice. "He leaves his left side unprotected. Especially when he starts jabbing. Wait for it, and it'll be a K.O. I promise you."

I nod, even though my muscles quiver with tension, warning me this isn't a good idea.

A thousand dollars.

A thousand dollars.

A thousand dollars.

Shaking my arms loose, I rotate my neck, gaze settling on my opponent as I school my features. *Don't show him anything.*

Just as I'm about to remove my white T-shirt, a familiar voice calls my name.

Elise.

I whip around, tugging the shirt back into place. Elise's mouth is wide open, Zay is laughing, and Nora's amber eyes shimmer with unshed tears.

"What the hell?" I grab Elise's elbow and pull her to the side. "Why did you bring them here?"

"What was I supposed to do? Nora saw you were about to get your ass kicked and dragged us away from the games."

"You all need to go. *Now.*"

She shakes her head, eyes wide as she looks me over. "You're fighting again?"

"It's a grand if I win."

She glances at the man standing on the other side and returns her gaze to me. "That's a big if."

I scoff. "Thanks for that vote of confidence. Now go, please. Take them with you."

Elise purses her lips as she grabs the two younger ones, ushering them out. Zay gives me a thumbs-up and shouts, "You got this!"

FOCUSING ON MY BREATHING, I enter the ring. We circle each other, neither one breaking eye contact; all I have to do is turn my brain off.

I've been here before.

Let my body do the work; don't overthink it, and it'll all be over.

The sharp ring of a bell barely ends when the burly man charges me. I sidestep just in time, avoiding his crushing force.

A smirk crosses my face as I fall back into old habits.

I've fought his kind. He *can* kick my ass, but he's all strength and nothing else. I'm guessing he lacks professional training; he doesn't know how to watch an opponent for weak spots. He's clumsy on his feet—a bull in a china shop.

Technically, I lack professional training, too, but my dad taught me how to fight when I was—no, stop. Don't go there. *Focus.*

We continue to circle each other as I study his body language. His face turns red the longer I watch him. Frustration—most likely—that I'm not doing anything. Or so he thinks. He doesn't shift his weight correctly. As a result, he can fall at any time.

He barrels toward me again, but this time he lunges.

His arms enclose around me, lifting me in the air and then slamming me onto the ground.

The air wheezes out of me, and it takes a second for me to react. It's a second too long since his fist connects with my nose.

Ow. Bastard.

He's kneeled over me, his arm pinning me down across my shoulders. My vision blurs as my eyes water, blood pouring from my nose.

But I smile, the iron taste filling my mouth, as his free arm retracts for another punch, exposing his right side.

Before he can release, I jab him in the ribs. He shifts just enough that I'm able to pull my legs in and kick him in the torso.

His grip slips from my shoulder, and I'm on my feet, smearing blood across my face and blinking away the tears.

The man is slow to get up, but once he does, he ambles toward me with his left fist guarding his chest and his right one ready to punch.

The oaf doesn't protect his face.

I shake my head as he draws closer.

He's going to tire himself out long before I hit my pain threshold.

He gets a few more jabs in as I bide my time. Grunting each time he connects. Once more to the face, a few times to the ribs.

Wait for it.

There it is.

The man's arms lower an inch, and that's my cue.

I close the space between us, getting in three or four punches before he can put his arms up. Then, when he protects his face, I aim lower.

When he drops his arms again—big mistake—I aim for his temple.

He drops.

I stagger backward until someone grabs my arm, raising it into the air. I shrug out of their grasp and approach the man who introduced me to this mess. He's sporting a wicked grin on his face.

He throws a towel at my chest as he sings, "Thatta boy."

"Where's the money?" I hold the towel up to my nose, wincing as the cloth brushes over a cut on the bridge.

He pulls out a wad of cash, counting it as he says, "You know, you keep fighting like that—"

"Not interested."

He *tsks* as he slaps the money in my hand, along with a business card.

"Ever change your mind... call me."

I drape the bloody towel over my shoulder as I quickly count the cash, then shove it—and the business card—into my pants pocket. There's blood speckling those, too.

After finding the bathroom furthest from the tent—in case they change their mind about letting me leave so easily—I wash the blood from my hands and face before donning my T-shirt. The bleeding has stopped, but the damage is done.

My nose is swollen and cut up. My knuckles have resplit, and bruises are already blossoming on my torso.

But we're a thousand dollars richer.

I let out a laugh, watching myself in the mirror. Between the world being *off* and being back in the ring... I can't help but think I've lost my mind.

Chapter Thirteen

Gemma

THE ELECTRICITY IN THE house has been running haywire since the funeral—bulbs flickering, the microwave flashing 12:00 every time the power restarts. The blender turns on when no one is in the kitchen. There's no doubt it's me, but no one else knows that. They have no idea; they're only suspicious, which scares them.

I've been unable to control the power that's been unleashed from inside me. Ever since I accidentally unlocked it, I've been shaking with—rage? Grief? Denial? I don't know what I feel anymore. Maybe a combination of all three. Whatever I'm feeling, the energy flows through my veins, looking for an escape. I wear fingerless gloves to cover some of the purple emitting from my hands since it's now more than just my fingertips, but it's only a temporary fix. How can I explain wearing them for the rest of my life? Especially in a hot and sticky state like Florida.

Trying to keep my feelings at bay has also been a struggle. The sorrow drowns me in waves, large ones that come extremely close together. I don't get a chance to breathe before the next one comes crashing down.

On top of that, I'm shouldering everyone else's emotions as well.

Judy and Dennis are terrified. For me? *Of* me? I don't know. They won't confirm their fears, but their voices carry when they think I can't hear them. Hushed whispers and urgent pleas. "*What are we supposed to do with her? She hasn't spoken a word since the night of the funeral. Should we call a therapist? A lot of weird shit is happening around here, Dennis. Do you think it's all connected somehow?*"

I can sense Amber's apprehension as well. We never had time to talk about what happened at the dress store, and now all of this. If I'm reading her correctly, there's even blame there.

You're right, kid. I should've kept my sister alive.

I don't know. Maybe I'm just projecting my own feelings onto her. Either way, Amber and I haven't spoken much. And she was always closer to Olivia than she was to me.

It doesn't help that I've mostly been trying to hide in my bedroom, keeping as far away from them as possible, lest something terrible happens and I explode something else.

A week has passed since the funeral, and most of the time, I think about dying, imagining what it would be like to join Olivia. Other times, it's ways of getting revenge on the person who killed her. The cops came up empty when trying to find her murderer. No mechanics in town have fixed up a red truck; no glassing companies have replaced a windshield. They have nothing else to go on. My blood boils whenever I let myself think about it. Hatred toward whoever hurt her fills me. I'm losing control, so I try to stop my thoughts—afraid of what will happen if I don't.

The dreams, though. The dreams still haunt me.

I'm not able to control my thoughts when I'm asleep, and all I do is relive her death. The red truck. The foggy road. Her broken body cradled in my arms.

I'm awoken every night by Dennis frantically shaking my shoulder, his face painted with concern as he tells me over and over again that I'm okay because, apparently, I start screaming aloud. I never know where I am in those first moments of consciousness. But then his eyes find mine, and my pulse slows just a little.

He stays by my side until I fall asleep again, for which I'm thankful.

But how long can we go on like this?

Last night, though, the dream changed. *He* stood at the bend in the road. Olivia ran right past him, and I watched him turn his head, look over his shoulder, and watch her go.

Why didn't he stop her?

I wanted to scream at him to *stop* her.

But of course, he couldn't. That wasn't what happened. And even if he could, he wasn't there that night. He couldn't have prevented her death.

His eyes met mine, and his mouth dropped open as if he wanted to say something when I ran by, tears blurring my vision. I already knew what would happen next because I experience her death every time I close my eyes.

In this dream, though, he stood behind me while my cries decimated the trees.

I felt his gaze on my back as I clutched Olivia, but her hand slipped from mine, and suddenly, the world shifted. We were no longer on the road. The fog dissipated. Olivia's body was nowhere to be seen as I frantically spun, searching for her.

It was only this boy and me standing feet apart in the middle of a vast meadow. The sky was gray, and wildflowers sprouted from the ground, their colors heightened. Pink and purple, a dash of blue, the yellow as vibrant as the sun that remained hidden by storm clouds.

My heart still ached for Olivia, my hands clenched into fists at my sides as I stood there. But I couldn't take my eyes off him. And how desolate he seemed while he watched me.

Shoulders hunched, he toyed with a piece of green wheat as if he couldn't keep his hands still. His lips formed, 'I'm sorry,' but the only sound was the howling of the wind and unspoken words.

I didn't know it at the moment, but now that I'm awake, I think this is my way of turning off my thoughts while I'm asleep, too. I didn't want to watch her death repeatedly, so my brain changed the channel.

It was the first time Dennis didn't have to wake me in the middle of the night, but he was still in the chair near the window when I woke up this morning, passed out with his head lolled back against a stuffed animal he used as a makeshift pillow.

My heart thundered at seeing him asleep like that. I've never felt... I don't know what the sensation is. Loved? Protected?

Whatever it is, I'm grateful. It's the first time an adult has genuinely cared for me, and now I know for sure that I can't stay here. I can't hurt him—or Judy or Amber, for that matter.

It might hurt them if I leave, but it won't hurt them as much as if I accidentally lose control. They deserve better than whatever I am.

⁂

OUT OF NOWHERE, THE cop from the hospital arrives at the house. Judy yells for me to come downstairs, but she isn't in the room when I enter. I find Officer Goodwin in the corner of the dining room, facing the hutch housing knickknacks and other mundane items Judy tends to collect from yard sales. He's reaching for something—a photo of all of us, I think—when I clear my throat.

He startles, and a soft thud vibrates from the cabinet. Craning his neck, he looks back at me and flashes a guilty smile as he rights the photo and extends a hand toward the dining room table to sit. I eye him warily as we take seats across from one another.

"I wanted to follow up on some things," Officer Goodwin starts as Judy scurries in with a tray loaded with a coffee pot and three mugs.

"Oh good, Gemma, you're here," she says, frazzled, her voice a higher pitch than normal, and a fake smile plastered across her face.

Officer Goodwin focuses back on me, eyes slightly narrowing as if he can read me like a book, and all I want to do is curl in on myself and disappear from view. This guy has done nothing to find my sister's killer. Yet he's here, wanting to know more from *me*? I lift my chin in sudden defiance, fighting the instinct to run and hide.

"How are you holding up, Gemma?" he asks.

My jaw clenches. I have nothing to say to him. How dare he ask how I'm doing? As if his time is better spent checking in on me than finding Olivia's killer. We continue to stare at one another, sizing each other up. Seeing him this close again, I'm definitely going to say he's in his late forties, his face covered in peppered gray stubble. He looks as tired as he did in the hospital. I frown in confusion the longer I study his eyes. Why do they seem so familiar? I had never seen him before Olivia died, yet something about his eyes pulls me in, lulling me into a false sense of security.

The tension in the room grows as I silently clutch the necklaces—two golden hearts with some weird symbol on the back and an inscription on the front—dangling from my neck. Judy gave me Oli's matching pendant after the funeral, and it's been a grounding lifeline during moments like this. I run my fingers over the text—Our love is forever.

Who knew forever could be so short?

I make a silent promise to myself to never take them off. These are the only items we had from *before*—before the foster homes, before the pain. I was too young when our parents died to remember where the necklaces came from, but we've always had them.

Now, I own both.

My eyelids flutter as I blink back tears. He won the staring contest because of my distraction. My eyes finally land on the table as another wave of grief threatens to drown me. Officer Goodwin shifts in his chair like he wants to say more, but since I didn't answer, he probably doesn't know how to proceed. Judy stands awkwardly in the corner, silently watching our exchange.

From the corner of my eye, I spot her hands fluttering to her neck, and then she clasps them in front of herself as she effectively breaks the silence. "Is anyone hungry? I have some cookies in the kitchen."

"Yes, please. That would be great." Officer Goodwin glances at her, giving her an award-winning smile.

I scowl when his eyes find mine again as Judy hurries out of the room. "Why are you here?"

"To help you."

His words catch me off guard, and I blink. "Help *me*? Maybe you should focus on helping yourself and your team so you can find who killed my sister."

His eyes flicker to my fingerless gloves. "I still think I can help you."

I slip my hands under the table, not understanding where he's going with this. *There's no way. He can't—*

"Do they know?" he asks, interrupting my thoughts.

A shock of panic zips through my heart, my scalp prickling in fear. Clenching my jaw shut, I curl my fingers into my palm, and the lightbulb in the corner of the room shatters.

Olivia's warning sounds through my head, *They'll ship you off to God knows where.*

"I don't know what you're talking about." I bite the inside of my lip, attempting to keep it still.

Judy materializes after the commotion, apologizing for the broken lightbulb and giving some half-thought-out excuse about how all the bulbs in the house need replacing lately, forcing a fake laugh as she does.

He rubs the stubble on his chin, narrowing his eyes at me again.

I shrink further into the seat, my heart thumping unevenly. I can't get any read on him. The terror is too loud in my head; the rest is static.

Judy jumps in to save me before Officer Goodwin can question anything. Explaining how I'm still shaken up over the whole ordeal, and she'll be sure to call if I remember anything from that dreadful night.

"Of course." Officer Goodwin stands to leave and turns to me. "I'm sorry for upsetting you. I'm only here to help."

While Judy ushers the officer out of the house, I bolt upstairs and cram my limited belongings into a backpack.

I'm going to leave tonight.

Not that I have any idea where to go. But I can't stay here. If he knows what I am, I'm not sticking around to find out what happens next.

The tingling in my arms has made its way up to my shoulders. After a second glance in the mirror, I'm unfazed when my eyes shift into a deep lavender. It keeps happening more and more, each time lasting longer than before, and I have an inkling that soon, they won't return to their regular brown. Changes are happening inside my body, and I'm confident they can't be good. I'm a bomb waiting to go off, and I won't risk taking the McIntyre family out with me. They're the nicest people I've met in my short life, and it's not fair to put them through this, to expose them to such danger.

They'll recover after I leave. It might hurt for a while, but eventually, they'll forget all about me, just like they'll mourn Olivia but move on.

They all do.

The two of us hardly stuck in anyone's mind; no one bothered to keep in touch over the years, not even the social worker assigned to our case. She didn't even spare me two seconds for insincere condolences.

But as badly as I need to leave, I can't right now; it's the middle of the day. I'll have to wait until everyone's asleep. Still, I scramble to pack everything, grabbing some of Olivia's things to ensure they aren't thrown out. Her favorite hoodie, a copy of *Jane Eyre*, the only book she would read again and again, her iPod, and lastly, her urn.

Slinging the backpack over my shoulder to test the weight, I count the money I have left.

Thirty dollars.

I'm screwed.

Chewing on my lip, I decide to fall back on past habits. I'll dip into Dennis's wallet tonight when I leave. Guilt gnaws at me. I don't like to steal anymore—it's why I gave Olivia such shit for it—but I don't have a choice.

Leaving is the only way to keep them safe, and I need money to do that.

Where will I go, though? Placing the bag gently on the floor, I flop onto my borrowed bed and stare at the ceiling. I could go to the bus station and buy a ticket. But to where?

Tears leak from the corners of my eyes and slide down my face. I sniffle, rolling over to face the wall, and before long, I'm drifting off to sleep.

❧ ☙

RUNNING. TERRIFIED. HAUNTED. SCREAMING.

The purple showers down on me, swirling around my legs, suffocating me. I cover my mouth, trying not to inhale, but then I cough, gag, and gasp for air.

Collapsing onto the ground, I fumble to take in my surroundings. Dirt, twigs, and rocks cover the hard earth. I'm crawling on my hands and knees until I spot a tree root. I use the pressure of the bark to guide myself back up and onto my feet.

With my back pressed against the oak, I surrender myself to the mist, allowing it to swallow me whole. The darkness grips me and ejects me outside of my body. Confused, I peer down at myself as I float in the air. The panic catches up, and I struggle to get back inside, but I'm denied. An invisible barrier prevents me from returning. I'm in ghost form, lingering, as I watch my human form move without my permission.

A branch snaps in the distance. My eyes, or rather its eyes, blaze purple when they open. She keeps quiet as terror pounds in my nonexistent heart, but through the connection, I feel stronger now. The haze empowering us in ways I didn't know was possible.

Another twig snaps.

The fog disperses.

He's here.

The body's shoulders slump with relief, already understanding she's not in danger. Within a second, I'm sucked back in and looking into the boy's gray eyes. For the first time in a while, I'm at peace.

His mouth hangs slightly open as he looks at me, eyes scanning my face like he's searching for something.

I don't move, but I hold my breath when he comes closer. We're face to face—the closest we've ever been. So close I can trace every detail of his features. To my surprise, there are specks of gold and brown within the silvery depths of his eyes. They're two storm clouds waiting to release the rain. There's a tiny scar above his right eyebrow and permanent frown lines I yearn to reach out and smooth. We both study each other as if we'll be ripped apart and are afraid of forgetting one another. Or at least that's how it is for me; I only hope he feels the same.

He reaches out a hand, my eyes fluttering to the ink covering his arm. After the briefest hesitation, he tucks a curl behind my ear. I gasp at the contact. All of this is so new; we've never been able to do this until now. What changed?

"Where are you?" he whispers.

I open my mouth, but nothing comes out. Why can I hear him now? Why can he touch me? This is only a dream. This can't be happening.

My vision blurs as the loneliness seeps in further. He was never mine, but at least I had Olivia before. Now it's only me and the figment of my imagination.

"Come to me." It's not a demand. It's an invitation. An escape. One I'd be too willing to accept if he were real.

"Come to me," he repeats as he fades into nothing.

I awake with a gasp, unaware of my surroundings. It takes a moment for my heart to settle, but then it jolts again when I spot Amber standing in the doorway, hand on her hip like she's suddenly not afraid of me, and the old version of her is back.

"What are you doing?" Accusation riddles her voice.

Yep, definitely the old Amber.

"Nothing."

"Then why did you pack a bag?"

My eyes flicker to the discarded backpack on the floor, zipper wide open, clothes peeking out. *Damn it.*

I lurch out of bed, pulse rushing as I repack. "Why are you going through my things?"

"Where are you going, Gemma?"

"Nowhere." I avoid eye contact as my throat constricts. Sensing the build-up, I turn my head, hiding my face in case my eyes flash purple from the flare. When my feelings simmer, I chance a glimpse back at her; she's staring down at her feet, fidgeting with the hem of her Star Wars T-shirt.

"Take me with you," she whispers.

My hand hovers over the zipper. "What?"

"Don't leave me here."

Shaking my head, I blink, realizing what she's asking. "I can't take care of you on my own. You're better off here with Judy and Dennis."

"No," she pleads. "I want to stay with you."

"You don't even like me."

"I do!" Her thin lower lip begins to tremble. "I'm not afraid anymore. I... I..."

I sigh. "Stop. You're not coming with me. I'm sorry, but this isn't a life for a kid."

"I'm not a kid."

"What are you? Like, twelve?"

"I'm fourteen."

"... a child. Yeah, no."

"You're not much older! You're a kid, too."

"I'll age out within a year, and then I'll be leaving anyway. You have years ahead of you; Judy and Dennis are trying to finalize the adoption. Stay here, go to school."

I pause, watching Amber's face fall. I make my way over to her, placing both hands on her shoulders. My sympathy mixes with her sadness. Her emotion beats against the edges of my senses, worming its way into my chest.

"They're good people. They'll take care of you. I just can't stay here anymore... I need to go."

Her round baby face looks up at me, big blue eyes filled with unshed tears. "Why?"

"It's not safe for any of you."

"You'd hurt us?"

"Not intentionally... no. But accidents can still happen." I understand that all too well. Judging by her quick look away as if remembering the exploding lights, I think she does, too.

"Will you come back for me?"

I allow a small smile to form on my lips. "Sure."

She frowns as if she knows I lied. "What do I tell them?"

"Nothing. You didn't see me, and you didn't know I was leaving. You woke up, and I was gone."

She nods sullenly and surprises me with a tight squeeze around my waist. I pry her arms off, convincing her to let me go, but my heart swells. Maybe she isn't so bad, but it's too late now.

KNOWING DENNIS SLEEPS IN my room, whether or not I have nightmares, makes this a bit trickier. Maybe he won't come tonight since he didn't have to wake me last night, but I worry he still will. Who knows how much of a head start I'll have if he notices my bed empty only moments after I've left?

As usual, he left his wallet in the kitchen, making it far too easy for me to snatch his money. Guilt churns my stomach, but I'm doing this for them. I repeat this lie until I'm sure everyone is asleep. If I'm honest with myself, I'm doing it for me, too. Sure, I don't want to hurt them. But I also can't stay in a place filled with reminders of Oli.

I sneak out of the bedroom window in the middle of the night and head for the bus station. Hopefully, by the time he realizes I'm gone, I'll be halfway to... somewhere far away from here.

But first, I find myself at the Mill. In every town we've ever lived in, Oli and I find one place and dub it our own. It's how we get away from everything, how we hide from the pains of life.

I follow the trail down into the woods until the mist from the gushing water seeps through my clothes and coats my skin. The streetlights fade the closer I get to the bottom, and I step over the jutting-out tree roots from muscle memory. I make it to the abandoned building, using my hands to guide myself against the grainy stone exterior. Left for so long, it's hardly even an establishment anymore. Half a stone structure lies in the middle of the woods, vegetation growing through the splinters of what was.

All I have to do is get around to the other side so I can dangle my legs over a mini waterfall, a human-made cascade of water funneling into a channel below. A smooth creek turned into a fierce whirlpool.

When Olivia and I first discovered the Mill, we devised a game where we'd both guess what the structure was used for. First, it was ordinary things like a clothing factory or maybe even a candy factory. Then, our imaginations grew wild as the weeks passed. Only two weeks ago, just days before she left me, Olivia proposed it was a place where angels came to rest.

I arched my brow. "Angels?"

"Yeah, angels need breaks too."

"From what? What could be so tiring?"

She sighed. "Everyone needs to escape every once in a while."

I settle my head against the rusted railing, questioning everything and wishing I could escape, too. We were supposed to graduate this year. Olivia would become my guardian, and we'd move away together. Travel for the summer, then figure out our next move. *Together, together, together.* Now I'm all alone, half of me ripped away.

We couldn't have been more opposite. When I rebelled, she steadied. When I pulled my act together, she went wild. We were balanced, sisters, best friends. Nothing could tear us apart, not even death. Or so I thought.

What do I do now?

The unrelenting water crashes against the building, soaking my feet as the waves splash. I'm too far away from town to notice someone's pain, so right now, the heaviness in my chest is entirely my own. I take stock of what I feel as if giving myself a medical diagnosis.

Heart? Broken.

Stomach? In knots.

Mind? Confused.

I take one more look around the Mill before saying goodbye, knowing I'm never coming back to this place. It belonged to us. And it doesn't feel right to be here without her. Maybe I wandered here to see if I could connect with Olivia. To see if she was right about it being a place for angels to rest, but that was a fool's dream.

I'm as alone now as I was back in the hospital.

Reluctantly standing up, I dust myself off and put one foot in front of the other toward the bus station.

THE BUS HEADING NORTH doesn't leave for another two hours. It makes my choice a lot easier since there are no other alternative routes. Having time to kill, I lie down on a bench and fail at counting the stars.

The terminal is nearly empty, save for the employee who sold me the ticket and a janitor sweeping the sidewalk. Every once in a while, the latter glances at me, and the worry of being caught puts me on edge. I probably appear too young to be sitting out here alone. Maybe I'll lie and say I'm eighteen already if anyone asks.

Not for lack of trying, but I'm hopeless at acting nonchalant. I swing my legs back down and sit upright, fixing my backpack onto my shoulders—only an hour to go until arrival.

The janitor walks over to me. "Are you all right, miss?"

I give a subtle nod, smiling without showing teeth. He's not giving off any creepy vibes, which is relieving, but I can discern his anxiety.

"Shouldn't you be home in bed?"

"I'm actually on my way home." After a second's breath, I add, "Vacation," for good measure.

"Oh, where do you work?"

Shit. My eyes widen. "The... laundromat."

"The laundromat?"

"…Yes. The one on 5th?"

"Oh, yeah. I walk past that one all the time."

"Cool." *Please don't ask any more questions; please don't ask any more*—sweat beads on the back of my neck. My breath is shallow as I wait to be busted.

"Well…" He shifts the broom handle to his other hand. "You be safe now, you hear? Enjoy your vacation." With one last skeptical look, he strolls away.

Letting out a long breath, I lean my head against the back of the bench and close my eyes. I don't entirely fall asleep, but a dreamlike occurrence happens to me anyway. I'm aware I'm sitting on the bench, but I'm completely immobilized. Paralysis seeps into my bones, and I can't shake myself out of it. Fear grips my heart, but the further I look inward, the more I can tell it's not just my own.

"Hello?" I call into the darkness of my mind.

Maybe my friend has returned. I want to call out to him, but he's still a stranger in some ways; I don't even know his name. How can I trust someone so thoroughly, yet not know who they are?

"Anyone there?" I ask.

A voice gurgles from afar, like it's coming from underwater. Straining to focus, I strive to find any semblance of a shape within the black but come up empty.

"What did you say?"

The voice is drowned out, but I can decipher what it says next. Ice runs through my veins. "Help?" I repeat the voice's plea. "Help with what?"

"Gemma?" the voice asks; it somehow sounds so far away yet also like it's directly in my ear.

"Yes?" I try to spin around, but I can't move. I squint, searching for any sign of who could be speaking to me in the darkness, but nothing forms.

"Help!" it screams before I bolt onto my feet.

The bus idles in front of me, the driver giving me an odd look. She snaps her fingers at me. "Are you coming or what?"

Shaken by the dream, I glance around the empty station. The janitor's cart is off in the corner, but he's nowhere near.

I shake off a shudder.

"Here goes nothing," I mutter as I step onto the bus, leaving Willow, Florida, behind.

Chapter Fourteen

Theo

"Theo! Your face!" Nora screams as she spots me behind Elise's shoulder.

Elise turns to examine me, already chuckling, and Zay covers his mouth, which has formed into an O, wincing.

Bright lights from the rides flash in the corner of my eye while the Tilt-a-Whirl spins around us. I lean against the fence surrounding the ride, dropping the backpack to my feet. "Yeah, yeah. I'm fine. Thanks for asking."

"So... no luck then?" Elise inquires, her tone implying she's holding back an 'I told you so.'

A wide grin stretches across my face, and I can't help but feel a little cocky when I spread my arms out. "What can I say? I'm just that good."

Elise punches me in the shoulder. "Shut up. You're joking."

Out of instinct, I rub the spot where she hit me. The rest of me hurts too bad to factor it in with the rest of my injuries. "Nope. I actually won." My chest feels lighter than it has in weeks. A thousand dollars won't last us forever, but it's more than we've had at once in years. "Who's hungry?"

Three pairs of eyes grow wider, and Zay lets out a holler for good measure.

My face hurts, my body aches, but seeing them so at ease for once will always be worth it. No matter what happens to me.

ZAY IS ON HIS fourth hamburger by the time the rest of us tap out. Nora idly picks at the cotton candy in front of her, but it's almost as if she's forcing herself to finish it.

I grin as she lets out a defeated sigh. "We can just bring it back, y'know. Don't make yourself sick."

"It's just so good. I don't want to stop." She fakes a pout and struggles to get the food back into the plastic bag.

Elise saunters toward the picnic table with four more refills of Coke and a giant bag of popcorn, announcing the fireworks should be starting soon.

"You know we don't have to spend *all* the money tonight, right?"

"Who said anything about money?" She gives me a wink. "His aura was glowing dark red. Now, now, before you give me that look, I only flirted."

I shake my head, sneaking a peek at Nora, who's now resting her face against her hand, eyes downcast. I wonder what color *that* is. And why Elise hasn't spotted it herself and stopped it. Nora is slightly younger, and we do have a weird dysfunctional family thing going, but give the girl a break at least and let her down easy.

I try to convey all this with one look at Elise, but she only shrugs at me. Whatever. It's not my battle; I'm not getting in the middle of it.

After glancing down at my watch, I close my eyes as the pounding continues in my head. My nose throbs, and I have a splitting headache. All I want to do is sleep, but we still have to walk home.

The longer I sit, the more my body locks up. Each time I shift, my ribs feel like they're cemented against the muscle, barely letting me move left or right.

This is going to suck so bad tomorrow.

Soon, fireworks fill the night sky, bursting into various shapes and colors: red, blue, and a dazzling white spark off one another, splitting into multiple directions. A boom cracks in the air and echoes throughout the fairgrounds.

The four of us gaze up, taking it all in before I lower my eyes to the crew.

Zay pops a handful of Skittles into his mouth as he watches, and I shake my head, smirking. The kid is a human garbage disposal; he won't stop eating if given a chance. Elise wraps her arms around her legs, and Nora leans back against the table. Both look relaxed enough that I hope the fireworks go on forever.

My eyes flicker up in time to see a magnificent purple explode against the black night sky. My breath catches in my throat; it's the same shade as *hers*.

I take a deep breath as my thoughts are dragged back to last night. I was able to break through the mental wall to dream of her again, but I couldn't understand what was happening. Why I was creating what I was. She looked at me with hatred blazing in her eyes as some blonde rushed past me, stumbling along the way.

Who was that, anyway? I've created two people now?

And I apparently killed one of them. I sigh. At least it was in a dream.

Bile burns the back of my throat as I recall her cries and how the purple surrounded us in a fierce storm. The way she clutched the bloody body to her chest.

I just wanted to make it stop.

I don't know why I was creating this hell for her... I never meant to hurt—I shudder. The movement sears my ribs, and I hold back a painful gasp. Once it passes, I glance around at the spectators.

Another firework booms overhead.

I search for her face as if she might be in the crowd, scrutinizing me, the one who created her only to destroy her.

I can't get over how real she felt. How much anger she clutched in those trembling hands as I tried to apologize. I somehow moved the dream's setting to a meadow, hoping the calm stillness would soothe her.

It was the first time I was able to change a dream in the middle rather than picking a destination when it began.

But it didn't work.

She didn't seem relieved. She appeared hurt. Scared.

I brought her to life by creating someone for her to lose.

What the fuck does that say about me?

There's an ache deep in my bones as my finger idly traces the tattoo spreading across my left forearm and climbing up my bicep.

I try to cast the guilt aside. She's not real. She's not real. She's. Not. Real.

You didn't hurt her.

My fingers dig into my arm. This tattoo is the first one I got after creating her.

It's of a small forest, with a tree fallen between the rest of the shrubs, where we sat all those dreams ago. Stars speckle a makeshift sky, intertwined between a few freckles that dot my arm.

I lift my head again, studying the firework's afterglow, the purple lingering before fading into nothing, and I suddenly know what to add next.

To make amends for what I've done to her in my dreams.

Her eyes as two fireworks exploding into a purple haze that will surround the forest, whipping in circles around the branches as it joins the tree roots.

Settled on the addition, I think about my next move. It's not hard to find a decent tattoo artist, considering I'm old enough, pay in cash, and tip well. No one asks for ID anyway. The hardest part is saving up enough money to get them done.

Every tattoo marking my body stems from my dreams—from the flicker of a bonfire to the twinkle of a star. To the single line that shaped her silhouette and the wildflowers from the field we laid in so many years ago. Who am I trying to fool? Every tattoo stems from my stolen moments with *her*—the stranger in my head.

Aren't I getting a little old to have an imaginary friend?

Sighing, I scratch my neck, wincing from the movement. This isn't healthy. I need to stop thinking about it. I need to stop thinking about her. I almost scoff out loud at myself; like that'll be possible.

As the firework finale explodes in the dark, smoke-ridden sky, I stuff our leftovers in my backpack, hiding the plates from view. I'm ready to head out, and hopefully, they are too.

I'M SWEATING AND SLUGGISH when we make it to the tree line. Every single muscle in my body seizes, screaming at me in fiery rage as if they alone are reprimanding me for the fight. Each step draws an unpleasant grunt from my mouth and a sigh from Nora.

Zay leads the way, clearing a path with only a flick of his wrist. His studies are paying off. He makes the trail as flat as possible so I don't have to maneuver around anything. Nora is directly behind me, and Elise, now carrying the backpack, brings up the rear.

None of us speak on the two-hour walk back. Why couldn't one of us have teleportation or something that could get us from Point A to Point B in the blink of an eye? I clench my bruised hands, sucking in a breath to keep myself from groaning out loud.

The fight was such a bad idea, even with the payoff.

By the time we make it back to the house, I'm ready to collapse in bed. Before I can, Elise demands she clean up my wounds. I sit at the table, and she shuffles into the kitchen with the first aid supplies I stole from Hilda's.

I pop a couple of painkillers as she bandages my hand and swipes alcohol over the cut on my nose.

It burns, not in the way a fire does, but it stings nonetheless, and I lean away from her, shaking the pain away. "Fuck, that hurt." I try to laugh, but nothing comes out. I'm too tired.

"Do you need something for your ribs?" She reaches for the hem of my shirt.

I swat her hand away, holding back another wince. "Nah, it's fine. I'll be good as new tomorrow."

Elise nods, repacking the supplies into the small first aid box.

Taking more effort than usual, I stand to say goodnight when something catches my eye. The tarp leading to one of the unused staircases fell again. How? I thought I nailed it up. In the dim light,

I can just make out that one of the spindles broke off, and it's now dangling loosely off the side. The wood from the step splinters upward as if a foot went straight through it.

Turning back to Elise, I ask, "Has someone been up there?"

She looks past me, examining the staircase. "No."

"Are you sure? That step wasn't broken before."

She shrugs. "It's an old house. Who knows?" Without another word, she picks up the first aid box and leaves me standing there alone.

I bite the inside of my lip, returning my focus to the shredded wood.

Something's not right.

But there's nothing I can do about it right now. My body screams for sleep, so I limp off to bed. Hopefully, I'll wake up more mobile tomorrow. And then I can get to the bottom of that mystery.

MORNING COMES, AND I'M slow to get out of bed. The pain from last night is still fresh, but at least I have more range of movement today.

Maybe I should spend the day in bed. The crew is fed and content somewhere in the Rib House, so why rush? I could rest for once.

Crap, the staircase.

Reluctantly, I roll to the side, grunting as I stand. My fingertips lightly caress the taut skin over my ribs, exploring the bruise that's swollen and darkening into a deep purple.

Unfortunately, that one is going to last a while.

I tug on a T-shirt and jeans and run my hand through my smattering of dark hair, disheveling it even more, but at least it doesn't look slept on.

The house is silent when I head for the kitchen and find it vacant. I check the bedrooms—empty. They're probably outside. Elise likes to lay out on sunny days when she's not giving Nora self-defense lessons. And when Nora's not getting her ass handed to her, she usually completes Zay's lessons in nature. It's easier to practice that way.

The fallen tarp and broken staircase taunt me as I approach the back door. Freezing, I cock my head to the side and study how the wood tilts unfavorably. Ready to crumble under the faintest pressure. If there were scorch marks, they'd look just like the staircase from my childhood home. The tarp crinkles under my footsteps. I sidestep a mound of lush, green moss growing through the foundation and stop at the foot of the stairs. The sixth one up has a hole right in the middle—the cracked railing and spindle are at the same level.

Someone fell and caught themselves just in time.

Frowning, I peer up the rest of the staircase. I don't trust the second level at all. The top of the stairs leads to a darkened hallway. Who knows if the floors would hold, given the state of the staircase? Why would anyone risk it?

I lean back, laying eyes on the door again, but no one has come back inside. Licking my lips, I weigh my odds.

I'll *probably* be fine.

But then again, if I fall, I don't know how much more impact my body can take right now.

Blowing out a puff of air, intrigue—and maybe a little worry—wins.

Keeping my back glued to the wall, I slide my way up each stair, testing the weight before moving to the next one. My arms stretch out on either side, keeping me balanced. I skip the sixth step altogether.

When I reach the top, I hold my breath as I fully plant both feet in the hallway.

Nothing happens.

Shaking my head nervously, I glance both ways and then choose right. Staying against the walls where the floor seems sturdier, I keep one foot in front of the other, and my hand glides against the cracked drywall. The hallway is dark, but light filters further down the corridor from another room.

When I make it there, the ruins of a nursery lay scattered across the floor. The entire wall facing outside is covered in disgusting, black mold that reeks, the smell snaking down my throat. I cover my nose with my shirt. Violet wallpaper peels away in strips, curling and exposing the glue. One wall looks like it might've been painted with a solar system mural, but there's a giant hole in the middle of it now, revealing the support beams inside.

A rocking chair, stained a grizzly brown, perches beside a shattered window. The glass litters the floor, reflecting rays of sunlight.

Piles of dingy, moth-ridden baby clothes clump together into sinister shapes in different corners. One lone stuffed animal is left in the wooden crib. Wood shavings cover the mattress from holes chewed through by rats.

I back out of the room and step into the one across from it.

Another child's room nearly identical to the other, except this room is colder somehow. Orange rotting wallpaper covers all four walls, but there's no special mural painted anywhere. The glass is also missing from this window, though there's no rocking chair. The rest of the clothes appear to be in the same condition.

At the end of the hallway is a door hanging from its hinges.

When I peek around it, a groan passes my lips at the sight of another staircase. What am I expecting to find, anyway? It's not like the Authorities are sitting up there, waiting for me. We'd know if they came here because we would've been taken or killed by now. I grimace at the thought.

I'm working up the courage to test fate when I hear the door close from the kitchen.

Fuck.

If they catch me up here, I'll never hear the end of it.

As fast as I'm willing to go, I slink back down the hallway, tiptoeing on the broken stairs, and just touch the floor when Zay pops his head in.

"What're you doing?"

I glance around, searching for an excuse as my gaze settles on the broken wood. "Just trying to figure out what happened here. You haven't gone upstairs, have you?"

Zay shakes his head. "Nah. I don't want anything to do with that." He scoffs, heading back toward the living room.

I follow him while Nora and Elise venture in from outside.

"Where were you guys?" I ask, hopefully sounding nonchalant so they don't suspect me of acting weird.

"We went down to the lake." Nora adjusts the bag on her shoulder. Then she does a double-take, rapidly blinking as her face scrunches up. "I have to tell you something…"

"Yeah?" Maybe *she* went upstairs.

"I saw something last night."

My eyebrows raise. "Oh?" She fusses with the bag's strap, not meeting my eyes. *Something's not right.* "What's wrong?"

Her gaze flickers to mine, and she swallows. "I don't know. You disappeared again, and I... I think someone is coming."

Chapter Fifteen

Gemma

After eight hours on the bus, I'm dumped out at a terminal in the middle of nowhere. Now comes the hard part—where do I go next?

Also, I'm starving. Dreading being cramped on another bus, I wander, searching for food and stretching my stiff legs. I have a few granola bars tucked away in my bag, but I'm saving those just in case.

The station has one bathroom, shared by everyone, and considering the thick layer of God knows what on the toilet seat, I'm guessing it hasn't been cleaned in years. My stomach turns. The unfiltered sunlight shining through the heavy bathroom door illuminates just how disgusting it is. A fat gray rat scurries toward my feet, and I clamp a hand over my mouth to stop myself from shrieking. Garbage litters the ground, from yellow-stained clumps of toilet paper to used... Is that a tampon? I grimace. The odor is so putrid my eyes water. Eff, no. I'm *not* using that bathroom. I'll hold it or take my chances in the forest.

Circling the terminal twice, I frown. There's hardly any food available, and the food they do serve is *expensive*. Ten dollars for a side of fries? I can't imagine what their kitchen looks like, knowing how *clean* they keep their bathroom. No, thanks. A lone vending machine stands near the ticket booth, forcing me to dig in my backpack for loose change. I come up short. *Ugh.*

Walking away defeated, I find myself overlooking a cliff. There's a single bench facing the spectacular view. It's maybe a five-hundred-foot drop? More? Less? Either way, it's deadly. But at the bottom of the valley, a small river winds through jutting rocks.

I peer over the ledge, my throat drying the closer I step until I gain enough sense to back away and sit on the bench.

This is weirdly dangerous.

How many people have died here? Just a bench mere feet away from a cliff, no fence, no signs, no warnings, nothing.

As I sit here, I stare out into the vast blue sky. There's a hollowness deep inside me I'll never be able to shake off. Olivia—my missing piece—is gone forever. My pulse drums loudly in my ears, and my arms, from fingertips to elbows, are completely numb. I suck in a breath, but my lungs refuse to welcome the air. I squeeze my eyes shut and let out a sob.

Oh God, I'm dying.

After a few minutes or hours, I don't even know anymore, my lips stop tingling. Clarity bleeds back into my brain, and I slump against the bench. The panic attack left me utterly drained, and I have to fight the urge to lie down and fall asleep.

It's been years since I've had an attack like that, where time means nothing, and I'm only a soul trapped in a body numbed by ice. I've learned nothing prevents them. I've tried meditating, taking deep breaths, counting objects. Nothing keeps the anxiety at bay. The last time it happened, I was in a fetal position on the bathroom floor for hours. Olivia found me and held me till it passed.

I let out a long breath.

Now, I'm left alone to pull myself out of the void.

My heart skips a beat, thinking of her again, but it doesn't escalate this time. The disquiet is out of my system. For now, at least. Who knows what the future holds? I rotate my neck, loosening the tight muscles in my shoulders. Everything is tied up in knots, and I shake my arms to regain full feeling.

Well, things can't get much worse from here. I *need* a plan. Counting the money I have left, I let out a sigh. My situation is bleak. I have enough cash for one last bus fare. But I don't know where to go, and I have no one to meet me when I get there, wherever *there* is.

I bite my lip, finally admitting I need to let some of the darkness back in to survive this. If I fall back into old habits, I can steal enough to get by. Gazing out into the trees below, a sudden thought of throwing myself off the cliff flashes in front of me, but I won't do it. Just the possibility of letting the evil in, though, makes me shift my legs.

It took years to become the person I am today: the quiet, responsible sister. But as a child? I was the wild one. And maybe, with any luck, I can survive this if I revert to who I was. Only a little, though; otherwise, who knows what else I'll accidentally explode?

Having no control of my empathic abilities sent me into a craze. I couldn't physically handle all the emotions tossed my way and had no guidance in learning how to subdue it. I would hurt those who were hurting me. It wasn't *their* fault that I was just as angry as them, but I took their pain as my own and then used it against them. So I got in fights, talked back to adults, and was hardened by something I never understood.

My head pounded so loudly most of the time I couldn't concentrate in any school environment, so I skipped class. Then, while roaming the streets, I started stealing. Nothing major—an apple from an outside cart because I was hungry. A book outside the library dropbox because I was bored, eventually leading to a necklace or two from a foster parent. Or maybe money from their wallet. Little things that added up over time.

Olivia never understood what I was going through, but she was never scared of me either. And that's one of the reasons I cherished her so much—someone who was so completely in my corner that she was unshakeable. I tried getting away from her for fear of hurting her or getting her into trouble, but she always clung to me. I would run away, and the following day, she'd be sleeping in the cemetery beside me, with a blanket draped over our legs.

I stayed on that destructive path because it felt good. It felt *right*. It was the only thing that quieted the noise inside my head and the pain I felt from others. The rush of emotions I didn't want to accept. The adrenaline charge would leave me feeling high each time I did something fairly reckless. I didn't understand I was feeding something dark inside me.

A cold tingle creeps up my spine. Sitting up straight, I peer over my shoulder to check if someone is watching me. My eyes land on a crow perched on a nearby branch. It tilts its head at me, but otherwise, we're alone.

Just like I'll always be alone now because who else will love me the way Olivia did? Who else is going to keep me balanced?

As the years passed, Olivia became as reckless as I was. We swapped places by accident. I started to straighten out when I noticed how uncontrollable she was becoming. I was the younger sister, but Olivia, solidly in my corner as always, never tried to change or correct me; instead, she became as devious as I was. We were a scary team. If a foster family was bad to us, we became equally terrible toward them. If they left us alone, we left them alone. Well, until Olivia started stealing and never stopped.

We bounced around a lot after that. Finally, maturity sunk in, and I could see the error of our ways. So, I developed a system on how to quiet the storm. The constant onslaught of emotions became a steady hum that pulsed against my senses from the outside, but it was manageable. It's white noise now, for the most part. Extreme pain or feeling will still rear its ugly head, but general moods go unnoticed unless I really try to get a read on them. Once I had that under control, I was able to relax. I didn't want to hurt anyone anymore.

But I already broke my sister by changing who she was.

And now she's gone. That's my fault, too.

An uneasiness comes barreling into me. I sling on my backpack and head for the terminal, picking up the pace as the prickling of danger cramps my muscles.

Heading straight for the window, forgetting about food, I purchase a ticket for the bus that's leaving in ten minutes. I don't even check the destination. I move to the left so I'm not in the way of the ticket seller but keep my eyes glued to the ground. There's only a handful of people here who've recently been dropped off, and I search their emotions one by one to find what I'm looking for.

My gaze leaps up, landing on a stranger's face as his apprehension knocks against me like it's asking to be let in. He's leaning against the wall, but his shoulders are bunched as if scared of me. That doesn't stop him from staring, though. He's older, at least in his fifties. Bald with pockmarks on his face and hard, unforgiving eyes. The muscle in his jaw twitches as he regards me. I have no idea who he is, but his eyes tell me he knows me.

I grip my ticket, paper crinkling as I gauge whether or not I should make a run for it. To where, though? I'm in the middle of North Carolina. It might as well be the middle of *nowhere.*

I chance a glance outside and then focus on him again. The others drain out of the building, seemingly oblivious to the danger radiating from this man. He straightens himself and pushes off the wall, fixing his leather jacket and wiping his sleeve. My pulse quickens with each of his movements, but I don't know what to do. The attendee also leaves her station, putting up a sign that says she's on break. It's only this guy and me.

Run.

I burst through the back door leading to a wooded area without a second thought. I only have to dodge him until the bus arrives. Heading straight for the tree line, I escape under the thick leaves and circle my way around the station to watch the front. The outside is empty, too; where did the few stragglers go after they funneled out from the building? I shake the question away. Who cares where they went? All I need to know about is the one man, and when I don't see him, I slump in relief.

Maybe I misread him?

But how? He was giving off some serious bad vibes.

My eyes scan across the parking lot, glancing between the few parked vehicles. When I land on a red pickup truck, my heart jolts. The twist in my stomach is unbearable, and I have to coax the knot out of my throat. It's just a red pickup truck. There's no damage to it. The windshield is fine. It's not like *this* red pickup is the truck that hit Olivia.

It's a coincidence.

But I can't shake the feeling that maybe it's not.

While I'm distracted, an arm snakes around me as a meaty hand smacks hard across my mouth. I try to scream, but his grip muffles it. I struggle against an impossibly hard body, attempting to elbow him in the stomach or stomp on his foot, but I can't land a blow. His grip remains solid. In one quick movement, he slams me against the tree trunk. My face splits against the rough bark. Warm blood trickles down my cheekbone as bile rises in my throat.

Fear vibrates within me, and my hands spark to life. I don't know what'll happen to him, but I don't have much time to think it over. I clutch the hand that's smothering me as black spots cloud my vision. Focusing all my energy on my fingertips, the man hisses in my ear, taking half a step back and loosening his grip an inch. It's not much, but enough to let me move my head to the side, inhaling life back into my lungs. Tears burn my eyes, but now isn't the time to cry.

I need to finish this. I need to finish *him*.

Energy surrounds me, calling to me, telling me to claim it. I can't feel whose it is, only that it's there for the taking. Closing my eyes, I open myself to it, sucking it into me. Electric power buzzes through my veins, making me gasp.

I've never felt anything quite like it before.

Losing all sense of urgency, I relax, letting a smile creep across my face as I calmly place my hands on the arm still wrapped around my chest. With the faintest squeeze, the bone crunches beneath my palms. The man howls, letting go. I spin to face him, watching him stumble backward into a tree.

He shakes his head, horrorstruck, as he cradles his injury. "He... he was wrong about you."

"Who?" I demand. The power continues to thrum, and I'm no longer scared. "Who sent you?"

"Draven." The man spits out the name between clenched teeth.

"Draven? I don't know who that is. What does he want from me?" He begins to sway, turning a sickly pale color as if he's about to pass out. Taking a step closer to him, I repeat myself. "What does he *want*?"

"He wants his power back." He collapses to the ground, landing on his injured arm. I hover over him, checking if he's still alive.

I suck in a breath of relief when I find his pulse and take in my surroundings.

The once lush, green trees around me are now ashen and black. The bark burned, the branches bare. A ring surrounds the stranger and me—scorched earth with one solid imprint where I initially stood. A piece clicks into place as the power drains away. It's obvious where I got this energy from.

What have I done?

Chapter Sixteen

THEO

"WHAT DO YOU MEAN, someone is coming?" I ask.

Nora shakes her head, her auburn hair shifting behind her shoulders with the movement, staring off into the distance, her mouth slightly ajar. A small *V* forms between her brows, telling me she's not currently in the room right now. Her mind is elsewhere.

Elise places her hands on Nora's shoulders from behind and guides her to the table, sitting her down. Nora blinks rapidly but doesn't speak.

Crossing my arms, I scan her face, looking for any signs of distress, but she doesn't move. I glance back at Zay. He's on the couch, leaning over the edge, biting his thumbnail.

No one speaks. No one moves.

The room feels like it's shrinking around me.

Nora needs to figure out who's coming.

Is it friend or foe?

A few minutes go by when Nora suddenly gasps, grabbing onto the edge of the table, her knuckles turning white from how hard she's gripping it. Elise rushes to get her water, bringing it back to her before Nora utters anything.

Nora shoves the water away, locking her eyes dead onto me. My stomach clenches as she stares right through me, the hairs on the back of my neck raising when her eyes fill with pity.

"Whoever's coming has to do with you."

"What... what does that mean?"

She shakes her head, unblinking. "I don't know. But I think it's why I can't see you in my visions anymore... You keep disappearing, and now I think it has to do with this... this person." She finally grabs the water with a trembling hand and takes a small sip. "I can't see them at all. They're powerful; I felt it. But I can't observe them. I don't know who—or what—they are. All I know is you have to meet them in the woods near us."

Elise and Zay watch me as my mouth drops open, and I try to process this.

"I *have* to meet them in the woods?" My eyebrows raise. "Why don't we just leave now?"

Nora shakes her head again. "I don't *know* why; I just *do*."

"Nora..." I start but close my mouth as words fail me. In the three years she's been with us, she's never once led us astray. But I'll be damned if I'm going to meet some *thing* in the middle of the woods who keeps making me disappear in Nora's visions. I haven't been in her head since she unknowingly spotted the real me the other night. So whatever she sees now is all her and has nothing to do with my dream hopping. "This seems like a horrible idea. I don't like it."

"We'll go with you," Zay offers.

I shoot a look back at him, and he raises his hands in surrender. "No one is going to the woods. This... thing can go fuck themselves, for all I care."

"Theo," Elise reprimands. "You know you're not going to leave someone like *us* out there."

"We don't know what it is! And this is nothing like before."

"You helped me," Zay adds.

I glare at him. "You're not helping," I spit out. "Plus, you were different. You were a fourteen-year-old grieving kid. You weren't some powerful being who made me *disappear*."

Nora rings the glass rim with one finger, studying the water vibrating inside. "I don't think it's... evil." She lifts one shoulder to her ear, cocking her head. "I mean, maybe, I guess. Whatever it is, it feels... lost."

"That settles it then." Elise shifts back in her chair, tossing her long blonde hair over her shoulder.

I drop both hands against my sides as I fight the anger rising in my throat. "That doesn't settle anything."

Zay makes his way to the table and sits with the other two. "We've always been a democracy."

His admission leaves me the odd man out with my back against the wall, literally. I whip my head around incredulously, looking at the place where we're currently hiding—the house that's in shambles around us. The fucking tarp that doesn't stay up.

They might have some pull, but not when it comes to decisions like this. "No, we *haven't*. Not when our lives depend on it. No. We're not doing this. End of discussion."

All three stare at me, letting the silence fill the room. I shift my weight, crossing my arms once more, turning away to stare out the duct tape-patched window into the tree line. The tape looks like it's breathing, inflating and deflating, swaying back and forth with the wind. I try to match its tempo.

The weight of their gazes burns a hole through my back. I'm not winning this one. Why don't they ever listen to me anymore?

Closing my eyes, I pinch the bridge of my nose, wincing as I squeeze the fresh cut. I inhale, holding the air deep in my lungs before letting it loose.

I can't believe we're risking this.

"When?" I finally ask, my voice coming out low and gravelly.

"Tomorrow. I'll show you where." Nora leaps up from the table, heading outside. Zay runs to catch up with her, leaving Elise and me alone.

I turn back around, leaning against the sink, and shake my head in defeat.

After stuffing my hands in my pockets, my fingers search for the comfort of the lighter. I study my shoes—worn-out black Vans, caked in mud with the soles starting to separate—then risk a peek at Elise. Her elbows are on the table, chin in her hand, while she watches me.

"Why are you doing this?" I ask her, hating how desperate I sound. "We've always seen eye to eye on matters like this."

She narrows her eyes. "You're scared. I can see it. Your aura is a vibrant, fearsome red."

I scoff. "Of course, I'm fucking scared, Elise. Some powerful entity needs to meet me in the woods, and if you forgot, I happen to vanish every time Nora catches me in her visions."

"It'll be okay."

Biting the inside of my cheek, I struggle to get the words out. My chest collapses in on itself, my pulse thrumming in my ears. "But... what if it's not?" My voice hitches, forcing me to clear my throat. "What's going to happen to you guys if I'm gone?"

Elise slowly gets up, her fingers toying with the edge of one long sleeve. She closes the distance between us, resting both her hands on my shoulders.

"Hey, look at me." Her eyes are crystal clear when I finally do as if she knows something I don't. "You're going to be fine."

"How do you know that?"

A smile tugs at her lips as she drops her arms back to her sides. "I just do."

Nora barges into the room, holding the map from the truck. She moves the now empty glass to the side and spreads the map across the table, laying it flat. She toys with her lip as she focuses on different areas, presumably finding the destination, which will *probably* be where I die.

I roll my eyes upward, studying the cracked ceiling. Dark water stains cover most of it, and it will likely come crashing down on our heads someday.

My gaze flickers back to the map.

"There." Her finger lands on a small wooded area right near the middle of town. "I can't tell the time, but it's around dawn. You'll want to be there before the sun rises."

I grunt as I study each one of the crew. Elise, with her steady gaze and Nora's pity mixed with concern. Even Zay's chestnut brown eyes are alight like he's eager to meet someone new. They all seem so sure that meeting this... thing... person... whatever the hell it is, is a safe choice.

But why do I feel like they're all sending me to my death?

I have no idea what dawn will bring, so tonight, I'm getting my damn tattoo.

A bell rings as I open the door to the shop. The mixture of smells crashes over me like a wave—a mix between soap, witch hazel, and latex gloves—one of my favorite combinations. No one is in the lobby, but a teal leather sofa runs along one wall, with a blond wooden coffee table in front of it. Various magazines litter the top, but I don't bother sitting down to read them. Photo albums perch precariously on the end table near a poorly lit lamp, and I've had enough work done in the past to know they contain drawings to inspire ideas for clients on what they might wish for. There's no need for me to look; I already know exactly what I want.

No one mans the register that sits behind a glass box filled with different styles of piercings—ear, nose, lip, and so on. A second cabinet occupies the furthest wall, filled with tattoo and piercing care.

"Back here," a voice calls out.

A door leads to the back of the shop, where Radiohead is blaring. I venture toward it, and the closer I get, the more the smell of rubbing alcohol hits me.

A man currently sterilizing some girl's belly button doesn't bother to look up when he asks, "What're you getting done?"

It takes a second to realize he's addressing me. "Tattoo. Forearm. More of an addition."

The man doesn't seem to care about what I'm saying, so I trail off, making eye contact with the girl on the bed. She offers a small smile when the guy jerks his head toward another door leading further into the shop.

"We Suck Young Blood" intensifies when I enter the room. The walls are covered in art, ranging from black and white pieces to some in vibrant colors. Blue LED lights line all the walls near the floor, and white tea lights dangle off hooks crisscrossing the ceiling. One bright spotlight angles over an empty chair.

Movement catches my eye from the corner of the room, and I turn, somewhat startled that I didn't notice her before.

In the low lighting, her hair appears to be black. It's pulled up and away from her face, and tattoos cover her neck. From what I can tell, the design mainly consists of a clock tower leading into vines that twist around, lowering to her shoulder and disappearing underneath her shirt.

Both of her cheeks are pierced where her dimples would be, two tiny diamonds shimmering as she closes a book.

When she stands, her band T-shirt reads *Cage the Elephant*. We're going to get along.

"Here for a tattoo?" she asks.

As she gets closer, I notice her hair has blue in it as well, matching the LED lights. Dark makeup rings her eyes; there's no way she's over thirty.

"Yeah," I finally manage. "If you're open."

"Lucky for you, I just had a cancellation." She looks me up and down. "You're eighteen?"

"Yes."

Biting her lip, she surveys my prior tattoos and nods. "Well, all right then. What're we doing?"

I gesture at my arm, filling her in on what I want to add. I settle into the tattoo chair as she begins washing her hands and setting up her supplies. My pulse thrums in anticipation, my heart skipping a beat when I hear the familiar buzzing as she tests the gun. Finally, she preps the area, and the needle touches my skin. I let out a relieved sigh.

We continue to listen to *Hail to the Thief* as she works on my arm, and I try to focus on the music rather than what waits for me in the morning. I close my eyes, head resting against the chair as the vibration speeds up.

"Who's the girl?" the woman asks, breaking me out of my thoughts.

"Hmm?"

She lifts her head, squinting at me, then directs her gaze back to the silhouette and the eyes she's now working on.

"Oh. I... uh..." There's no way to explain it without sounding insane. "Just someone I wish I knew."

"Are you sure you don't? Seems like you know her pretty well if you're going through all this."

I sigh. "It's a long story."

"Longer than the one about what happened to your face?"

A grin tugs at my lips when I peek at her, and she dips her head back down, continuing her work. Rolling my head against the back of the chair to face the wall again, I chuckle. "That story is shorter. I won it in a fight."

"You sure you won? That's quite the shiner."

I let out a full laugh now. "Yeah, I'm sure."

We talk about music the rest of the time, and she fills me in on all the concerts she's been to. She's easy to laugh with, but there's a sinking feeling in my gut that I won't ever get stories like that of my own. I mean, sure, we could probably risk going to concerts, but why? We're always on the run, constantly looking over our shoulders, making sure the Authorities don't catch up to us. What's the point? It would be even worse in a crowded space and so risky it wouldn't even be worth it.

By the time she's finished, I stare in amazement at the purple haze spinning around my arm. It's so much *more* than I expected, so I end up tipping double what I usually would.

She gives me a card, telling me to come back, and I say I will, even though it's a lie.

Tomorrow may be the end of me, anyway.

Before heading back to the Rib House, I pay someone off to buy me a six-pack. None of this is hard; people don't care what age you are, they just want the money.

Slipping the case into my backpack, I venture into the familiar woods that will most likely be the scene of my downfall. I study the trees, searching for any changes, like whatever is going to happen is much more sinister than a person arriving in the morning, but none have come yet. This night doesn't feel different from any other.

Instead of going back inside the house when I arrive, I walk past it and go to the small dock overlooking a lake.

Sitting on the edge, I open one of the beers and stare into the darkness. The fog hangs low and heavy, and I can't see anything across the lake.

I lose sense of time, downing each drink as I try to thaw the ice in my veins. Idly playing with the lighter, I study the flame and how it dances in the dark.

I'll be gone before the crew wakes up tomorrow, so I haphazardly scribble a note on a piece of paper I found in my bag, instructing Elise to head west if I don't come back, and leave the rest of the money tucked into the folded note. I hope it buys them enough time to make it to wherever's next on the list.

Elise would poke fun if she could see me now, calling me dramatic, but an aching deep in my chest understands that *something's not right.*

Chapter Seventeen

GEMMA

Leaving the man unconscious in the woods, I bolt onto the bus and find a middle seat so I'm away from the window. The bleeding has stopped, but I use my hair to cover the gash anyway to avoid drawing attention to myself. There's hardly anyone on here, but better safe than sorry.

Hunkering down, I focus on the floor, searching people's emotions around me for any signs of danger. My hands stopped glowing the second I wanted them to, which is reassuring. Maybe I can learn how to handle this.

That power, though.

I shudder, thinking of what I've done. I've broken a man's arm without concern—and with no strenuous effort. It just shattered beneath my touch. I didn't mean to suck in nature's energy, either. It was like I could see the pipeline around me, calling out, tempting me. There for the taking, so I took it. I didn't bother to stop and think about what would happen; I only knew I needed to escape a bad situation. Was this nature's way of protecting me? Or did I force that power to become available?

There are so many unanswered questions; all I can do is burrow my face in my hands. As if I didn't have enough problems, now there's one more. *He wants his power back.* Who's Draven, and why does he think I have his power?

I lower my hands to my lap but can't look away from them; they caused so much destruction with no remorse.

Movement jolts me forward, and I settle back into the seat, slightly relieved the stranger didn't make his way onto the bus. Here's to hoping I'm leaving him behind.

TEN HOURS LATER, I stumble off the bus, legs numb from the constant sitting, fatigue hanging heavy on every limb. My hunger vanished when I was attacked and hasn't come back yet. The thought of forcing myself to eat makes me nauseous, but it's necessary. Also, I want nothing more than to crawl into a hotel bed, but I can't afford it.

I inhale sharply as fear encloses me. What was I thinking? I'm eighteen hours away from the people I'm closest to. Referring to them as my family is a stretch, but at least I knew where I would sleep each night. Thankful for the four months the McIntyres gave me, I regret not giving them a proper goodbye. I only allow myself a second to think about calling them but decide against it. I can't go back there, not without Oli. And especially not now that someone is looking for me.

Immediately suspending my thoughts, I stop the grief in its tracks. Right now, I need to figure out what I'm doing. But no matter how much I keep it at bay, thoughts of the man from the bus station come flooding back. What if there are more people like him? And what if that guy somehow followed me after he woke up?

Scanning the terminal, I spot a locker room of sorts. I creep in silently, unsure if I'm even allowed to be in here or if I need to pay first. It's a combination of toilets, showers, and lockers. After checking every stall, I discover I'm alone—probably because it's nearly midnight—and it's the first time in a while that my breath comes slightly easier. I close my eyes, and the world tilts beneath my feet—drained of the power from the forest, my own natural energy spent, and from lack of food. I open my eyes as I sway and catch myself on the wall before falling.

I check the lockers with shaky hands to see if anyone has accidentally left anything that might be useful. Unfortunately, all I find is an old baseball cap with "Disneyland Resort" on it, but I snatch it up anyway, only semi-grossed out. It's unclear how the guy found me the first time, and I'm worried he'll be standing there waiting when I walk out of here. I try not to shudder as I test the hat, pulling it down low to cover most of my face, seeing if it'll help disguise me. It doesn't fix all my problems, but it's something.

Taking a second and then a third look at the closed door, I rush into a stall and quickly strip out of my clothes, tossing the hat onto the pile, and let the cold water wash over me. Goosebumps cover my arms, my head pounds, and my eyes burn from fatigue, but the chilly shower gives me some life back. I'm more alert, at least. I gently wash the blood off my face, wincing as the cold water beats down on the cut on my cheekbone. I'm in and out in minutes, putting my clothes back on without fully drying off. Throwing the hat on, I dash out before I'm discovered.

Stepping outside into the fresh air, I take a moment to lift my face toward the moon. It's a moment of refuge—one I'm not entirely sure I have to spare—but I cling to it for now.

I'm in Thornbrooke, Indiana. I've never even heard of it. I have no idea where I am or if there are any nearby cities. I'm out of money and have no plan in mind.

Continuing to wander, I wrestle between planning and despairing, eventually deciding to make do outdoors for tonight.

Thankfully, it's semi-warm out.

Roaming the small, darkened town, the only place open is a tattoo shop, which doesn't help me. I glance up at the flickering neon sign glowing in the window, then spot a line of trees. I'm not sure how deep the woods go, but I might be able to take cover until the morning—hidden by thick foliage and twisted tree branches that remind me of the southern live oaks back in Florida.

I head into the trees and eventually pick a spot on the forest floor, digging out one of the granola bars from my backpack's pocket and eating it in two bites, ignoring my stomach flipping in protest. In a moment of weakness, I scarf down another one.

I'll have to find a job. Or steal. My heart drops thinking of the latter. It'd be so easy, *too* easy, to head down that path again.

I wrap a hoodie around me, using the pack as a pillow. Making myself as comfortable as possible, I ignore the pain radiating from my face and aim to get at least a little sleep before the morning comes.

DARKNESS SEEPS INTO THE woods, expanding over every inch, weaving its way closer to me. The moonlight disappears, hidden behind the fog. Tossing and turning on the ground, I dig rocks out from underneath me that pierce between my shoulder blades. Lying there gazing up into nothing, I let the silence of the woods soothe me.

It takes me far too long to realize that the darkness is no ordinary lack of light. This is something else. At the same instant, a voice—sounding a lot like Olivia—screams at me to run.

A jolt of adrenaline has me on my feet in seconds. I'm not entirely sure what's happening. This could all be a dream, but the fear is real.

The dread presses into me, clouding my thoughts. I have to run.

Spinning in circles, I throw on my backpack and pick a direction. Everything is based on my gut at this point, and it's pulling me deeper into the woods.

My feet pound the earth, not knowing when to stop, or if I can, who is chasing me, or why. Only Olivia's echo of a voice remains.

Run, run, run.

I reach out into the unknown, expanding my mind and feelings to sense my sister's presence, but nothing is there. The fear is too strong; I can't get around it. *Focus on surviving*, I remind myself. *Worry about the rest later.*

I'm slowing, running out of air. I chance a look over my shoulder. There's nothing. Stopping, I double over, clutching my knees. A lick of embarrassment causes my cheeks to warm.

My dead sister came to me in a dream. Is that what it was? Or was it real? Dawn is breaking, so I must've fallen asleep at some point. Regardless, she told me to run, so I did. No questions asked because I'm an idiot. Glad no one is around to question my sanity, I search the sky to try to find my way back into town. Lost, with no sun visible to get my bearings, I laugh.

"This is great," I say aloud, throwing my arms out to the side. "Just great."

Sudden rage slams against me, and my body shakes with fury, hands sparking to life. My brows furrow as I raise my hands and study them; they're glowing brightly.

Whose anger is this?

Slowly, I turn.

My breath stills as I watch a black cloud morph into a shape. Human-like but featureless. I've never seen anything like it, but I'm frozen to the ground. Fear paralyzes me as a silhouette of an arm reaches out. Blood returns to my legs, and I take a step closer, wanting—no, *needing*—to take the hand that's offered.

My head cocks to the side as I study the black vapor coaxing me closer. I don't understand *how* it's doing it. I only know that it *is*. The arm continues to reach for me, searching, and all I want to do is help it. I can feel their struggle, their pain, their *anger*.

Clarity finally comes, startling me backward. I trip over myself when I'm able to fully turn around and run.

What was that?

The further away I get, the more the fury diminishes. Separated by distance, it doesn't have quite the same hold on me.

I have to get out of the woods and away from whatever that is.

Up ahead, a man is walking. He's entirely out of place—but he's an actual human, not whatever that shadow figure is.

I can't leave him behind, abandon him to whatever's chasing me, but how can I explain? I'll leave town and pick a different place after I get him to go. He'll never see me again. Yes, that could work.

Sensing the darkness on my heels, he, it, whatever it is, is catching up to me.

Oh, God. We don't have time.

"Run!" I start screaming at the person. His head snaps up, and when he notices me, a spark of his alarm zaps into me, but he doesn't move. "Run!" I repeat, out of breath. He still doesn't move; terror and shock mix into one expression now plastered on his face.

I run past, grabbing his arm and tugging him forward. "What don't you understand about 'run'?" I snap, dropping his arm quickly—at least my hands stopped glowing, but I'm still afraid of hurting him.

He humors me for a second before I'm yanked backward. "Stop!" he orders.

I crane my head every which way, searching the woods for the darkness that doesn't come. Shaking from head to toe only makes him grip my arms harder.

"Let me go! Let me go!" I scream. I can't hurt him; I *won't* hurt him. When my gaze finally falls on his face, we both recoil away from each other. I perceive his shock as much as my own.

"It's you," I whisper. This person isn't a man like I'd initially thought, but a boy whose gray eyes are currently wide with terror.

He stands far away, both hands on his hips, shaking his head. "This isn't possible."

The darkness is suddenly forgotten since I can't take my eyes off the stranger—the stranger who's been in my head, in my dreams, for years.

"How are you here right now? How are you..." His voice fades away. He rubs his eyes, slightly groaning to himself when he takes another look at me.

"Real?" I finish for him, knowing it's the word dangling from his lips because it's also dangling from mine. I'm gasping for air, chest heaving. "I..." Lost for words, I close my mouth but continue to gawk.

He takes a step closer to me, eyes wide and wild as if he doesn't believe what's in front of him. He holds out a tattooed arm, and I stand frozen, afraid of his touch, yet craving it all the same, just like in my dream. This is it; he's going to touch me for real this time.

Instead, he reaches for the brim of my hat and reads aloud, "Disneyland Resort?" He smirks while asking the question, and I don't know how to respond.

Heat creeps up my neck, and I let out a harsh laugh. I run my hands through my hair, gaining some semblance of order, knowing I look like a hot mess from sleeping in the woods all night and running from... My eyes widen as I whip around again, kicking myself for being shocked into forgetting.

Movement rustles in the distance, and a small yelp escapes me. It was foolish to let my guard down even a second; how could I forget the darkness and its rage?

"We need to go," I tell him.

His jaw clenches as he peers out into the empty trees. "What's wrong?"

"I don't know. Something was chasing me, and I have a feeling it's still out there."

"Follow me."

Seeing him here, in front of me, is so strange that I don't hesitate. It's like I already trust him from the years we've spent together, but that wasn't real. And this is. We should both be asking a lot of questions right now, but any words die on my lips because he's *here*.

We walk along in silence, me two steps behind, studying every inch of him. I should be afraid, but I'm not. He's exactly how he appears in my dreams—broad shoulders, slightly messy hair, stubble along his jawline. My knees weaken—those gray eyes...

Shaking the thoughts away, I finally ask the question I've been dying to know all this time. "What's your name?"

"Theo Goodwin."

I freeze.

There's no way. There's no possible way he's related to the cop.

Theo glances over his shoulder, noticing I stopped, and doubles back. His brows furrow as he silently takes me in, but he doesn't bother asking why I'm just standing here.

I size him up, trying to determine the age difference between him and Officer Goodwin. Is Goodwin a popular surname? I don't freaking know. How could it be a coincidence, though? But I'm eighteen hours away from Florida; they can't be related. I continue internally arguing with myself before deciding to see where he's taking me first. Maybe I'm about to meet his parents, and my questions will all be settled.

"Gemma," I finally respond. "...Gemma Roberts."

His eyes shift to the ground, lips quirking into a small smile, but he doesn't say anything. Instead, he turns to resume walking.

Once we leave the woods, we enter a large field filled with wildflowers. It's breathtaking, and for a moment, I forget my troubles. Ironically, it reminds me of one of my dreams with Theo. It's like I've been here before. I want to stay in this moment forever, soaking up the sunshine. This place is calm compared to the chaos of my heart. My fears, faults, and worries bleed out of me into the soil, and all I want to do is enjoy it while it lasts.

"So, Gemma Roberts," Theo says, breaking my reverie. He's plucking a flower apart, keeping his eyes on anything but me. "You exist." It's not much of a question, more like an observation he can't wrap his head around.

"So do you," I challenge. "Why didn't you ever tell me?"

Theo frowns as he seems to think about it. "I didn't know how. Or why would I, for that matter? I didn't know you were real."

"You've been visiting my dreams for years but didn't think I was real?"

"I didn't purposely visit. I just... I *created* you. You weren't real. Or so I thought." His voice comes out as defensive.

"You told me to come to you."

The look he gives me is unnerving. Hairs rise on the back of my neck when he responds. "No, I didn't."

Blinking away unwanted tears, I consider the horizon and how the pastel colors melt together in the distance, focusing on my breathing so I can calm down. "This doesn't make sense. In my dream... you... you..." Not wanting to say how close we were or how excited I was, my cheeks warm, and I spill out the rest. "You said 'come to me' when I had nowhere else to go. And I've been drawn to this town ever since, apparently, with fate leading the way. I thought it was a sign..." My voice fades toward the end, and I realize how childish I sound as he shakes his head.

"Gemma." He chews his bottom lip as if considering his next words carefully. "That wasn't me."

"Oh." Sucking in a breath, I wrestle with what this means. The person I've felt connected to all these years doesn't even want me here. He didn't say those things to me in my dream. I made it all up, which somehow led me to find him even though I didn't think he existed, and I wasn't sure what I was even searching for.

How is that possible?

As if echoing my thoughts, he asks, "How?" His eyes seem to search mine for something as his voice softens. "If you didn't think I was real, how did you get here?"

I have no answer to this. I don't have answers for anything.

I shrug. "All I did was get on a bus."

A slight grin tugs at the corner of his lips again, but it slips away as he pulls a twig from my hair. "You can stay with us." He doesn't wait for my response as he twirls the twig between two fingers and turns away from me to walk across the field.

"Us?" I squeak out, but Theo doesn't answer.

Chapter Eighteen

Theo

Gemma. *Gemma*. Her name rolls around in my head, dangling from my lips, and I resist the urge to speak it aloud. *She's real*.

What the fuck is happening?

This doesn't make any sense.

She follows me, not saying a word, but the crunching of autumn leaves under her booted feet tells me she's still there. Inches away from me. Living and breathing, in full color.

My heartbeat hasn't steadied since she grabbed my arm, screaming at me to run.

What was she running from, anyway? And does it have anything to do with the cut on her face? My fingers twitch at the thought of something harming her, but I ball my hands into fists to keep myself from doing something stupid.

I open my mouth to ask her, but nothing comes out. I can't wrap my head around the fact that she's real. It's too much to handle, let alone dealing with whatever else she was talking about.

It's not... possible.

Chest heaving, my breath comes in gasps as I swipe a hand over my face.

Calm down. Get it together.

Is Gemma the one Nora saw? Is she the all-powerful entity that'll be my undoing?

My hands turn damp, electricity running through me, and all I want to do is grab her. Feel her skin. Touch every inch of her to make sure she's here. This isn't in my head; it can't be. Please.

Hell, she's *already* my undoing.

A groan comes out before I can stop it, and her soft voice floats my way. Its musical infliction entrances me, and I completely miss what she asked.

"What?" I glance back at her, trying not to meet her eyes. Those eyes that I now have tattooed on me. Ugh. That's going to be hard to explain. She's going to think I'm some sort of stalker weirdo.

"Are you okay?" she repeats.

"Yeah, why?"

"I don't... sorry. Forget I asked."

I lower my chin, focusing again on our makeshift trail. I glance back at her a second time and frown. The gash on her cheek does look fresh. Maybe it's from that thing she was running from back there. I open my mouth to say something again but don't. My mouth snaps shut instead. Why can't I just talk to her?

The onslaught of questions buzzes around inside my head, making it nearly impossible to think straight.

How are you here?

Where did you come from?

What were you running from?

What happened to you?

Why do you make me disappear?

Maybe she won't kill me after all. Perhaps Nora saw whatever Gemma was running from.

I'm satisfied with that for a split second until I realize it doesn't solve any problems. Something is coming after her, and I'm now directing it to the Rib House.

Our lives just got considerably more complicated.

Thinking of putting the crew in danger finally brings words to my lips. I spin around, and Gemma nearly trips over herself, backing away from me, arms retreating behind her back like she's making sure she doesn't accidentally touch me.

Her eyes.

It's like they can't decide if they want to be brown or violet, the colors blending together and changing depending on which angle I look from.

I was wrong. The words still don't come. So instead, we stare at each other; only the cicadas chirping in the distance ground me. I could get lost in her eyes, and that terrifies me. My jaw ticks, but something softens in my chest the longer I study her.

Steeling myself, I inhale deeply. I need to keep my head straight. I can't do whatever it is that's happening right now. I have to think of the others.

I rock back onto my heels, shaking my head to clear it, not knowing where to begin.

Gemma bites her lip, grinning like she's about to start laughing at me.

"What?"

She squints. "You are not handling this well."

"Oh, and you are?"

"I mean, no, but—"

Scoffing, I reply, "But what?"

Her cheeks flush as she rapidly blinks, but she doesn't continue. "What were you running from?"

Crossing her arms, she looks away from me. "I don't know."

"Not good enough. I need to know how you're here and what you left behind back there before I endanger them."

Her eyes narrow to slits. "Who?"

"Just answer my questions."

By now, we've somehow managed to close the distance between us. I don't remember moving at all, but if I just lift my arm...

Gemma has her hands placed behind her back, her eyes narrowed up at me. She tilts her head as if considering something before she lets out a small admission. "You were a lot nicer in my dreams, you know."

My mouth twists as I nod, considering her words. "That's all it was. *Dreams*. It was never supposed to come to this."

I turn away from the hurt in her eyes, continuing toward the house. I'm nowhere closer to answering the mystery, but what am I supposed to do? Leave her in the woods?

Gemma continues to follow, much further behind this time, and I can't help but think I've already ruined everything.

Chapter Nineteen

Gemma

Neither of us has spoken since Theo walked away from me, and the silence becomes harder to break as it grows. I clear my throat, but that doesn't do anything to prompt conversation, so I huff out a sigh instead. He still doesn't take the bait.

I finally work up the courage to ask, "Where are we going?"

"Back to the house."

Nodding, even though he can't see me, I mumble, "Right." That makes sense; why would I possibly need further clarification?

A thought has been worming its way through my brain, unscratchable, since we started this journey. I've been too afraid to ask, worried about his response, but not knowing the answer becomes unbearable, and I have to voice it. "Why were you standing there in the woods?"

Theo glances back at me before staring straight ahead again and continuing on his way.

"Clearly, you weren't out for just a walk."

Still nothing. I bite the inside of my cheek, refusing to let him rile me up. I can't let him see my hands come to life.

"Can you just answer the question?" I ask.

"Nope."

Puckering my lips, I have a sudden urge to hit him. He was never this annoying or mean in my dreams. We might not have talked at all, but he was always... calming. Consistent. Loveable.

My eyes narrow in on his back, and I stop walking, but it takes him a while to notice I'm no longer following.

He throws his hands up, making his way back to me. "What? What's wrong?"

"I need a little more information before I aimlessly follow you." Anger drips from my words, and I'm unsure if it's solely mine.

His emotions don't seem to attack me from the outside like others do. It's like he's already inside my chest, sort of how Olivia's were. Maybe being in my head all these years allows his emotions to run freely to mess mine up as well. It probably doesn't help his mood that I didn't answer his questions, either.

Why is this so confusing?

His eyes flash to mine, something unreadable in them, but they soften a second later. "You were doing just fine before."

"I've come to my senses." I raise an eyebrow at him. "Where are you taking me? And how did you know to be in the woods at the same time I was?"

He rakes a hand through his hair and looks past me into the distance. "There's an old abandoned house not much further ahead, and I currently stay there with three friends I'm sure you'll meet later. So that's where we're going. And I... don't know why I was in the woods."

"You don't know why..."

"Look, it's—" He cuts himself off, kicking his tattered shoes into the ground. "Will you please just come with me, and we can figure it out at the house?" He looks back into the wilderness, concern shaping his mouth into a grimace. I haven't felt the darkness anywhere near us, but it's almost as if he senses something himself. My gaze darts all around, then settles back on him. Can I unquestioningly follow someone I don't know? I have no reason to trust him other than knowing I already do. Can I live with that?

"We're close," he repeats. "You can eat, shower, sleep. Do whatever. And then we'll figure this all out, all right?"

We make eye contact, and for a moment, nothing else matters. My heart flutters, and all I want to do is reach out and hold his hand. Reassure myself he's truly standing before me, that it's not a dream this time. He's actually here.

"Okay, fine. And thanks for finding me, by the way." I pause. "Even if you didn't mean to."

His lips quirk as he starts walking again. "No problem."

WE MOVE FROM AN open field before returning into the woods, but only for a minute, the trees thinly veiling a house that appears out of nowhere.

The dwelling is a Victorian-style mansion, painted a deep blue with black trim around the door and windows. A room on the second floor—furthest to the right—is shaped like a tower. It's circular with long rectangular broken windows and a pointy roof, but cutting through the blue are five white painted stripes wrapped around the outer structure, all split in half down the middle. They almost look like ribs.

Dropping my gaze to the wrap-around deck covered in different kinds of plants, I notice that most of the wood is rotted away. The entire house looks like nature has devoured it.

And that's the last thing I notice when the world turns white.

Searing pain tears my brain apart, and I clasp my ears to get the screaming to end, but I hardly register that the screams are coming from me.

I collapse to the ground, curling in on myself.

I would do anything to get it all to stop.

Blinking rapidly, squeezing my eyes shut, keeping them wide open. Nothing helps. It's all white. A high-pitched whistle blows and my eardrums feel like they'll explode any second. My body shakes uncontrollably.

I don't understand what's happening to me.

Within the whiteness, a figure appears. It makes its way to me slowly, too slowly, and I can't move—blood gushes from my nose, and my eyes water.

This is it. This is the end for me.

The figure morphs into Olivia, and I choke back a sob. Am I imagining all of this? She's how I last saw her—when she died in my arms—but there's no blood this time. She's as perfect as ever.

"Oli?" I question the figure. She nods but doesn't say anything. Instead, she hovers over me, her brows knit together, and her lips turned down. "What's wrong?" I ask her, though clearly, *everything* is wrong.

Her face softens, pity filling her eyes. "Oh, G," she finally whispers. "I'm sorry, darling, but you have to keep running."

A sob racks my body again. The nosebleed won't stop. Blood, mucus, and tears all mix together, suffocating me. "Running from who? What's happening to me?"

"You won't ever be safe here. He's coming."

Olivia's head snaps up, and she stares off into the void. I can't see what she's looking at, but she spares me one last glance, mouthing, "Run."

I gasp awake, clutching at the damp grass beneath me as the world settles back into view. I find myself on the ground with Theo panting above me. His chest heaves as blood drains from his face, and he looks away, wiping at the corner of his eye. My upper body rests on his thighs as he kneels awkwardly. He has one arm wrapped around my neck, supporting my head. Blood coats his shirt, probably from my nosebleed. My cheeks warm as I blink at the red staining his clothes, failing to block out the embarrassing fact that I bled all over him.

If he notices, he does a good job hiding it.

"What happened?" I ask as a new face comes into view.

I study the girl standing next to us, estimating we're around the same age, but the stranger is unearthly beautiful. She has blonde hair cascading down her back and emerald eyes, and with a start, I realize she reminds me of Olivia.

It was *definitely* Olivia that I saw just now. I blink, trying to clear my head. Or was it somehow this girl?

No, the dress. It had to be Olivia. She called me G; she's the only one who does that. Also, this girl wouldn't even know my name, let alone have a nickname for me.

I'm still lying carelessly across Theo's lap, so I shift away from him and out of his arms. The world spins around me.

"Easy now," the girl says. "I had to give you an antidote so the wards would stop kicking your ass. It's going to take a bit before you feel good again."

"W-who are you?" I stammer out, mind reeling from everything that's happened. I wipe my face with the back of one fingerless glove, attempting to get some of the blood off, but judging by my skin's stickiness, it doesn't work.

"Elise Beck, at your service." She sticks out a hand to shake, but I limply hold up mine that's covered in filth. "Right..." she teeters off. "Well, let's get you inside. It should be safe now."

She and Theo both tug at an arm until I'm fully upright. Elise lets go, and I slump into Theo, leaning all my weight against him. I have no strength left in me, and my legs are numb. Sighing, he scoops me up, and my head lolls against his shoulder, eyelids fluttering shut.

Other voices swim into my brain, but I barely register them. My focus is gone, and I feel like I could sleep for a year. As I'm lowered, Theo lets out a grunt, a stiff mattress pressing against my spine before I'm out cold.

Chapter Twenty

Theo

I check on Gemma's breathing from time to time, leaving her and pacing outside the bedroom. She's been unconscious for nearly twelve hours.

The rest of the crew should be returning anytime now. They left for the day to give Gemma space, not realizing she wouldn't be awake, so it didn't even matter.

Flopping onto the couch, I run both hands over my face, rubbing my tired eyes and ultimately failing to wake myself up. My brain feels waterlogged, thinking back on how long today's been and the whirlwind of emotions I wasn't prepared for.

I left before the sun rose, with only the shiniest of stars breaking through the dense fog to guide me, thinking I might never make it back here. I never once imagined I'd be bringing *her* back with me.

Then she collapsed.

I shudder as I recall her screams. Her cries tore a hole straight through me, and she lost so much blood. I honestly thought she was dying. None of us has had any problems stepping onto the property before. So, what changed? I need to talk to Elise and ask her how the hell she knew there were wards around the house.

I thought I lost Gemma. I didn't even realize she was someone I *could* lose until today, yet she almost slipped through my fingers so easily.

Please wake up.

I'm lost in my thoughts, staring at the wall, when the back door opens, and the crew comes filing into the kitchen. None of them say anything. They just look at me expectantly, like I should have all the answers by now.

I raise a hand in defeat, then drop it onto my thigh. My head rests against the back of the couch, and I don't have enough strength to lift it.

"She won't wake up," I whisper.

Nora and Zay both plop down on either side of me. Zay slaps a hand onto my shoulder, tightening his hold. "She will. Just give her time."

I allow a small smile—no use arguing the point—when I roll my head to the other side to eye up Nora. "Is she the one you saw?"

She shrugs, tugging on her lip again. She's going to make it bleed if she keeps doing that. "Gotta be. No one else was in the woods, was there?"

"Gemma said she was running from something, but I have no idea what."

"I don't sense anyone else."

I hum a noncommittal noise. None of this makes any sense, and all I want is to go back to when things were easier. Okay, so maybe things were never *easy*, but they weren't this fucked up.

Elise has kept her hands busy, rearranging papers on the table this whole time.

"How'd you know about the wards?" I ask her, raising my voice enough for her to hear me from across the room.

She stills, but she doesn't look at me. Then, she continues shuffling the documents. "I sort of put one up when we first moved in, and I forgot..."

"You forgot?"

"I wasn't sure it was going to work! It was a spell I've been messing around with over the years, and I never got to actually test it." She claps her hands together, letting out a weak chuckle. "Surprise! It works!"

"A warning would've been nice when you first put it up."

"It wouldn't hurt any of you, so I didn't think I needed to. And she's fine, isn't she? I gave her the antidote I *also* made as a precaution. You're welcome?" She lifts both her eyebrows, cocking her head, waiting for a *thank you* she's not going to get.

"I don't know, Elise. Is she fine?" I spit out.

She doesn't say any more as she sulks out of the room, Nora in tow, to do God knows what. Nora casts one last look at me, lips thinned like she's disappointed in me. She always chooses Elise's side when we have little tiffs, so I'm not that surprised.

My blood boils mainly from anger, but maybe there's fear, too. This isn't Elise's fault. Putting up a ward was a good call. I just wish she'd told me.

Zay is sitting so silently that I nearly forgot he was there until he nudges me in the side.

"Take it easy on her, wouldya? She's only looking out for us. She takes after you, you know." He gives me a wide grin, relaxing into the couch. "Your girl is going to wake up any moment now. Happily ever after and all that jazz."

I furrow my brows at him while frowning. "My girl?"

Zay's curls shake as he clutches his stomach in an exaggerated laugh. "Play it cool. All right. Whatever. We all saw what you looked like when she was dying out there. And isn't she the girl on your arm?" His laughing stops as my throat closes. *My secrets will come out now. It was only a matter of time.*

He eyes me for a moment like he wants to say something, but thankfully, he doesn't push the topic any further. Instead, he hits me on the leg. "Just go apologize to Elise."

"Yeah, yeah. I will."

Biding my time, I wait a while before summoning the courage to address Elise. Even without the ability to read my mood, she has a way of knowing almost every thought that goes through my head, and I don't want to lose my temper again.

With the last two beers—a peace offering—I knock on her door, and it opens a crack, revealing she's poring over a large book she's kept with her for years now: her spell book.

Elise has been studying potions and tarot cards ever since I met her. She seemed disappointed she could only read auras, so she threw everything she had into learning more about the craft, hoping to strengthen it someday. I never knew what to say, especially when she tried to figure out why I wasn't disappointed that I had no gift of my own, so I just let her have at it and said nothing at all.

I lean against the doorframe, studying her as she sprawls across her bed. She knows I'm here, but she's ignoring me. *Rightfully so.*

Sighing, I stare down at the broken wooden floor below my feet. The slants reveal the foundation beneath. "I'm sorry."

"For?" she asks.

My eyes snap up to hers, and her gaze is locked onto me now, but there's a grin across her face. I deflate some, knowing she's not actually pissed at me.

"For being an asshole."

"And?"

I hand her a beer. "... And for... doubting you? I'm sure your antidote works fine. She's just, well... I don't know. I don't know what's wrong with her." I bite my lip, confused by my sudden rush of words.

Elise sits up, tapping the cushion next to her as she takes a sip, and I sit, sprawling my legs the same way she does. Our backs against the wall, we face the window we had to repair—also with duct tape.

"I know it doesn't seem like it now, but everything is going to work out."

I arch my brow. "Did Nora see something else?"

"No, but I have a good feeling about this. I think things are going to change for the better soon."

I pick at the scabs on my hands from the fight. One starts bleeding again the more I dig. "That's optimistic of you. Where's this coming from?"

She shrugs. "Gut feeling."

"Mm." A few seconds go by when I finally relent. "Good call on the wards. It was smart and kind of cool they worked, even if... well... you know."

"I wrote it down so I'll remember what I did. And I'll whip up more antidotes, just in case."

I clink my bottle against hers. "Well, here's to not having any more visitors."

Chapter Twenty-One

GEMMA

I STARTLE AWAKE WHEN a door slams. My heart hammers against my ribcage as I try to place where I am. I have a pounding migraine and can't get my thoughts in order. Flipping the covers off, I groan. My clothes are blood-stained and ruined. I bolt upright, and a wave of vertigo overcomes me.

Cautiously getting out of bed, I search the room to orient myself and get the vibe I'm safe and sound in Theo's bedroom. Nothing tells me that exactly, but it's familiar to me. I think we hung out here in one of our dreams. Thinking of Theo, memories slowly come back—the pain, the gushing blood, Olivia. I suck in a breath. *Olivia*. Was that real or just a dream when she told me to run?

My hand shakes as I reach for the door handle. I should stay put. Who knows what's waiting for me out there? Another unseen attack? Whatever happened to me outside, I do *not* want it to happen again. Also, I don't want to walk out there like I own the place.

Sitting back down on the bed, I tap my fingers on my knee and make up my mind. I'll wait until Theo comes back.

But what if he doesn't?

What if he's waiting for me to leave his room?

I push those thoughts to the side. He has to come back eventually.

THE DOOR SLOWLY CREAKS open. I straighten my spine, lifting my head to see Theo side-step in, face schooled into an expression of fierce concentration. His shoulders are bunched as he quietly closes the door, letting out a breath when it makes no noise.

I bite back a smile. He's trying to be quiet. He recoils, finally noticing me. I lift my eyebrows at him and no longer contain my grin.

"Sorry." His breathing doesn't seem to slow, his chest rising and falling quickly as he tries to get words out, stumbling along the way. "I didn't want to... wake... disturb you."

"It's all right." I lift a shoulder. "I woke up a little while ago."

"Oh." He scratches his head, then shoves his hands deep into his pockets as he leans against the door.

Neither of us speaks until he does a double-take at my shirt. Reaching over, he snags a black T-shirt off the chair and hands it to me.

"You can wear this if you want. It's clean. I don't know if we can get"—he points at all the blood on my shirt—"that all out. Elise probably has extra clothes you can have, too."

When I take it from him, our fingers brush, and it's like an electrical current going down my spine. My lips part as I'm forced to turn away, worried my eyes are about to flash from the sudden surge of emotions. Seconds later, the feeling settles, and I focus back on him.

"Thanks," I try to say, but my throat is suddenly dry, and I can't get any words out. Clearing my throat, I give him a slight smirk instead.

Theo looks down at me with hooded eyes, biting his lip. "Right," he whispers like he's saying it more to himself than to me. Then, shaking his head, his voice comes out slightly louder. "I should give you some space to change. If you want to come out after, I can introduce you to everyone."

I nod, twisting the shirt in my hands. I don't want to meet everyone. I don't ever want to leave this room, *his* room. And I don't want him to leave either.

But he does, closing the door behind him.

I stand there frozen, staring at where he stood—tall and lean, with tattooed arms and dark hair just long enough to curl slightly at the ends. It looks so freaking soft. He's real! My stomach clenches, thinking of our fingers brushing, and I try to hold back the smile spreading across my face until the unwanted thoughts creep in.

Get it together. You can't touch him, you freak. What if you hurt him? The longer I scold myself, the more the anxiety and fear twist inside me, which only confirms my point—*look at your hands glowing.*

Stripping out of my top, I tug his on as the scent of citrus soap and... something else wafts around me. I can't quite identify it, but it smells like... the outdoors—crisp fresh air from hanging on a clothesline mixed with the woodsy scent of pine. I close my eyes, inhaling deeply as the smell wraps around me like a cozy sweater.

Shaking out the tension—and glow—in my hands, I swap out my fingerless gloves for a clean pair, ditching the stained ones. I swing the door open and curl my fingers into the bottom of the shirt so they remain hidden. I can't let them see me glow. Who knows what would happen? They might kick me out.

Where would I go then?

But I can't stay here either. Olivia's voice comes back to haunt me, *Run.*

As I take a tentative step into the hallway, the broken floorboard squeaks under my weight, and I stiffen. My pulse thrums in my neck. I give myself less than a second to calm down before convincing myself to continue.

A conversation drifts from the other room; someone laughs. There are... one, two, three, four different voices. I take several deep breaths, calming my nerves. I'm capable of meeting four strangers. Well, two. I already met Theo and that other girl... What was her name? Esme? Elsa? Elise!

See. *I can do this.*

After ten seconds of inhaling through my nose, I turn the corner into the room, and all eyes fall on me as their conversation dwindles. My face heats the longer they stare at me, but Theo's soft gaze encourages me to take another step toward them.

I snake one arm across my body, my hand clutching my other elbow as I raise that hand, providing a weak wave. I drop my palm back down as the words leave me, and I fail to even offer a small 'hi.'

Great first impression. I pass out, and then I'm rude. Stupid.

As if noticing my hesitation, Theo finally steps in, starting the introductions.

"You've already met Elise." He points to the unearthly goddess whose face I saw when I first woke up after being given the antidote. As I study her features now, I realize she isn't as identical to Olivia as I first thought, but the similarity is still there. She has a pinkish tone to her skin, almond-shaped eyes of the purest green, a sharp nose, and blonde hair lighter than Olivia's that slips down her back. Her part is flipped to the side, giving her a disheveled look, but it's the perfect kind of messy. My scalp tingles as I note the first hint of jealousy I used to feel when comparing myself to Oli when we were younger.

My gaze drifts to the smaller girl sitting next to her, and I'd guess she's maybe a year or two younger than me. Her amber eyes fit perfectly with her beige round face and pointed nose. Her auburn hair is parted into two elaborate French braid pigtails and gives her more of a child-like innocence. She chews on her lip as we consider each other, but eventually, she flashes me a quick smile.

"Nora Sanders," Theo says, his eyes then shift to a boy with brown skin and coiled hair. He has chestnut brown eyes and a button nose sprinkled with freckles. He grins at me, his friendly face immediately pulling me in, and I already know we'll be good friends. His affection pours out of him, and in my uneasiness, I soak it in greedily, hoping it'll calm my nerves. His grin must be contagious because Theo's face splits into a dazzling smile, taking my breath away. "And this is Zay Lewis, the youngest of the crew."

"At least I'm not the newbie anymore." Zay strolls over, throwing his arm around my neck, towering over me by a foot or more.

I freeze, not knowing what to do.

I don't want to shrug him off because *that* wouldn't look good. I'm already zero to two with my first impressions, but I don't have complete control over my power yet, either. *What if I hurt him?*

My shoulders bunch, and the panic creeps in as they all joke about something. I can't tell what they're saying because I'm too busy focusing on the desire to keep the purple energy at bay. At least, I think they're joking with each other because everyone's laughing. But I don't know. I don't know *them*. They're all strangers.

What am I doing here?

Theo's grin fades as he catches my gaze, concern crinkling the corners of his eyes. He pulls a chair out for me next to him at the table, breaking up the conversation.

Zay drops his arm, retaking his spot, and I shuffle over after him, lowering myself in the seat as my heart rate settles back to normal.

I'm sitting between Theo and Nora, and I can't get over how strange this all is. The five of us as if they just accepted me, no questions asked.

Something's got to give.

My gaze darts around the kitchen, and I take in my surroundings. They've done well for themselves, considering. We're seated at an oval table, the wood weathered from overuse and time. Mismatched chairs surround it, but at least it's somewhere to sit.

Looking at everyone sitting here, I notice their clothes all look like hand-me-downs, too. Theo only sports a white T-shirt paired with torn jeans, but the rest have layers. Elise is still somehow fashionable even though she has a maroon T-shirt on top of a purple long-sleeved sweatshirt. Zay has a brown sweater beneath a green hoodie with a gray collar popping out from underneath. And Nora is swimming in a sweater that looks like it's three times too big and comes from someone's grandma—a lone flower printed right in the middle of the chest.

Glancing down at myself, I grimace at my own attire—Theo's black T-shirt and my blood-stained pants.

What looks like plastic wrap surrounds the windows, held together by duct tape. The ceramic flooring is intact for the most part, but parts are chipped away, exposing the foundation below. White string lights dangle above us in the open layout, making their way into the attached living room, where the hallway leads to Theo's bedroom. The ceiling is cracked, moldy, and stained.

I swallow, thinking of how unsafe it probably is to stay here, but it beats being homeless.

Canned goods line the counter, and the refrigerator gives off a low hum. So, they obviously have power somehow. That's good. Hopefully, they have running water... Theo did mention I could take a shower.

God, I want to take a shower.

My eyes land on Nora as she glances at me, but she quickly looks away, and a ball lodges in my throat, forcing me to swallow a few times to work it loose. It's like I'm scaring Amber all over again. My heart tugs thinking of her. I wonder what happened after I left.

I block out any more guilty thoughts of the McIntyres, instead focusing on the kids in front of me. "So... you guys stay here?" I ask.

Theo says, "Not for long," at the same time Elise responds, "Yes."

They stare at each other while no one else says anything. When I glance across at Zay, he only lifts his eyebrows at me, shrugging.

"Okay..." I start, trying to figure out what I want to ask next, but the tension from those two seeps into me, and I can't focus.

"We can't leave now. Gemma needs to settle before we have her on the run with us. She just lost her sister. Give her a minute," Elise continues.

My head snaps up to look at her. "How did you know my sister died?" Theo turns to me, mouth gaping, and he leans his head back slightly like he just figured something out. "How did you know that?" I gasp.

The electricity in my fingertips flares to life, the pins and needles steadily growing. I stuff my hands under my thighs for good measure.

"I saw your necklace... considering you're wearing both and were lost in the woods..." She rolls her eyes as if not understanding—or caring—why I'm suddenly upset.

Tears hang on my eyelashes, and I dry them on my shoulder before they slip free. "I wasn't lost," I snap. But who am I kidding? I was definitely lost, with nowhere to go. I don't like her having this sudden advantage over me, knowing something about me when I know absolutely nothing about them. How could she put two and two together so quickly? The necklaces don't even say 'sisters'—it makes no sense.

Maybe she has powers, too.

Without saying another word, Elise gets up to refill her glass of water. Theo reaches out a hand, sliding it across the table toward me, but then seems to think better of it because he draws it back into his lap.

Nora whips her head toward me with sudden vigor, forcing me to lean away from her. "I'm a clairvoyant. I knew you were coming."

Not entirely over the shock of what Elise said, my mouth hangs open as I try to figure out what to say. *Thank you? Are you different, too? How many people out there are like us? How did you know I was coming?*

Instead, my voice comes out in a whisper. "You knew?"

"Well, sort of. I didn't see you exactly, but I knew something powerful was coming. And then Theo brought you home." She shrugs while pulling at one of her dark braids as if this all makes perfect sense.

Home. Powerful. My hands clench underneath my legs. This has to be a mistake.

Theo turns his attention back to me, and I try to ignore the pain in his eyes and the sorrow leaking from him. It reminds me too much of pity, and I don't want it. He clears his throat. "What were you running from out there?" He leans forward, elbows resting on the table, and interlocks his fingers in front of his mouth.

"I don't know... I've never seen anything like it before. It was this... black mist."

Everyone is silent now, and it's as if it's only Theo and me alone in the room.

"Black mist?"

I nod, unsure how else to describe it. "When it reached me, it kind of... got in my head, like it was luring me into coming closer. I wanted to go near it." I pause, thinking about how badly I wanted to reach out and touch it. "Then an arm kind of took shape?" I wince as I say this, knowing how stupid it sounds.

"Did you touch it?"

"No. My senses finally returned, and I got out of there. The draw to it seemed to lessen with distance. And that's when I saw you standing there."

Theo makes a humming noise as he leans back in the chair like he's thinking it over. This sounds so wild even to my own ears. There's no way they'll believe me.

"Do you think..." I glance between him and Nora. "Maybe that's what you saw in your... uh, whatever it is? Maybe I'm not powerful, maybe *that* is."

"Well, that's just great," Zay chimes in. "A super-powerful mist. Not ominous at all."

Elise doesn't say a word as she narrows her eyes at me.

Nora plays with her lip again—a dot of blood appearing at the surface. "I don't think so. I don't know, though. I have visions of sorts. Some come and go. Some are just a feeling. Others... disappear." Her gaze flickers to Theo, and my stomach drops. *What does she mean by that?* "I sensed something in the woods. It was powerful and felt lost in the world, which is why we sent Theo."

I resist the urge to hide my face in my hands. Nora thinks I'm powerful, and Elise voiced my own fear aloud—lost. Both words sum me up *great.*

Nora looks at Zay. "Your turn!"

"Let's just show her all our secrets," Elise mutters.

I cut her a glance as Zay says, "We'd have to go outside."

My eyebrows knit together. "For what?"

Nora reaches for a plant sitting in the middle of the table. "Just show her on this."

"I'm not good with potted plants yet."

Rolling her eyes, Nora continues, "You're good *enough* to show her."

Zay takes the potted plant with a sigh and a curse and deeply inhales. Closing his eyes, he sets the plant on the table with his hands hovering over it. The pot trembles and my eyes grow wide. I nearly fall out of my seat from stretching forward to witness everything.

Nora snatches the pot just as a bud appears. She places it on the ground, and a vine grows straight up, attaching itself to the wall as little green leaves sprout everywhere. It only makes it about a foot up, but a wide smile spreads across my face; I've never seen anything like it.

Zay's face twists in concentration, sweat beading on his forehead when he finally lets out a breath. As soon as he does, the leaves shrivel and die, turning black and falling to the ground in heaps of dust.

I blink. "What happened?"

Zay narrows his eyes at Nora. "I told you I wasn't ready for that yet." He brushes his hands on his pants and then smirks at me. "I can alter the elements. Not much right now, but I'm working on it. I'm hoping to get a handle on all the natural elements, but I'm focusing on plants right now."

"That's... that's amazing."

Zay shrugs as if it's no big deal.

Nora straightens in her chair, turning toward Elise. "Elise can see people's auras; the colors depend on their general mood and personality."

Elise throws her arms up in disbelief. "Why are you telling her all this? Maybe wait a day before we tell her *everything*?"

So, Elise can see people's auras? I probably look like a freaking rainbow to her. I internally groan, afraid I won't be able to keep my secrets for long. Maybe I'll just tell them about the empath part of me if it comes up. Considering their abilities seem relatively harmless, I don't think exposing how I broke a man's arm with a single touch is wise.

That leaves one person. I bite my lip and turn toward Theo.

"What about you? What else can you do besides..."

The fear in his eyes is undisguisable, and a rock settles in my stomach. His jaw clenches, and a rush of terror fills me. I don't know if it's his or mine because it's so tightly wound together; I can't tell where his feelings start and mine end. Do they not know about our connection? Why wouldn't he tell them about his dream ability?

The need to protect him overpowers any other thought, and I trust him enough to know there's a good reason for hiding it. My chest tightens, knowing I might've just blown his cover. Maybe they didn't notice his reaction. Hopefully, his aura didn't change colors.

I stammer out the rest of my sentence, trying to save him, "...having the ability to find me in the middle of the woods?"

His nostrils flare for the briefest moment as he takes a deep breath in. His gray eyes thaw with the tiniest hint of relief, but my heart still thunders inside my chest.

He shifts, leaning back in his chair. "As Nora said, that was all her."

I nod as I look down into my lap, letting my hair fall around my face like a curtain, and hope I didn't do any lasting damage. I silently pray to anyone and anything that might be listening, *Please let his secret stay safe.*

After what feels like an unbearable amount of silence, Elise announces she's going to bed. Nora follows behind, and Zay grips my shoulder on his way out, smiling. "Have fun, you two."

Chapter Twenty-Two

THEO

GEMMA STEPS OUT OF the bathroom—thankfully, the one fully standing room in this hellhole—and cautiously runs her fingers through her hair. It's wet enough that droplets fall away, and the top of her shirt, my shirt, is soaked. She's also changed into sweatpants and has her ruined jeans tucked underneath her arm.

She freezes when she spots me, and even in the dim lighting from the tea lights, I can trace the rosy blush coloring her porcelain cheeks when she catches me staring. She's beautiful. The gash on her cheekbone is raw and tender, with a bruise forming around it, but she's still perfect.

Clearing my throat, I ask if she needs anything for her cut, which I probably should have done hours ago. She shakes her head. I want to ask her what happened and who hurt her, but I don't.

Instead, I nod at my bedroom door and point over my shoulder to the lump of furniture behind me. "You can sleep in there. I'll take the couch."

I consider my own injuries; the cut across my nose is almost healed, and some bruising is left, but thankfully, my ribs don't hurt nearly as much. I don't think I could tolerate the couch otherwise.

Gemma ducks her head, readjusting the pants clutched in her hands. "Thanks. Well, good night then."

"Sweet dreams," slips out of my mouth as I raise my hand in an awkward half-wave. I internally groan. *Did I really just say that?*

Then, I make matters worse by continuing to stand there like an idiot, wishing she'd stay awake but too scared to talk to her or answer the questions she must have about this place. About us. But what do I do? Absolutely nothing.

When the door clicks shut, I run a hand over my face and collapse onto the sofa to stare at the ceiling.

I should've grabbed my headphones first. *Shit.*

Putting my hands behind my head, I follow the cracks in the plaster and observe how they venture off into separate directions. Some come together from all angles, forming a spiderweb design, and others jut out by themselves.

This place might tumble down on us at any moment.

I close my eyes, envisioning everything crashing down on me, burying me alive. The second-floor nursery becoming the lid to my coffin. The solar system mural laying over my body like a blanket.

It's all going to come crashing down.

It's not a matter of if but when.

My thoughts drift toward the abyss.

Flames now lick the ceiling rather than the spiderweb cracks. My eyes water from the smoke, and I can't see anything. I want to try the stairs, but they're gone. They collapsed. I can't get—

"Theo?" Her voice shatters my spiraling, and it's like I'm coming up for air. She saved me from burning, if only for tonight.

I roll onto my side, leaning all my weight on my elbow. Gemma stands in the bedroom doorway, now only in my shirt, which is long enough to cover the tops of her thighs. She has one leg bent, her foot perched against the other, and her arms folded across her chest. Christ, she *is* my undoing.

When my gaze finds her face, a knot forms in my throat—her brows are furrowed, a frown tugging at the corner of her lips, and her eyes have a sheen to them like she's about to cry at any second.

Sitting up, alarmed, I throw my blanket to the side. "What's wrong?"

She bites her lip while shaking her head.

I'm at her side in an instant, but she won't look at me. Instead, she takes a step back.

"Did something happen?"

Another shake of her head, but no words come. She blinks away tears when she meets my eye. "I'm sorry. This seems stupid... and embarrassing. But could you..." She shifts her weight. "Could you stay with me tonight? If that's not... if that's not too weird? I know we don't really know each other—"

"Yes." It comes out so easily. She's right. We don't know each other, but in some unorthodox way, we do.

I feel like I've known her for years.

Gemma sniffles, heading back into the bedroom as I follow a step behind, my heart pounding with each footstep.

She lays down first, curling into a ball and facing the wall. I stretch out beside her and pull the blanket up to cover us. We're so close that the honey scent from her shampoo surrounds me, and I breathe it in.

She's made herself as small as possible as if she doesn't want to touch me. I do the same. My fingers itch to reach out and find her hand, but she's made her boundaries clear, and I don't want to make her uncomfortable. So I fight the urge and turn to the side, facing away from her—our backs mere centimeters apart.

After about ten minutes of silence, she finally asks the question I've been dreading.

"Why don't they know?"

An answer is already waiting on the tip of my tongue. "No one does."

"But why? Don't you trust them?"

"Of course I do."

Gemma flips over, facing me, so I return to my back, sticking one arm underneath my head to stare at the ceiling once more.

"I don't understand," she whispers like she's not trying to wake anyone even though we're alone.

I glance at her from the corner of my eye before screwing my eyelids shut. I swallow hard when the words get stuck in my throat. Then, opening my mouth, it takes a second to coax them out. "Being different isn't a good thing. I think anyone here would tell you that. If any of us had a choice, we'd all choose to be... ordinary. Typical boring teenagers who can go to school, hang out with friends, and do whatever stupid shit stupid kids do."

I bite the inside of my cheek, reigning in my temper. It's not *her* fault we're stuck in this situation.

"But we don't have that luxury. And my... *ability*... is easy to hide. So, I've never shared it. They know... enough... about me, so they understand why I'm here, why I am the way I am. I don't want anyone to know the truth about me, though." I place my free hand on my chest, attempting to slow my pulse. "A larger target's put on your back when people know. And then they'll come for you." I turn my head to look at her fully now, and her brown eyes—mixed with the faintest hint of violet—are wide in fear. "If you want to talk to me about... it, I'm here for you. But don't let anyone outside of this room find out about you. Promise me."

Gemma doesn't say anything at first, but neither of us breaks eye contact. *What is she thinking? Will she confide in me?* She has to realize I saw her glowing hands.

Doesn't she?

Maybe she has no idea I was ever standing in that room with her the night she accidentally burned me.

"I don't make promises," she finally says, echoing the words I previously uttered to Nora. A humorless smile tugs at my lips before she continues. "Who will come for me?"

"The Authorities."

"The what?"

"They're people who track and kill *gifted* people like us. We dismantle the system, and we're impossible to control. They're scared of us, and they'll do everything they can to keep us a secret."

"Like a cop?" she asks.

I nod, glancing back up at the ceiling. "Possibly. The Authorities can be anything. They hide in plain sight, waiting to catch someone. Whoever knows about our kind is dangerous and should be avoided. End of story."

She shifts, stuffing her hands underneath her pillow and stretching out along my side. "None of them try to help? Are there more of you? Do you know why we're like this? Are there any adults we can ask for help?"

"I'm not willing to figure out the answers to any of those questions."

"But..."

"No." My eyes flash over to hers again. "It's too much of a risk. We move from place to place, stay under the radar, and keep our mouths shut."

I spot her biting her lip, and she closes her eyes. My bones suddenly feel heavy from snapping at her. She doesn't say any more, and the longer the silence drags on, the worse I feel. Finally, I relent on her first question. I should give her *something* so she's not entirely in the dark.

I inhale a large breath, and the words come rushing out on the exhale. "The crew doesn't know about my abilities because the last person who knew is dead. Well, until now, I guess. But you don't count since I didn't know you existed."

"Who was it?" she asks.

A thick knot forms in my throat again, and I have to coax the words out. "Riley, my little sister."

Gemma lifts her head off the pillow. "What happened?"

"I was thirteen; she was eleven. She, uh, was powerful, too. Not like me. Different. She couldn't hide it. So my parents got... I don't know... scared or something? And they called the Authorities. They... they turned her in. It's all their fault she's gone. Mine, too, I guess. I was supposed to protect her."

My hand quivers as the memories come flooding back, the smell of smoke lingering in the air—suffocating me.

"She was so scared. I tried to calm her down, to tell her every-thing would be all right, that I would find her, but..."

Gemma is fully sitting up now, legs crisscrossed, facing me. Her hair hangs to the side, nearly brushing my arm. She reaches a hand out, and my pulse quickens, waiting for her touch. But it doesn't come. Fixing my gaze on her shoulder, I continue. "She lost control of herself—of her powers—and set everything on fire. Our childhood home went up in minutes. They never found her body."

I scratch at the outside corner of my eye, hoping to relieve the building pressure. I've never shared this much with anyone. The crew knows about Riley and my parents, but only to a certain extent. They know the outcome, and that's it. But with Gemma, I want her to know *everything*.

"I ran away after that and never looked back. I was scared my parents would turn on me next if they found out about my abilities, and I couldn't forgive them for what they did to Riley.

"Then I found Elise by chance. Well, actually, she found me. She walked up and said something about my aura." I cough out a laugh. "Two years later, Nora found us—thanks to her visions—and earlier this year, she led us to Zay."

Shifting, I find her eyes, and they're dead set on me. I flash her a grin, trying to lighten the mood. "And now you."

"And now me," she repeats. After a beat, she adds, "I'm so sorry about your sister. That's terrible." Her voice cracks. "You were so young."

"It was a long time ago," I lie, not wanting to linger too long on Riley. "Still, I keep us on the move in fear of them finding us. I've seen firsthand what the Authorities can do. I won't let it happen to anyone else." The taste of ash fills my mouth, and I have to swallow back the bile. The next words tumble out. "I'm sorry about your sister, too. Do you... do you want to talk about it?"

She lifts a shoulder, tilting her head to study the fabric twisting between her fingers.

"She was hit by a truck... and I was there. It's all my fault. If I would've just done *anything* different that night..." Her voice trails off, and she blinks rapidly, wrinkles forming between her brows.

My chest aches. There are so many things I could've done differently, too. I could've saved Riley. Somehow. I could've gotten her out of the house before the Authorities came.

But I was too weak.

I reach out a hand, setting it on hers. She glances at me and then diverts her gaze.

"It's not your fault," I tell her. "There's no way you could've known what would happen."

"I guess you already knew what happened, though, didn't you?" she asks.

"Hm?"

"The dream. You watched it happen, but then you... I don't know. Changed it or something."

"Oh... uh, yeah... I guess. I mean, I didn't know it was real at the time. I just felt terrible for, uh, making you experience it. I thought it was something I did."

She nods, jaw ticking, but doesn't respond, so I continue.

"Look, I know what you're going through right now and how impossibly hard it is to get through each day. But maybe that's why you're here. Maybe we can find a way to move forward—together."

Gemma lays back down and turns toward the wall.

Her breathing doesn't slow; we're both lying there awake, but neither one of us bothers to continue the conversation.

I guess we've both had enough to process for one night.

Jolting awake, my hand searches for Gemma in the dark, but she's not there. I'm alone, and for a terrible moment, I think I've made it all up.

She was never here.

I frown as the brain fog wears off and lift my head to look at the space she occupied. A small indent is in the pillow, and her honey shampoo lingers in the air.

Relief loosens the hold on my chest, and I lay my head down, drifting back to sleep. Maybe she went to the bathroom or something.

A few seconds later, a thud crashes from overhead.

Oh, no.

I already know it's her up there; who else would it be? The others know better. Groaning, I'm out of the bedroom instantly, but I stop at the bottom of the stairs.

"Gemma?" I whisper, not wanting to wake the others. I wait a few moments. Nothing. "Gemma?" I repeat louder this time.

Don't make me go up there. Fuck.

I'm eyeing the stairs, retracing my route from before, shaking my head incredulously that I have to attempt them again when another crash echoes from the upstairs hallway.

All hesitation is forgotten; I run up to the second floor. "Gemma?"

The rooms are empty, and a tingling fear climbs up my spine.

"Seriously, where are you?" I mumble to myself. My footsteps creaking on the unsteady floor beneath me is the only noise in the soundless house. The attic door—still broken—is open a tad wider than I found it last time.

I run a finger down the splintered wood of the frame, edging around it, and start climbing the steps.

My heartbeat thuds in my ears, and my hand grips the handrail that hangs loosely off the wall. I let go of it, afraid it will do more harm than good.

Halfway up the steps, a crow flies above me, swooping down low, then flying out of the broken window—this damn house. Now we have a bird problem? Shaking my head, I continue upward.

When I get to the top, my blood turns to ice.

There's Gemma, perfectly framed by the moonlight cascading through a shattered window. Her back is to me, and she's just... standing there.

"Gemma?" I ask again, unsure how to proceed.

No response. Is she ignoring me?

I inch my way closer to her. Half in fear of whatever the hell she's doing but also concerned *she's* not the one doing it by how still she stands.

She looks like she's possessed.

When I'm close enough to see what she's looking at, I stop a foot away, trying to process the scene. A heap of books has fallen over, but one remains open at Gemma's feet.

The air reeks of must. Black mold coats the spines and covers of the books, but it must've been the moisture from the elements that ruined them.

I bend down and pick up the discarded book at her feet, scanning the contents and eventually peeking at her. Tears pool in her eyes, one hanging off an eyelash, but she makes no noise.

Furrowing my brow, I study the book.

It's a diary of sorts, the handwriting fading with time. But the right side of the page is covered with the same object over and over, blurring together like the pen was pressed down so hard at times that it tore right through.

I'm not following.

Another glance at Gemma. Why is she so distraught over some long-lost diary? And what the hell is this drawing?

The object reminds me of an alien head. That's all I can see, anyway. It has two dots like eyes with a curved line above them, which would be the forehead. Then, a line goes straight up in the middle of the two dots, like an antenna or something.

I flip the diary closed, keeping my fingers tucked between the pages, and chew on my lip as I stand directly in front of Gemma.

Before I can say anything, though, she rips a necklace away from her throat and dangles it from her fingers.

The gold pendant reflects the moonlight, slowly spinning in a circle. A cold fist closes around my throat when I notice what's on its back.

My mouth gapes as I tear open the book and look at the image again.

The alien-looking symbol is on the back of Gemma's necklace. I glance between the two. "How? Wait. What does this even mean?"

Gemma snaps out of it, tugging the journal out of my hand and flipping it to the front, showing me the name *Belinda*. "Belinda and Calvin Roberts were my parents. Their names and these necklaces are the only things Olivia and I had from our past."

"Is this... no. This can't be your house, can it?" My mouth twists as I try to guess the odds of that. The two nurseries underneath our feet, though. And the fact magic even exists. *Anything* is technically possible, but *why?* What's the meaning behind all this?

Why was she led here?

She snaps the book shut, dust spewing from the sides. Her chest heaves as she paces back and forth. Her empty hand flies to her throat as she gasps for air. "I can't breathe. Oh my God, I can't breathe."

I grab her hand to stop her from choking herself. "Stop, breathe. Look at me." I follow her eyes that dart every which way until they finally settle on me. "Breathe."

She takes a shallow breath and nods, tears still shimmering in her eyes. I tug her along, and at first, she seems like she's going to pull away. But her fist slightly loosens in mine, and she follows me back down to the first floor.

I usher her into my bedroom, coaxing the diary out of her grip and placing it on the chair. She sits on the cot as I begin to pace. At least we didn't panic at the same time. My brain spins as it tries to rationalize any of this, but it doesn't make sense.

Gemma's eyes—slightly swollen and red now—follow me as I walk in circles. Pulling out my lighter, I spin it between my fingers to focus. I can't get lost right now. *Stay present.*

"So, wait, let's back up here. You thought I told you to come find me, which I didn't. Then you get here and find your mother's old diary. That can't be a coincidence. Someone has to be pulling the strings." Stopping, I squat down in front of her. "What happened to your parents?"

She shrugs. "They died. No caseworkers ever told us how. We know nothing about our past. I was barely one, Oli two. I tried looking them up when I was older but couldn't find them online. No records. Nothing. It's like they never existed." She stares at the broken necklace in her hand as her bottom lip juts out.

"Why were you even in the attic?"

Without meeting my eye, she shrugs again. "I... I don't know."

"You don't know?"

"I woke up and felt like I needed to go up there. So I did."

"Well, don't go up there again. It's dangerous."

Her pretty eyes turn icy as she glares at me. "My mother's journals are up there."

"I mean... they're mostly ruined."

She leaps off the cot, shaking her head and shoving her hands inside the bottom of her shirt, twisting the fabric to cover them, and I realize once again, too late, that I'm an idiot.

"All right, all right." I hold my hands up in a placating position. "We'll go back up there to grab them tomorrow, but we bring them down here to look at them. Okay? The less time up there, the better."

She nods once but doesn't turn back to face me. I snatch the watch from my nightstand. It's nearly three in the morning. "Lo ok... let's try to get some rest, and we'll figure this out when we wake up."

One shoulder rises then falls, and I take that as acceptance, even if she doesn't seem particularly enthused about the idea of sleeping.

I crawl back into bed as she takes her spot next to me, but this time, she's more in a sitting position, the diary cradled in her lap. Minutes pass as I drift off to sleep with the image of her reading by moonlight seared into my mind.

Chapter Twenty-Three

Gemma

A WEEK HAS GONE by, and I'm no closer to figuring anything out.

I've read my mother's diary enough times now to have what I can read memorized. Half the ink has faded away or been smeared into illegible scribbles. The other half is incoherent passages written by someone losing her mind. It doesn't exactly instill confidence about where I come from.

The symbol from mine and Olivia's necklace covers entire pages; the rest are a mixture of spells and ingredients, at least from what I can tell. Theo gave the diary to Elise—ignoring my protests since she's the "expert"—and she came up blank, too. She only knew that the symbol on my necklace is a moon glyph for "blood."

Theo also brought down more journals for me, but he was right; they've all been destroyed. Some are impossible to open, like the pages were glued shut.

I'm having a hard time wrapping my head around everything. Literally everything. The fact Olivia is gone, for starters. That Theo is real. The Draven guy who thinks I have his power. My mother was an unstable witch of some kind. And now, learning there's a deeper meaning for my being here.

Is this really *my* childhood home?

I pick at the scab on my cheek as I lean against the railing, slightly comforted by the lake lapping against the shore. The smell of rotting fish is bothersome but not bad enough to return to the house yet. For a brief moment, I think of dubbing this my spot. Somewhere I can go when I need the escape. Just like Olivia and I used to do.

My breath catches in my throat, and I want to cry out at the pain lancing through my heart.

I don't want a spot without Olivia.

This is all wrong.

Footsteps approach, thudding against the wooden landing, and I quickly steel myself, tucking my emotions away, not wanting to seem dramatic that I'm about to lose it over a dock. But I'm taken aback when I turn to see it's Zay and not Theo.

"Oh, nice face." He mocks a pained expression. "Sorry I'm not him."

A smile tugs at my lips. "My bad, I just assumed."

Zay leans against the banister next to me, bumping my shoulder. "Nah, it's cool. We haven't talked much since you got here. I wanted to see how you were doing."

I shrug, gazing back out at the water. It's such a murky brown, it's impossible to see anything underneath the surface. "All right, I guess."

"We can do better than all right, surely?"

"It's a lot to take in. A few weeks ago, my life was normal—well, sort of—and now it's just..."

Zay nods, looking down at his feet and scraping the mud from his shoes against the edge of the wood. "I get it. It's how I felt after my gran died, too. I ended up here because she told me I couldn't trust anyone. I didn't know where to go, but this place seemed to pull me in." His gaze flickers to me before rolling his eyes. "Obviously, I didn't listen very well, but still. I don't know where I'd be without them. You should give them a chance."

My jaw drops. "I am! I—"

"Yeah, yeah, let me guess, you're shy or something?" He nudges me again. "We'll warm you up in no time."

Grinning, I pick at a thread coming undone from my fingerless glove. "Hey, I have a question for you."

"Shoot."

Turning my back to the railing, I lean my elbows against it, giving him my full attention. "How does your power work? The way you made that plant grow..."

He gives me an easy smile. "I'm magic, baby."

It's now my turn to roll my eyes at him, but I still let out a laugh. "Come on. I want to know."

He chuckles, too, but he shakes his head in response. "I don't know. I've been working with Nora. Something in the dirt calls out to me like I somehow know if I give it some of my energy and coax it a little, it'll do what I want. It's not easy, though. The second I lose my concentration, everything dies."

I try not to fidget as he describes it. It's almost identical to what I do, except for a mirror image. I take in the energy; he expels it. "So, what else can you do besides make plants grow?"

"I can manipulate anything in nature, it seems." He flicks his wrist, and a rock tumbles off the side of the dock. "But it has to be nature. Like soil, rocks, or air... " A large gust blows through my hair as he says this, and I shake off a chill. "But, say, like... a beer bottle or something." He nods toward one that lies abandoned on the shore.

Zay drops his hands to the side. "I got nothing. I don't get how it works."

My cheeks burn, and I'm afraid of the answer since I already know. It's already happened to me. "And all powers grow?"

He slaps his hands back onto the railing. "I have no idea. Elise can only see auras, and that hasn't changed. Nora's visions are getting stronger, I guess. But that's it. Why? What you got?" He lifts an eyebrow at me when his mouth splits, perfect white teeth creating a dazzling smile.

I slowly turn to face the water again, jaw locking up at the thought of telling him, so I pick a half-truth. "I'm an empath."

"Really?"

I nod, but a female voice cuts in before I can say anymore. "No shit. That explains why you look like a rainbow to me."

I glance over my shoulder to see Elise standing at the tree line, her face betraying nothing, but her piqued interest surrounds me.

Zay shrugs. "That's cool, though! Probably a little overwhelming..." He trails off as if sensing the tension now surrounding us.

There's something about Elise that makes alarms go off whenever I'm near her. There's something about her I can't put my finger on yet. But whatever it is, I have a bad feeling.

The three of us stand in silence until Zay pushes off the wooden post. "Right, well, I'm starving, so I'm heading back. You coming?"

"No, I'm going to stay out here a little while longer. Thanks, though."

He waves as he disappears into the tree line, Elise right behind him.

Irritated and unable to shake off the vibe from Elise, I head toward the water and stick my fingers in it. It's freezing, even though it's not winter yet, and I snatch my hand back out and wipe it on my jeans.

I begin to walk, unsure what to do or where to go, keeping the lake to my left.

AFTER WANDERING FOR SOME time—lost in my thoughts of how out of control my life has become—I realize I've strayed too far from the house. I don't know where I am.

Stopping, I take in my surroundings, breathing in the pine trees that stand like a wall to my right. Between them, more live oaks twist and turn, and the monster's limbs are there, beckoning me closer, calling me home.

I glance to my left and right as I disappear into the woods. A small voice in my head tells me this is a terrible idea, but if I don't lose sight of the water, I should be fine. Once the canopy of the red and yellow leaves blocks the setting sun, I'm transferred into a seemingly different world. The greenest moss wraps around tree trunks, while grass half-matted with brown fallen leaves covers the forest floor. The silence is so deep that the world seems still. Not even a tree branch quivers. It's like I'm standing in a photograph and, all at once, returning to a place where I'm comfortable, a place where I'm free to be me.

A circular stone structure looms in the distance, and intrigue leads my feet without my brain catching up. A rusted gate comes into view, covering the opening of the circle and blocking the entrance to whatever this formation used to be. It's in shambles now, like a bomb went off, leaving half the rocks crumbling to the ground. As far as I can see, a matching stone wall travels along each side of the round entrance, but it's only ten or so feet high. Over the arch is a metal plate with large letters embedded into it, "Coven of Firelite

Grove." The symbol beneath the lettering is the same as the one on my necklace—the moon glyph for blood.

I have to know what's in there.

Judging the distance of the fence again, I chew on the inside of my cheek and decide I can climb it if needed. I shake the metal bars, and to my surprise—and relief—the gate swings open. I step inside, and my blood runs cold.

It's a cemetery.

The tombstones vary from the 1800s to the early 2000s, but there aren't many—close to thirty, if I had to guess, unless there were more that have been lost to the destruction of this place.

What happened here?

I glimpse a few names, all foreign to me until I spot my parents, Belinda and Calvin Roberts. I inhale a sharp breath, my eyes glossing over as my legs buckle beneath me. I drop right on top of their graves, landing in front of two twin headstones that state nothing but their names—no mention of being a beloved husband and wife or caring parents, nothing, just words tattered and misaligned on the plainest of rocks.

Tears beg to be unleashed, but nothing comes. Yes, they're my parents, but I didn't know them. Can you mourn a stranger? My heart tugs, wishing for things to be different, but I can't rewind time.

This is *nothing* like losing Olivia.

I don't know how long I sit here, staring at their headstones, but I eventually lift myself off the ground. The wind finds me through the trees, forcing me to bite back a shiver. As I head for the exit, my focus is fixed on not tripping over anything, but my gaze flickers over the pillars of stone, catching the last tombstone in the row.

Draven Wilkins.

I freeze as a lump forms in my throat. Draven. Could it be the same person who wants his powers back? It has to be. Who else has a name like that? I stumble backward, tripping over a rock, and fall, scraping my palms on the hard ground as I try to catch myself.

I can't tear my eyes away from his name as the worst feeling claws its way into my stomach. I can't describe it since there are so many fluctuating emotions. Hatred, mainly. So much hate mixes with sorrow, anger, and *fear*. My heart pounds so hard it's painful. I need to get out of here.

My hands tremble as I try to orient myself when a burst of cackling laughter pierces the air. The hair on the back of my neck stands up as my feet stiffen. I literally can't move, like something has frozen me in place.

"Hello?" I ask weakly, my voice betraying me by shaking.

No response.

"Is anyone there?"

Glass shattering echoes from my right, and the spell breaks. Yelping, I jump back as if scorched by fire. The pain in my hand burns right through, and I remind myself it's not real. My stomach is queasy, and my head spins a little. I can just make out that *I'm* fine, but someone nearby isn't.

Spinning in circles—blinded by the dark—I curse myself for not being prepared. The leaves hide the moon from sight, and shadows dance all around me.

"I know you're here. Are you okay?"

More laughter. Deranged. Unpleasant.

Scrambling over loose rocks and branches, I'm out of the cemetery, heading straight back in the direction I came from. Once I reach the water, that should lead me back to the pier behind the house.

The temperature drops dramatically, and my eyes slowly adjust to the dark, but the only noise is the lapping of the lake.

My lungs stop working, seizing up on the air that will no longer come, and it takes everything in me not to cry out. I run as fast as I can toward where I last saw Theo.

Please, let this be the right direction.

The contours of the pier, or at least I think it's the pier where I was standing with Zay, come into view when someone snickers.

Jumping, I twirl, but no one is behind me. Only trees and leaves.

My pulse quickens even more as the knowledge of being in danger seeps into me. Not just danger. Violence. Someone wants to hurt me—a warning courses through my veins at the threat.

Vaguely remembering where Zay and Elise disappeared into the tree line, I bolt toward it, pushing myself harder, hoping, *praying* it'll take me back to the house.

Someone is still following me. The warmth on my neck makes it seem like they're catching up. I'm almost positive if I turn around to look, someone would be right there. With each ragged breath, I force air into my lungs as my feet hit the grass in the backyard.

So close. So close to the house.

The queasiness doesn't pass; if anything, it's getting worse the more I try to escape it.

My legs ache, and stitches spread up my side. I'm ready to collapse.

I can't outrun whatever's chasing me. I finally burst through the kitchen door, and the feeling disappears all at once. I fall against the counter, gasping for air. Sweat drips down my back and clings to my top.

Theo dashes past me and runs outside. I yell for him to stop, but he doesn't listen. *Please don't get hurt.* The knot in my throat makes it hard to breathe, and the other three stare at me dumbfounded from the kitchen table. But I'm too on edge to care.

He slinks back inside moments later, watching over his shoulder as he does, and I slump in relief. "No one was out there." He closes the door behind him, locking it.

My heart hammers, but this time it's from the anger boiling in my veins—I went from nervous to absolutely hating him for how foolish he was in a matter of seconds. What a freaking death wish! Squeezing my eyes shut, I clench my jaw when I can no longer hold in my outburst.

"You don't even know what I was running from, and you just run out there like a goddamn hero?"

My cheeks flame as everyone continues to gawk at me.

"Well, I wasn't going to let whatever it is come in here," Theo spits back.

I put a hand to my forehead, breathing through my nose, trying to tame my temper. "It's gone."

"How do you know?"

"I can feel it." I shove past him and head for the bedroom. The other three don't move from the table, still not saying a word.

I slam the bedroom door shut and shake out my glowing hands. Frantic, I pace, intermittently kicking the cot. My blood continues to boil, and I want to scream. I can't seem to calm down, and my heart thuds harder at the thought.

I'm out of control.

Grabbing a pillow, I sit on the edge of the mattress and hide my hands just as Theo comes storming in.

"Oh no, no. We're not playing that game. What the fuck just happened out there?"

"I don't know."

His chest heaves as he grinds his teeth together. "Who was chasing you?"

"I don't know!" I hide my face from him, using my hair as a curtain so he doesn't see the vibrant purple spark in my eyes that will inevitably come with my power this heightened. My entire body trembles from his anger seeping into mine. The light in the corner of the room flickers, its pace increasing. My heart crashes against my ribs, frantic. I need to calm down or something is going to explode.

"You seriously aren't going to tell me how you're more than an empath, are you?"

Freezing, I hesitate a moment too long. "I don't know what you're talking about."

He tugs at the pillow I'm clutching, and I let out a muffled cry as I try to hold on, but he's too strong and tears it out of my hands. Purple lights up the bedroom walls.

I quickly stuff my hands under my thighs, fighting off tears. My head spins, and I squeeze my eyes shut, trying in vain to block it all out.

Anger, frustration, and fear blend together, but there's something more now, too—awe, wonder, *love*.

I peek up at Theo's soft gaze, and he's slack-jawed as he focuses on my hidden hands.

"I *know*, Gemma. When I told you not to tell anyone, I meant"—he runs a hand through his hair before pointing toward the wall—"them. You don't have to hide it from me. I already know."

I bow my head as the tears come, and an invisible weight slides off my shoulders. Someone else knows my secret, someone who's not Olivia.

"How?" I croak out.

"I saw you. You were sitting at a table in a small room. You were in a dress and a jacket. I thought it was a dream, of course, but you lit up the entire room. And then you... then you burned me when I held your hand.

"When I was... I don't know... me again, I had small blisters on my fingers, like it was real. Between that and your gloves... it doesn't take a genius to figure it out. Christ. I've just been waiting for you to confide in me."

I choke down a sob, swiping at my eyes. "That was *you?* I felt the pressure on my hand and saw... something—a figure of sorts. I thought it was Olivia... Theo..." I shake my head, not understanding what any of this means. "I wasn't asleep then. I was at the hospital when you saw me. That was the night she died."

His face falls, lips turning downward. He stares at the wall behind me, not saying a word.

After a few moments of terrible silence, I confess. "I didn't know how to tell you. It *terrifies* me, and I can't hurt you. I won't let myself. You need to stay away from me."

Snapping out of it, Theo scratches his neck and sits next to me on the cot. He doesn't voice whatever thought that was bothering him. Instead, he says, "I'm not going anywhere, you know. We'll figure this out."

With him this close to me, I see it. Really see it. The tattoos on his arms...

I brush my thumb over what I'm guessing is my silhouette encased in purple and then correct myself, pulling away my now dull hand.

Inhaling sharply, I ask, "Is that me?"

Theo nods sheepishly. "Weird now, huh? I only got them because I didn't want to forget. So, I tattooed a few of our spots over the years. I'm sorry if that's creepy."

Biting my lip, it takes everything I have not to cry again. This past week has been a whirlwind, and now everything is pouring out of me. The fact he's cared enough to tattoo our memories. Or how he's not scared of me. I didn't think he could be any more perfect.

What's the catch?

"It's not weird," I gasp. "I love it."

He glances at me, shocked. "You do?"

I nod, even though I can't get the words out. I hastily wipe away the tears from my face, my cheeks raw and chapped from crying. The slow healing gash aching.

"Since I'm being honest... there's more you need to know." I bite my lip as he slides back to lean against the wall, but I stay still so I don't have to face him.

"I think someone might be coming after me to"—I make air quotes—"get his power back. And... a cop might know about me, too."

I glance back, and Theo's face has grown pale, but he doesn't move.

"And he had your last name," I finish in a rush.

Chapter Twenty-Four

Theo

Slack-jawed and about to throw up, I slam the door shut behind me and slump against it, trying to stay upright as black spots overtake my vision. A frozen fist wraps its deadly fingers around my heart and crushes it.

And he had your last name.

My dad found her.

And she came here.

Breaking out in a cold sweat, I push off against the door and storm into an empty kitchen. "Elise!" I grab the coffee can from the top of the fridge, where we hid the rest of the money I won from the fight.

She creeps into the room. Nora and Zay are two steps behind, concern plastered onto each of their faces.

"What is it? What're you doing?" Elise asks as I fumble with the lid, my hand slipping off the top.

"We need to go."

She lets out a groan as her shoulders sag. "We've been through this already."

"No. We haven't." My eyes lock onto hers. "My dad knows where we are."

Zay swears as Nora runs back to her room.

I return to counting the money as Elise rushes over, stilling my hands. "Whoa, wait. How do you know this?"

"He knows about Gemma."

"And..."

"He's a *cop*." My eyebrows lift, waiting for her to put two and two together. "This is literally his job. He knows about people like *us* and found Gemma before she came *here*." I freeze. I'm too loose-lipped about using the word *us*, but thankfully, she doesn't seem to catch it. Otherwise, she'd have way more questions right now.

Elise's gaze drops to the floor, and I can practically see the wheels spinning in her head, trying to come up with an excuse to stay like she always does.

"Plus, remember? Gemma wasn't alone out there when I found her. Someone else is chasing her."

Nora reappears with her dark red traveling backpack strapped to her back, bulging from how much she's crammed in there. Gravity might tip her over any second. She clutches her winter jacket in her hands. *At least someone gets the urgency.* Zay chews on his thumbnail, eyes wide, probably waiting for instructions. He hasn't moved with us yet. He's not familiar with the drill like Nora is.

"So..." Elise huffs, hip leaning against the counter as she faces me but nods over my shoulder. "She's the problem."

I glance to see Gemma standing in the doorway. She must've followed me out of the room. She crosses her arms and hunches her shoulders like she's trying to make herself as small as possible.

"What? No." I shake my head. "That's not what I'm—"

Gemma bows her head. "No, Elise is right. I should go."

The coffee can slips from underneath my arm and clatters to the floor. I drop the money onto the counter as I turn to face her fully, frantically searching her face for any signs indicating she's kidding. But her eyes are clear; the decision has already been made.

"No." My voice is surprisingly steady, even though my heart rages. "No one is leaving. Wait, ugh." I run my hands through my hair, jaw clenching, as I try to get my thoughts in order. "I mean, we're *all* leaving. But no one is splitting up. We stick together."

"Let's put it to a vote." Elise smirks, but there's no humor behind it.

My eyes practically bulge out of their sockets. "Seriously?" *What's with all this voting shit?* "Why do you want to stay here? He's coming, Elise. You know what he can do."

Ignoring me, she turns to the younger kids. "Nora?"

Nora chews on her lip as her eyes flicker from me to Elise. Her cheeks turn pink as she caves under the pressure. "I... uh... if Elise is staying, I want to stay, too."

"I'm sorry for putting you all in danger. I didn't know... I would've never come here if..." Gemma shakes her head, cutting herself off. "I vote on leaving. *Alone.*"

I open my mouth to have an entirely different argument with her. As if I'd ever let her leave by herself, especially with two threats against her, but Zay finally enters the conversation, wiggling his finger back and forth between all of us. "Uh uh. Nope. No way. I'm not going to be the deciding factor."

"There is no deciding factor," I hiss. "We leave tonight."

Elise snaps her attention to Gemma. "What did Theo's dad say to you?"

Gemma's eyes grow large as she whips her head toward me. Of course, she already knew the last name was the same, but she probably didn't guess the relation, especially after learning about the fire.

Her brows furrow as she blinks rapidly, and it takes her a second to respond. "Nothing. I mean, he definitely hinted he knew I was... different." Her eyes dart to mine, and her face pales. "He seemed like he wanted to help." She lifts one shoulder in a half-shrug. "He was the cop assigned to my sister's case, but he seemed more interested in *me* than trying to catch her killer."

"And then what happened?" Elise prompts.

"I... left. Two bus rides later, and I'm here."

"Can he follow that?" Elise slides her questions back to me. "That's not a great trail."

"Only one bus left the station, and that took me to North Carolina. So, if he figured out when I left, he could probably follow me there. The second station had routes going all over the country, but I booked the next immediate departure because I"—Gemma picks at her fingerless gloves as she stares down at her hands—"had a bad feeling."

Nora tilts her head. "It'd be hard to pick what route she took if they went all over the place. I think we'll be okay. I haven't seen anything, at least."

"Someone can identify her, though—the ticket seller or the bus driver. They might remember what route she took. Or there might be cameras with footage showing she was there." The number of possibilities... It's suddenly too warm in here. Sweat beads at the back of my neck as my fingers search for the lighter in my pocket, clenching it when they find purchase. Panic rips through me as I think of all the ways my father could show up here.

Elise claps me on the shoulder. "You think too much. It's going to be fine."

"Don't forget, Elise also has wards up." Zay's grins. "Badass."

Elise clears her throat at this but doesn't respond, only giving a stiff nod.

Am I going to lose every fight from here on out?

What is happening?

I lick my lips, my mouth suddenly dry as I mull it over, failing to tame my breathing.

"Even if my dad isn't a problem—which he is—what about the second issue? Something else was in the woods following Gemma. It's probably the same thing that was out there tonight. We don't even know what it is. Or why it's coming after her."

"Yeah, so let's pack up and leave so we're defenseless. Smart." Elise rolls her eyes as she leaves the kitchen, ending the discussion. Nora follows behind her. Zay gives me an apologetic shrug as he goes, too.

Once again, Gemma and I are left alone.

The silence swells the longer we stand there. She shuffles a foot forward, shattering the quiet. "Theo?" She takes another step closer. "I think..." One more step. She's nearly in front of me now. "I think you should let me go."

My eyes snap to hers, and her gaze has the same stubborn clarity. I shift away, not even dignifying the statement with a response, as I sort out the money still lying on the counter.

"Theo, please. It's better for everyone."

"It's not better for me." My voice grates, dripping with emotion that I try to swallow down.

"You have the others to take care of. And I'm only going to endanger the rest of you. I don't belong here. I don't belong anywhere."

I turn back toward her, hoping she'll recognize the pain in my eyes as my heart breaks a little more. I didn't know she actually existed a week ago, yet I've already fallen for her. Truth be told, I fell for her years ago when we were still strangers in each other's heads.

"You belong with me."

She smirks as she reaches out a hand but tucks it behind her back after a split second. "You have no idea how much I wish that were true."

"It is. We can figure everything out. I promise." My stomach drops as the words slip out.

I don't make promises.

She bites her lip, nodding. "Okay," she whispers. "But if something happens, I'm gone. I won't be responsible for anything happening to you. Or them."

I reach out, pulling her into a hug before she can turn away. Her shoulders tense, but she slowly relaxes into me, arms slipping around my back. She nuzzles her head against my shoulder as I breathe in her honey shampoo, and I'm pretty sure I could stand here, lost in her embrace forever.

ALL I CAN THINK about the following day is how much I've weakened since the night the world shifted off balance for me. Which apparently is the night Olivia died.

There has to be a connection.

Gemma was *awake* when I saw her at the hospital, and I wasn't asleep either. Was I? I still don't know if I fainted or what happened in that gas station.

All I *do* know is Gemma entered my life, and it's now like I'm a new person, terrified of letting her slip through my fingers.

Gross. I need to get it together.

Our crew never had discussions before; we never had *votes.* Elise and I were a united front; whatever we said happened. Now, we're on opposing sides, and I no longer have pull. Which means I can no longer protect them. I don't like it.

It has to do with this house. Elise has fought to stay here prior to Gemma even showing up in our lives, but there's no way it's a coincidence that it's also Gemma's childhood home. But Zay found it first. How does he fit into all this?

I rub my temples, attempting to dispel the brewing headache. None of this makes any sense, but something has to change. We definitely can't stay here.

Since when did Elise and I start disagreeing about things, any-way? Everything was fine until we decided to stick around this place. We should've grabbed Zay and continued on. I wouldn't have met Gemma, though.

Frowning, I continue running the thin wire toward the next base of the tree.

If we're not leaving, I can at least set up traps. The rattling of cans might be just enough to alert us of any company.

Huffing, I kneel and secure the empty tin cans so they're dangling off the ground, and then I cover them with branches to obscure them from view.

Standing, I brush the dirt off my hands and gaze around. I've lined the perimeter of the house, so if anyone trips the wire, we'll at least get a ten- maybe twenty-second warning until they're in the backyard. Depending on how fast they're moving, I guess.

My lungs burn at the thought. Even imagining seeing my father again makes my throat close. I break out in a sweat as my blood runs cold, and the memory of smoke fills my nostrils. I imagine all the different ways I can kill him.

After what he did to Riley...

My hands turn clammy as I reach for the matches in my pocket, forcing me to wipe the sweat off on my T-shirt.

I must've forgotten my lighter somewhere in the house.

I light a cigarette, focusing on the flame, but I don't actually smoke it, not this time. Instead, I let it burn as I watch the flame devour the paper.

My heart rate settles by the time I drop it onto the forest floor, stomping on it to make sure it goes out.

I round the perimeter one more time for good measure, ensuring everything is working correctly while my thoughts continue to circle over the never-ending problems.

My dad might know where we are.

Something is after Gemma.

Elise is acting strangely attached to this house.

Said house continues to fall apart daily, the tarps putting up a poor fight against the wind, and winter is inevitably coming.

But no, I'm the crazy one for wanting to move.

Before I came out here to put up the fence, I passed out orders to everyone, and if I'm honest, I'm a little concerned that when I go back, I'm going to see them lounging around with nothing done.

My hands instinctively flex, clenching into tight fists, forcing me to work them open. *You're getting ahead of yourself.* I don't know if they aren't listening; they very well could be.

Gemma should be going through all the journals again, trying to see if there's a connection between the thing following her and this house. Elise should be continuing to work on Nora's self-defense moves. Knowing what might happen before it does *could* help, but her visions can't be relied on like that. And I trained Elise years ago since her ability is absolutely useless in a fight.

And Zay. Sighing, I head to where Zay should be practicing in the yard. If he can get it under control, it would be a game-changer for whatever we're up against.

I tap the spot where my lighter would be in my pocket as I step over branches, my thoughts settling on whatever power Gemma has. What can she do? The risk of letting anyone else know, though... Huffing, I kick a rock in frustration. We'll keep it a secret for now, but we'll need her if things go to shit.

Chapter Twenty-Five

GEMMA

It's time to face the facts—the journals are worthless.

The only non-English word that's decipherable, thanks to Nora's library books, is imperium, which is Latin for "power." Anything remotely readable is lists of random ingredients—like herbs, roots, and salts—that are completely useless. The rest of the scribbled cursive is illegible, and some sections have faded so much that the ink has disappeared altogether.

It's easy enough to put all the pieces together, though: the matching blood symbol everywhere, my parents' names, the partial lists of ingredients that could be spells, and lastly, the sign above the cemetery. They belonged to the Firelite Grove Coven. I wonder if they all packed up and moved or if the entire group is buried in that cemetery.

After Theo tasked me with spending all morning scouring through the diaries for the millionth time, I drop the current journal I'm holding; it lands on the table with a soft *thud*. I'm getting nowhere, and as much as I try to summon my power, hoping *that* leads to anything, it won't come unprovoked. It's pointless. All of this is pointless—the journals, my curse. What am I supposed to do with powers I can't control? Clenching my hands into fists, I stomp outside for some fresh air.

Alone in the yard, Zay twirls a large branch in the air with only the slightest twitch from his fingers. He stands as still as a statue otherwise. If I didn't know any better, I would assume the branch is doing it all by itself.

I glance toward the garage for the others, but no one else is around. Pulling my long sleeves down, I cross my arms and shake off a chill.

The graying skies threaten rain, but for now, all is still and dry. Thunder sounds in the distance, but it's miles away. The sun remains hidden behind the storm clouds.

I sit cross-legged in a cool patch of grass, peering up at Zay, who seems to enjoy having an audience for his magic tricks. He introduces more and more objects to his performance as he shouts, "Watch this!"

He adds yet another rock to the tornado of elements, a dozen stones, a few branches, leaves, and dirt spinning all around us in a fierce wind, forcing me to shield my eyes as it traps us in the eye of the storm.

My breathing hitches as I think of how *impossible* this is, but a smile tugs on my lips as it seeps in that *this is magic*.

I don't feel so alone anymore.

I've found people like me.

Even if they don't know everything I can do, I have a place where I fit in.

The lightness in my chest makes me want to twirl and dance. I'm tempted to jump up and hug Zay, but my heart stalls, flickering and then going entirely dark.

How can I be happy when Olivia is gone?

My throat closes at the thought. It hasn't even been a month yet. One second—a single moment of reprieve—and now a crashing wave is dragging me under. How could I forget her so soon?

My lips tingle, and I clench and unclench my hands to gain feeling again. I'm going to hyperventilate.

The objects spinning around my head make me dizzy, and black spots blur my vision.

Focus on Zay, focus on Zay. Don't glow.

I breathe in and out, willing my heart to slow down.

After a few minutes, the episode seems to pass, and Zay is none the wiser.

I need to get out of here. But how do I leave without offending him? Or without getting hit by an object?

"You're doing great!" I shout up at him, encouraged by the progress he's already made in the short timeframe I've known him, but my heart isn't in it.

I just want to be alone.

He grins as he locks eyes with me, and the swirling doesn't even slow. He can split his concentration now. *Nice job.*

Well... while I'm stuck here, I may as well enjoy it.

"What else can you do?" It seems slightly foolish to scream, but the draft he's creating pummels my eardrums, and I can hardly hear myself over the harrowing wind tunnel.

Zay shrugs. "What else can I try?"

I click my tongue, thinking. An idea quickly takes shape, but uneasiness washes away the excitement. However, the thought of destroying something right now lifts my spirits. "How much control do you have?"

"I don't know. A lot?"

"You're sure?"

Zay's eyes narrow in on me, lips pursing in suspicion, but he nods anyway.

"Slow it down a bit." I nod at the rocks whizzing by, digging for Theo's lighter in my pocket. I scooped it up this morning when he left it in bed. I meant to return it to him, but I haven't seen him since he handed out the orders.

The fake storm calms, everything dangling high above us in slow motion.

I lift the lighter in the air. "What about flames?"

Zay's eyebrows lift as his eyes sparkle dangerously. His grin is wicked and contagious. *Challenge accepted.*

"We just need to keep it under control, yeah?" I drill my eyes into his. "Do *not* lose focus."

What am I doing? I'm acting like his trainer, and I don't even understand my own power, let alone his. *Drop the lighter! Drop it!*

Although, if he can control fire with his mind and actually master it? That's a serious advantage to anything coming our way.

"I'm going to light this stick on fire, so just see if you can, like... move the flame or something. Don't get crazy with it," I warn him again.

Worst case, I'll stomp out the flame.

I shake my head. That's definitely not the *worst* case, but I'm either being hopeful or just stupid. If Theo isn't around, though, and the Authorities show up, or whatever that thing was chasing me comes back... At this point, the danger is endless. Any amount of self-defense is better than none.

My thumb presses down on the wheeled mechanism, and a quick spark shoots out, but nothing happens. I shake the lighter and then hold it beneath the branch, trying again. This time, it works.

I'm twirling the stick as the flame stretches along the wood, inching toward my hand, when Theo's grave voice shatters the silence.

"What the fuck?"

I jump, and the branch slips loose. I catch it for some stupid reason instead of letting it fall to the ground. The hot wood burns my palm before I'm able to let go. I hiss, clenching my fist as I stomp on the piece of wood to make sure it doesn't catch anything on fire, then turn my glare on Theo.

Zay must've also been taken off guard because everything comes crashing down around us. I throw my hands over my head to protect myself as Zay whispers, "Oops. My bad."

My anger vanishes when I notice Theo's scowl equaling mine. His gray eyes steel themselves as he glowers at us. If looks could kill…

My heart skips a beat as fear sinks in. We've seriously pissed him off, and the lingering silence is swallowing us whole. It's scary that he's *not* talking. He has a bewildered expression on his face, chest heaving, like he can't believe we're this foolish. Then it dawns on me. *This fear isn't mine.*

Zay and I exchange glances, and I lean my head to the left, indicating he should leave. His eyebrows pull together, questioning me, but I nod. Theo stares at the ground—still not talking.

When Zay walks away, I stand in front of Theo, stuffing one hand in my back pocket, and wince when the fabric scrapes against my burned palm. The other clutches the lighter, and my arm hangs limply by my side. "I'm sorry…"

"Do you know what happens when a fire isn't controlled?" he whispers, slipping the lighter out of my hand.

A rock settles in my stomach as I sharply inhale.

I was too involved with thinking of how much of an advantage it would be if Zay could manipulate fire, not even bothering to remember how Theo already lost someone who could do just that.

I'm such an idiot.

"Theo..." I start, but I trail off as I worry my lip. "I'm so sorry. I didn't even think. I was impressed with Zay and wanted to see... I thought he could help if..."

I let the excuse die on my lips.

His eyes finally snap to mine, and they're just as hard as before.

"Don't blame him. It was my idea—a stupid one. You're right. He could've lost control."

When he doesn't say anything, I continue rambling. "You should see him, though. He's getting really good. I think he would've done okay—"

"You don't figure it out by lighting a random fire in the middle of the woods," he cuts me off.

Then he huffs, and we're standing so close his breath ruffles my baby hairs, some tickling the side of my cheek. He tucks a lock of hair behind my ear before I have a chance to do it myself, and his touch sends shivers down my spine.

I chance a peek up at him. His gray eyes have melted into warm silver again, and I remind myself to breathe.

We hold each other's gaze for a beat longer. He shakes his head, breaking the connection and stepping away from me. "I had a reason for coming over here. I almost forgot."

I school my features, hoping the look of disappointment isn't written across my face. Of course, I can't touch him, but oh, do I want to.

"Come with me." He turns away, heading further into the woods and glancing over his shoulder, inclining his head for me to follow.

"If you're still mad at me"—I follow behind like a lost puppy—"just remember Zay knew I was with you last, so if I go missing..."

Theo's hands are shoved deep into his leather jacket pockets, so when he turns around, spreading his arms in a "so what?" gesture, his jacket opens, revealing more of his skin-tight gray T-shirt.

I swallow hard.

"Do you honestly think Zay would rat me out?" Theo aims for seriousness, eyes narrowed and jaw clenched, but the quirking of his lips gives him away.

"That's not funny," I say, also fake pouting.

Theo's laugh wraps me in a warm embrace. That simple sound calms my nerves and somehow reassures me everything will be all right. I could listen to it forever.

I stifle back a chuckle, but now we're both standing in the middle of the woods, grinning at each other like fools.

"All right, well, if you're not murdering me, what are we doing?"

"I want to try something."

My face warms as I force myself to stand still. "And that is?"

"Do you trust me?"

It's no longer butterflies in my stomach; I have full-on bees buzzing in my body from head to toe. "Yes," I breathe.

Theo moves closer until we're a hairsbreadth apart. His lips are so close to mine that my eyes shut of their own accord, thinking this is it.

Instead of kissing me, though, he whispers, "I want to test your powers."

Reeling, I stumble backward, shocked out of my daze. "You want to *what?*"

He closes the distance between us again. "Just trust me, I have a theory."

"Do you plan on sharing that with me?"

"No," he chides. "*Trust* me."

I shake my head. "This is a bad idea. You don't understand. I could hurt you."

"But you won't." His finger drags from beneath my ear, down my throat, to the top of my collarbone. Goosebumps cover my arms, and it's getting harder to breathe.

"I don't think you'll hurt me because you like me." His voice is like velvet as he circles me. The back of his hand brushes mine, and I want nothing more than to lean into his touch. He stands in front of me again, and he's so close. *So close.* His mouth brushes my cheek, and I think my heart will explode.

Just kiss me already!

His teasing continues relentlessly, with little touches here and there. I don't understand the point of any of this, but I want him—all of him.

Knowing I can never have him makes my cheeks burn. I can't ever risk hurting him. What if I lose control? The crunching of the man's arm echoes deep inside my brain. I will never forgive myself if I hurt Theo...

"Theo," I breathe. My chest is rising and falling as I battle myself. I could hurt him if we touch, but every fiber in my body is screaming at me to do so. I can also feel his need mixing with mine, overwhelming me. My legs turn to jelly as my resolve weakens.

He takes a few steps away, and the concern crinkling the corners of his eyes confuses me. The steely gray comes back, giving me a cold stare, and it's like all of the tension in the air between us shifts into something darker.

"What's—what're you doing?"

He doesn't say anything.

I take one step forward, and he takes another back. I give a fake laugh, not understanding the game.

"How'd your sister die?" His voice comes out no louder than a whisper, but it's like he screamed it at me. The words vibrate through my bones.

"What?" I gasp, my hand flying to my throat as it suddenly contracts.

"How did your sister die?"

I shake my head. "You already know..."

"Why didn't you help her?"

He drives a knife straight through my heart. Tears well in my eyes, and I shake my head again, afraid of letting them loose. "I tried."

"You didn't try hard enough."

Anger intertwines itself with my ribcage, and my heart pounds. It's something I've been telling myself all along. It's a black cloud that never leaves me alone, always dangling right above my head, but hearing it from *him?* Bile rises in my throat. "You don't mean that."

He doesn't respond. Instead, he continues to watch me like this is some kind of science experiment.

"Why are you doing this?"

For a horrible moment, I think this isn't Theo. Maybe it's whatever that thing was from the dream that led me here. But Theo's concern leaks into me. Why is he saying these hurtful things if he doesn't mean them? Or am I reading him wrong? Maybe he's concerned for the others, not me.

"What happened to your parents?" he continues.

"I don't know."

He folds his hands in front of himself like he's finished a presentation. "So you don't have parents, you couldn't save your sister, and now you're an orphan girl all alone in the world."

I scoff just as my vision goes red.

My body shakes with fury, and my hands light up, glowing a vibrant purple in the overcast. I don't need a mirror to know my eyes have also turned violet because Theo's face melts into something else entirely. The night from his bedroom comes back to mind, and he's all-encompassed by awe and love again. And I *hate* him.

The emotions are too much to control, and I collapse in on myself, letting out a whimper. Never-ending tears stream down my face; all I want to do is hurt someone. I want someone to feel *my* pain.

And there's only one person here.

No, not him.

I wrench my head away from him when he closes the distance, kneeling near me.

"I'm so sorry," he says, but the words don't land. Why would he do this to me?

I'm a monster let out of her cage.

There's no going back now. That pipeline of energy appears, just like it did when I broke that man's arm—energy for the taking. And I let myself have it.

I'm more and more powerful with each second that passes, and I'm hungry for the thrill of it all. I suck it in, envisioning the strength around me filling me up, empowering me. The pain ebbs away.

"Gemma, stop," Theo's voice orders from off in the distance.

I don't listen.

The tears have dried on my face, and now I'm laughing. Actual laughter. The threat of being alone doesn't bother me anymore. Not when I feel this good. I'm high on it. I never want to go back to being the sad sack of shit I was—the one who couldn't even save her sister.

This... this right here.

This is right.

"Enough!" Theo's voice sounds a bit crazed, and it makes me laugh harder. He's the one who did this to me. I pull myself up, brushing the dirt off my pants; the energy pipeline is still there.

I'm about to dive in for seconds when I notice its pulse.

I stop just long enough to focus. I've never noticed the musical melody attached to the power before.

It's comforting.

The tempo is a bit fast but somehow soothing all the same.

Horror ricochets in my chest. It's not just energy from nature, like last time. It's *Theo's* energy, and that pulse is his heartbeat.

I stumble backward, away from the noise. At the same time, Theo wraps his arms around me.

I shove him off, losing my balance, and fall to the ground.

My already scraped hands reopen on impact, and blood drips from my palms, but they no longer glow.

I whip around to find Theo facing me, and he looks *okay*. He's alive, at least. But his eyes are wide and full of fear, shattering my already broken heart.

What did we do?

"Are you... are you okay?" I grip my hands against my thighs to staunch the bleeding.

He nods as he collapses to his knees in front of me. "Are you?"

"I didn't..." I shake my head, trying to get my thoughts in order. "You shouldn't have grabbed me like that. Don't *ever* do that. I could've hurt you. Killed you." *I wanted to kill you.*

"You didn't, though."

"*I could have.* I broke a man's arm without a second thought when he attacked me."

Theo rocks back onto his heels. "Wait, what?"

I point at my face, where the mostly healed cut lingers. "Someone attacked me, and my"—I wave my hands, not knowing how to describe whatever I'm cursed with—"helped me. I used nature's energy to draw in strength and snapped his arm in seconds."

Theo's jaw drops as he stares at me, running a hand along the side of his face. "Well, I didn't know *that*. But I, uh, I think I proved my theory."

I'm too exhausted to want to know more. My body is heavy, fatigue tightening its grip on me like I just went into battle. My muscles ache, and I feel like I could sleep for days—but my lower lip trembles, defeat flooding through me. I *need* to know. So I pick the skin off my scratched hand, working up the courage.

"Why did you do that to me?" I glance up at him, and he avoids making eye contact.

"I'll hate myself forever for doing that to you. But I had to know. *You* had to know."

"Know what?"

"Your full powers. It's your grief and your anger. And now I'm assuming, based on *that* story, that when you're scared or don't feel in control, your powers trigger in a bad way. In self-defense, if I had to guess. But when I was flirting with you... not a flicker."

I frown as I study my hands. He has a point... They've never glowed just from being happy—yet, at least.

My head keeps replaying his words over and over, *But when I was flirting with you... not a flicker.*

"You can learn to control this. I don't think it has to be as bad as you think." He tucks his hands into his pockets again. "But you need to learn to grieve your sister and put it behind you."

"I can't," I choke. *I can't put Oli behind me.*

"You have to. It's dangerous, Gemma. It's dangerous for everyone."

"Are you going to tell the others?"

"No." He shakes his head, jaw tightening. "This stays between us."

We sit in silence until a loud crack of thunder jolts me.

"I'm so sorry," Theo whispers, edging closer. "I didn't know how else to make you angry. We needed to know."

My mouth turns downward as I stand up, looking anywhere but at him. "I get it."

I do. I really do get it, but it doesn't make any of this easier.

Why do the ones you love have so much power over hurting you?

My stomach sinks when I think of the word *love*. Could I love him this soon? In some ways, it's been years, but in others, it's been weeks.

A raindrop makes its way through the leaves and lands on my cheek. Another one splats on my shoulder. Soon, the drumming of the rain bouncing off the leaves surrounds us.

Lightning cracks overhead, and thunder rumbles two Mississippis later. The storm isn't far now.

Theo glances up through the trees. "Did you do that?"

"No." *Oh God, I hope not.* "It looked like it was going to storm earlier."

"Do you forgive me?"

Letting out a sigh, I lock eyes with him. Just seeing him softens my resolve; there's no way I can stay mad, even if it might take a while to recover fully. He did voice my greatest fears aloud, but his nervousness and anxiety that I might hate him seep in, and knowing he's sincere lightens the burden, if only by a little.

I give him a small smile. "Yes, I forgive you." My shirt is already beginning to soak through as the leaves give beneath the weight of the rain.

I only make it two steps when Theo's breath hitches as he grabs my elbow. "Gemma?"

I turn to him, and he's. Right. There.

As close as before, but this time, he wastes no time.

His lips meet mine, and everything else is forgotten.

There are no powers, or experiments, or risks.

Fireworks explode in my chest, and the bees are back, buzzing in my brain.

I melt into him as he encloses his arms around me, lifting me. I wrap my legs around his waist and rest my elbows on his shoulders, my hands finding their way through his hair as our kiss deepens. It's as soft as I imagined.

I don't know how long we stay like that, but we're both completely drenched by the time we break apart.

Chapter Twenty-Six

THEO

I TUG GEMMA ALONG behind me, fingers intertwined as the rain continues its onslaught. We're already soaked, so we're not in a huge hurry, but she's shivering whenever I glance over my shoulder.

The ground squishes beneath our feet; we're almost back to the house when Gemma slips, letting out a yelp as my arm is tugged backward. I turn, catching myself on a tree branch for balance to prevent her from falling into a mud pit.

"Thanks." She lets out a breathy chuckle as she pulls herself closer to me. "That was a close one."

My hand is caked in filth from holding onto the tree, and I give her a crooked grin. Raising my eyebrows, I ask, "Why? Afraid to get a little dirty?"

She narrows her eyes right as I lightly sweep my hand across her face, leaving a smear from her hairline to the corner of her lips. She gasps, breaking out in the most pleasing laugh I've ever heard.

"Theo!" she fake scolds between the hiccups of laughter.

I chuckle, too, but quickly sober up. She's drenched from head to toe, her hair sticking to the sides of her face—now covered in mud—and she's *flawless*. Her laughter teeters off as we stare at each other in the storm.

I grab her chin with my thumb and pointer finger, tilting her face toward mine. "You're beautiful. You know that, right?"

She closes her eyes, and a blush creeps across her cheeks.

"I mean it, Gemma," I whisper. I'm not even sure she can hear me over the downpour.

Her eyelids flutter open, her lips crashing into mine. I spin her so her back is against the tree and deepen the kiss.

The girl from my dreams is in my arms. And I'm never letting her go.

She comes up for air first as she lets out a giggle. "I'm freezing."

I blink up at the night sky as rain pelts my face. It doesn't seem to be slowing—lightning flashes in the distance, the rumble of thunder echoing through the trees. I should probably check on that stupid tarp.

"Wait. I almost forgot. I have something for you."

"Oh?" she questions, tilting her head.

I dig in my front pocket and pull the necklace out. She snapped the chain when she wrenched it off her neck in the attic, and it's been sitting on the floor next to the mattress this entire time.

There's a quick inhale when she catches it dangling in front of her; tears well up in her eyes. She takes it from me, slipping it around her neck.

"Thank you," she whispers, running her fingers along the fixed clasp. "I was worried I'd never be able to wear it again." She pauses. "I never did say thank you for before either... so, thank you."

I squint down at her. "For what? I haven't done anything."

She sighs as she glances around the forest, biting her lip. "When you were still... in my head. You came to me whenever I needed you. I don't know if that was on purpose or not, but if it weren't for you and Oli... I don't know what would've happened to me back then. I owe you." Her lips quirk upward as she settles her gaze on me.

"You don't owe me anything, Gemma. You saved me, too."

She nods, the blush on her cheeks deepening. Her teeth chatter as she fidgets with the second pendant hanging around her neck. I tug her arm forward, our fingers intertwined. "Let's get you inside."

I open the door to let Gemma in first, and her Converse slide on what's left of the ceramic kitchen floor. She tilts back into my chest, and my arm snakes around her waist to steady her. We're both grinning until we notice everyone sitting around the kitchen table.

Zay has a smile plastered on his face. Nora is tugging at her lips, trying *not* to smile, but her eyes are alight with mischief.

And then there's Elise. She rolls her eyes. "Great. So this is a thing now?"

Before I answer, she stands up, empties her cup into the sink, and stalks to her bedroom.

Shit.

Gemma snaps out of her good mood, and it's almost like I can see her feet returning to earth, leaving cloud nine.

"I'm going to go shower," she says, running off.

Zay waves at her as she passes, but she keeps her head down.

Nora shrugs. "I like it."

My eyes flash to hers, and I allow a slight grin. "Me too."

Zay's smile hasn't faltered as he sits with his arm raised, waiting for a high five. "Come on. Don't leave me hanging."

I shake my head, chuckling. "Not gonna happen." As I head for Elise's room, I walk past him, slapping his shoulder with my clean hand.

Inhaling a steadying breath, I hold it for a few seconds before knocking on the door. When there's no answer, I crack it open. "It's me." I open it wider when she still doesn't respond. She's sitting on the bed, glaring at me. "I'd sit, but I'm filthy."

"What do you want?" she snaps.

I lean against the doorframe. "Are we good?"

I rub the back of my neck. *Did I do something wrong?* I never imagined running a potential relationship past Elise to make sure she approved. But then again, I never imagined I'd be in this position.

"What do you even know about her?"

I study Elise's eyes—worry mixed with something else I can't put my finger on—as I fidget with the lighter in my pocket.

There's never been anything between Elise and me, so it's not jealousy. We've always been like siblings to one another, nothing more.

I cautiously answer, not wanting to elaborate. "I know enough."

"What if Nora's visions are correct? What if she's dangerous?"

"That's not..." I shake my head. "Trust me. I'm well aware of what I'm doing."

"Fine. What happens when she's gone?" As soon as the word slips out of her mouth, a brief flash of panic spasms across her face. She schools her features as if it never happened.

Frowning, I shift my weight as a stone settles heavily in my stomach. "Gone?"

She shrugs. "Like if you two break up or something, and she leaves."

We stare at each other. Leaving is different than *gone*.

"Nothing is going to happen, all right? Everything will work out."

"I don't want you to get hurt."

Fear and doubt tangle in my chest at the idea of Gemma ever being *gone*, but Elise's protectiveness makes it a little easier to breathe. She's only worried we're going to break up. I need to check with Nora to see if she's seen anything she failed to mention to me, though.

"I like her," I whisper.

Elise rolls her eyes. Again. "Yeah, yeah. Your aura is bright blue." Her lips twitch. "It's disgusting. She's not even that cute." She cracks a small smile at the end, toying with me.

I hang my head, grinning as I fiddle with her doorknob.

"So we're okay?" I peek at her as she seems to mull it over.

She takes a deep breath. "Yeah, we're fine. Close the door."

Nodding, I say goodnight and leave.

GEMMA EMERGES FROM THE shower, slipping into the bedroom as I reinforce the tarp to ensure it holds for the rest of the night.

I hurry to shower and return to the bedroom to find Gemma lying on her back, listening to my iPod. Her gaze flashes to me, but her focus returns to the ceiling. I stretch out next to her, breathing in her honey shampoo. She hands me one of the earbuds Arctic Monkeys is blaring out of.

After moments of being lost in the music, she glances at the door, still slightly ajar, whispering, "Is Elise your ex or something?"

"God, no. Nothing like that. I swear."

"Hmm," she muses. "I wouldn't be surprised. You're both very attractive. You've been on the run together for years..."

"Stop." I place my hand over hers. "I promise. *Nothing* has ever happened, and it never will. She's just worried about..."

Gemma sits up. "About what?"

"Nothing."

"Tell me."

I flip onto my back, stuffing my hands behind my head. "She's just worried we might break up or something. I don't know."

"Break up?" She tilts her head at me, giving me a teasing smile. "Wouldn't we have to be dating to do that?"

I place a hand over my chest. "You wound me." This somehow feels extremely unimportant but also so *right*. "Let's make it official then." Reaching up, I toy with a piece of her hair. "Gemma Roberts." I fight a smile. "Will you be my girlfriend?"

Gemma leans her head back, smiling while shoving me. "Yes, you dork." She bites her lip, then leans down to kiss me.

❧❧❧❧❧ ❧❧❧❧❧

THIS IS THE FIRST time in five years I've woken up in a *good* mood. That's not to say I've been miserable all the other days I've been on the run, but something has clicked.

I'm... hopeful?

For once, I'm not worried about where our next meal will come from or if the Authorities are nearing. Everything has shifted into place, and I can breathe.

Gemma isn't in bed anymore, so I roll over, stretching out before sitting up. I'm running a hand through my hair when there's a knock on the door. "Come in."

Nora pops her head in, already tugging at her lip.

No. *No.* Give me a break.

I sigh. "What is it?"

She glances over her shoulder, closing the door firmly behind her. "You disappeared again last night."

"When?"

"Shortly after you got out of the shower. I heard you go into your bedroom, and then, as I was falling asleep, you poofed—just disappeared. Like you blinked out of existence. I can't figure out what's happening, but I don't like it."

I run a hand along my jaw, trying not to get worked up. I don't remember doing anything. Hell, I don't even remember my dream last night. *Don't take my good mood from me, kid.* "I'm sure it's fine."

The corners of her lips turn down. "I don't know..." Her eyes grow large as the rest of the words tumble out. "I can't figure out what that powerful being was from the woods, either. I thought it had to be Gemma, but if she's only an empath..." She trails off, then switches gears. "I'm pretty sure it's connected to you disappearing. I just don't know how."

My stomach tightens. Gemma could destroy me in a heartbeat, in more ways than one.

Nora narrows her eyes at me, picking at the skin on her lip. "You're *sure* Gemma isn't it?"

I open my mouth, but nothing comes out. What the hell am I supposed to say to that? I don't want to lie to her. I scratch the back of my neck. "How about you just leave the super-powerful being to me? Don't worry about it. Nothing is going to hurt me. I'm sure whatever was following Gemma and me disappearing is just a coincidence. They aren't related."

"I thought you didn't believe in coincidences."

I give her a sly smile to try to lighten the mood. "Well, I do now."

She rolls her eyes. "If you say so."

She's about to leave when the unbidden question pops out. "Hey, you haven't seen Gemma disappear at all, right?"

What happens when she's gone?

The anguish in her eyes chills me to my core. She lifts one shoulder. "I don't see her at all."

Chapter Twenty-Seven

Gemma

WHAT'S HIDING IN THE darkness? The unlit hallways? The rotted attic? Something is brewing inside this old Victorian house, and the quiet seeping through the walls bleeds right into me.

I didn't bother to wake Theo when I got up this morning, but I should probably inform him that something led me back to the attic last night while he was asleep—how the magnetic pull is too strong to resist.

Scanning the attic now—in daylight—I search for any signs of danger, but nothing seems out of the ordinary. Mold covers everything. Old wardrobe cabinets, boxes packed away with who knows what, even an old dollhouse sits in the corner.

I creep over to investigate, and I'm shocked to see my birth mother's name carved into the attic floor, exactly where I'm standing now. It makes sense that she owned the dollhouse; this was her home, after all, but why carve your name in such a bizarre place?

I step back when I notice it's this Victorian house, just a mini version. *Interesting.* I circle it a few times, then leave it alone.

When I reach the far end of the room, the furthest away from the stairs leading me back to safety, I spot a door high above my head hanging in thin air. It lays horizontal to the floor, but I can't see what suspends it—*could it be impossibly fine wires hard to see with the naked eye?* I try to shrug the mystery off, but the pit in my stomach tells me that can't be it.

Will a ladder reach it? And if it does, then what? Do I try to open the door? Would I even be able to? I do quick calculations of opening a door hanging sideways in the air while balancing on a ladder.

"Hm," I muse aloud.

Why am I even interested? It's a door in the middle of an attic! If I open it, all I'll see is the rest of the roof.

My gut twists with sudden anxiety. I break out into a cold sweat and screw my eyes shut to stop a wave of nausea from overwhelming me.

I have to get out of here.

I whip around to leave, but there's a black cloud hovering above the stairs, blocking my path. My heart pounds as I lick my lips to tame my nerves, but unpleasant energy radiates from the matter, keeping me uneasy. This is the thing that keeps luring me here; I'm sure of it. It's appeared to me too many times for it to be a coincidence. But what does it want from me?

Steeling myself, I summon all the courage I have.

"Do you have a name?" I ask the swirling black mist. I'm not sure if whatever it is is fully human, but with the amount of emotions it's poured into me lately, it has to be remotely sentient.

It's currently full of dark, withering hate. Maybe if I can help, whatever it is, it'll leave me alone.

I edge closer, and it doesn't move. "I'm Gemma."

Still no response.

"I can try to help you if you'd like?"

The swirling speeds up a fraction and then slows back down. I can't sense if that's good or bad, in agreement or disagreement, an acceptance or a warning.

"Are you stuck like that?" I continue. The anger increases a notch, and my hands shake. The rage is directed at *me*. I back up a step when my fingers spark, and it all clicks—the man who attacked me at the bus station, the fog chasing me in the woods, the cemetery outside.

My voice quivers as I ask, "Draven? That's your name, isn't it?"

The black cloud frantically swirls, moving away from the stairs, as my hair whips against my face from his strength.

"Draven Wilkins," I say, recalling his full name from his tombstone as I inch closer to the exit.

His pain and betrayal sear through me. I yelp and stumble down the first few stairs, catching myself on the railing. I find my footing and race downward.

When I get to the door, it says, "Stop."

I suck in the air, goosebumps covering my arms. I'm terrified and thrilled at the same time, angry and excited—too many emotions for one person—I must be feeding off of it still. I slowly turn; a person stands at the top of the stairs.

"You're..." *No way.*

A boy my age stands there, weeping. At least, it looks like he's crying. Dark streaks, almost like dried mud, mark his skin. It's so pale it appears translucent. His hair is white and cropped short on the sides, but the top is longer and smoothed back. He keeps blending back into a mist and then reforming. He can't seem to stay in human form for long, like there's a bad connection and static is filling the air.

Was this how he looked when he was alive? Or is this his ghostly form? Can people have different forms? My fear vanishes. I'm too excited to see him standing in front of me to continue feeling afraid. If he can come back, then maybe Olivia can, too. If I help him and learn why he's here, perhaps I can find a way to bring her back to me.

My heart surges with hope. If I can see Oli again, at least one more time... I can tell her how I'm doing okay without her.

I grit my teeth. *Okay* isn't the right word, but I'm surviving, as painful as it is sometimes. Maybe I can have more than one conversation with her. Maybe I can keep her with me.

Draven's ice-blue eyes meet mine, and I don't know what to say. *You're a ghost? You're no longer a mist? What are you exactly?*

I take a tentative step up the stairs, and he flinches.

"I'm not here to hurt you," I offer. "I want to help."

"You can't."

I gasp at hearing his voice again.

"Why not?" I take another step, daring myself to inch closer.

"No one can help me."

"Are you stuck here? Like... can't you cross over or something?" I inwardly kick myself—what a dumb question to ask. I don't know how the afterlife works.

His eyes flash blood red when the door behind me whips open. Electricity zaps me as I back away, startled—right into Theo. His hands latch onto my arms as he pulls me backward and down the stairs. Before I can process what's happening or stop him, Draven's mist flies through the attic door. And not the one leading downstairs, but the one hanging directly above.

Theo drags me down the hall as my eyes stay glued on where Draven disappeared.

"What the fuck was that?" Theo hisses when we reach the first floor.

"I don't... Draven." My mind is spinning too fast to make coherent sentences.

"Who the hell is Draven?" he asks, bewildered.

"The person who wants his powers back," I whisper. My legs turn to jelly as the reality of the situation crashes down on me. I was just standing face to face with the boy who believes I took something from him—the entity that somehow sent a real-life person after me. I could feel his anger, but he didn't seem threatening when he shifted into human form. He seemed... scared. I shake my head. "He just appeared."

"I told you not to go back up there!"

"I... know." I don't have an excuse for this morning; that was my own choice. But last night, I had no control. "He calls to me. I can't explain it. I found myself in the attic again last night while you were sleeping."

The look of horror on Theo's face makes me turn away. I pick a spot on the floor to stare at instead.

"I'm sorry," I grumble. "I don't exactly have a choice in the matter."

He sighs. "Are you okay?"

I peek up at him, gauging how mad he is. His eyes are wide, his mouth slightly open like he can't believe what he's hearing, but him being overwhelmed and lost bleeds into me more than anything.

"I'm fine." I shrug. "He didn't do anything to me. I think he's just stuck here. I want to help him."

"Help him?" Theo scoffs. "How?"

"I don't know," I snap. "But this is somehow my fault! He thinks I have his power. He's *stuck* here. He'll go away if I can help him cross over or something. Or..."

"Or?"

"Maybe I can get Olivia back. He appeared... why can't she?"

"No." Theo shakes his head as if to emphasize his point. "Don't even go there, Gemma. You're only going to end up hurt. You have to let her go."

His eyes drill into mine as my hands shake. I don't *want* to let her go.

And if Draven can show me a way to get her back...

"I'm sorry," Theo murmurs. "I know how hard it can be, but you need to move on."

Nodding, I swallow the lump in my throat as I go to the back door. I need fresh air.

I need to find Draven.

Theo moves, but I spin around, stopping him. "Please don't follow me. I need to be alone right now."

He frowns, but I give him a quick peck on the cheek and run outside. I don't know what I'm going to do yet, but whatever it is, my *boyfriend* isn't going to approve of it.

I chew on the inside of my lip. He'll forgive me. I think.

I VENTURE BACK TO the cemetery. I'm sure he's the one who chased me out of here the first time. But now he's shown himself, so it'll be different this time... hopefully.

Passing by my parents' tombstones, I hardly spare them a glance and continue straight toward Draven's. His doesn't say much either, only his name crudely marked in stone.

My eyes scan the tree line before, like a fool, I whisper, "Draven?" My cheeks warm from embarrassment, even though I'm alone. "... Draven?" I ask again.

Is this how it even works? Can he appear whenever he wants? I don't need to do a seance or something, do I?

The minutes pass, and the only sound is the wind rustling the dying leaves.

Since I'm already out here embarrassing myself, I take a chance.

"Oli... are you here?" I ask.

Of course, no one answers.

Sighing, I return to my parents' graves and stare at their names. I don't feel anything toward them. I should be more upset than I am, shouldn't I?

My shoulders slump as fatigue seeps into my bones, guilt worming around the edges. I don't know how long I've been out here, but my eyelids droop like I haven't slept in days. I turn to leave, and there he is.

Draven—in his full human form—stands next to the rusted gate of the cemetery entrance. My fingertips tingle as we stare at each other, long and hard.

"You're here," I whisper.

He nods.

"You..." What do I even say? *You ran off?* No, he straight up turned into a black cloud and vanished through a door. "...left earlier."

A smile tugs at the corner of his mouth, but he still says nothing. He's dressed in all black—a shirt with a blazer on top, tight jeans, and black Vans. His hair is the same snow-white shade, but his ice-blue eyes draw the most attention. It's painful to look at them. They're filled with so much remorse it makes my stomach turn.

I lick my lips, working up the nerve to ask my next question. "Do I have your powers?"

He nods again.

"Can you... talk?"

"Yes."

Okay... "H—How did I get them?"

He cocks his head, another smile teasing his lips. I can't tell if it's sinister or not. My pulse quickens the longer he looks at me like that. Fear, hatred, and intrigue all mix together. He steps closer, circling me once, twice. One hand strokes his chin; the other is shoved deep in his pocket while he studies me. The hair stands on the back of my neck, and I can sense a build-up. I'm going to spark soon.

He stops behind me, and a shiver runs up my spine. He leans down, whispering in my ear, "They're never going to accept you."

I bite my lip, freezing in place.

"No one accepted me either. No one *understands* our power. You'll always be alone, but I can help you."

"How?" I choke out.

"You only have to give it back."

Fear vibrates my bones as I whip around to look at him. We're inches apart as he towers over me. My voice shakes as I ask, "How do I do that?"

He flashes a loathsome grin as he slowly fades into nothing. I cough out a breath, trying to still my beating heart, when Nora's shriek echoes through the trees. My scalp tingles as I break into a sprint, heading in her direction.

"Nora?" I scream, but the sound has stopped. "Nora!"

I spin in circles as crows appear. Their harsh caws blend together as they dive-bomb my head. I struggle to wave them off, when a faint whimper comes from behind a boulder. I edge closer, and Nora's cries become louder. Draven's circling black mist whips at her from every direction. She's on the ground, hands covering her ears as she curls into a fetal position.

Purple electricity closes around my fists as I jump between them. I shake my head to block out Nora's fear. I need to focus. Draven's bitter laugh grates the air, and he increases his speed.

"Stop!" I yell at him. "You have a problem with me, not her. Let her go."

Rocks, branches, and leaves kick up in a flurry. I cover my head as Draven continues his attack. Nora stares at me from the ground, tears in her eyes.

"Run!" I shout.

She tries to fight but can't fully stand up. She rocks back and forth like she's battling against an invisible barrier.

I don't know how to beat Draven, but I need to for her to escape.

Time slows down as I hold my palms outward and surge all the energy I can into stopping him. The energy pipeline reappears, but I'm too afraid to take it. I don't know whose energy it is. What if it's Nora's?

But what if it's not?

I turn back toward her, and she's on her feet now.

"Run!" I scream at her again.

Her body trembles in fear. "Come with me."

"I'm right behind you," I lie. I'd say anything to make her leave. If she's not here, then I don't have to worry about killing her with what I'm about to do next.

She bolts in the direction of the house, and a surge of relief heightens my powers.

The purple glow flashes white, and Draven's black mist shifts backward.

I take two steps forward, closing in on him.

He laughs.

Why is he doing this? Why did he attack Nora when I was right here? It doesn't make any sense. He's slowing down, shifting back into human form, and I tentatively lower my hands.

When he's himself again, my temper ignites.

"Why are you doing this?" I scream. "What do you want from me?"

He pinches his bottom lip between his teeth and then grins. "I want them to see what you truly are."

"What?"

Nora reappears in my peripheral. She's about to grab me when I gasp in horror, turning sideways. Out of instinct, I push her away. My hand barely grazes the area between her collarbone and neck... and it's still glowing.

She lets out a scream as the rest of the world stands still.

Draven vanishes. The wind stops. The birds disappear. And it's just the two of us in the woods. Burns are already surfacing on her skin, where a perfect imprint remains of *my* hand.

"Nora!"

The sparks dull immediately, but it's too late. The damage is already done. She backs away, hissing in pain as tears flow down her cheeks.

"Oh my God, Nora! I'm so sorry." I choke back a sob. "I'm so sorry."

I'm too afraid to touch her, but I need her to get back to the house. Theo can fix this. I don't know how, but... Oh *no*, he's never going to forgive me for this.

Nora grimaces in pain the entire way back. She's covered in sweat, but I push her lightly to keep her moving forward. When we're in the backyard, I shout for help.

Everyone bursts outside at the same time. Theo's eyes flash from the burn to me as he grabs Nora and pulls her inside. Elise swears as she runs after them. Zay stands there with wide, fearful eyes.

What do I do?

I do the only thing I can think of. I run.

AN HOUR LATER, ZAY finds me on the dock. I *was* going to leave, but I had nowhere else to go. I didn't want to return to the house, so I just sat. And I've been sitting here, hating myself, ever since.

I *would* find a way to mess everything up. I finally found people like me, and then I went and burned one of them. What is wrong with me? I should give these powers back to Draven. I don't want them. They've always been a curse, and now it's even worse.

Zay sits down beside me, too close, considering what happened. "Are you running away?"

I shrug. "I want to."

"Nora doesn't blame you. She told us everything that happened."

"She should blame me." Tears well in my eyes. "I'm the one who hurt her. Is she going to be okay? Is it going to leave a mark?"

"It's going to scar. But Elise had some salve she put on it that took the pain away." He lightly bumps his shoulder into mine. "She's okay."

I sniff. "That's good. I'm glad she's not in pain." A stone settles in my stomach. She's going to have a scar because of me. I permanently disfigured her. And Theo didn't come; Zay did. "Does Theo hate me?"

"Yeah, like that's possible." Zay scoffs. "He hasn't left Nora's side."

It's probably for the best anyway.

"I can't go back, Zay. All I do is hurt people."

"Who else have you hurt?"

"My sister." More tears fall. "She died because of me."

He sits in silence, staring at the water. "I thought Theo said she was hit by a truck?"

"She was."

His eyes cut to mine. "Were you driving it?"

"Well, no..."

"Exactly. Not your fault then." He leans against me, shoulder to shoulder. "We'll figure this out, okay? But you can't leave. I'm just now learning you're a *badass*." He smiles at me. "For real. No one wants you to go. Come back with me. You'll see."

"Elise didn't like me to begin with."

"Ehh..." Zay laughs. "I'm sorry, there's nothing I can do about that. This will blow over, though."

He jumps up, wiping his pants off, then holds a hand out, but I don't take it.

I reluctantly follow Zay back to the house. Elise is sitting at the kitchen table with her spell book—ingredients spread out in front of her—and the look she gives me makes me want to turn around and go right back outside. She says nothing as Zay walks by, but as I pass her, she whispers, "Just give him his power back. Then all of this will be over."

I freeze mid-step. How would she know that's what Draven asked for? My lungs squeeze out any leftover oxygen as my mind races in a million different directions. I get back to the room and collapse against the door.

Theo never comes to bed.

Chapter Twenty-Eight

THEO

NORA'S BREATHING IS EVEN as she sleeps on her back, the top of her shirt ripped open to air out the burns. Elise applied more of her salve and announced Gemma was back as she headed to bed herself.

I left Nora's side once to check on Gemma, but I couldn't bring myself to open the bedroom door. I stood there, resting my forehead against the wood, taming my breathing, eventually turning around and returning to Nora's room.

This never should've happened to her.

I sigh, scrubbing my hands over my face and leaning back in the chair.

What am I going to say to Gemma?

What the hell are we going to do about Draven?

It's not her fault, but it's not *not* her fault either. If she could just learn to control herself... But I'm responsible, too. Nora wouldn't have been out there if it weren't for me. She wouldn't have been looking for her if I had just told her the truth about Gemma's power.

I screw my eyes shut as my fingers find my lighter. I squeeze it tight. Nora's burns. In the shape of a perfect handprint. A shudder runs through me, recalling the burns left on my hands all those years ago.

But this wasn't a fire.

Not this time.

This was her.

She said Draven lured her into the attic. How? Through her dreams? Maybe I can stop him if I'm there. I don't want to fall asleep, though. If Nora wakes up, I want to be here, waiting.

But what if Draven is in Gemma's head? I clench my hands into fists, then shake them loose.

An hour. That's it.

Stretching out on the floor next to Nora's cot, I close my eyes, and the fatigue of today's events quickly drags me under.

I would normally pull Gemma into my dreams—or so I thought before I ended up at the hospital with her—so this time, I concentrate on going to her.

Darkness swallows me. It's not even a room. It's a void. There's nothing here but me.

I tap my fingers against my leg, pick a random direction, and start walking. Water splashes under my feet. I stop, circling in the darkness as a wave crashes against my ankles.

Okay...

I turn around and head away from the water. A circle of light blooms in the distance, growing larger as I draw closer. By the time I'm next to it, the light is as big as me. I step through it, and I'm at a beach. Parents stretch out in lawn chairs, with picnic baskets scattered on towels. Children run in and out of the water.

There's a cool breeze against my face, and gray clouds loom ominously above.

I scan every face for Gemma's but come up empty until I hear a scream. As I run toward it, I whip my head from side to side as all the families disappear. Only two little girls remain, around age ten, if I had to guess. One has blonde hair, the other brown. And the smaller one's hands are glowing purple.

This must be Gemma.

She chokes on water as it spews from her mouth. The other girl—Olivia?—drags her back onto the shore. Olivia collapses next to her, pounding her on the back as Gemma pukes up more water.

"You almost drowned," Olivia mumbles, freezing in place. "G... your *hands*."

Her eyes grow large as Gemma lifts her hands, purple circling around them.

Gemma's bottom lip juts out. "What's happening to me?"

Olivia frantically peels off her wet sweatshirt, covering Gemma's hands to hide the glow. "I don't know, but it's definitely not normal!" She panics, head whipping around to make sure no one is looking, her eyes wide with fear. "No one can see this. It's not..." Olivia trails off as if she genuinely can't think of a word to explain the phenomenon. *How could she? She's so young...*

Gemma whimpers as she stuffs her hands further into the cloth. "Does it hurt?"

Gemma shakes her head, but her body trembles. "What's wrong with me?"

Olivia is about to say something when they both fade into the wind. I watch the place where they were sitting as it sinks into me. Almost drowning must've activated something.

Her power has always been fear-based.

I take a few steps when the scene changes, and I'm now in a school hallway. None of the students can see me as they bustle from room to room. Gemma's eyes are trained on the floor when I spot her leaning against a locker at the end of the row. I'd guess she's probably twelve here.

When I'm standing next to her, Olivia's voice drifts around the bend.

I poke my head around the corner to find Olivia standing with two other girls, all three of them giggling.

Olivia continues, "She's a freak. But she's my sister, you know? No one else is going to be friends with her. She doesn't fit in, so I'm stuck with her."

The other girls laugh as Olivia smirks.

I glance back at Gemma. She toys with the end of her hoodie sleeve, then fixes the backpack strap on her shoulder. She runs off in a different direction.

The hallway fades away, and we're on a road. Gemma is in a black dress—the same one she wore that night at the hospital—and she's running toward the bend. A red pickup truck flies past us.

My heart drops when the scene unfolds.

Gemma clutches Olivia's dead body.

The purple storm rages around her—she's fully unlocked now. Her grief is unmeasurable.

The skies open up.

I lift my face toward the downpour and close my eyes.

I'm so sorry, Gemma.

The last scene that plays is Draven telling her, "They're never going to accept you. No one accepted me either. No one *understands* our power. You'll always be alone, but I can help you."

My heart aches. He's wrong. I hope she doesn't believe him. She'll never be alone. I won't let that happen.

We'll figure all this out... somehow. She just needs to learn to control herself.

My eyes spring open, and I'm back in Nora's room. Daylight creeps through the blinds, and I shield my face with the crook of my elbow.

Is this what Gemma dreams about when I'm not altering them?

The cot shifts next to me, and I peek from under my arm to see Nora staring down at me. "I'm okay, Theo."

"Does it hurt?"

She shakes her head stiffly as her fingers lightly touch the surrounding burn area. "I need more salve, though."

"I'll get it." I pick myself up off the floor, stretching and yawning. But by the time I open the door, I'm rendered useless. Elise barges in and takes over caring for Nora.

I find myself sitting at the kitchen table, staring at the bedroom door. Gemma hasn't come out yet, and I haven't gone in. I'm more mad at myself than her, but what am I going to do? Say it's fine when it isn't?

I flex my hands, finally jumping up. I need to rip the bandage off and get it over with. I wrench open the door to find the room empty.

She isn't here.

I'M BACK AT THE kitchen table, creating a maze of matches, waiting for Gemma to return when Nora comes out from her room, making a beeline for my door.

"She's not in there," I say as she opens it anyway. Flexing my shoulders, I return my attention to the matches. They all stand up, their red tips aligning, creating an arrow. I'm so on edge that when Nora speaks, my hand spazzes, and it knocks over the nearest match. They all go down like dominoes.

"You let her leave?" she asks incredulously.

"I don't know when she left." I shrug. "She'll be back soon."

"Her stuff is gone."

My stomach flips when I leap up and push past her into the room. "What do you mean, her stuff is gone?"

Nora raises both arms and lets them drop to her sides. "Her backpack. It's gone."

I didn't even think to look. I just assumed she went for a walk... Her words come back to me, *But if something happens, I'm gone...* A chill creeps down my spine, and my lungs stop working as I try to suck in a breath.

Gone.

I've been sitting here waiting while she's been running. *Goddamn it, Gemma.*

I yell at Nora to stay there as I bolt out the door. I check down by the dock first, but the shore is empty. Panting, I scan the horizon, wondering where the hell she would've headed.

She came here on a bus. That's probably how she'd leave, too. Where'd she get the money, though? My heart pounds as I struggle to decide what to do.

Fuck.

I don't know what way she would've taken toward town, or if she even knew the way, considering I led her here.

She could be lost right now.

Or she could be fine and on a bus. Out of my life forever.

Why didn't I check on her last night?

If I go back and get the others, we can split up. But that's wasting time. Groaning, I run my hands through my hair, spinning in circles. It's time to decide. I take off, deeper into the woods, toward town.

MY VOICE IS HOARSE by the time I hit the pavement. I zig-zagged as much as I could without breaking away from the fastest route, calling out for her the entire time, forced to slow down at points because my heart felt like it was imploding.

It still does.

With the last bit of air in my lungs, I race to the bus station. Nearly empty. Inside and out. I put my hands on my head, dragging in large breaths as I try to slow my racing heart. She actually left. My jaw locks as I try to shake the betrayal off since it isn't all her fault; it's mine, too.

My breathing hiccups at the thought of her lost in the woods. Or with Draven. I guess both are still a possibility.

But maybe it's easier to believe she left me. I tend to lose the ones I care about most; at least this way, she's still alive.

I slump down onto the bench next to the window selling tickets. An older lady gives me a warm smile but doesn't say anything. I focus on my clasped hands, forcing them not to shake.

It's worth asking, at least.

I approach the window and ask the lady if she's seen her. I hold out my hand. "Yea high? Seventeen? Dark curly hair?"

The old lady continues to nod, smiling, but doesn't actually say anything.

I don't... What does that mean?

Giving up, I drop my hand and turn toward the exit. Gemma stands there, eyes sweeping the area as if she wants to bolt.

"Jesus Christ," I mumble, covering my face with my hands before they drop to my sides. I close the distance between us, pulling her into me and crushing her with a hug. "I thought you were gone."

"I tried to be," she admits. "I'm only two dollars away from a ticket. But I'm running out of people to ask."

"Why?" I let her go, stepping back and exploring her eyes. "Why are you leaving?"

Her lips flatten into a straight line. "You know why."

"Nora's fine."

"That wasn't the deal." Her voice trembles. "I can't risk it, Theo. The thought—"

"Stop. We're going to figure this out. Everything is going to be fine."

Gemma's eyebrows furrow. "You can't possibly know that."

I hang my head. She's right. And I have no idea where to even begin on solving this, but I can't lose her. Not when I just got her. "Don't leave me. *Please.*"

Her voice comes out as a whisper. "Theo..."

My hands shake as I fumble for the correct words. I didn't want to admit this so soon, but it might be the only thing that gets her to stay. I don't want her to only be a stranger in my head again. "I love you, Gemma." I search her eyes as I confess the rest. "I think I always have, but I thought you didn't exist. But now..." I pause, my heart racing. "I don't want to think about only seeing you in my dreams again. I want you here. With me. You have a place here."

She glances away. "How can you love a monster?"

"You're anything but." I pull her into a hug again, resting my chin on her head. "Come home."

Before returning to the house, I stop walking, pulling Gemma toward me. She looks up at me with doe eyes, and it's hard to believe that so much power can come out of someone as innocent-looking as her.

"I'm sorry I didn't come to check on you last night." I tuck a piece of hair behind her ear. "I was angry. More so at myself, since Nora wouldn't have even looked for you if I told her the truth, but…"

"You were angry at me, too."

I release her and blow out a breath. "I didn't want to be."

Gemma's eyes fall to the ground as she kicks a rock. After the silence builds, she bunches her shoulders near her ears in a half-shrug and looks up at me again. "So, I guess we should've told the truth, huh?"

"I guess so." I exhale. "The cat's out of the bag now, but I still don't like it."

"I'd rather them know and stay away from me than risk getting hurt."

I lace my fingers through hers and squeeze. "It won't be like this forever."

The crew is at the kitchen table when we get inside.

"I'm calling a family meeting," Nora declares.

A family meeting? What the hell? I glance at Gemma, and her eyes fix on the handprint-shaped burn on Nora's chest.

Nora meets Gemma's gaze and gives her a soft smile. "I'm all right, honestly."

Gemma nods but apologizes anyway. I let go of her as we sit at the table, waiting for someone to begin. Gemma opens her mouth but closes it. Her cheeks color as she leans back in the chair, focusing on her nails.

When the silence becomes unbearable, I slap my hands on the table. "So? What's up?"

Nora pointedly looks at each of us before returning her gaze to me.

"Here's what we know: Gemma is powerful as *hell*." Her voice has no malice; it's more like awe as she glances at Gemma. Gemma bites her lip, but she doesn't respond.

Nora continues. "She and Draven are connected somehow. And you disappearing in my visions may or may not be related. What we don't know is how, or why, any of this is happening."

Gemma's head snaps up, and her eyes drill into me when Nora mentions me disappearing, but I keep my face trained forward, not sparing her a glance. Nora's visions could mean nothing; why worry her about it?

After another second of feeling her gaze burn into me, her voice strains as she speaks up. "Draven wants his powers back..." When everyone turns to look at her, she wrings her hands. "Some guy attacked me in the woods before I met you all and said I have Draven's powers. I don't know how I have them or how he sent that guy after me."

"Right..." Zay's eyebrows furrow as he narrows his eyes on the cup in front of him. "We should probably start there then?"

Gemma gives an unamused smile as she continues. "And my parents and Draven are buried in the same cemetery out back, and I'm only guessing at this point, but I imagine they were all a part of the same coven."

Nora leans forward. "Why do you think that?"

"The name of the cemetery is 'Coven of Firelite Grove,' and the symbol on the sign matches my mother's journals along with"—Gemma hesitates, grabbing the two necklaces dangling from her neck, flipping them around to show us the backs with the moon glyph—"it means blood," she finishes.

"Oh, hell no." Zay shakes his head, throwing his arms up. "This is getting strange."

Nora toys with her lip as she squints at the wall like she's trying to piece the puzzle together. Elise hasn't said a word. Actually, she's leaning back in her chair, filing her nails like she couldn't care less about this entire conversation.

Weird.

"So, it's time to do some digging." Nora nods as she says this like she's formulating a plan. "We go to the library or ask people around town if they know about Gemma's parents or Draven. Maybe we'll find someone who was part of the coven?"

"No." I shake my head. "We can look into it and see if there are any old records, but we don't involve outsiders. This stays between us."

"Can we head to the library now?" Nora asks.

I glance at my watch. "By the time we get there, it'll be closed."

Nora lets out a huff, shoulders sagging. I can tell by the light in her eyes that she's excited by all of this, which isn't the response I expected. Draven—whatever he is—made Gemma burn the shit out of her. But she almost seems *happy* to solve the mystery. Like we're the Scooby Gang?

Elise hums a song as she gets up to clear the dishes. I've never heard the tune, but Gemma recoils so hard she almost falls out of her chair.

"Why are you singing that?" Gemma gasps.

Elise looks at her, a smirk sliding across her face. "'Lloyd, I'm Ready to Be Heartbroken'? It's one of my favorites." She turns back to the sink and starts washing dishes as Gemma scrambles away from the table, dashing into the bedroom.

I follow her, confused. "What's wrong?"

Gemma's chest heaves as she paces around the room. "That was Olivia's song. She would sing it every time she got drunk."

"Sit." I pull her down onto the bed. "Just breathe. It probably just shocked you to hear it. It's all right."

Gemma shakes her head. "I think Elise knows something. I don't know how. But she already knows about Draven. And now Olivia's song."

I lean away, staring at her. "What are you saying?"

Gemma's eyes glisten as she looks at me. "I don't *know*. But something isn't right. Elise—"

Elise's scream comes from the kitchen. "Theo! The cans!"

It takes a second before I register the tinkling of metal cans crashing against one another. My stomach heaves as my heart kicks into overdrive.

Someone's here. Someone who *isn't* Draven, if they have a body that can trip the wire.

Gemma and I rush into the living room, and all eyes are on me, waiting for direction as the sound haunts us.

Instincts kick in, and I'm on the move.

I rush over to the brick wall surrounding the fireplace and use the side of my fist to hit one brick loose until the other end pops out. The rough edges bite into my hand, but I hardly register it. I take out the block next to it as well before reaching in and pulling out a pistol.

"Elise!" I bark as she takes a step forward, putting on a brave face even though tears gather in her eyes. I check the gun's ammunition, then sprint over and grab more from the cigar box on the counter. I shove the gun into her hands and dump bullets in her hoodie pocket. "Take the kids and go upstairs to the attic."

Her hand trembles as she wraps it around the pistol, nodding.

"Do you remember how to use this?" I search her eyes, and she gives another stiff nod.

"Be careful. Don't come back down until I tell you."

Hopefully, I'll be here to tell them. Otherwise, they'd stay up there as long as possible, but once it becomes clear I'm not coming back, be it a few hours or a day, depending on whatever threat we're against and what they'll overhear, Elise will stick to our plan and get the hell out of here.

"What're you going to do?" Elise asks me.

I back up until I'm at my bedroom door. Twisting inside, I pull a shotgun down from inside the closet.

"You're not going out there!" Gemma hisses.

"Elise." I lock eyes with her. "Go. Now."

Elise grabs Nora by the shoulder to push her forward, and Nora grabs Zay's hand. But before Nora takes a step, she wrenches away and runs over, throwing her arms around me.

My pulse slows as if time stands still. I want to ask what she sees right now, but it's too late. The cans continue to clang together, which doesn't make any sense. Whoever it is should be here by now. They're toying with us. Unless Elise's wards already took the trespasser out?

"Promise me you'll come back," Nora cries into my shirt.

I give her a tight squeeze, then pry her arms off me. "Go with Elise," I say softly.

Elise comes over, grabs Nora's wrist, and drags her out of the room. Zay waves goodbye as he disappears behind the tarp.

My gaze lands on Gemma.

Gemma. Shit.

My heart stills, knowing I have to leave her, too. Right when I got her back. I look away, checking my gun as I attempt to steady my breathing. My voice comes out hoarse. "You need to go with them."

"I'm not leaving you."

"Gemma," I spit out, glaring at her. "Go upstairs."

Her eyes flash purple, and she sets her jaw. "You're not going out there alone." Her fingertips dance with electricity as she nods toward the weapon. "I'm probably more dangerous than you are, even with that thing anyway."

"If something happens to you..."

"You're stuck with me now." She closes the distance between us, her hands losing their purple tint before she places them on my chest. "So, shall we see what's waiting out there for us?"

Clenching my jaw shut, I wait by the kitchen door, straining to hear which direction the cans are coming from. When I'm sure which tree it's at, I creak open the door, gun at the ready.

"Stay behind me," I whisper to Gemma.

She holds her hands out in front of her like she's brandishing a weapon, which I guess she is, in a way.

My finger hovers over the trigger as we approach the tree line. I can just make out the wire bouncing up and down, but I don't see anyone.

I shift sideways to come in at a different angle. A man is stepping on the wire, jiggling it up and down, hands on his hips. His head is down, and he sports a police uniform.

My heart hammers as I cock the gun.

They're here. The Authorities finally found us.

"Theo! No!" Gemma gasps as she reaches around, grabbing the barrel and pointing it toward the ground.

At the same time, the man's head snaps up, and his gaze finds mine. I swallow bile.

He raises his hands in surrender, a smile tugging at his lips as tears shine in the gray eyes that match mine.

I think I've stopped breathing. The world stands still, and I don't hear anything other than the beating of my heart. It's frantic, ready to stop at any second.

Riley screams my name as I'm dragged away.

I rush to get back inside, but the doorknob burns my hands.

I kick the door in.

The stairs collapse.

Flames lick the ceiling.

The smoke catches in my throat as I gasp for air.

Tears run down my face as I'm pulled out of the burning house.

The smell of smoke stays with me forever.

Sweat beads on my neck, and the world snaps back into focus. Gemma's rubbing my arm, trying to get my attention. I don't break eye contact with John Goodwin. I shove Gemma away from me and raise the gun back in the air. I cock it and point it straight at him.

The smile slides off his face, and fear takes over.

Good.

I want him to know the fear we felt.

I want him to suffer.

I want him to burn.

My hands shake as I hold the gun in position. *Just shoot him already. Be done with it.* But Gemma steps in front of me before I can bring myself to do it. "Theo! Enough."

I don't move. "Get out of my way."

"I'm not going to let you shoot your father."

"He's not my father."

She steps closer to me, the gun pointed straight at her chest. The idea of her being on the other end of my rage snaps me out of it. I lower the weapon to my side. My voice breaks as I try to get the words out. "You don't understand. He's *with* them."

"I can explain," John adds.

Gemma whips around to face him. "You don't get to talk!" She turns back to me and says softly, "We can figure this out. Don't sink to his level. You're better than him."

I give her a bitter smile. "I just had a gun pointed at you." My stomach turns, acid coating my tongue. *I pointed a fucking gun at her.*

"Stop that." She grabs my hand, pressing it against her chest. "Feel that? My heart is still beating. You didn't do anything, no harm done. And now we're even."

I don't know what to say, so I don't say anything. Panic inches through every fiber of my being, and I'm about to lose control. I haven't seen John in five years. Five years of being on the run from him and people like him, and now he's standing in the yard.

If only Elise would have fucking listened to me. We could have left before he found us. My hand grips the gun so tightly that it aches. Dried blood from the bricks coats my torn skin.

"Go back inside," Gemma whispers. "I can get rid of him."

My eyes flash to hers, horror digging its claws into me. I can't leave her alone with him.

"Trust me. It's going to be fine. I already dealt with him back in Florida, remember? He won't hurt me."

"There's someone you need to see, Gemma," John interrupts.

Our heads turn in his direction, and he coaxes someone out from behind the tree. It's a girl with blonde ringlets, and now I'm super confused.

Gemma gasps. "Amber! What are you doing here?"

The girl runs away from John and throws her arms around Gemma.

Gemma clings to her like a life raft and touches nearly every part of her body. "Are you okay? Did he hurt you? What are you doing here?"

"He brought me here. Well, kind of. I ran away, and he found me on my way to you."

"How did you know…" Gemma trails off, hugging her again. She might not wholly control her abilities, but knowing when her hands are about to spark seems more manageable for her now.

Gemma glances at me. "This is my foster sister. Who I left behind *on purpose* back in Florida." She turns her attention back to the younger girl. "Where do Dennis and Judy think you are?"

John chimes in. "That's been taken care of. They know Amber is safe and sound. I told them she was with me after she made it nearly across the country before I caught up. She has a day or two until I need to take her back, or they'll get suspicious." He gives Amber a stern look, holding two fingers up. "I mean it. Two days tops." Then he faces me. "No one knows we're here. I swear. I'm staying at the Voyager Inn in town. Please, come see me. There's a lot we need to talk about."

Yeah, like that'll fucking happen.

Chapter Twenty-Nine

Gemma

THEO GOES UP TO the attic to get the others as I pace around the
kitchen, chewing on my thumbnail, not believing my eyes. Amber
sits at the table, her head bowed.

"What are you even doing here?"

Jutting out her chin, she tilts her head up to look at me. "I came
here to be with you."

"But *how?*"

Her proud appearance falters, apprehension flashing across her
young face. Her large blue eyes blink rapidly. "I..." She wrings her
hands together. "Someone told me."

"Who? That's impossible."

"Just believe me," she whines. "You have to."

My brows furrow as I study her. Who could've told her, and why
isn't she telling me? Shaking my head, I face the window and try to
wrap my head around this.

"This is like kidnapping, you know. No one will ever believe I
had nothing to do with this. What were you thinking?" After a few

soundless seconds pass, I glance over at her. "What about Judy and Dennis?"

"I couldn't stay there anymore." Her lip quivers as she sucks in a deep, shaky breath. "I just... I had to come find you."

I focus on her, *really* focus, and drown out my own confusion over everything to get a read on her. Her fear creeps in, and I stiffen. Memories of what I've endured at other homes surface: the screaming, the hitting. *No.* There's no way Judy and Dennis are like that. I would have sensed that back when I lived with them. *But what is she so afraid of?* Heat licks my fingertips, and I stuff them behind my back to hide the potential glow.

"Did they hurt you?"

She fixes her gaze on the table. "No..."

"Amber. Did they hurt you?" I repeat, my voice stern, demanding her attention.

After letting out a sigh, she shakes her head. "No. They're fine. They're the same old Judy and Dennis. I don't think they're capable of getting mad. But I'd still rather be with you."

I let out a breath. *Thank God.* However, the facts don't change a thing. She can't stay here with me. It's too dangerous, and I couldn't provide for her even if it wasn't.

"You have to go back."

"I'm not like them! I'm like you!"

I freeze. "How?"

"I'm different. They wouldn't understand."

"How are you different, Amber?"

When she doesn't respond, clarity dawns on me. How did I not figure it out sooner? Maybe there are more people like us in the world than I imagined. I went from being alone to knowing four others who were *different* in a matter of a day. Why not one more?

"How did you know where to find me?" I crouch in front of her so our faces are level and offer a small, encouraging smile. "It's all right. You can tell me."

"I can talk to Olivia."

The air is sucked out of the room, my knees buckling at Amber's confession. That is *not* what I was expecting. I thought maybe she could see things like Nora or would say she has excellent tracking skills. I don't know—anything but *this*.

Anything but speaking to Olivia.

My words halt on the way out. "You... You can talk to her... now?"

Amber slowly nods. "She told me to come to you. She said you needed me."

My vision clouds, and I'm lightheaded from her revelation. I turn away from her, afraid of passing out. Leaning on the counter, I shake my head. I don't believe this. Amber can talk to Olivia.

My chest squeezes. I swear, if this is a cruel joke... I spin toward her, narrowing my eyes, balling my hands into fists, and fighting through the panic clawing at my throat. *Don't light up, don't light up.*

"So you can talk to ghosts? Is that it? Is Olivia here now?" I scan the room, fixing my attention on an empty corner. Angrily, I spit out, "Hi, sis, glad you're back."

Nothing happens. I throw my trembling hands up in defeat, facing Amber, who promptly rolls her eyes at me.

"She's not here *now*, like in the room, but she's here in general."

"Even if I believe you—which I don't—why come all this way?" My voice is an octave higher now. "What did she say? Why do I need *you?*"

"How can you not believe me?" Amber's face bunches up like it used to when Olivia and I would kick her out of our bedroom. She crosses her arms, glaring at me. "I'm here, aren't I?!"

She has a point.

How else would she have known where to go if it weren't for Olivia? And I thought I saw Olivia after almost dying from Elise's wards when I first arrived. Maybe Olivia *is* still here. Maybe she's acting as my guardian angel or something. Tears burn at the back of my eyes, and I don't know if I'm happy or sad. Happy she's still *here*, but also... why? Is there nowhere else to go? Is there no afterlife? What happens after you die? My heart rate doubles in speed, sweat beading on my neck as I gulp in the air.

Oh God, what if she's stuck here?

Like Draven?

Amber yells my name as I bolt out of the kitchen door and into the backyard. My hands clutch my knees as I bend over, willing my frantic heart to slow down. I can't breathe. The pins and needles travel from my fingertips up to my elbows, and soon my lips are numb. I'm hyperventilating.

Just breathe.

Voices from inside drift through the open door. Theo appears by my side, placing a hand between my shoulder blades. I squeeze my eyes shut. The warmth of his skin bleeds through my thin shirt, and as the seconds pass, my heart rate slows. I stand upright, dragging in a large breath, as he turns toward Amber.

"What happened?" he asks.

Amber's eyes shift from him to me, and I nod, giving her the go-ahead. I place a hand on my forehead, still trying to tame my nerves. My heart jolts every couple of beats; I might spiral again. I won't be able to get the words out.

"I, uh… told her Olivia is the one who told me where to find her." Her eyes cut to me. "She didn't take it too well."

Theo frowns. "Olivia, as in…"

"Olivia," I say curtly.

"Now, that's cool," Zay's wonderstruck voice cuts in. "Can you see other dead people or just her?"

Nora elbows him in the stomach. "You can't just ask her that, dummy."

Much to my own surprise, I burst out laughing. It's either this or crying.

Theo grimaces. "Are you okay?"

"No." I chuckle some more. "My foster sister is talking to my dead sister. I'm not okay at all. But at this point, it'll take a lot for anything else to shock me."

I shake my head in a daze, covering my face with my hands. Where to begin? Draven? Olivia? Amber? John? By the time I drop my arms to my sides, only Amber and Theo are left standing there, watching me.

Amber and I have to figure everything out about Olivia, and maybe because of her ability, we can deal with Draven as well. All that leaves is John, who is definitely Theo's problem.

"I can stay here with Amber. You should go talk to your dad."

Theo's shaking his head before I even get the full sentence out. "He's not my dad."

"Fine, John, whatever." I place a hand on his shoulder. "You should still talk to him."

"I have nothing to say."

I open my mouth to argue but don't have anything to say either. If he *was* responsible for Riley's death, and he's working with the Authorities, I don't blame Theo for his reaction. I wouldn't want to talk to him either. But John said he could explain, so maybe Theo doesn't have the full story. I pucker my lips, unsure how to say that without upsetting him.

"It's your choice…" I shift my weight from foot to foot. "But I think it's worth at least finding out what he knows. He said no one knew he was here. Maybe you can learn more about his involvement with *them?* Might be worth knowing if we have to leave soon."

I shrug like it's no big deal, even though I'm right and am sure Theo will see its validity. The frown lines on his forehead increase the more the idea sinks in. I can basically see the wheels spinning from here.

"I'll think about it," he mumbles. Then, glancing between Amber and me, he scratches his neck. "I'll let you two catch up. But I have to ask. How did John know I was here, too? You two came looking for Gemma."

Amber's smug smile flashes across her face. "Olivia told me."

I cover my mouth with my hand, biting back a laugh and avoiding eye contact as Theo's gaze burns a hole into the side of my face.

"Your ghost sister ratted us out? Unbelievable." He shakes his head, stalking off.

Amber and I approach the front of the house, sitting on the broken steps as we dive into the heavy stuff. Maybe I should've introduced her to everyone, but I'm sure Theo brought them up to speed in the attic. We can worry about introductions later.

Spotting the front of the house brings me back to the first time I saw this rotted wrap-around porch, seconds before the blinding white light and the nosebleed.

But Amber's fine. John was fine.

Did Elise take down her wards? I gnaw on my lip as the suspicion eats at me. I never got to finish my conversation with Theo about Elise.

Ugh. *Focus, Gemma.* One crisis at a time.

Sitting beside Amber, I ask, "Why does Olivia think I need your help?"

"She didn't say. She's..." Amber squints at the tree line. "I don't know how to explain it. We can't have a full conversation, and she's not as clear as I see you, but she's come to me three times now telling me where to find you.

"Every time she appears, it's only for a couple of minutes, and then she quickly vanishes. She gave me your location, who you were with, and said you need to run." Amber's eyes flash to mine, then focus on the woods again. "She didn't tell me who you were supposed to run from or where you're supposed to run to, but she made it pretty clear you shouldn't stay here. Also, she mentioned *Draven*, but she disappeared after that. And before you ask, I don't know what that means either."

My blood runs cold at the mention of *his* name.

"She didn't say anything else about him?"

"Him?" Amber looks at me, confused.

"Draven. He's a ghost. Here. I guess."

She shakes her head. "No, as soon as she mentioned his name, she vanished into thin air. I haven't seen her since."

Is Olivia warning me away from him? Is that why she wants me to run? But how would Olivia know about Draven unless she's here, too? I think it over, trying to make sense of everything as we talk.

"So, how'd you cross paths with John?"

"He caught me at the bus station. He was already there when I showed up in North Carolina... Recognized me from being around the house. Judy and Dennis haven't stopped looking for you, you know. They've been in constant contact with John. He visited the bus terminal several times to find a lead on where you might've gone."

My heart sinks at the mention of Judy and Dennis. Guilt chips away at me for leaving them how I did and now taking Amber down with me. I can't imagine how they're handling any of this right now. At least John has told them Amber is safe.

"Did you tell him about Olivia?"

She nods, setting her chin on her knees and picking at her shoelaces. "Olivia led us here... and I had to give him directions. He wanted to know how I knew where to go." Her gaze cuts to me. "Should I not have?"

I bite down on my lip, thinking. Theo says he's with the Authorities. But if that's true, why would he have brought her here and not taken her in?

Well, if he followed her, he could catch more of us.

But he didn't. Not yet, at least.

Why would he give us time to escape, though? It doesn't add up. Maybe he's telling Theo the truth. Ugh, why is this so confusing?

She swallows, seemingly understanding my silence, and switches topics. "Judy and Dennis are worried. Come back with me if neither of us can stay here."

A pang of guilt spears my chest again. "They're better off without me. And so are you. You need to go back without me." Even if it's not with John, we need to get her back, somehow. She'd be in danger if she stayed here with me.

"I know you're special like me."

My lips thin into a straight line. "Let me guess—Olivia?"

"I'm not dumb." Amber crosses her arms, full of satisfaction, sticking her nose in the air. "Olivia tried to convince me the dress shop was a fluke. But once all the weird shit started happening in the house after... you know... I knew I was right. You're different, too."

"Hey, *language.*"

She rolls her eyes at me, and I stifle a smile. Old habits die hard. Judy and Dennis wouldn't let us swear. I guess that's the least important problem we're currently facing.

"Well, did you happen to see the handprint burned onto Nora's neck?" I grit my teeth. "That was me, too. You can't stay here. It's too dangerous. *I'm* too dangerous."

"Don't make me go back alone." The desperation in her voice tugs at my heart.

"I don't think I have a say," I whisper. "John will come back for you. He's an adult. I'm not. I can't take care of you."

But I do have to have a conversation with him before I let her go.

Amber pouts as she wrenches away from me, jumping to her feet and storming down the broken stairs. She bolts into the backyard. The kitchen door slams shut by the time I round the house.

"Just make yourself at home," I call out, exasperated.

Everyone carries on, as usual, unfazed by Amber being here. It's another mouth to feed for now, but no one says a word. Maybe it's just for my sake. I'm grateful since she'll be gone soon anyway.

The rest of the evening creeps by with no hiccups. Zay asks Amber a million more questions about speaking to dead people—it's not just Olivia; she can talk to any ghost that presents themselves to her—and she answers them with a creeping blush that's brightening with the attention Zay gives her.

Theo never goes to see John, and I try to corner him about Elise, but he busies himself with some meaningless task every time I approach. I don't know if he's avoiding a confrontation or still upset about me trying to leave. Everything has happened so quickly that neither of us has had a chance to stop and breathe.

I can't even plan on talking to him tonight because Amber is sleeping with me, and Theo is taking the couch. Hopefully, we can right ourselves tomorrow and return to... normal.

Whatever that is these days.

After everyone has gone to bed, I find myself in the attic again. I clench my fingers at the thought of Theo catching me, but the magnetic pull is too strong. I can't help but follow when it calls. I don't *want* to be connected to Draven like this, but I do have his powers. It makes sense that we're attached.

I spin in circles, studying the empty attic before he appears. The mist takes shape until he's fully formed, leaning against the wall. I grit my teeth, prepared to fight him this time. I won't let him fool me as easily.

I won't let him make me hurt anyone else.

"What do you want from me?" I growl.

He tilts his head, ice-blue eyes filled with curiosity. "Do you want to see where Olivia is?"

The air leaves my lungs. Unsure I heard him correctly, I sputter, "...see? I can really see her?"

"Of course." He gives me a wicked smile as he holds out his hand. "I can take you to her."

I lick my lips, nervous to follow him, but the surge in my heart is unstoppable. Finally—all this time, I've wanted to see Olivia again, and here's my chance.

Taking a tentative step forward, I place my shaky hand in his. I gasp a little at the contact, still unable to process how I'm touching him. How can a ghost have a sturdy hand like this? It defies logic.

Draven wraps his slender fingers around mine and gives a gentle tug, urging me closer to that bizarre attic door hanging above us. I stare up at it, unsure how we'll get up there, when he snaps his fingers, and it comes crashing down.

I brace myself, cringing against the sound of the impact, but nothing happens. When I open my eyes, the door is now dangling in the middle of the room, fully upright. How did he do that? I glance at him, but he doesn't say a word.

Warning bells sound in my head, but I block them out. I can't turn back now. I'll never get this chance again; I have to see Olivia. I have to know she's okay.

I hesitate... What if he's lying? *But what if he's not?*

"Just a little closer now," he prompts.

I slowly approach the solid oak door. Nothing stands out; it's a plain old door with a copper handle. Draven stands closely behind me, letting my hand drop. I reach for the knob, but the door opens on its own.

A swirling wind blows my hair back. Purple and black mix together on the other side. I think I see stars, but everything is moving too quickly for me to pinpoint. I glance down, and there's nothing there. I'm afraid to take a step; I'm scared to fall.

Draven gives me a gentle push, and I'm in. I wait to drop, but nothing comes. Instead, I *become* the black and purple mass; energy runs through my veins. This is the strongest I've ever felt, even more so than when I sucked up nature's power. I'm full of pride and determination. I'm greedy. I'm hungry.

I look back, searching for Draven, recognizing those feelings inside him.

"Go on now, little mouse," he states calmly.

I take another step forward, and the scene changes abruptly. I'm standing in the middle of the woods, and Draven's gone. Panic floods my chest. Where am I? *What did Draven do?*

I run, but the scenery doesn't change. Everything is cast in a darkish hue, not entirely black and white, but the color that should be here is still missing.

"Olivia?" I shout. "Draven?"

My stomach twists into something awful, almost causing me to cry out. The pain is sharp and burning. Sweat trickles down my back, and soon I'm winded. I slow down, searching for anything that might point me in the right direction.

Laughter pierces the air—deranged, unpleasant—the same laugh that chased me in the woods. I spin around, and there—the 'Coven of Firelite Grove' sign dangles in the air. We're at the cemetery; the decimated stone structure surrounding it isn't there yet.

Voices grow louder up ahead, and I crouch down into the branches, edging closer until I can see better. There are two men and one woman. The one male has his back to me, but the faintest familiarity nudges me when I look at the two others. They seem to be in their twenties, and though I've never seen them, there's something about them... *Do I know them somehow?* I'm afraid of approaching because their faces are screwed up in anger.

The one with his back to me pleads with them, but I can't make out all the words. The female's voice cuts him off, and one word drifts up to me—"power."

The frightened one turns to glance behind him, and I swear he's looking right at me. My heart skips a beat.

Draven.

I'm about to stand up when the stomach pain is back, and I double over, gasping.

I peer back through the branches, and the female slowly inches away as she chants something. I'm too far away to catch all the words, but it sounds like a ritual. Draven begs them not to do this.

Do what?

The unidentified man pulls out a knife while realization comes crashing down on me. Draven brought me here to show me his death. Where is he now, though? The ghost Draven? Surely he's not reliving this? Can I stop it? But how? Is this time travel or only a dream?

I have to try. I can't sit back and watch this happen. Clenching my hands into fists until my nails bite into my skin, I swallow the fear. I'm unsure if it's mine or Draven's, or maybe it's both of us combining our emotions into a heavy load.

Rushing down to the group, I stumble as my legs threaten to give out. The blood thickens in my veins, and I'm stranded in slow motion. I struggle to get the words out of my mouth.

"Stop!" But no one does.

Draven screams out for Belinda.

By the time I hit the trail and process the name, we're face to face. Time seems to stand still for me, but not for Belinda. She runs right through me as if I'm not even standing there.

I watch her run away, stunned and overwhelmed by it all.

They can't see me. They can't hear me. But maybe they can feel me?

My hands spark to life as I focus all my attention on Belinda leaving. "Come back! Save him! Come back for him!"

Belinda stops. She felt it! She heard me! But after a second, she says, "Calvin, finish it."

Then she runs away, never looking back.

I whip around. Calvin smashes a beer bottle on the nearest tombstone, slicing his hand in the process. I hiss as the phantom pain slices through mine, but Calvin *laughs*. It's *his* deranged laugh that chased me in the woods. It was *his* beer bottle I heard smashing.

I choke on bile as the scene unfolds. Draven struggles against an invisible barrier, just like Nora did that day back in the woods. He's trying to escape, but it's proving impossible. He's outmatched by something that's not even there.

Calvin punches Draven in the face, and blood spurts from his nose. My face reacts to the pain, and I can't see through the tears clouding my vision. I get between them, but I'm only a ghost. They don't even notice me.

Calvin grabs Draven's chin, forcing it upward, smearing blood across his face, and punches him again. Draven's head hangs, both men's blood now mixed and dripping.

Draven's not going to last long. He's not nearly strong enough.

Why doesn't he use his powers?

What did they do to him?

I grit my teeth, summoning everything in my power, a guttural growl escaping me. If only for an instant, Draven's eyes meet mine; this time, he can see me. I stare at him helplessly, unable to do a thing. His eyes remain locked on mine as the knife stabs him in the stomach.

The piercing pain I felt before is back. My stomach is torn to shreds. I collapse to my knees. At the same time, Draven falls and mirrors me. Calvin rubs his face with the back of his hand, smearing their blood on his nose.

I inch my way toward Draven, trying to apply pressure to the wound as a sob racks my body. My hand goes right through him; I'm still not here. Blood trickles from Draven's mouth as he looks helplessly at the monster who did this to him.

The monster—*my father*—shows no remorse. His eyes are void of emotion.

I'm flooded by everything. Draven and I are one now; his thoughts are in my head, and he knows it's too late for him. "Why is it taking so long to die?" he asks himself.

The pain consumes him like a fire he thought would be extinguished by now. Aren't you supposed to go cold when you die? The blood is draining from his body, yet flames consume him.

I fight for my life as well, racked with Draven's pain. I remind myself this is him, not me. I wasn't stabbed. I'm perfectly fine. But no, I'm not fine at all, am I? Though he can no longer see me, I place my hand on his. I hope he knows he's not alone, but he is, isn't he? I wasn't here all those years ago.

This is only a memory—the worst memory.

Calvin leaves as Draven lies there, staring at the stars through the branches—the brightest stars he's ever seen—and a tear slides down his cheek when the cold finally comes.

"At last," he thinks. His voice rings aloud in my head.

Draven's dead.

The pain is gone. I sit up numbly, arms wrapped around my legs as I stare at his body.

How could my parents *murder* him? I cover my mouth, swallowing the vomit. How could such evil give life to Olivia and me? What does that mean for us? *For me?* I choke back a sob.

I was thirsty for power and enjoyed the feeling of strength when I sucked in nature's energy. Is that from them? Am I tempting the darkness within my soul?

I was right.

I *am* a monster.

The trees surround me, and I look to them for guidance. To soothe me like they normally do, but this time, they don't. Instead, they suffocate me, judge me, and I don't want to be here anymore.

Why hasn't Draven come back for me? Is there something else I'm supposed to do? Where's Olivia?

I can't convince myself to get up yet. I'm frozen to the core, unblinking. I commit every detail to memory, but a tree branch snapping jolts me out of my stupor.

Belinda has come back.

She has a young face with smooth white skin, a small nose, and thin lips. Her hair lays flat and flows down to her waist, the same golden shade as Olivia's. Even in the darkness, I can see the similarity through the moonlight.

"Draven?" Belinda whispers. She stops about a foot away. "Draven?"

No movement.

She kneels and starts performing another ritual. I can't even begin to guess what tongue she's speaking in. I can't take my eyes off her, not that it matters; she has no idea I'm here.

Draven's mouth dangles open, and a purple glow spills freely into a bottle Belinda has placed below his chin. The words she utters are coaxing it right in. It swirls inside, trapped.

I'm filled with inexplicable anger as I put the pieces together. My parents murdered Draven to get his power... to give it to *me*.

But why?

I stand up, brushing myself off as I search for answers.

"Draven!" I glance back down at the body when Belinda disappears down the path. "Draven! I know you're there somewhere."

A figure steps out from behind the trees—still as flawless as the last day of her life. Blonde hair tucked behind one ear, still in the same old stupid ballgown.

The air leaves my lungs as my knees threaten to buckle. This can't be happening. Is she actually here right now, standing in front of me? My heart hammers against my ribs as tears gather behind my eyes.

"Hey, G," the voice says. It certainly sounds like her, but is it?

"Oli?" I'm the only person in the world who could call Olivia by that nickname.

Olivia offers an impish grin. "It's me."

I rush forward, throwing my arms around her. I couldn't care less if she's only a materialized ghost—somehow tangible—I need to be held by my sister.

We hug for an eternity while the wind plays with our hair. I'm too afraid to let go, worried I'll wake up any second now.

As if reading my mind, Olivia lets out a laugh. "It's all right. You can let go."

I slowly let my grip loosen. I sniff a few times, swiping at my eyes, taking a full step back to get a better look at her.

"Oli..." I start but then quickly break down in sobs. I can't get the words out. There's too much to say in too little time.

"Shh," she coos. "It's okay. I'm okay."

"How are you here right now?"

She lifts one shoulder, giving a half-shrug. "I'm here. That's all that matters."

I nod, wiping my nose with the back of my hand. "I've missed you so much."

She gives me a sad smile as she takes a step forward. "We don't have long." She clutches both of my hands. "Draven is going to be back soon. He thinks I'm here to convince you to return your powers, but you must leave here immediately."

"I-I know he does..." I stammer out. "I want to give them back. What our parents did—"

"No!" She cuts me off. "You can't let him have them, G. Whatever you do, do not give in to him."

"Why? It'd be easier for all of us if I were just normal."

Olivia shakes her head. "Listen to me. We're both in danger if you give them back. I'm bound by something he did to me, so I can't explain. I'm lucky I've even gotten this far." She begins to flicker as the grip on my hands loosens. "What have I been telling you since day one?" she asks, determination fueling her words.

"Oli? You're fading."

"*Embrace* them, Gemma. For both our sakes."

I let out a whimper. "I can't. I don't want—Oli! Don't go!"

"I love you," she says, but she's already vanished. It's more of a whisper in the wind. My arm is still dangling in mid-air, grasping at nothing, when I'm suddenly back in the attic—alone.

Chapter Thirty

THEO

I WAKE TO THE crunching of gravel outside. I lay there listening until it dawns on me it's a vehicle pulling into the overgrown driveway.

Shit.

I jerk to the side, forgetting where I am, and fall off the couch. The bedroom door swings open, and Gemma leans against the frame, arms crossed, watching me spin in a circle of dazed, sleep-induced confusion.

"Someone's here," I panic as her eyes squint at me like I'm insane.

"It's probably John," a voice drifts into the room. Amber slips out from behind Gemma and heads toward the kitchen door.

Right.

Amber's here.

John.

I groan, running my hands through my unruly hair, failing to tame it.

There's a reason I didn't meet him at the Inn. And that reason doesn't mean he should show up *here.* The pit in my stomach is already growing, knowing he's just on the other side of the wall.

The others drift out of their rooms, following Amber outside, curiosity piqued as they talk about meeting my dad.

Why are they all excited? How can they be *laughing* right now?

"Traitors," I mutter under my breath.

My eyes roll upward, focusing on the ceiling. I huff and pick up the discarded material I used as a blanket last night. I remind myself not to get mad at them. Of course, they know, but I can't expect them to resent him as much as I do.

I glance at Gemma, who hasn't moved, then concentrate on folding the fabric. I give up and toss it to the side.

"I don't want to talk to him." The words scratch like sandpaper on the way out.

She nods, stepping closer to me. When she's close enough for her honey shampoo to calm me, she hugs me, whispering, "I think you need to."

My arms instinctively tighten around her, but I don't say anything.

"I'll come with you if you want." She nuzzles into my chest, tilting her head back to look up at me with those pretty chocolate and lavender eyes. "But you need to face him."

I inhale deeply, letting her scent fill my lungs, and kiss her forehead. Then I let her go.

"You're right," I murmur, heading outside.

My stomach turns with each step I take. I pull the lighter out of my pocket and twirl it between my fingers as I try to tame my breathing.

I've avoided this for so long. I don't know how to face it. How to face *him*.

At the front of the house, John has the back of his cab open, and the crew surrounds him. He leans against the side of the truck, smiling about something, and my stomach clenches.

Elise's high-pitched laugh travels over to me, and I resist the urge to hit something. I shove my hands into my pockets to avoid bunching them into fists.

They're all so... calm? They all know what he did—who he had killed.

Well, I doubt Amber does.

John's gray eyes meet mine, and I come to a halt.

Gemma runs straight into me, apparently not realizing I stopped. She almost falls but catches herself by grabbing my arm, and I steady her without breaking eye contact.

John's no longer laughing. He's straightened himself to his full height.

From my peripheral, I spot the crew presumably noticing the tension brewing, their eyes trying to focus on anything but us as we all silently stand there. Nora is the first to step away, picking at her lip.

Zay swivels his head between us like he can't decide what to do. "Theo, he brought groceries!"

We aren't out of food—yet. But another run is needed soon. "We don't need his groceries."

"Yeah, we do," Elise cuts in. "We're not idiots." She steps in front of me, blocking out most of John. "Right, Theo?"

My lips part on a sharp intake of breath. I want to say the number of things racing through my head, but I can't get them out. Everything—Riley, my parents, my past—burrows as deep as it can into the depths of my brain, and it feels like I'd need a shovel to dig through all the shit in my head to make sense of any of it.

John orders the kids to take the bags inside. Nobody moves. Nora chews on her lip as she watches me, waiting.

Gemma tightens her hold on my arm, and I focus on her touch.

I briefly shut my eyes, giving the slightest nod, and the three younger ones all rush to grab bags.

Elise slaps me on the back. "Good boy." She smiles, following them inside.

Gemma hasn't said a word, and I'm grateful she stays beside me instead of running off with the others.

After the silence stretches—only the crows cawing in the distance fill the air with noise—he turns to close the cab to his truck and then brushes the dirt off his hands.

He lets out a breath, turning to Gemma. "Could you give us a minute?"

Her eyes cut to me. I lace my fingers through hers, stilling her before she even has a chance to move. I can't do this alone.

I can't do this without *her*.

The motion finally breaks something in me, and the words pour out. "What are you even doing here?"

John's eyes drift around the property, frowning as he takes stock of the run-down house. My shoulders bunch as he scrutinizes the place.

His gaze lands on me. "I can help you. I think you guys need me."

"No thanks." I grit my teeth together, loosening my grip on Gemma's hand when I notice her fingers are turning purple. And not from her glow. But I don't let her go entirely.

"You're a bunch of kids out here on your own..." He shakes his head. "It's not right."

"I haven't needed you for five years now." My voice is low, dangerous. "We're doing just fine."

"Half of this house is missing."

I clench my fist tighter around the lighter in my pocket. "We're not staying here for much long—" I cut myself off with an exasperated growl. "Why am I even explaining myself to you? Go. And don't come back. I didn't need you then, and I don't need you now."

He scratches his chin and then sets his hands on his hips. "I've been looking for you this entire time. Every time I thought I was close, you were already gone." He lifts a shoulder. "I admit, you're doing better than I would've at your age, but I'm your *father*, Theo. I'm not going away, not after I've found you."

My chest heaves as the rage boils in my veins.

As if Gemma knows I'm at a breaking point, she rubs the back of my hand with her thumb in small circles.

"You're my *father?*" I say incredulously, bursting into a manic laugh.

I throw my lighter as hard as I can at him, but he ducks out of the way. It's such a stupid, immature move, but it's all I have on me, and all I want to do is hurt him.

"Were you Riley's father when you called the Authorities on her? When she burned to death inside that God-forsaken home because you were *scared* of her?"

I suck in large gulps of air, hoping the squeezing in my chest subsides. I picture the gravel rocks bursting under the tires' pressure and feel like my ribs are about to do the same.

"Well, guess what?" I continue. "*She* was scared. *I* was scared. Where was our father then?"

"I'm so sorry. You shouldn't have been alone in that. But it wasn't me." His throat bobs. "That was your mother who called. She turned Riley in."

"I don't give a shit! She's *gone*." The words are more of a howl. "Riley is gone." My voice cracks when I say her name, and I'm a step closer to unraveling.

Somewhere through the haze of grief, Gemma's hand squeezes mine as she continues making her circles.

"I lost both of my children that day." He steps closer to me, palms raised in surrender, tears glistening in his eyes. "I didn't know who called them at first. But I left your mother when I found out it was her, and I've been looking for you ever since."

I shake my head in disbelief. He's lying. He's trying to manipulate me.

He takes another step. "I was never a part of them, Theo. You have to believe me. But I *do* know where they're at. I can help you, keep you off their radar." John pauses before his voice comes out, thick with emotion. "All of this—the damn world is a mess out there, kid—this is much bigger than either of us."

The tension in my chest increases, teetering on unbearable, and I have to back away to get more space. It doesn't make any sense because we're outside, but there's somehow not enough air.

He takes another step closer to me, and I'm ready to collapse.

How can he show up all these years later and expect me to forgive him for what happened to my sister? Expect me to let him help us?

Riley's gone. Riley's gone. Riley's *gone*... Those silly giggles that sounded like music. Those stories she told when she was bored and how she dreamed of being a writer someday. Sneaking into my bed when there was a thunderstorm. Those big hazel eyes. Gone.

My hands itch as I think of the flames.

Sweat pools on the back of my neck, reminding me of the heat.

Gemma releases her grip on me and steps between the two of us, arms raised. Her hands are dull, and I latch on to an inkling of hope that she's in control. I don't want him to know what she's capable of.

"That's enough." Her voice is icy, a frigid rage. "You said your piece, now go. Can't you see he doesn't want you here?"

John nods once, taking a step back. He shifts his footing, opening his mouth like he wants to say more. But he doesn't. I cling to that gratitude. He walks around his truck, stopping by the driver's side door. "You know where to find me if you want to talk more." He pauses. "If not, I'll be back tomorrow for Amber."

He gets in his truck and drives away. As his taillights disappear into the woods, Gemma moves across the yard to where John last stood.

I'm still panting and drenched in sweat by the time she makes her way over to me, but my pulse is slowing, and the fist gripping my heart releases its pressure.

Gemma smiles sadly as she brushes the dampened hair away from my forehead. "Well, that went well."

I chew on the inside of my lip as I work to slow my breathing. "Do you... do you think it was my mom who called the Authorities?"

She shrugs. "I don't know." I spot a deep sadness in her eyes. "I don't think there's a right answer for that. It happened, one way or another. You need to do what's right for *you* now, whether that's forgiving him or writing him off forever."

I frown, letting her words sink in. She's right. It doesn't change anything; Riley is still gone.

"I need to blow off some steam." I turn on my heel, heading for the garage. "I'll see you back inside," I throw over my shoulder.

"Wait!" she calls out, running to catch up with me. She quickly kisses my cheek, slips something into my front pocket, and then darts back to the house.

I recognize the weight of my lighter without even having to check if that's what she returned to me.

Inside the garage, the hatred, the anger, and the *pain* still rattle deep in my bones, and I strike the tires, imagining they're *him*.

My knuckles reopen as the tension ebbs away—the familiar motion lulling me into comfort.

Once my hands are dripping in blood, I stop, exhaling. I study them as they throb, the blood spreading into the black ink covering my skin. Tree roots and vines from Gemma's and my encounters inch toward my fingers, covering the scars from the burns.

I tried to hide my past with memories of her, and now it's caught up to me. Elise no longer has a choice in the matter. We have to leave. No votes. No arguing.

He knows where we are.

It's time to move on.

Chapter Thirty-One

Gemma

Amber said she came here to see me but spent the past hour with Zay. He's showing her his comic books—the one thing he took with him when he left home.

I'm sprawled out on the couch, trying to read one of Nora's free library books, but I can't focus. Two particular men circle my brain: Theo and Draven.

Thought one: Theo's sad, remorseful eyes as he asked me, *Do you think it was my mom who called the Authorities?*

Thought two: my parents murdered Draven.

Anxiety gnaws on my stomach, thinking of Theo alone in the garage. I wish I knew what to say to make things better, but I don't. I don't think anything could make it better anyway.

My blood runs cold at the thought of my parents. I shake off a chill, knowing I came from such evil. No wonder why Draven wants his powers back; I'd want them back, too.

Around and around and around. Theo and Draven. Theo and Draven—like a damn merry-go-round.

The kitchen door slams open. I leap up from the couch as Theo storms in first with Elise on his heels.

Theo rounds on her. "Stop. It's not up for discussion. We're leaving tomorrow."

"But we can't," Elise whines.

"Do you actually think John is just going to leave us alone? He *found* us. I wouldn't be surprised if he's alerting the Authorities now."

"He wouldn't do that."

Theo's eyebrows shoot up. "Oh, because you know him so well?"

Zay turns to me, raising his eyebrows as well, leaning his head toward them.

I shrug. What am I supposed to do about it?

He motions with his hands like he's urging me to break it up.

I roll my eyes, then nod toward the bedrooms. He gives Amber a gentle nudge, and they sneak down the hall, away from the argument.

Elise has her hands on her hips, spitting words out at Theo that I can't understand. Her tone is too high-pitched and frantic.

Theo—if he even understands her—doesn't look impressed. His arms are crossed against his chest as he glowers down at her. Then he spins on his heel, storming off to the bathroom, and slams the door shut.

Elise follows, banging on the wooden frame. "We're not done talking!"

When he doesn't respond, she turns her glare on me. "Would you talk some sense into your *boyfriend?*"

All I can do is blink before she shoulders past me and disappears behind the tarp.

She's going up to the attic.

Draven.

Scrambling, I follow, racing to catch up with her. "Elise! Wait! Don't go up there."

She's already up the attic steps by the time I climb the rickety stairs to hit the second floor. Damn, she's fast.

"Elise!" I hiss as I climb the last set. I can't make my voice any louder, fearful of Draven being up here and hearing me. But when I reach the top, the air is knocked out of me.

Draven is in his human form, facing Elise, and she's *smiling.* It's a sinister smile, a manipulative one, that chills me to my core. My steps falter, and time seems to slow as I process what's happening.

"Hello again, little mouse," he purrs.

Just give him his power back. Then all of this will be over.

"Lloyd, I'm Ready to Be Heartbroken"? It's one of my favorites.

I freaking knew it.

No wonder she doesn't want to leave here; it all makes sense now.

"What... what's going on?" I ask, unsure how to address this. I had a feeling all along, but now that it's a reality, I'm at a loss.

My fingers tingle. Elise was working with him. Even after he made me hurt Nora? I thought they were close, but if she's working with Draven...

I don't know what that means.

Is it bad? *Is she bad?*

Elise turns to me, morphing that blood-curdling grin into a sweet, innocent smile. "It's okay, Gemma."

My hand clutches the newel, knuckles turning white. I'm ready to turn and bolt down the stairs at any second. "Does Theo know about this?" It's the only question I can manage to get out. Of course, he doesn't. He'd never allow it, but I need to ask anyway.

Elise ignores the question. Instead, she replies, "Draven can help us. Just hear him out."

My gaze flickers between her emerald eyes and his ice-blue ones.

How many times can Theo forgive me for screwing up? I sigh. I don't trust this—them—but I nod once.

I need answers.

✦✦✦✦✦✦ ✦✦✦✦✦✦

I THINK I'VE SOMEHOW entered a bizarre alternate reality. I'm cross-legged, elbows on my knees, with my chin propped up by my hands as I sit in a triangle formation with Elise and Draven in the attic.

I must be dreaming.

I pinch the skin under my chin and wince. No, I'm definitely awake.

Draven stretches out his long legs and leans back, using one arm to support himself. The other hand keeps fidgeting with a chain around his neck, but it mostly lays beneath his black shirt, so I can't see the rest of it.

Elise has both legs bent in front of her, and she wraps her arms around them, resting her chin on her knees and staring at me.

Odd.

I feel like I'm about to be sacrificed, which is certainly a possibility.

I shift my focus away from her, creeped out by the vibes she's sending. I can't tell if she hates me or is only jealous. Either way, whatever she's feeling isn't great.

Draven seems relaxed, which is even stranger.

For my benefit, he starts at the beginning, or at least where my parents come in. He says this is the only way I can truly understand. I need the full picture, apparently.

"The Coven of Firelite Grove had about thirty members. It wasn't always like that. It used to be twelve—with the Devil as their leader, of course." He smiles as he says this, the wicked glint in his eyes creating goosebumps. "But then, I don't know; our Coven got popular somehow. Everyone wanted to be a witch. So we grew."

Of course everyone wanted to be a witch. It's all fun and games until someone gets hurt.

"I was the only member who had *actual* powers—"

I cut him off. "Where did you get them from?"

"Not important."

I open my mouth to argue, but he shoots me a look. "Don't interrupt me."

Okay, jeez.

"Most of the Coven were eclectic witches with a whole blend of methods, using different sources like earth or cosmic energy to fuel their craft. But others were... different." His eyes flash to mine, then back to the dollhouse, but they don't appear focused.

He continues talking, but it's like he's back in time, reliving it all. "A select few began dabbling in blood magic. Nasty stuff." He shakes his head, scrunching his nose. "I shouldn't have even been there. No family tied me down. I was alone in the world. I could've been a drifter.

"But I decided to stay because even though I wasn't like the others, I was still closer to them than any other ordinary humans out there."

"So you aren't human?" Draven's eyes snap from the dollhouse back to me, and I shrink at the malice in them. "Sorry," I whisper.

No interruptions—got it.

I glance at Elise, and she's studying Draven in absolute awe like she's literally swooning for him. Now it's my turn to wrinkle my nose. *Great.*

Draven starts again. "Blood magic didn't seem to be enough for them, and they wanted more power." He runs a finger across his lower lip before pulling out the necklace. It's a solid silver circle, with the moon glyph for "blood" stamped on the front.

"Ironically, your parents gave me this necklace." He frowns. "I can't seem to get rid of it."

He stares down at the pendant, unmoving, and I'm not sure if I'm allowed to speak yet. I let the seconds pass, and I get more and more anxious, waiting for him to go on.

"They murdered me as an experiment," he whispers. "They wanted my power. But they were too scared to give it to themselves at first, not knowing what would happen. It could've killed them, for all they knew. That's why they gave it to you." My heart climbs into my throat as he lets the next words slip out. "You were expendable."

Bile burns my mouth, and tears gather behind my eyes. That can't be true. *Can it?*

Draven—ignoring that the room has suddenly lost all oxygen and I can't breathe—continues. "There was a divide in the Coven after the others found my body. They went to war with each other. Your parents were condemned for murdering one of their own. And some, namely those scared of me, defended them because I was different."

He holds my gaze, and I can't seem to look away. "We're different, little mouse—you and me. No one will ever understand us. But I understand you. I *was* you."

A spike of anger bubbles inside me, but it's not mine. I cut a glance toward Elise, then focus back at Draven. "Stop calling me that," I snap. I don't need more reasons for Elise to hate me.

"Why?" His lips twitch into a grin. "I like playing with you." His focus drifts to Elise, and when I don't bother responding to his bait, he continues his story. "Most of the Coven lost their lives that day. Those left alive scattered far, far away from here. Except for one. He buried anyone who fell and still works for me. Actually, the guy you met." He flashes a grin again. "Sorry about that."

Something tells me he isn't all that sorry.

I interrupt again, but this time, he lets me. "How did you send him after me?"

"I told him where to go." He shrugs. "It wasn't that hard. I knew where you were by sensing my own power, but I couldn't come to you myself, so I told him to fetch you for me."

"Why couldn't you come? You're here now... in a form of sorts."

"Your parent's handiwork won't let me leave town. I can only go so far from where I'm buried." He smiles sadly at this.

My lips twist as I consider his words. "The man you sent then... does he own a red pickup truck?"

Something brief flashes in Draven's eyes, but he holds my gaze. "Why?"

"A red pickup hit and killed Olivia. A red pickup was at the bus station before your friend attacked me."

Draven holds up a hand, stopping me. "For starters, he wasn't supposed to attack you. Just kidnap you."

"Okay, yeah, that's better." I roll my eyes. "Did you order your henchman to kill my sister?"

"My henchman? I'm not a mob boss, little mouse."

I raise an eyebrow at him. "That's not an answer."

"Fine," he sighs like I exasperate him. "I didn't order her death."

I frown as I try to get a read on him, but no alarming emotions come through. I don't want to believe him, but he seems genuine—his shoulders are relaxed, his eyes clear. Could the red pickup be a coincidence? *Doubtful...*

"*Anyway*, as I was saying... Little did your parents know, they didn't take all of my power. They only weakened me. I died, sure, but I've been"—he gestures toward his body—"this ever since. All I need is my power back. Then I can be alive again."

I lick my lips, mouth dry, as I wait for him to go on. When he doesn't, my voice comes out as a whisper. "What happens to me then?"

He waves my words away. "Everything will be fine."

Everything will be fine? Not *you* will be fine. That's not reassuring. Oliva's warning rings out in my head, *We're both in danger if you give them back.*

I rub my sweaty hands on my pants. "I don't know... I mean, I'm sorry. I'm *so* sorry that happened to you. What my parents did was..." I can't even finish the sentence because nothing I say will undo the horrible things they did to Draven.

I'd question why my parents decided to do this to him, but I saw them in the woods for myself. The malice in Calvin's eyes, how Belinda ran away without a hint of guilt.

These weren't people; they were monsters.

And I—their own daughter—was expendable.

Screw them.

"Draven can help find out who killed your sister, though," Elise cuts in, breaking up my thoughts.

Draven gives her a sidelong glance but doesn't say anything.

"Wha... what do you mean?"

"If Draven has his full powers back, he can do *anything.*" Her eyes sparkle in admiration. "He's like a *God.* He can find out who killed Olivia. He's even going to give me powers to avenge my parents."

"Elise..." I shake my head.

This seems dangerous. Like we're venturing down a path where there's no turning back. And I'm not sure I want to travel *anywhere* with Elise.

"Do you even know what happened?" she asks incredulously, slipping into a darker mood, her words dripping with hatred. "I watched my parents die. They were shot point-blank in our basement as I hid in the closet. The Authorities didn't know I existed—they didn't know to look for me. But my parents were executed for being different." Her voice hitches. "Don't you want a better life for us? We could take the fight to them instead of running all the time."

"God, Elise. That's terrible." My heart breaks for her, and I would do mostly anything to make it right, but I don't think *this* is it. Whatever *this* is. "Isn't there something else we can do, though? Find some other way?"

She gives me an icy glare, and the moment of us ever having a chance of being friends is gone. I did *not* say the right thing.

"I'm doing this for Theo, too," she snaps. "Don't you love him?"

I squirm, wringing my hands as conflicting emotions tug at my heart. I do want to know who killed Olivia. Theo's sister... Elise's parents... Draven.

But an eye for an eye? Doesn't that make me as bad as them? As bad as my parents?

"I can do better than giving you Olivia's killer..." Draven's voice comes out almost as a whisper. "I can bring your sister back."

My spine straightens as I try to process his words. "Bring her... back? Like... she'll be alive again?"

He nods, his ice-blue eyes shining. "I only want a second chance at life. Your parents stole my chance of growing old... from being"—his hand waves frantically in the air, like he's searching for the right word—"something, from being *someone*. I might've not been a human, with my powers and all, but I had a *life*. And Olivia's life was stolen, too. You can bring us both back. You can give us another chance."

I scrub my hands over my face, not knowing if this is the right choice but not knowing what else to do either.

I can have Olivia back.

My chest swells with hope that she can see me now and witness who I've been forced to become after losing her. I'm not the shy, timid girl anymore. While I might be rid of these powers soon if I give in to Draven, I've still learned to accept them for the most part. She can see how happy I am with Theo and finding others who are different. And while they haven't filled the void of her being gone, they still accepted me for *me*.

If Olivia came back, I'd have it all. I'd be whole again.

But these are large ifs, and I worry about wishing for too much. I don't want to lose Oli all over again.

Sighing, I regretfully ask, "What do we need to do?"

Draven smiles as he sits up, leaning toward me. "We're running out of time. We need to do this tomorrow before the Draconids meteor shower."

"The what?"

"It's the next celestial event, and if we don't do it before then, we'll both be stuck like this forever."

I bite my lip at the sudden rush, and Draven must sense my apprehension because he gives me an encouraging smile. "You don't even want these powers. I've been watching you. You're miserable. It's a win-win for everyone."

Blinking, I ask, "How long have you been watching me before you sent that guy?"

"Since the night of the accident."

I lean away, frowning. "Why didn't you just talk to me? All that chasing? Hurting Nora?"

His eyebrows furrow as he glances down at his clasped hands. "I didn't know if I could trust you. I was scared and slightly worried you would turn out like your parents and you'd finish the job and banish me for good. I'm... sorry."

He's choking out that apology as if it physically pains him, but I open myself up to his and Elise's emotions anyway.

Draven's face darkens but not from rage as I've felt so many times from him—no, this is more like misery, making my stomach plummet. I don't blame him for being afraid of me after all my parents took from him.

Even Elise, for that matter, seems relieved now that I've agreed. She stopped glaring at me, at least. No sense of danger emanates from either of them, but that doesn't calm me. Something still doesn't feel right.

What am I getting myself into?

Draven's been watching me for so long, I can't help but wonder... "Was it you who led me here?"

"It was," Draven says, nodding. "It was fate that brought your dream friend here in the first place. Lucky for me, he had a connection with you."

Elise doesn't seem phased by this at all. She must've known about Theo's gift all along, or at least since she met Draven.

"But I thought you couldn't leave town?"

"Ah, *I* can't. But my mind can. I was only in your thoughts."

Well, that's not weird at all.

Another question bubbles out of me. "Do you know why Theo and I are connected?"

"Some people just are." Draven gives me a long, hard look, and I get the inkling he's sincere for once. "Your strings have been tangled together long before I came into the picture."

Pressure loosens in my chest that I didn't even realize was there.

At least what Theo and I have is real. Draven didn't manipulate our dreams, didn't manipulate us into loving each other.

That's a plus.

But Theo's going to kill me for this.

"Tomorrow, you and Elise need to bring the dollhouse to the cemetery. Then we can begin."

My gaze flickers to the corner of the room where the massive replica looms and then back to him. "Why the dollhouse?"

"You'll see why."

Draven dissolves in front of us, leaving Elise and me alone.

"Are you sure about this?" I ask her.

I don't even know why I'm bothering to ask *her* of all people, but none of her emotions have me on edge. Also, Theo trusts her. And I trust him.

If this works out, we'll all get what we want.

She glances over at me. "Oh, I'm *very* sure."

As promised, John shows up to collect Amber the next morning. I'm already sitting outside, waiting for him to pull up the driveway. I need to make sure I can trust him before letting Amber go. Theo's hesitations drift in my mind, but John has had two days to alert the Authorities to our whereabouts and hasn't.

John also seemed genuine back when we were in Florida; his helplessness over Olivia's death flooded into mine, but I was so angry at him that I didn't register it. I couldn't admit to what I was then. I was running from my powers, never once thinking I'd end up somewhere like here.

John's truck turns the bend, and his lips slip into a smile when he's close enough to see me. I straighten myself out, standing tall and crossing my arms in front of my chest.

When he's out of the truck, he takes his sunglasses off and tucks them into his shirt pocket, narrowing his eyes like he's studying me. "Is Amber ready?"

I sniff, clenching my hands into fists, knuckles digging into my ribs. "She is. But we need to talk first." I feel like I'm betraying Theo's trust by relying on his dad, but I need to make sure he has Amber's best interests at heart.

"I wanted to talk to you, too."

His response takes me off guard, and I adjust my weight, shuffling my feet. "You did?"

"I wanted to update you. Well... I guess it's not much of an update. But we haven't found anything to do with Olivia's killer." The rush of sadness pouring out of him makes my lips tremble. "We've looked everywhere for a red pickup truck, and nothing has come up. I think whoever it is left town right after the accident."

He takes a large breath, his eyes finding mine again.

"I'm so sorry, Gemma. I've tried calling every station in the surrounding areas, but there's nothing. They vanished."

A knot lodges itself in my throat, but I nod anyway. I did want to know about Olivia's case, but a part of me had a feeling nothing would ever come of it. I was scared to ask, afraid of knowing the truth.

I swallow a few times and clear my throat. "Thanks for, uh... keeping up with it."

He bows his head. "Of course. I want to catch the asshole as much as you do."

I lock eyes with him—gray eyes so similar to Theo's—and I can sense he's being honest. He's not holding anything back from me right now. I can trust him even if Theo can't.

And that breaks my heart.

I'm not going to push Theo into anything he's not comfortable with, so I'll keep this secret to myself, but at least I feel better sending Amber home with him.

"Keep Amber safe," I whisper.

"I will." His voice is so sure I don't even need to read his emotions to believe him. "Do you want me to tell Judy and Dennis I found you?"

Unclenching my hands and letting my arms fall to my sides, I shrug. I think it'll only hurt them more if I choose not to go back. But it's not fair to let them worry about me. "Do whatever you think is best." I don't elaborate, assuming he has to understand by now. John knows we're all different, and being different in an ordinary house is dangerous. I turn to leave. "I'll send Amber out."

"Gemma?" he asks, his throat catching. "I'm sure Theo's told you about his past. And I've said all that I can right now. He'll either forgive me in time, or he won't. But I'm not going to give up on him."

I don't say anything to this, but he continues.

"But I'm… glad he's found you. Keep him safe, too, will ya?" A small, humorless smile flashes across his face. There one second and gone the next.

I nod, blinking back unshed tears.

I will do anything in my power to keep that boy safe.

John stays in the front yard as I go to grab Amber. She wraps her arms around me, unwilling to let go, and I basically have to drag her out front with *mostly* everyone following behind. Theo has already said his goodbye and is hiding in the bedroom.

I wrench Amber's arms away from me. "Amber, you need to go with John. I'm sorry. But you can't stay here."

Amber's no longer putting on a brave face, and she sobs.

I brush a blonde curl behind her ear, tilting her chin up. "Hey, look at me."

Her bottom lip trembles, and she sniffs a few times.

"I'll come back for you. Okay? It just can't be right now."

"Do you promise?"

I stare long and hard at the girl who used to give me so much grief back when we shared a home. But I'm so sure now, I can feel it in my bones. Yes, someday, I will go back for her.

Being the only one *different* is hard, feeling like you're alone in the world. I can't do that to her.

Grinning, I realize I'm not lying to her like I did when I ran away. "I promise."

She nods slowly, wiping at her eyes. At least she looks like she believes me this time.

Nora steps forward, wrapping an arm around her shoulders. "In two years, you can get emancipated."

"Nora," I scold. "Don't put ideas in her head."

"Hey, I'm just saying. She's already in the system; she can go through with it." Nora squeezes her once before letting go.

I chew on my thumbnail as Zay takes a step forward. His usual smile is replaced with tight lips, his eyes creased with worry. My heart tugs as they hug each other.

"Amber, it's time to go," John says, breaking up their embrace.

Zay steps backward, and I pull him into me, curling my arm through his. "It'll be all right." He nods but doesn't say anything.

Elise waves goodbye as they get into the truck, and then they're gone, disappearing around the bend.

A knot forms in my throat, but I work it loose.

I can't get emotional now.

I have a celestial event to get to.

THEO OFFERED TO TAKE Nora and Zay to the library so Nora could find information on the Coven. I didn't have the heart to tell her I already knew all I needed to.

Not to mention, this was *perfect*.

There's no chance in hell Theo would allow me to go through with what I'm about to do.

I kissed him about five extra times before he left, and he laughed them all off, so I'm glad he doesn't suspect anything, but my stomach turns at the thought of betraying him.

Ugh.

It'll all be over soon. I'll be back to my powerless self. I won't hurt anyone anymore. It's fine. He'll understand, eventually.

Regardless of what he does or doesn't understand, though, if there's even a chance of getting Olivia back, I have to try.

Elise snaps me out of my musings. "Are you going to help with this or...?"

Turning, I find her circling the dollhouse. We need to get it out to the cemetery for Draven.

"Can't he do this?" I groan. "I thought he was as powerful as God or something."

She snorts. "He's still a ghost." Struggling to get the roof off, she sets it to the side.

As we stumble down the stairs without falling through and dying, I gasp out the words that have haunted me all morning. "Do you really think"—I hiss in air as my grip slips, and I clench my teeth together to hold back the pain from my fingers being pinched—"he can bring Olivia back?"

Elise grunts but doesn't answer until our feet are firmly planted on the floor. We set the base of the house down, catching our breaths.

Panting, she leans against the wall. "If he says he can, he can."

"Why doesn't he bring *your* parents back then?"

Her brows furrow, eyes darting around the room, landing on anything but me. "He has limits. I've asked. He said they've been dead too long; their souls are already long gone."

I frown, weighing her words. It makes sense, I guess.

Huffing, we bend over at the same time, heaving the stupid dollhouse back into the air.

It takes two trips, but we're able to get the house and the roof outside to the cemetery. Sweat drenches my shirt by the time we have it set up near Draven's headstone.

I wipe my forehead off with my sleeve. "I still don't understand what this is for."

"He needs it for the ritual."

"Yeah. He already said that." I narrow my eyes at her. "But *why?*"

She shrugs. "It's almost time. I left my spell book back at the house. I'll be right back." She takes off through the iron gate, leaving me alone, surrounded by tombstones.

I wander over to my parents' graves and look down at them in disgust.

They filled me with powers they didn't even understand, too scared to do it to themselves. Willing to sacrifice *me* if it went wrong.

What kind of parents were they? Maybe Olivia and I were better off in our foster homes—go figure. If only we'd had parents like Judy and Dennis. I wouldn't be where I am today, that's for sure.

Now, here I am, giving away my powers to seek revenge on others.

I'm as bad as my biological parents.

I want to throw up.

Draven materializes next to me, turning me by the shoulder and directing me toward the dollhouse. How is he touching me? I held his hand previously, too. How does he turn it on and off like that? Sometimes, he's almost human, and other times, he's very much not.

We stop in front of the dollhouse, and he pulls the necklace out from underneath his shirt. "About time we get rid of this," he mutters.

My heart skips a beat as I instinctively reach for my own. I don't have to get rid of mine, do I? I can't part with Olivia's.

I can't. *I won't.*

Draven pulls out a dagger from inside his jacket pocket. My eyes go wide as I tense, shoulders bunching. He holds it up, palms out, in a non-threatening way. "Just need a little blood, is all. Don't worry, little mouse."

I nod, more unsure than ever, as he continues with his list of items.

He pulls out a sheet of paper next, which I can't read, but he flashes it toward me. "The spell."

"Don't meteors happen at night?" I blurt out.

It's such a stupid thing to ask, especially now, but I'm starting to panic, and I'm regretting everything. I should've told Theo.

Stupid. Stupid. Stupid.

"We have to do it *before* the celestial event."

"And we... we can't wait until the next one?"

He clenches his jaw. "Nope."

I grip my hands together, taking a deep, reassuring breath.

I can do this.

It's what I always wanted—the chance to be normal.

Chapter Thirty-Two

Theo

The house is silent when we get back from the library.

Which is... disturbing.

I can't remember the last time this place was quiet unless everyone was asleep, and even then, there was always noise, whether it was the tarp blowing in the wind, the walls creaking as the house settled, or bugs chirping from outside.

It's never *silent.*

"Hello?" I call out. No answer. My chest tightens.

I glance back at Nora and Zay, who give helpless shrugs as they dump their books on the table. None of them have to do with Draven or the Coven because we found them all in the free book box outside in the library's yard. However, I *was* able to pay off the librarian to let Nora use one of the computers without signing up for a library card.

It wasn't a total lie. I told her my little sister needed to look something up, and we'd be leaving town soon. It's pointless to sign up for a card we'll never use.

She argued it was free, so it didn't matter.

I argued that it *did* matter.

The librarian didn't seem pleased, but she eventually gave up and became thirty dollars richer. I grimace. Thirty dollars for an hour's worth of computer use—ridiculous. Nora couldn't find much, only old news articles about the massacre of 2004.

The local authorities knew the victims were "within the same group" but didn't speculate on how or why the murder occurred. Instead, all they did was promise the public they were "relatively sure" the town was safe and there wasn't a serial killer on the loose.

Fine police work.

My scowl deepens. Even John could do a better job than these idiots. I drop my coat on the back of a kitchen chair and then check my bedroom. It's empty.

I knock on Elise's door.

"Come in," she says with a singsong voice.

After opening the door, I find her sprawled out on her stomach, propping herself up on her elbows, listening to my iPod. Her spell book is open on her pillow.

"Where's Gemma?"

She turns the page without looking at me. "No idea."

"Did she say anything before she left?"

Elise shakes her head.

Maybe she went down to the lake or something? I close the door as I try to keep the anxiety at bay. I can't keep panicking every time she steps out of the house.

But Draven is still out there.

I last all of two minutes before I'm pacing around the house, rubbing the back of my neck. I try to distract myself by doing the dishes, my gaze drifting to the window to scan the yard every few seconds.

Where is she?

I give up. I wipe my wet hands off on my jeans, grab my jacket, and head for the door.

"I'm going down to the lake." I take a deep breath. "If Gemma comes back when I'm gone, tell her where I am."

Nora and Zay nod as they exchange books, discussing which one they each want to read first.

I'm barely to the tree line when I hear that familiar crunching of gravel again. But this time, it's fast—a sudden, urgent noise—something barreling right toward us.

A vice-like grip clutches my heart as I drop my coat on the ground and run over to the side of the house to get a better look.

John's back.

Seriously?

He left hours ago, or he should have, at least. Why is he here now? I still don't want to talk to him, but then I notice Amber in the passenger seat, her face contorted in fear.

John leaves the truck running as he whips open the door.

"Get your friends. We have to go."

"*What?*"

"They're coming."

Icy fingers trail up my spine, sweat beading at my neck. He doesn't have to say another word because I already know who he's talking about.

"Are you sure?" My voice is thick.

Maybe this is a trick. Maybe he's lying to get us to go with him. We can leave here—I *want* to leave here—but we're not going with him.

"My buddy from Carson City called. He knows I'm out here, looking for you. And before you start, no. He's not working for them either, but he said they mentioned our coordinates over the CB radio. It doesn't sound like they're sending more than a squad or two because they think you're only a handful of kids. But we need to go."

The dread sinks in, the pit in my stomach growing. How else would they know who we are and where we are?

And why do I feel so betrayed right now?

Maybe somewhere deep, *deep* down, I wanted to trust him. I wanted a father.

But I should've known better.

"This is your fault," I spit out at him. "I knew you'd be the one to destroy us."

I break for the house, shouting everyone's names, yelling that they're coming.

Nora is already grabbing what she can when I make it inside. She holds her red backpack in front of her, stuffing in the new books, trying to make them all fit.

"Get in our truck. Don't go with John," I bark out as I make for mine and Gemma's belongings.

Gemma.

Fuck.

She couldn't have chosen a worse time to disappear.

The only one not scrambling is Elise. She hasn't even come out of her room.

Practically kicking in her door, I freeze when I notice her standing in the corner of the room, facing the broken window.

What the hell?

"What are you doing?" I shout. "Come on. We have to go!"

"I'm not going."

"Don't be stupid." I close the space between us and yank her wrist to tug her along.

She wrenches out of my grip. "I'm not going, Theo."

Our eyes are locked, and something about her seems... different. What is it about this house that makes her want to stay? I don't understand.

"Theo!" Zay yells from the kitchen. The panic in his voice snaps me out of my turmoil about Elise. "Theo!" he shouts again.

I crane my neck from side to side, looking from Elise to the door. I have to decide: figure out what's wrong with Elise or see what's wrong with Zay.

After one last look into her stubbornly clear eyes, I let her go, bolting into the kitchen to see John gently shaking Nora by the shoulders. Nora's expression is blank—she sees something.

"Get away from her," I growl.

I slide between them and guide her to a chair. She grips my upper arms, her fingernails digging into my skin.

"What is it? What do you see?" It comes out as a whisper, but my heart rages inside my chest. Maybe the Authorities sparked something. Maybe she knows how far—or close—they are.

"Come on, Nora." I coax. "Snap out of it. Talk to me."

Zay continues to panic behind me, his voice climbing higher and higher. "This is the longest one she's had yet. What's wrong?"

I turn my head to face him, Nora's grip still holding me in place. "It's going to be fine. Pack the rest of the stuff."

His throat bobs, but he nods. His eyes scan the room, but he doesn't move. His shoulders bunch as he continues to nod, still looking around. He's totally freaking out.

Hell, *I'm* freaking out.

"Zay." He stops to look at me. "It's going to be fine," I repeat. "Just get everyone's stuff."

He blows out a puff of air, jolting into action. He grabs the bags, piling them all by the kitchen door, then grabs the coffee can with the money.

"Should I run to get Gemma?" he asks.

"I don't know where she is. She might be down by the lake, but I don't want you going out there alone."

Glancing over, I see John grabbing the bags and heading outside. I shake my head. He's probably putting them in his truck. I don't have time for this.

John's voice carries from outside. "Hey! I told you to stay in the truck."

My eyes land on the door when Amber comes bursting inside. "Olivia! She's here!"

My mouth drops open, but Nora gasps, throwing her head back, her fingernails drawing blood. I drag an arm away from her grip, leaving red scratches blotted with dark red.

"Zay! Get her some water." I cup her head as she comes to. Her eyes glisten with tears as they find mine. "You're all right. Here, have some water."

Zay helps her sip some as I face Amber.

I can't handle anything else right now. I can't.

Where the fuck is Gemma?

"What about Olivia?" I ask.

"She's here." Amber's lips are trembling. "Draven has Gemma."

Nora adds, "She's going to give him her powers."

The world stops moving. The ringing in my ears is so loud I can't tell if anyone else is talking. All eyes are on me, and it feels like I'm about to fall. I stumble backward, hitting the counter. My surroundings snap back into focus, and Nora is screaming for Elise.

And she's *angry.*

I've never heard her so upset before.

It still feels like I'm stuck in slow motion, my legs heavy with lead, but I shove past John, who's now standing in front of me, eyes crinkled with concern.

"How could you?" Nora accuses her when I make it to Elise's room. Tears swim in her eyes. "I *loved* you! How could you do this to us?"

I can't wrap my head around what Nora is saying. My brain is shutting down, and I can't think. Unable to comprehend anything but the fear drowning me.

Draven has Gemma.

The Authorities are coming.

Get it together. You can't lose it right now.

"Nora," I cut in, focusing on the problem at hand.

Nora whips toward me, her face full of hurt and betrayal.

Her eyes are wild as she points at Elise, spitting out, "She's working with Draven. She's known all this time."

I inhale sharply as my legs threaten to buckle again. "*What?*"

"I can see it all now." Nora's voice is icy. "I couldn't before because I only saw the power. I never saw Gemma or Draven, only the energy they share. That's what I saw in the woods that day. It wasn't either one of them. It was the magic. The most powerful magic I've ever seen." Nora's voice comes out in a rush, like we're running out of time, and she wants to catch me up.

The scary part is we *are* running out of time. On both accounts—we have to stop Draven and disappear before the Authorities get here.

Nora continues. "Elise let Draven out of the dollhouse. He's been here since he died. Gemma's parents trapped him with a binding spell after they gave his powers to Gemma. When freed, he set everything in motion to get them back."

Nora takes a large gulp of air, her eyes frantically darting back and forth like she's replaying the vision in her head.

"He had Olivia killed. It started everything—it unlocked Gemma's power. It scared her. Convinced her to run. He knew you two were connected, so he lured her here through you. Then Elise helped convince Gemma to give up her powers."

The tightness is back in my chest. "Where is she now?"

She shakes her head, licking her chapped lips. "I'm trying to find her."

I round on Elise now, blood boiling. "Where. Is. She?"

"I don't know."

"Stop lying!" I shout at her. My voice cracks, the desperation bleeding out of me. "Why? Why would you do this?"

Elise shifts from foot to foot, looking me dead in the eye with no sign of regret. She lifts a shoulder. "He promised me power."

My jaw drops as I try to wrap my head around it. I clench my hands together, refraining from punching a hole through the wall. I refuse to believe she's this foolish. This gullible.

"You did this for *power?*"

"I did this for us. We can finally get revenge for all the pain they've caused—what they did to my parents, to Riley..." She lays a hand on my arm. "Then we can stop running, Theo. Think of how happy we can be."

I back away from her, disgusted. "I don't want revenge, Elise. I want us to be left alone. All I ever wanted was for us to be safe. And you've ruined that."

Elise's face falls, and she takes another step closer to me, apprehension filling her gaze.

"I trusted you." I edge back to keep the distance. "We all trusted you."

"You'll see this is the right thing!" she argues. "I did this for us!"

"Elise created wards that would only affect Gemma," Nora adds in a quiet voice. "She never expected her to live. If the wards killed her, then Draven would already have his power back."

A knife carves its way inside my chest, forcing me to turn away.

I can't look at her.

My best friend.

My sister.

Five years of running.

Five years of hiding.

We've lost everything.

Amber barrels into the room. "Gemma is in the cemetery!"

I'm pretty sure I yell at everyone to stay there, but my feet carry me off without a second thought. We can deal with Elise later. Right now, Gemma needs me.

I head straight for the tree line, the shortest distance to the cemetery—to her.

Please don't let me be too late.

Please.

Chapter Thirty-Three

Gemma

The cemetery is quiet.

There are no birds. No wind.

The trees—with their monster limbs—surround me in utter stillness.

Draven goes about his business. He hasn't spoken to me as he arranges everything for the exchange on the top of his tombstone.

Not weird at all.

I turn away from him, hugging my arms across my chest, and take in my surroundings. I walk the perimeter of the graveyard and come across a small patch of wildflowers. Magenta and purple bloom in stark contrast to the orange and brown leaves littering the ground.

I didn't even know wildflowers could bloom in the autumn, but however they're alive, they're breathtaking. They remind me of Theo and the first day we met. The memory of his smell curls around me, crisp fresh air from his clothes hanging on a clothesline mixed with the woodsy scent of pine. A smile tugs at my lips, breaking through my terror of what'll happen next.

How different am I going to feel being ordinary?

Will Theo still love me?

He has to. I won't be a monster anymore. I won't be capable of hurting anyone else. I won't have the curse I didn't ask for, given to me by abominable parents.

I can finally be *me.* Plain, old, boring me.

"Ready?" I startle at Draven's voice. He's just behind my shoulder.

No.

I'm not ready.

I wring my hands together, giving a brief nod as I follow him back to the dollhouse.

"Can you just walk me through what's going to happen?" My body vibrates with fear, and a tiny voice in my head tells me not to do this.

"You're going to cut your palm"—my eyes flash to his—"only enough to draw blood as you say these words, and then you're going to smear your blood on the paper before lighting it on fire."

"And the dollhouse?"

He smirks. "We'll get to that part."

I glance at the objects balancing on the tombstone: a dagger, a piece of paper, and a matchbook.

"And this spell just... takes the power from me and gives it back to you?" I chew the inside of my cheek. "Will it hurt?"

He gives a teasing smile, and fear rolls down my spine. "You won't feel a thing."

"Okay..." My voice shakes, betraying me. "Now?"

He nods, hands behind his back, watching me.

My palm is sweaty as it wraps around the blade. I readjust my grip, steeling myself to cut my palm. Draven leans toward me, grasping his necklace in one hand, pulling hard on it like he's about to snap it off. His once teasing smile now spreads into a full grin.

And I don't like it.

I hesitate for too long, and his eyes narrow, turning into an icy glare. "Just do it."

The dagger vibrates in my hand. *What the?* It's shaking like it wants me to let go, only causing me to grip it harder. Is this him doing it? I glance around, frowning, and my heart falters when I notice Olivia standing behind Draven.

She's faint, barely even noticeable, but blood streams down her nose as she stretches an arm out toward me, her hand clenched in a fist. My hand springs open, and the dagger falls to the ground.

"What are you doing?" Draven asks. "Just cut your damn hand already."

Giving a subtle shake of her head, Olivia mouths, "No."

I take a step back, and Draven snaps. His icy-blue eyes turn red. Black mist surrounds him, but he's still human-shaped... This is something *more.*

And it's coming right at me.

"Give me back the power, Gemma." His voice booms across the graveyard.

I take another step back, tripping over myself, fear echoing in my bones. When Olivia drops her arm, she comes into better focus and finds her voice.

"Don't do it!" she screams.

Draven whips around and lunges for her.

"No!" I jolt forward, but Olivia disappears.

She reappears on the other side of the field. "He's going to trap you in the dollhouse!"

Draven lunges for her again, but she vanishes.

He lets out a frustrated growl, spinning toward me. "I'm not playing games anymore." The red in his eyes swirls as he shifts into the black haze; the static circles me in a crazed frenzy. "You know, I wasn't lying. I didn't order him to kill your sister, per se. I wanted something that would unleash your potential to ensure my powers were still up to par. That your parents didn't do something to them while giving them to you. But, honestly, this isn't worth the trouble anymore. He should have saved me some time and killed you instead," he snarls.

My heart hammers against my ribs, anger coursing through me. Both of our rages fight against one another deep inside my chest. I drop to the ground, covering my head, leaves kicking up around me. The wind circles me like a tornado. It shifts away for a moment, and I glance out, noticing the black is now entangled with something white.

Wait.

It's not something white at all.

It's Olivia.

The two colors blend together, fighting each other off. I don't know who's winning. My hands spark to life. He will not hurt my sister. I pull myself up off the ground, and the energy pipeline presents itself.

Oh, thank God.

The only two out here are already dead, so I siphon the power greedily, which calms me. The frantic beating of my heart slows as my hands glow. Then my arms. Then my entire body.

"Stop," I demand.

The power flowing through my veins makes me foolish enough to think I'm in control—that no one is stronger than me right now.

The two figures come to a halt, but when they reappear fully, Draven has his hand wrapped around Olivia's throat, and she's dangling in the air.

My heart skips a beat again, and it's like I'm two people. The frail version of me is whimpering, while the one sucking in the energy around her is unstoppable.

One is weak.

One wants revenge.

Which one do I choose?

Which wolf do I feed?

The fear of losing control of myself overrides everything. I stop draining the nature of its energy. "Let her go," I plead.

"Not until you give me the powers back."

Olivia gasps for air, which is ironic, considering she's already dead.

She claws at his hand. "Don't, G." She struggles to get the words out. "We'll both be trapped forever."

"If she's not enough of a reason, then you should know the Authorities are on their way to take your little friends."

The purple haze flares, and his eyes widen for just a second. "Ah... there we go. There's a reaction. I had my friend give them a call and drop a hint about where to find you." He gives me a tantalizing grin, squeezing Olivia's neck tighter. She wheezes. "Just finish the spell, and this will all be over."

My eyes lock with Olivia's.

"Let me go," she whispers, but it shocks me as much as a yell would have.

She's speaking to me, and only me. Not Draven, who's got his deadly ghost hand wrapped around her throat.

Me.

She wants *me* to let her go.

A blade twists in my heart, and the pain is too much to bear, tears freely falling. I don't want to let her go. She's my sister. My best friend. Who am I without her? I grit my teeth as a ripple of pain seizes my chest.

The purple haze explodes around me.

And then the entire graveyard goes up in flames.

Chapter Thirty-Four

THEO

I'M TOO LATE.

By the time I make it outside the cemetery, smoke is billowing up into the sky. I can't see anything through the haze. Fear freezes me in place, and I think my heart stops beating.

I'm right back to staring at my childhood home engulfed in flames.

I can't save Riley.

Sweat beads at my temples as the burns on my hands itch. I choke on the smoke filling my lungs.

Riley, I'm coming.

I scream out for her, but she can't hear me.

I stumble forward, gasping for air, trying to get to her.

But I'm too late.

Gemma's scream snaps me out of it, bringing me back to the here and now. The burns on my hands aren't real. Long ago healed, hidden by ink. The smoke *is* real, though—a suffocating vapor swirling inside my lungs, clogging my airways.

I let out a dry, hacking cough, covering my mouth and nose with my shirt, and force myself forward.

I won't lose her, too. I couldn't save Riley, but I can save Gemma.

My hands tremble as I struggle to get closer. As a guide, I stretch out an arm to avoid running into anything. My feet—as if by instinct or muscle memory—carry me toward the iron gate leading to the graveyard.

Once I'm inside, I spot her through my itchy eyes. But even more than that, I notice the purple light surrounding her.

Little patches of fire litter the ground, spreading to the nearby trees. This place is going to go up in flames, and there's no stopping it.

Gemma's standing ramrod straight, her shoulders shaking with violent sobs. Beside her, there's some kind of mixture of white and black intertwined. I can't tell from where I'm standing what it is, but my heart stops at the sight of Gemma crying, *begging*.

I choke down a cough, not wanting anyone to know I'm here. I sneak around the back of the black figure, ducking behind tombstones, to get into Gemma's line of sight.

My steps falter when I'm this close to her.

She's like a... supernova.

There's no other way to describe it.

She's a star that exploded.

She's still *her*, but she's also... not.

Purple exudes from her pores, her eyes beaming a bright violet. Her tears are lavender as they stream down her face. Even now, she's the most beautiful thing I've ever seen.

Oh, Gemma. What did you do?

I recognize Draven from Gemma's dream; there's no mistaking him. Anger laces through me, but I don't know what to do. *What can I do?*

In Draven's grasp is a... ghost? She's translucent, fading in and out like she's losing strength, but his grip never budges. She squirms, gasping to Gemma, "Let me go, or we'll both be trapped."

Gemma cries harder at this. *Olivia.*

Gemma's entire body shakes, and more fire shoots out of her hands. I rub a hand over my face, trying to wipe the sweat away. There's a fifty-fifty chance that making myself known is a terrible idea. On one hand, Gemma will know I'm here, so I can try to calm her down. On the other hand, Draven will probably just kill me.

A hand touches my shoulder, and I nearly jump out of my skin. I whip my head around, and see Zay with a bandana tied around his mouth.

He lets go of me, holding his palm facing up, and then uses his other hand to draw a circle above it with his pointer and middle finger. He continues this over and over, and the wind around us shifts. Along with it—the smoke.

He directs it toward Draven.

I pat him on the shoulder; it's a solid plan. Wheezing, I cover my mouth with my shirt again, trying to save what oxygen I have left. I have to get to Gemma while Draven is distracted. Or at least, I hope he will be. Maybe he can see through smoke, too.

I dash across the open space, standing directly in front of Gemma. My throat constricts when she doesn't even glance at me.

"Gemma," I say her name like a prayer. "Look at me."

Her eyes flash a brighter violet, but she doesn't move.

"Gemma!" I reach out to her but don't know where to touch. Her entire body is alive with light. My hand hovers over her as I'm rendered useless. "*Please.* Come back to me."

The wind shifts suddenly, and the smoke billows in our direction, along with a black mist. I shield her from Draven.

He morphs back into a human, laughing. "Clever trick with the boy."

My heart sinks. *Zay.* "What'd you do to him?" I spit out.

Draven waves a hand, the other one now grasped firmly around Olivia's wrist. She continues to struggle, but it's futile. Even as a ghost, he's too strong.

"Oh, nothing he won't recover from." His lips curl. "Can we get on with this now? The sooner your little girlfriend gives up her powers, the sooner this will all be over." He shrugs, dismissing the scene around us. "I'm getting bored."

Olivia's white form turns to me, pleading. "She needs to let me go."

Her eyes drill into mine with such urgency that I don't know what to do. I've been trying to get Gemma to let her sister go for weeks. But that's easier said than done.

Draven rolls his eyes. "God, will you shut up?" He turns his attention to me. "Elise already made a deal with me to get revenge for her parents. I can give you something, too?"

His voice is so genuine and nonchalant I'd imagine it's like making a deal with the devil. You don't realize what you've done until it's too late. I'm not surprised Elise fell for his shit. His bright red eyes shift into the color of dark blood the longer he studies me.

"Now, don't give me that look." He tilts his head. "Every human desires something. It's your worst quality." His mouth twists into a bitter grin. "So, what's yours?"

I don't say anything, afraid of saying the wrong thing. Instead—in a seriously dicey move—I turn my back to him and face Gemma.

"Gemma, listen to me." The words rush out of me. "I love you. You know that, right?"

The purple haze around her flares, and I stumble backward, shielding my eyes from the brightness. When I'm able, I take another step closer.

"You're not scaring me off that easily," I try to joke, but the laughter crawls out of my throat and dies, turning more into a whimper mixed with a cough.

"You need to let her go, Gemma." Another step. "Olivia is suffering here. *Let her go.*"

In the tiniest movement, Gemma shakes her head. It's so faint, but I saw it. She's listening. She can hear me! I glance back at Draven, who's trained his eyes on me, a snarl on his face. He tosses Olivia to the side, and she falls to the ground, flickering.

Oh shit. Hurry up, Gemma.

My heart thuds as I think of anything to say, anything to get her to listen. I race to get the words out. "She won't be in pain anymore! She'll be free from here." My chest aches at the uptick of my pulse combined with the smoke. "And you'll never be alone. You'll have me, and Nora, and Zay, and Amber. You'll have a family with us, Gemma. I promise."

Draven is nearly next to us, glowering as he begins to shift back into a mist.

"Gemma, listen to me." I'm frantic now, itching to reach out and shake some sense into her. "You have to stop this. Only you can save us."

Draven's mist is about to collide with my chest when Gemma shoves me backward.

The world goes dark as the fire rages around us.

Chapter Thirty-Five

Gemma

THE SMOKE SURGES so heavily that it may as well be nighttime. I can't see Theo anymore. I hope I didn't hurt him.

But it's better if he's away from this, away from *me*.

Draven still swarms around me in a frantic haze, but I ignore him. Instead, I move closer to my sister, who's fading in and out.

"Embrace it, G." She looks up at me from the ground, giving me a sad smile. "I've been telling you all along."

I kneel next to her and smooth her hair back. I'm relieved I'm able to feel her skin beneath mine. It's not warm like it used to be. It's ice-cold. She's so transparent I'm worried my hand will slip right through.

"Does it hurt?" My words echo hers from the day at the beach.

She gives a half-shrug, but a grimace creases her pretty face.

"Was this my fault?" I ask her. "Did I keep you here?" Tears cling to my eyelashes, ready to crash onto her cheek, but I smudge them away. It's a selfish thing to ask, but I need to know.

"Draven kept me here," she says softly. "But it's up to you to let me go."

I nod. Although a large part of me still doesn't want to, it's my only choice. I lean forward, my lips brushing her forehead. "I love you so much."

She cups my cheek. "I know." Her body flickers again. "I won't be far. It'll be like I'm right by your side the entire time. Whenever you think of me, I'll be there. But... but just let me go, okay?" Her voice cracks at the end. Even in death, she's trying to put on a brave face for me.

A few tears escape as I cup a hand to my mouth to choke back the sobs.

It's like I'm losing her all over again, but her favorite drunken song slips between her lips in a faint hum, giving me the last bit of courage I need.

Clutching the necklaces dangling around my neck, I stand up. I take a second to scan the area for Theo, but I still don't see him through the smoke.

Please be okay.

"Draven!" I shout. "You win!"

I pace in circles as my body begins to glow again. There are a few things I'm certain of now:

Letting Olivia go is the only way for us to move forward into our new adventures.

I'm ridiculously and wholeheartedly in love with Theo.

And as much as I used to think I was, I'm *not* a monster.

Draven shifts into his human form, eyes back to ice-blue. "I'm glad you've come to your senses, little mouse." He hands me the dagger. "Shall we?"

I hold out a hand, ready to grab for it. The plan is to either stab him or myself if the blade doesn't affect him. He can't have my powers if I don't surrender them. That has to be it.

Otherwise, he probably would've just killed me himself by now.

His silver necklace catches my attention, the memory of his words in the attic ringing out in my head, *I can't seem to get rid of it.*

I blink in surprise. I should've realized it earlier. The plan changes in front of my eyes. I lunge for the necklace, ripping it off his neck. At the same time, I break the two chains holding mine and Olivia's together.

All three necklaces. All three moon glyphs have the symbol for "blood" on them.

They vibrate in my hand, alive with energy.

Draven yells, "No!" when I close my fist around them, burning them—turning them to ash. The dust settles at my feet.

I wasn't sure what would happen, but something about it felt *right.* I had to sever my only connection with Olivia to let her go. And in doing this, I hope I also severed something with Draven.

The smoke from the fire turns as a strong wind blows in, clearing the sky briefly. Across the yard, Zay stands with his palms outstretched, brows furrowed in concentration. Nora is behind him, tugging Theo to his feet. Elise runs toward Draven, but he's now a cloud of black, inky smoke, and the dollhouse is sucking him back inside to where he belongs.

"No!" Elise screams, dropping to her knees. She clutches the dollhouse, shaking it.

We're still surrounded by fire, fire *I* started, but Zay keeps the smoke and flames at bay, encircling us in a patch of daylight.

I glance at where Olivia was lying, but she's gone now. A pang in my chest moves to my stomach as reality settles over me. She's gone. For good this time.

"I'll miss you, Oli," I whisper.

Maybe wherever she is now, she's still looking down on me. Perhaps she's still my guardian angel.

I make my way toward the group. Thankful for them. Thankful we're alive. And fully relieved this is over. I don't know how to put out the flames, but then I remember Draven called the Authorities.

"Theo!" I screech.

Zay and Nora drag Elise away from the dollhouse as Theo digs in his pocket, yanking out his lighter. He wipes his hand off on his jeans and then ignites it, holding the fire to the corner of Draven's prison.

A tiny flame blooms, and he holds it to the roof of the dollhouse, lighting the wood in sections, spreading the fire bit by bit as if hoping it catches.

With Zay distracted, the smoke cloud falls on us again, and we all begin to choke. One hand flickers to life, and I gasp at how much easier it feels to control now. I use it as a light until I reach Theo. He pulls me into him, kissing my hair.

"We need to go," I gasp. "The Authorities are coming."

He steps back, his face falling. His confusion thrums through me, and he looks like he's about to say something, but then John bursts through the cloud.

"Oh, thank God," John pants. He's drenched in sweat, and soot speckles his cheeks. "I couldn't find you." He backs away, coughing into his elbow. "Where's everyone else?"

We turn, scanning, but without Zay's wind, we're all lost in the same gloom.

"Zay?" I call out.

At the same time, Theo shouts, "Nora!"

White lights reflect through the haze from every direction. What is that? Theo closes my hand, slightly hissing, effectively snuffing out the glow. Only our heavy pants break the silence. After a second, I realize the white lights are flashlights.

And we're surrounded.

"Theo," I whisper, my voice cracking.

They've found us. We have nowhere to go. I can't even see them. I only know they see us. Their lights don't budge anymore; they all hold steady, all trained on us.

After an eternity, the light directly in front of us moves. It dips lower, and heavy footsteps fall. I hold my breath as it comes closer.

Will they kill us or take us with them?

My heart thunders inside my chest as a person dressed in all black breaks through the fog. They wear a helmet with goggles and a mask attached, their entire face covered. And it's not a flashlight they're holding. It's a gun with a light fixed on top, pointing down the barrel.

My throat burns between the smoke and the fear.

I'm suffocating.

I turn away, burying my face in Theo's arm. He holds still but squeezes my hand.

This is it.

The seconds are excruciatingly long as nothing happens, but then Theo gasps. His grip on my hand tightens, almost causing me to cry out. I glance up at him, and his eyes are wide with panic. Grimacing, I force myself to face the person standing in front of us. She's removed her helmet. Her head is shaved on one side, and her hair on the other side is pitch black, still cut short, but hangs to her chin. She has a malicious smile as she locks eyes with Theo. Something about her seems familiar but *wrong*—her face twists with betrayal. Her eyes gleam with something sinister.

Hatred radiates off her and into me, but she smiles, showing perfect white teeth. Their kind doesn't seem to like us, but this feels *personal.*

John stumbles forward, covering his mouth. His throat bobs as he cries out, "Oh my God." When he's face to face with her, he whispers, "Riley."

I inhale. *Riley?* The weight of Theo's hand disappears. I reach out to grab him but grasp air instead. I turn, but he's no longer standing next to me. My heart leaps to my throat as I spin in circles.

"Theo?!" I cry out.

Where did he go?

What did they do to him?

Those dressed in uniforms rush toward me. I light up both hands, trying to keep them back. And I run.

"Zay! Nora!"

I can't find anyone.

The fire surrounds us all in a circle, and there's nowhere else to go. I'm blocked in. The smoke still rages on, and lights beam in every direction, glowing against the smoggy sky. I snuff out my glow and stand in the darkness—alone. I count ten flashlight beams, watching their sweep of the graveyard as I figure out what to do next.

Then a burst of fire appears directly in front of me. I stumble backward, away from the heat blazing from it. Elise appears in my peripheral seconds before she disappears, too.

Gone.

What...?

Riley stands in front of me, snapping her fingers. Another fire explodes into life next to me. Then another. She's trapping me. She cocks her gun. But John is right there before anything happens, pushing me out of the way.

I fall to the side, but familiar arms wrap around my waist, catching me so I don't hit the ground.

Theo's back.

I breathe out a sigh of relief as we step back into a darkening void. I don't know what's happening, but we're surrounded by pitch dark, except for one tiny hole of the real world in front of me. A picture-sized frame of the fire and destruction we're leaving behind. And within that picture, I watch John take the bullet meant for me.

I scream as Theo drags me out of the void—or whatever we were just in—into an empty field.

The sun is already setting, and no cloud is in sight. The moon slowly comes into view. The green grass stretches until it hits a parking lot. Elise, Nora, and Zay all stand in front of me. All battered. All covered in sweat and grime, looking like they're about to collapse.

Theo is behind me, clutching his knees.

"What just happened?" I ask no one in particular.

How did we get out of there? And where are we? And John...

John.

My heart sinks at the thought. Did Theo know he was leaving him behind? Did he know his father was just shot? I turn toward Theo; his body shakes. He's inhaling large gulps of air, swaying left and right as he bends in half.

"You okay?"

"I don't know what I just did. I... I..." he falters, trying to get it all out. And then he vomits.

I rub his back in small circles as his dry heaving continues. Before long, he slowly stands up.

"I saw Riley, and I panicked. I just... blinked out." He wipes his forehead with the back of his hand. "Suddenly, I found myself here."

"Your powers grew," Nora whispers.

"Powers? What powers?" Zay asks.

A sorrowful smile flashes on her dirty face. "Theo can teleport now, which is why you disappear in my visions. You were never *gone*; you just went elsewhere." Her shoulders sag as she lets out a breath like she's satisfied her visions haven't failed her.

Theo pales as if he's about to faint. Before I can panic about him, though, a terrible thought occurs.

"Oh my God!" I clutch his arm. "Amber!"

Theo huffs, scratching his head. His face is still ghastly. "She must be at the house. I'll go get her."

"What if the Authorities are already there?" Zay asks.

"There were ten in the cemetery. There might be more," I warn him.

Theo nods, chest heaving. "I'll be careful."

And just like that...

He disappears.

Chapter Thirty-Six

THEO

I stumble out of the field the fair was at and into the woods near the Rib House. My legs shake from the transport, and my stomach sours, ready to vomit again. I'm not sure if it's from the physical act of traveling or the thought of it.

Energy drains out of me. Each time I hop, I lose a little more strength. It's an effort to stay standing right now, and I'm bone tired. But I don't have time to be tired. I need to keep moving.

Gritting my teeth, I push myself forward, closer to where the tree line meets the backyard. I came in on the opposite side of the cemetery, unsure if the Authorities found this place yet.

I hope not.

When I'm close enough to see the garage, the side of the house, and the two trucks, I pause, hiding in the shadows of the trees.

Waiting. Watching.

How did I not know I could teleport? Is that what happened the night of the accident? When I found myself at the hospital, before falling back into the kitchen of the gas station?

I would know, though.

Wouldn't I?

None of this makes sense.

My head swims, and I lean against a tree to keep myself upright—the traveling. Riley is alive. John is... gone. I stop myself. I can't get worked up about him. Even after everything, I consciously chose not to go back for him. Maybe he didn't alert the Authorities. How would Gemma know they were coming if it was him? But still, I couldn't risk it. I couldn't risk being captured and forced to abandon the crew.

I can't help but wonder, though... Did I seal his fate?

My throat closes as I shake the images out of my head, focusing back on the house. All seems quiet. It doesn't mean no one is in there, though. Would they hold Amber hostage? What if she followed us into the woods?

My heart jolts.

Riley's alive.

How? How is that possible? They didn't find a body after the house burned... but I thought that meant she burned with it. Not that... God, I left her behind, and now she's working for *them*.

I should have checked. I shouldn't have left her.

I screw my eyes shut, failing to block out the images of the staircase collapsing, the smoke burning my lungs as bile rushes up my throat. The image in my head transforms into her now—armed with a weapon, fury warping her face into something wicked.

Besides the hatred, she was the same as when I saw her last... just five years older. Her face didn't change, though—her hazel eyes and high cheekbones matched our mother's. She looks even more like her now that she's older.

Except she's angry. Extremely angry.

What did they do to her?

Guilt eats away at me, and I'm about to hurl again. From the corner of my eye, a blonde head of curls pops up from the front seat of John's truck.

Amber.

I creep along the tree line, leaves crunching under my feet as I close in on the truck. When I'm in line with the driver-side, I make a run for it. Amber yelps when I whip open the door, sliding into the seat next to her and ducking down. Of course, they would've heard the noise if anyone was nearby. But maybe they'll overlook us if we don't move.

"Where is everyone?" Amber asks as she waits low to the floor, mirroring me as I stay down.

I do a double-take when I notice she's engulfed in my jacket. At least she didn't leave it laying in the yard. "We have to go get them."

She flips her hands up, chiding me. "Well, what are you waiting for?"

"Do you know if anyone is inside?"

"I don't think so, but don't go in there." Her voice is on the verge of begging. "*Please.* I've been freaking out here."

"I need to grab some things."

"We already got everyone's bags. They're in the cab."

"Are you sure? Everyone's?"

"Yes. Well... I don't know if Elise packed one. John grabbed everyone else's by the door, though."

"I'll be right back."

"No," she whines.

"It'll only take a second."

I open the truck door slowly and leave it cracked open. I inch toward the back of the truck, peering out into the backyard.

No one is here. But they have to be coming soon.

I dash for the kitchen door, forgetting all sense of stealth, and storm inside, figuring I can blink out if someone comes.

That's how this works, right? Do I have a quota on how many times I can do this? Will it eventually kill me? Thankfully, I don't need to find out since the kitchen is empty. I grab the shotgun from my bedroom and double-check that everyone's backpack is truly gone, along with the coffee can Zay grabbed.

My last stop is Elise's room.

She doesn't deserve this. After what she's done, we should leave her behind. I hate myself for taking a step inside her room. And then another.

But before I can leave, I grab the picture of her parents from next to her bed and shove it in my pocket.

***

It doesn't take long for us to get back to the field since I'm driving this time.

The crew looks desolate as they all sit on the ground, except for Zay, who's sprawled out on his back. Elise is sitting about twenty feet away with her back to everyone.

Gemma hops up, pulling Nora to her feet when she spots the truck.

When I park, Amber scurries out, wrapping herself around Gemma and hugging Zay, who's finally on his feet.

It takes me all of two seconds to pull Gemma into my arms and hold her close.

The bitter stench of smoke masks her honey shampoo, but I don't even mind. This has been the longest day of my life, and I still feel like I might pass out any second.

"What do we do now?" Nora asks, tugging at her lip.

"We find a new spot." I glance over my shoulder. "At least John's truck doesn't have stolen plates. We can go farther this time before swapping them so he can't track us. Start over."

Gemma stiffens beside me, her eyes fixed on her shoes. She looks up at me and then shifts her gaze elsewhere.

I squeeze her into me. "Are you okay?"

It seems stupid to ask. What we all just went through... Gemma exploded into a fucking star. I'm sure she's anything but okay.

She tucks a piece of hair behind her ear. "Can we... I need..."

Then she takes my hand, pulling me to the other side of the truck, away from everyone. Okay, now she's scaring me. "What's wrong?"

She squeezes my hand in between both of hers. "I saw..." She swallows a few times, seemingly struggling to get the words out. "When we went through... the void or whatever. I saw..."

"Yeah?"

Her chin wobbles, and she looks into the woods, blowing out a breath. "I saw Riley shoot your dad."

I bite my tongue as my vision clouds. My throat constricts as I try to process what she's said. I knew this was a possibility, didn't I? I left him behind. But knowing the truth...

Gemma adds, "He saved my life."

"Are you sure?" I finally ask. "It was him? He was shot?"

Her gaze flickers to mine, and she nods. "I'm so sorry, Theo. We were already stepping through before I could do anything."

The lump in my throat grows, but I don't want to cry in front of her. Not now. We need to keep moving.

Hell, I don't even know *why* I want to cry.

I need to figure my own shit out before I get her involved.

"No, no... it's not your fault." I clench the hand she's holding into a fist. "I chose not to go back for him."

"You couldn't have known..."

"Either way, I left him behind." I lift one shoulder. "It's done."

"Are you... are you okay?"

I pull my hand free from hers, rubbing my knuckles as I nod. But I'm *not* sure if I'm okay. My sister—who I thought was dead until an hour ago—killed my father, who I wrote off five years ago. "It's complicated."

She kisses me on the cheek. "I understand. I'm here whenever you're ready." Then she leans back, her fingers running through my hair, brushing it back from my forehead. Concern settles on her face. "You look awful."

"Thanks." A humorless smile tugs at the corner of my mouth. "You look great, too."

"No more teleporting until we figure this all out, got it?" She drags me back toward the silent group, and it breaks my heart to take in their faces.

Zay, normally happy-go-lucky Zay, keeps his gaze lowered, frowning. Nora's optimism is now faded as she keeps her eyes on me, pulling at her lip and causing it to bleed. Amber looks the best out of all of us—she's clean, at least. But she's also the youngest and is visibly shaking. She wraps her arms around herself and keeps glancing over her shoulder, looking into the trees.

Gemma must get the same impression as I do because she pulls the younger girl into her arms, tucking her into her side.

Elise hasn't bothered to move. I don't know what to do with her. She can't be trusted.

Gemma is the first to break the silence. "I've been thinking... It might be nice to go back to Judy and Dennis's."

Amber snaps her head up, breaking out into a grin. "Really?"

Gemma nods as she turns to me. "They're safe. We can trust them."

Everything in me tells me not to do it.

Adults ruin things. Adults try to take charge. Adults call the Authorities.

Zay's face lifts at the notion, and Nora looks at me expectantly, basically pleading with her eyes for me to say yes.

"What about her?" I nod toward Elise.

Zay scowls again, kicking at the ground. "I say we leave her behind."

Nora smacks him on the arm. "What she did was wrong, but she's still family. We can't just abandon her."

"Is she, though?" He turns to glare at Elise's back as her shoulders hunch more. "Family doesn't try to get its members killed."

Elise finally turns toward us. "I'm sorry, okay?"

My teeth clench together. "No. It's not okay." Her gaze flashes to mine, and I have to look away. After all we've been through, it's too painful for us to end like this.

But she knew Gemma would die this entire time, and I'll never forgive her for that.

Nora asks, "Are we voting?"

I roll my eyes. The fucking votes. Again.

"I say we bring her with," Nora states.

Zay shakes his head. "I'm against."

I chew on my lip, the turmoil eating away at my insides. It's been Elise and me since the beginning. She's been with me from day one on this hellish nightmare ride.

She was my best friend, my go-to, my confidant.

I walk over to where she's sitting. She looks up with such a hopeful expression it almost makes me sick. I dig in my pocket and pull out the photograph.

She takes a deep breath as I hand it to her, tears brimming. "Thank you, Theo."

When she pulls the photograph from my fingers, I step back, casting my vote. "I'm against."

Her mouth drops open. I turn away from her, stuffing my hands deep into my pockets, and make my way back to Gemma.

Amber's tapping her chin. "I don't know if I get a vote, but I feel kinda bad leaving her in a field. So I say yes."

Two-two.

All eyes turn toward Gemma.

"She was going to sacrifice you," I whisper. "It's okay to say no. You don't owe her anything."

Gemma stares at Elise, long and hard. Her face is expressionless. I can't even begin to guess which way she's leaning.

"I say she comes."

Nora lets out a breath, and Zay shakes his head.

"We're not them," Gemma insists. "We're better than that."

"If you say so," Zay says as he shuffles past her, heading for the truck.

Everyone else follows suit—Elise included—until it's just Gemma and me standing in the field. I glance down at her. "So it looks like we're going to Florida?"

She gives me a coy smile, pulling me in for a kiss. "Maybe when we get there, we can just be teenagers for a while. I'd like a few regular days."

I let out a soft laugh, and it feels like it's the first time I've laughed in weeks. It's hard to believe all the events that have transpired in *one day*.

Gemma cups my cheek. "You look beat. Seriously. I don't know if that blinking out is good for you. Let me drive."

"Are you sure?"

"Mhm. Dennis taught me how to before I ran away."

"Do you know where you're going?"

"Probably no more than you do." She smirks at me as she turns away, heading to the truck.

Elise, Amber, and Zay sit in the back seat. Nora is plopped in the middle of the front seat with the map already in her hands. I direct Gemma back to town. We fill up the gas tank, load up on snacks, and then we're on our way.

Goodbye, Thornbrooke, Indiana.

WE'RE AN HOUR INTO the drive, and I struggle to hold on. My eyes close, flutter back open and repeat. Everyone in the backseat is passed out as well. Elise leans against the window. Amber's head is on Zay's shoulder, and his rests against the seat.

Out cold.

Nora is wide awake next to me, studying the map. I close my eyes, resting my head on my arm against the door.

I'm almost out when I hear Gemma ask Nora in a low voice, "What's your story? If you don't mind me asking? I know how everyone else ended up... here."

The map crinkles a bit as Nora replies, "I knew they needed me."

"So... what? You left home?"

"Home was fine, but I had a vision of this lost boy. He was fifteen at the time and only had one person in his corner. Something called to me so strongly that I knew I couldn't ignore it. It turns out he needed me more than my family did."

Gemma breathes out, "That's incredible. So your family didn't bother to look for you? I find that hard to believe."

"I made everyone forget I existed. I'm not sure how... it just happened."

I open my eyes to study Nora's profile. She never told me *that* part.

"I didn't want them to hurt, so I wished for them to forget who I was." She blinks. "I have visions of them sometimes, and it's like I was never there."

Gemma glances between her and the road. "Wow... I'm so sorry. That must've been difficult for you."

She shrugs as if it's no big deal. "It's okay." She turns to look at me, catching me staring, and slips her hand into mine. "It all worked out for the best."

GEMMA AND I TAKE turns driving the eighteen hours to Florida. We sleep when we can and only stop when we're forced to. When we're ten minutes out, Gemma frantically asks me to pull over. Her face is flushed, and her chest heaves.

She hops out of the truck as soon as I'm parked and starts pacing on the sidewalk.

I glance at the others in the car, and they all watch me silently before staring out the window at her. Unbuckling, I get out of the truck.

The Florida heat beats down on us as she continues to pace, her hands fluttering around.

We're way too far in for her to be changing her mind. "What's wrong?"

"What if they're not happy I'm back? What if they hate me for leaving?"

I place my hands on her shoulders, forcing her to stop walking. "They're not going to hate you."

"You don't know that."

She's right. I don't. But I don't think anyone could ever hate her... Besides Elise, I guess.

"You said they're good people, right?"

She nods. "They are."

"Okay. So we go. And if they don't want us? Then we'll leave. Easy."

She blows out a breath and fixes her hair. I almost want to laugh, considering we've spent eighteen hours in a truck after nearly dying in a fire and then almost being captured by the Authorities. Running fingers through our hair will not fix any of our appearances.

I tighten my grip on her shoulders. "It's going to be fine."

She nods again, getting back into the truck. "Let's do this."

Chapter Thirty-Seven

GEMMA

I CAN'T DECIDE THE best way to handle this… maybe it should just be Amber and me.

Wait, no, just Amber.

I try to untangle the rat nest growing in my hair from my curls tangling together but end up groaning in frustration. We're parked outside Judy and Dennis's house, and everyone's staring at me, waiting to see what we're doing.

For the millionth time, my thoughts circle back to deciding to let Elise come. I chew on the inside of my cheek, hoping I didn't make the wrong decision. I meant what I said. We *are* better than the Authorities. We don't discard human lives because they're different from us. We can be accepting—forgiving.

Theo didn't forgive his dad, and now he'll never get the chance to have him in his life again. And who knows, maybe Elise will be better without Draven influencing her.

So, yes, we should forgive her.

But forgetting?

That might be a different story.

Elise will have a lot to prove before I trust her, and I understand why the others felt so strongly about leaving her behind—Theo, most of all. I can't imagine the kind of heartbreak that came from so much betrayal after five years of friendship.

But it isn't my place to be judge, jury, and executioner.

I just hope she doesn't do anything stupid while we're under Judy and Dennis's roof. *If* we're under their roof. My thoughts divert back to the fact we're just sitting here. I need to make a decision.

I've spent so much time running away from them, worried about their safety, and now I'm bringing even more baggage—and danger—to their doorsteps. But they're the only adults who've ever made me feel safe, and from the horrors we just witnessed, I really want an adult to tell me what to do. Tell me it'll be okay.

I take in everyone's dirty and heartbroken faces. We're all so *young*. We've been through way too much already to be denied. Judy and Dennis have bleeding hearts; they have to let us in.

I shake my head, not believing this is about to happen, but finally coming to a decision. "We all go. They can't say no to a sad lot like us."

We're all bunched together on the front porch, but I can't gather the courage to knock or ring the doorbell.

Amber rolls her eyes at me and pounds on the screen door. "Wuss."

The door cracks open, and there's Judy, hunched in on herself. Her wavy strawberry blonde hair is tossed up in a messy bun; her hooded eyes are ringed with redness. Her expressionless gaze lands on Amber first before flickering up to me. And then she breaks down and sobs.

"Dennis!" she yells. "Get in here!" She opens the screen door, pulling Amber to her. "I'm so glad you're okay," she mumbles into her hair. After letting her go, she reaches for me.

Instinctively, I stiffen, but Theo pokes me in the back, stirring me forward.

She wraps me in a bone-crushing hug. "I'm so glad you decided to come back." She lets go, wiping her eyes. "Dennis!" she yells again.

"I'm coming!" a familiar voice hollers back from further inside the house.

Judy seems to notice the four standing behind me for the first time. A ripple of shock spasms across her face, but she recovers. "Oh, right! Come in!" She holds the door open as we usher into their two-story house in a single-file line.

It's been less than two months since I've left here, but it also seems like it's been years. I repress a shiver, thinking how different it is now. I ran because I couldn't control my powers, scared of hurting someone. Now I'm back with more control—*hopefully.*

My, how times have changed.

I'm doing better than I thought I would've, but it's still... strange.

A piece of me will always be missing with Olivia gone, but being here feels like coming *home.*

"You're back! Both of you!" Dennis cries out as soon as he enters the room. The relief on his face makes my throat constrict. His brown eyes are still filled with warmth. He pulls us both in for a hug simultaneously, then looks at the other four standing in the corner. "Who are your friends?"

I break away, pointing everyone out. "Judy... Dennis... this is Theo, Zay, Nora, and Elise."

Dennis's smile doesn't falter as he bobs his head. "Okay, sit, sit, all of you."

None of them move, and Theo glances down at his filthy clothes.

A pang of sadness grips my chest when I watch him. His bottom lip juts out the slightest bit, his jaw twitching with tension. It's been five years since he's been inside a real home. His hair droops across his forehead, and he seems so young and vulnerable right now, so different from the one in charge back in Indiana.

I want to cry for the little boy who ran away all those years ago.

Theo glances at the others. "Thank you, but we're okay standing."

Judy stands next to Dennis, looping her arm through his. "Nonsense. Who cares if something gets dirty? We'll just wash it."

A look of surprise spreads across Theo's handsome face, and he nods toward the others. The four squeeze onto the couch as Amber and I take the loveseat adjacent to it.

Dennis sits in the recliner, with Judy propped up on the armrest.

Theo meets my eyes as everyone settles, and his anxiety rolls into me. He's on the verge of panic. I flash him a small reassuring smile as if I'm saying, *"It's all right. We're all right."* He bites his lip, clenching his hands together like he's trying to rein it in.

Judy starts with the questions first. "Where have you been? We've been so worried. And we lost contact with John."

I rub my hands together, unsure how to proceed or where to start. I should've asked Theo what he wanted me to say.

Too late now.

"A lot has happened... and uhm... well, John didn't make it."

"What do you mean *he didn't make it?*"

"He... uh..." I cut a glance toward Theo. *Crap.* We should've come up with a plan, but he gives me a subtle nod. "...died."

Amber turns to me, startled. "No one told me that!"

Judy blanches. "Oh my God, that's horrible. What happened?"

"That's a long story. And I promise I'll tell you everything. But we really need somewhere to stay... secretly."

Dennis leans back in his chair, one hand covering his mouth. His eyes narrow, and his concern rolls into me, but more in a fatherly way than a 'we don't want you here' way.

"Are you in trouble?" he asks.

I hesitate, my hands fidgeting. "In a manner of speaking. But it's not what you think."

Judy turns toward the four on the couch. "Where are all of your parents?"

"We don't have any, ma'am," Theo answers for all of them.

"You're all in foster homes, too?"

He tenses. "We're not in the system... and we'd like to keep it that way."

Judy and Dennis exchange glances with their own sort of secret language. Then Judy shakes her head. "I don't know... we should call *someone.* Maybe—"

"Judy, don't," I cut in. My hands tremble as I gather the nerve to show them what I can do. I wanted to keep it a secret for so long. But this is the only way...

They have to understand.

It's the worst possible time for this to happen, but an unbidden thought comes to mind—the night of the homecoming bonfire, which seems like eons ago now. Olivia and I argued over whether we should tell our foster parents about my powers. She was so adamantly against it, so I didn't. And now she's gone.

If only I had been brave enough to show them sooner.

My voice shakes on the way out. "You always suspected something was different about me. I could sense it. And you weren't wrong."

I hold up a hand, focusing on a plant in the corner so I don't accidentally drain anyone else's lifeline. I might be in better control, but there's still so much left to figure out regarding these powers—the purple sparks to life.

Judy's mouth drops open in shock, and Dennis leans forward, eyebrows raised.

I curl my hand into a fist, snuffing out the purple glow before I continue, "We're all… different in our own way, and there are people out there who don't like us. Who want to hurt us—or worse. Please don't tell anyone we're here."

Judy's mouth stays open as she turns her head toward Amber. "And you're… *different* too?"

Amber nods. "I can talk to dead people."

Dennis snorts. "Okay, well, this is getting interesting. Honestly, I'd love to ask all of you about your abilities, but I feel like that's prying."

Frowning, I shake my head. "I'm shocked you're both taking this so well. I tell you we have powers, and you're… okay with it?"

Judy gives me a soft smile. "To be honest, I'm freaking out. But you weren't wrong. We always knew you were different. Just not quite to this level." She gives a high-pitched, nervous laugh. "But we always wanted you to feel welcome here. I'm relieved you came to us with this."

"We'll figure this out, kiddo," Dennis finishes.

I nod, a stone loosening inside my chest. "Thank you."

Dennis bobs his head, slapping his thigh. "Right, well, you kids must be starving. How about we order some pizza?" Zay's face splits into a wide grin, and Dennis chuckles. "I'll take that as a yes."

"I'm going to run to the store and pick up some supplies." Judy hops up from the armrest, grabbing her purse from the end table.

She starts making a list out loud: "Food, drinks, toothbrushes, hair-brushes, clothes." She stops, turning toward the crew, scanning them like she's checking their measurements. Then she snaps her fingers. "Sheets! Sheets. I should write all this down."

Warmth floods my chest as I watch her. Tears gather at the corner of my eyes, and for once, it's not out of sadness.

I hop up, shouting, "Wait!" I cross the room to Judy, giving her another hug. "Thank you. Thank you for everything."

She smiles, tossing some of my hair over my shoulder. "I'll be back."

Dennis leaves the room as well, leaving the six of us alone.

We sit in silence for a few seconds as the feeling sinks in. The sense of comfort, of safety. The thought of sleeping somewhere warm tonight.

Even the idea of pizza.

I glance at Theo as he nudges Zay with an elbow, the two of them grinning. Then Theo finds my gaze and gives me an earth-shattering smile.

My insides melt a little as I return his smirk, resisting the urge to curl up on his lap.

I might need to give Dennis and Judy a night to digest everything they've learned so far before informing them I brought a boyfriend home, too.

Nora turns toward me, breaking the silence. "What do we do next?"

"There's enough room here; I'm sure we can stay for a while." I take a deep breath. "I'll work out the specifics with Judy and Dennis later."

Theo shakes his head. "We shouldn't impose. It's already nice of them to be doing this now."

"I was thinking..." I start but then pinch my bottom lip between my teeth, cutting myself off.

"What?" Theo asks.

I shrug. "Well... I mean, there are already six of us in this room. A twist of fate brought us together. But there has to be more of us."

Theo frowns, answering slowly, "I guess..."

I point to Nora. "Could you look for more?"

"I can try."

Elise has been deadly quiet this entire time, but she's watching me intently. She gives me a small smile, not malicious this time, more grateful because somehow, she already knows where I'm going.

Maybe she can read it in my aura.

What's the color for determination? For courage? For power?

"Well, maybe if there's more of us, we can stop *running*. Maybe someone can help us figure out our powers? Someone who knows what they're doing."

Theo shifts, wiping his hands on his pants. "Okay... and then what?"

Zay and Amber turn toward me, excitement written on their faces, waiting for me to spill the plan.

Nora smiles; maybe she saw it, too.

I lean toward Theo, resting a hand on his knee, and take a deep breath.

"And then maybe... we take the fight to *them*."

Acknowledgements

I put off writing my acknowledgments until the last possible second. I wrote a whole book; you'd probably think, what's a few hundred more words to thank those dearest to me? Well, apparently, it's the toughest part of the job. At least for me. I'm so thankful to so many people, and if I forgot anyone on this list (another reason I held off for so long!) I'm so, so sorry.

To my husband, Chris: Thank you for keeping me sane and being my voice of reason. Thank you for celebrating the highs and understanding the lows. I couldn't do any of this without you—publishing, life, all of it. You keep me grounded.

Sarah, you're my person. You've been my rock for nearly two decades now, and I can't thank you enough for everything you've ever done for me. I'd end up filling another book if I tried. Thanks for always believing in me. Tammy, it's not an island, but I still want to say thank you for always being there as well.

To my old Newfane crew: You have all saved me in more ways than one back when we were kids, and I'll never be able to repay you for that. I wish I had known back then that our lives would take different paths because I would've held on tight and never let go.

Lara, none of this would be possible without your support. Thanks for being my biggest cheerleader and solidly in my corner. I'm so happy fate brought us together, twin! Your friendship and guidance means so much to me.

To my fellow awkward/anxious monkeys: Kate, I will gladly stay at any weird hotel with you and have a drink on their gazebo. Whether we're driving for hours to attend an author event or crossing borders to see Arctic Monkeys, I'm so glad our paths have crossed. Thanks for being my first-ever reader and not giving up on me. Mary, your unwavering support means the world to me. I cherish our calls and all your pep talks and can't wait to give you the world's biggest hug someday! I love you both.

Nicole, Michelle, Erin, Rina, Marissa, Em, Bria, and the wonderful writers of SPPP and the Women's Writing Group: Some of you are early readers, but you're all friends. Thanks for making me better. And speaking of early readers, thank you, thank you, thank you to anyone who has read earlier versions of Strangers. It might have been years since you first read it, but we finally made it, friends. Also, shout out to my amazing hype team; thank you for being as excited as I am about bringing Strangers into this world.

Aileen, I can't remember which one of us was "Bitch" or "Jerk" (#Supernatural), but either way, I'm so grateful you came into my life all those years ago! I'll get piercings with you any day, and I can't wait for more sleepovers.

Kristin, no notes! (#NewGirl) I cherish our coffee dates! I love how you're always one of my first readers. Your support has carried me through three novels now!

Ashley, thanks for dealing with my anxiety and taking my author photos. You're a wonderful photographer and an amazing friend. I'm lucky to have you.

To my brother, Billy, thank you for the killer music taste. I owe you for more than that, but it's a pretty big one. Also, to the other family members (in-laws included!) who've always been there for me. You know who you are. Thank you for being so supportive.

To my editor, Jennia. I appreciate you talking me off many cliffs over the past few months! I'm thrilled we worked together on this story, and your visions helped make this world the best version it could be. To my cover artist, Emily from Emily's World of Designs, thank you so much for giving me the book cover of my dreams. You took my measly little ideas and ran with it.

There's so much I could say, but some things are better felt than said. Miss you, Lys. Always.

And lastly, thank you, dear reader, for taking a chance on me and helping my dreams come true. I'm overjoyed to share this little bit of magic with you.

Go Bills.

Strangers in Our Heads Playlist

Music plays such a huge role in my life, especially in my writing. So far, two of my short stories have been fully inspired by hearing a particular song. So, of course, I have an entire playlist for Strangers that got me through the years of daydreaming, writing, and editing the final version of the book. Here's the list that always reminds me of my chaos crew:

The Hunted - Slipcast
How To Disappear Completely - Radiohead
The Void - Muse
Dance Of The Clairvoyants - Pearl Jam
Say Nothing - Pianos Become The Teeth
Staying Up - The Neighbourhood
Oceans - Seafret
Where's My Love (Alternate Version) - SYML
I Found - Amber Run

Be There - Seafret

Drown - Seafret

I Found (Acoustic) - Amber Run

Particles (Piano Version) - Nothing But Thieves

Saturn - Sleeping At Last

Lloyd, I'm Ready To Be Heartbroken - Camera Obscura

You - Keaton Henson

5AM - Amber Run

Fear of the Water - SYML

Skin and Bones - Cage The Elephant

Can You Keep a Secret? - Ellise

Panoramic Girl - Young the Giant

Relax My Beloved - Alex Clare

Ode To The Mets - The Strokes

Under Cover of Darkness - The Strokes

What Ever Happened? - The Strokes

Automatic Stop - The Strokes

Call It Fate, Call It Karma - The Strokes

Goodbye - Cage The Elephant

Oblivion - Bastille

In My Veins (Feat. Erin Mccarley) - Andrew Belle

Wicked Game - Gemma Hayes

Silhouette - Aquilo

I Of The Storm - Of Monsters and Men

Neptune - Sleeping At Last

Broken Boy - Cage The Elephant

How Not To Drown - CHVRCHES, Robert Smith

In My Head - Peter Manos

Mx. Sinister - I DONT KNOW HOW BUT THEY FOUND ME

You Are a Memory - Message To Bears
So Close To Magic - Aquilo
We Suck Young Blood - Radiohead
Forever Nevermore - Sea Wolf
Beautiful Crime - Tamer
In Flames - Digital Daggers
Repeat Until Death - Novo Amor
Your Blood - Nothing But Thieves
Little Do You Know - Alex & Sierra
Insomnia - IAMX
Come as You Are - Prep School
Demons (Philosophical Sessions) - Jacob Lee
Through the Valley - Shawn James
Hypnotic - Zella Day
Hurts Like Hell - Fleurie, Tommee Profitt
We Have It All - Pim Stones
Moondust (Stripped) - Jaymes Young
Earth - Sleeping At Last
The Deep End - Scary Kids Scaring Kids
I Don't Like People (& They Don't Like Me) - Boston Manor
Hollow Tune - Brick + Mortar
Every Day Is Exactly The Same - Nine Inch Nails
R U Mine? - Arctic Monkeys
Come a Little Closer - Cage The Elephant
In Dreams - Roy Orbison

Ashley Staley Photography

Bri Eberhart is a contemporary fantasy writer, and her stories are published in the *Scarlet Leaf Review*, *Variety Pack*, and *Neuro Magazine*. She has a BA in cultural studies with a concentration in creative writing and literature from SUNY Empire State. She's also an editorial assistant for an online marketing website and currently resides near Buffalo, NY, with her husband and two cats.

You can find her on Instagram and Twitter at bri_eberhart or at brieberhart.com.

www.ingramcontent.com/pod-product-compliance
Lightning Source LLC
Chambersburg PA
CBHW030114310726
48970CB00004B/1273